BY MELANIE BENJAMIN

THE CHILDREN'S BLIZZARD

The
CHILDREN'S
BLIZZARD

A NOVEL

MELANIE
BENJAMIN

DELACORTE PRESS

NEW YORK

The Children's Blizzard is a work of fiction. All incidents and dialogue, and all characters with the exception of some well-known historical figures, are products of the author's imagination and are not to be construed as real. Where real-life historical persons appear, the situations, incidents, and dialogues concerning those persons are entirely fictional and are not intended to depict actual events or to change the entirely fictional nature of the work. In all other respects, any resemblance to persons living or dead is entirely coincidental.

To Alec

CONTENTS

Book One

A DISTURBANCE
IN THE WEST

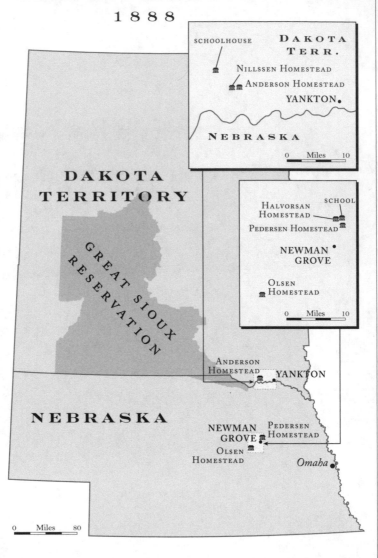

NEBRASKA
and the
DAKOTA TERRITORY
1 8 8 8

SCHOOLHOUSE

DAKOTA
TERR.

NILLSSEN HOMESTEAD

ANDERSON HOMESTEAD

YANKTON

NEBRASKA

0   Miles   10

DAKOTA
TERRITORY

HALVORSAN
HOMESTEAD

SCHOOL

PEDERSEN HOMESTEAD

NEWMAN
GROVE

OLSEN
HOMESTEAD

0   Miles   10

GREAT SIOUX
RESERVATION

ANDERSON
HOMESTEAD

YANKTON

NEBRASKA

NEWMAN
GROVE

PEDERSEN
HOMESTEAD

OLSEN
HOMESTEAD

Omaha

0   Miles   80

They came on boats, on trains, great unceasing waves of them—the poor, the disenfranchised, the seekers, the dreamers. Second and third generations of farmers eking out an existence on scraps of farms divided up among too many sons. Political agitators no longer welcome in their homelands. Young men fleeing conscription in a king's army. Married couples starting out. Bachelors from towns with few women. The poor from tenements with air so stifling and foul there was no room to breathe, let alone dream.

Come to Nebraska! Dakota Territory! Minnesota! Come to the Great Plains of America!

The pamphlets showed up mysteriously in the towns of the countries they'd left. Or in the tenements of the city that was the portal to America. Pamphlets handed about, passed around from family to family until the pages were as soft as fabric. Pamphlets that were read over, prayed over, that led to sleepless nights and days of planning, parsing, calculating: What can I get for this old piece of land that's worn out from generations of farming? How much will passage cost? How long will it take to get to these Great Plains? Will my old mother survive, will the newborn make it, can I take the cow, my wagon, her spinning wheel?

And they came. Entire villages packed up and left. Tenements *cleared out. They disembarked from the boat or walked across town and they got on a train. The train. The great snorting, pawing iron horse, the endless miles of track that led west. They packed themselves tightly into cars with only benches, they brought food for the journey, bread and sausages and cheeses, although they longed for* bløtkake *and* stollen *and* kanellängd.

They were strong, these immigrants from across the sea, stronger than their traveling companions from the cities whose bodies were bent, skin so pale, lungs so squeezed. The ones who'd first arrived on boats were big and healthy with open faces, Nordic brows, white teeth. Women with abundant braids crowning their heads. Men with red beards. Children with hair so fair it was almost white. Blue, blue eyes.

Other eyes watched them get off the trains, darker eyes set in darker skin. The tragic eyes of the people whose land this had been. But nobody paid any attention; the Indian wars were over. White people lived on their land now.

They came to seek their fortunes, to plow a farm on acres— hundreds of acres!—that would remain in the family for generations. They were the new hope for America. The only way the land would settle, the country would grow, territory by territory, state by state, was if it were settled by immigrants.

They came.

They came full of promise.

They came because of a lie.

What happened to them once they arrived was of little interest to the industrial towns in the East, the government that counted their bodies and took their money, the boosters who cheered them when they got off the trains, and the stockholders of the railroads whose very existence depended on them to keep coming—

And then never gave them another thought.

JANUARY 12, 1888, 12:15 A.M.

SIGNAL OFFICE
WAR DEPARTMENT,

SAINT PAUL

———

Indications for 24 hours commencing at 7 A.M. today.

FOR SAINT PAUL, MINNEAPOLIS, AND VICINITY: warmer weather with snow, fresh southerly winds becoming variable.

FOR MINNESOTA: warmer weather with snow, fresh to high southerly winds becoming variable.

FOR DAKOTA: snow, warmer, followed in the western portion by colder weather, fresh to high winds generally becoming northerly. The snow will drift heavily in Minnesota and Dakota during the day and tonight; the winds will generally shift to high colder northerly during the afternoon and night.

CHAPTER 1

· · · · ·

THE AIR WAS ON FIRE.

The prairie was burning, snapping and hissing, sparks flying in every direction, propelled by the scorching wind. Sparks falling as thick as snowflakes in winter, burning tiny holes in cloth, stinging exposed skin. Her eyes were dry and scratchy, her hair had escaped its pins so that it fell down her back, and when she picked up one of those pins, it was scalding to the touch.

Everything was hot to the touch, even the wet gunnysacks they were using to beat out the flames were sizzling. When Raina glanced back at the house, she saw the dancing, hellish flames reflected in the windows.

"To the north," her father called, and she ran, ran on bare legs and bare feet that stung from earth that was a fiery stovetop as she beat out a daring lick of flame that had jumped the firebreak with all her might. Just beyond the hastily plowed ditch, the emerging bluestem grasses hissed;

some exploded, but the fire did not look as if it was going to cross the break.

"Save some of that for the others, Raina," her father called, and even from that distance—he was at the head of the west break—and through the sooty air, she recognized the twinkle in his eyes. Then he turned and pointed south. "Gerda! Go!"

Raina watched her older sister leap toward another vaulting flame, beating it out before it had a chance. It was almost a game, really, a game of chicken. Who would win, the flames or the Olsens? So far, in ten years of homesteading, the Olsens had come out victorious every time.

Gerda smiled triumphantly, waving back at Raina, the outside row of vulnerable wheat, only a few inches tall, between them. At times like this, when the air was so stifling and smoky, Raina didn't feel quite so small, quite so inconsequential as when the air was clear. On a cool, still early summer morning, the prairie could make her feel like the smallest of insects, trapped in a great dome of endless pale blue sky, the waving grasses undulating, just like the sea, against an unbroken horizon. But Gerda, Raina knew, never felt this way. Gerda was stronger, bigger. Gerda was untouchable, even from the prairie fires that flared up regularly in Nebraska, spring and fall. Gerda would know what to do in the face of fire, or ice. Or men. Gerda—

Gerda wasn't here.

Raina blinked, gaped at the McGuffey Reader in her hand. She wasn't on the prairie; she was in a schoolhouse. *Her* schoolhouse. The second class was droning the lesson:

God made the little birds to sing,
And flit from tree to tree;

'Tis He who sends them in the spring
To sing for you and me.

Raina sat straighter, tried to stretch her neck but it was no use; she was smaller than the biggest boy sitting in the last row of benches. Her pupils—precious minds that were hers to form, or so she'd been told in the letter accompanying her certificate. But the oldest one was fifteen, only a year younger than she. And the way he looked at her made her shiver, made her think of a well that was so deep, the bottom would always remain a mystery.

No, it wasn't this boy's eyes that made her think that; this boy's eyes were blue, his gaze was measured, and if there was a wildness in them—only at times, for he was a well-brought-up lad—it was a wildness she believed she could tame.

His eyes were chocolate brown and soft with an understanding Raina had never before felt she needed. Until she first beheld that fathomless gaze.

Gerda would not feel so silly. Gerda would not allow herself to be so—understandable. But Gerda was teaching in her own school across the border into Dakota Territory, three days' travel away, and boarding with a family there. A family not at all like the Pedersens, with whom Raina found herself sharing a roof, food, and air that was becoming too polluted with glances, sighs, and tears. And beds, beds upstairs, beds downstairs. Beds without borders, without walls, too exposed to those glances and sighs.

Her mother should have prepared her for this, Raina sometimes thought. Her mother should have taught her, warned her as she used to warn Raina not to wander into the tallgrass prairie when she was little, not to touch a hot stove,

not to eat the pokeweed berries that flowered late in summer; her mother should have prevented her—

From what? From going out into the world? That was the
dream her mother most cherished: that Raina and Gerda
would never have to homestead, that they could go to college, then live and teach in a city someday. But life in this
new country was hard and expensive and they had no relatives to act as a cushion. First, the two girls had to teach and
save their wages.

Her mother couldn't have prevented this, and Raina
knew it. Her mother had met her father when they were
barely out of childhood. Her mother was soft and childlike,
in the best way—she loved to sing songs and make up games
as she went about her work. Her mother wasn't meant for
homesteading, for harsh environments and cruel blows; the
entire family, Raina and Gerda included, tried to protect her
as best they could in this elemental place, a place of life and
death and not much in between except backbreaking work.

As for her father—well, she couldn't even meet his eyes
on the weekends he came to take her home. Steffen Olsen
was a man but he was a god, too, a Norse god, untouchable,
unknowable except in wise words and stupendous feats of
physical labor. He could tie a mile-long barbed-wire fence
in half a day. He could plant an entire field of wheat in twice
that time. He could eat enormous meals and at sundown fall
into a blameless sleep that would leave him refreshed and
ready to go at first light.

Her father was not a man but a myth.

Gunner Pedersen, however, was *real:* flesh, blood, sinew.
He was a man in the way her father was not, a man to dream
about, to hunger for. To imagine in your arms. A man who
would pause in his work to tell a funny story to a frightened

girl boarding out for the very first time. A man who would fill a glass with cattails and prairie grass, because he thought it looked pretty, and present it to her without a word, only a kind look that told her he knew how lonely she must be.

A man with a wife who saw these things and stored them up. The way Raina stored them up, as well. But for what purpose? Neither woman, at least in the beginning, could answer that.

After this past week, however . . .

A sound like a thunderclap startled her. Little Anette Pedersen had dropped her reader on the floor; the girl jerked her head up, a red spot on her cheek where she must have been pressing it against the desk. She had probably fallen asleep again.

This was another thing no one had prepared Raina for; it hadn't been covered in any of the textbooks or on the examination she'd passed with flying colors. In all her studying, she had never come across what to do if one of your pupils was so mistreated and overworked, she fell asleep during class.

Raina stood; the children all put away their readers and looked up at her. Carefully, in her best, most precise English, she instructed the children to go outside for recess; the weather was warm enough, this January day, for them to get some fresh air. It was so unexpected, this gift of a day, the temperature hovering around thirty degrees, the sun shining so brightly this morning although it was turning cloudy now. It would do everyone good to play outside.

Raina could never tell if all the children understood her; she longed to talk to them in Norwegian, even to the Swedes and the Germans, because surely they'd pick out a word or two, these languages were so similar. But the school superintendent had warned her that this was the most important rule for a prairie schoolteacher: *English only.* These children of immigrants had to learn; their parents could not teach them.

The children rose, dutifully went to the cloakroom—just a tiny shed, no bigger than a broom closet tacked on to the main room—and brought out their light coats. It had been so warm this morning—comparatively warm, anyway—they all had come to school clad as if it were May, not January. After the long cold snap last week that kept everyone cooped up at home, this day had a holiday feel to it. Chattering excitedly in a mixture of languages, they ran off in groups to the bare little schoolyard that the biggest boy, Tor Halvorsan, had swept without being asked. Raina was pleased to see little Fredrik Halvorsan, Tor's younger brother, tug on Anette's apron strings as the two of them ran off together.

Raina longed to join her pupils; it was only last year she was a pupil herself in her home district, sitting with her friends on a tree stump during recess and chatting about dress patterns and boys, occasionally allowing her dignity to fall off her like a discarded shawl to play tag with the younger students. She still felt stiff and awkward sitting alone at her desk inside while her pupils played. She should go outside and take in the fresh air herself; after the stifling nightmare of this last week, she needed it. But she felt like an intruder as the children played their games; they would grow shy whenever she ventured outside, afraid to be themselves in front of the schoolteacher.

Raina also had a headache, a throbbing at the base of her neck, radiating up to the top of her head, already aching from the heavy pile of her braids. She began to restlessly walk about the room, wishing it were spring already, plant-

ing time, and school was out, and she was back home. Away
from Anette's hungry, sad eyes.

Away from *him*.

SUMMER WAS WHEN THEY MET. Summer, with the haze of
the fires still hanging in the air so that nerves were tense,
tingling—*anticipating*. She was wearing her first dress with a
skirt that brushed the ground; her mother had made it for
her the week before. She felt like she was playing dress-up,
with her hair piled heavily on top of her head in an elaborate
twist instead of the usual braided bunch at the base of her
neck or streaming down her back. She pinched her wrist,
trying to stop the giggles that bubbled up on their own; she
felt like an imposter. Absurd.

It was summer, and Nebraska homesteaders were hopeful that this year, unlike the year before, and the year before,
and the year before *that*, the crops would come to fruition
before twisters, grasshoppers, fire, or hailstorms decimated
them. Or lack of rain withered them.

Summer, and the prairie flowers that Raina loved were in
bloom—not even the fires could kill them, they defiantly
sprang back up from the scorched earth—and when he came
in the house clutching a bouquet of them, prairie wild roses,
black-eyed Susans, purple larkspur, she'd gasped and almost clapped her hands.

"Teacher!"

Raina jumped behind her desk, her heart racing; Fredrik
Halvorsan was standing before her, panting.

"Come look! Look in the sky, Teacher!"

Raina shivered—the wind must have picked up, for it was

noticeably colder than it had been earlier in the day—and followed him outside.

ANETTE PEDERSEN HAD RACED OFF with Fredrik the moment Teacher released them. It was only when she was sitting still that her legs cramped up and the weariness overcame her, that bone-drenched weariness that was a constant companion ever since she came to the Pedersens.

And it was only when she ran that she felt joy. Well—then, and whenever Fredrik Halvorsan sidled up to her, told her a funny joke, helped her with that foreign language that was so clumsy on her tongue.

Teacher tried to help her learn; it was fortunate, she said, that they lived in the same house! But even when she said that, Anette saw in Teacher's eyes a guarded confusion. And she wondered how anyone could use the word *fortunate* to describe the Pedersen household.

"We go to a visit," Anette's mother had said that summer day a year and a half ago, when she told Anette to pack her scant belongings—some petticoats, two faded dresses that were almost too small, two pairs of mended stockings, a coat, mittens, and her rag doll—and climb up on the wagon. Ten years old at the time, Anette couldn't help but notice that her four half-brothers did not pack their belongings; couldn't help but notice that her stepfather laughed tauntingly at her and her mother as they rode out of the yard, away from the tiny dugout.

Anette's mother didn't say a word the entire journey, not even when they stopped to give the horses a rest and eat their lunch, and neither did Anette. She felt she'd done something wrong. Had she looked at her stepfather that certain way he accused her of—"like a damn idiot," he would say whenever he caught her staring off into space, her mouth half-open? Had she jumped away from him too abruptly when he crept near? Had she angered her mother somehow, either by not taking good enough care of her younger brothers, or simply by being herself, ugly Anette, pockmarked Anette, the rough craters from the smallpox still too visible across her high cheekbones?

She didn't know, she didn't dare ask, and before it was dark she found herself in a strange house, bigger than the dugout—a real house made of wood, with two stories—with her carpetbag on the floor next to her.

"I go now. Be good, don't make trouble. That's all I can give you," her mother said, before she left the house without even touching her daughter in farewell and climbed back up on the wagon, turning the horses around and leaving Anette with her new family—Mother Pedersen, small and beautiful, too beautiful for Anette to even understand; she'd only seen such pink and gold and dimpled beauty once, on a postcard. On a person, it was a beauty almost too vivid to bear; Anette wanted to shade her eyes or look away. But she didn't dare; she knew instinctively that this would be considered an affront. Mother Pedersen also had the most bountiful hair Anette had ever seen, thick and golden, so many braids in an intricate twist that flattered her pretty, but unsmiling, face.

Father Pedersen was big and handsome with little streaks of grey in his hair and crinkly lines at the corners of his eyes that made him look slightly puzzled, yet kind. And three little Pedersens crawled about, already tugging on Anette's skirt. "You're Anette Pedersen now," Mother Pedersen informed her as she marched her up to her "room"—a faded curtain divided the unfinished upstairs into two sections with a bed, a washstand, and a rush rug on each side. No window, no tar paper for insulation in winter, and not even the warmth from a stove pipe, which vented straight out from the kitchen, not the roof.

Anette nodded. She went to bed that night in the stifling attic. She cried—silently—and couldn't sleep. When the sun rose, she was summoned by a big cowbell from downstairs and put to work. Washing, fetching water, throwing slop out into the ravine behind the house, tending to the children, sewing—Mother Pedersen looked over her shoulder as she tried to darn a sock, and said something under her breath that Anette couldn't quite make out—cooking, clearing away.

That night, exhausted, Anette slept.

When school started up for the summer session, before the crops had to be harvested, she was told that she could attend when she wasn't needed at home. Mother Pedersen gave her a slate and a shiny new lunch bucket but warned her, "They cost a dime. A whole dime, do you understand? If you lose them, you can't go to school anymore. And come right home after. No dawdling." Anette ran the mile north carrying the slate and bucket along with a flicker of hope, cradling them carefully, terrified that all three would be snatched from her, or fall to the earth and shatter.

But school hadn't turned out to be much better than her new home; she couldn't understand English, her over-worked muscles cramped up from sitting at the bench for so long, and sometimes she fell asleep without warning. The other children—twelve assorted Norwegians, Swedes, and Germans—were polite, but they all knew that she was only a hired girl with no family. So they kept their distance.

Except for Fredrik Halvorsan. Who, one day, instead of

running around with his brother and the other boys, suddenly peeled off, pulled on Anette's apron string, and said in Norwegian, "Tag, you're it!" And Anette ran toward him, she tagged him easily, and he was so astonished—because he prided himself on being the fastest boy in school—that he blurted out, "You're my friend now," and he kept that promise. He sat next to her at lunch, they chased each other at recess, sometimes he even raced her home, even though he then had to turn around and run another mile and a half back north to his farm. He was the only good thing in her life, but Anette couldn't tell him that for fear of inviting too many questions for which she had no answers.

Teacher was also nice to her, when she was allowed to be. Ever since she started boarding at the Pedersens' this last school term, she had tried to help Anette with English. But Mother Pedersen wouldn't allow it. "This is not school," she told the younger woman, as she gave her one of her needling looks so at odds with the china-doll delicacy of her face. "Boundaries must be respected. Anette is mine here."

Mother Pedersen was always claiming ownership of things, people—even ideas.

Father Pedersen was different. He had tried to be kind to Anette, and to Teacher. But he was outside most of the time with the horses he loved. Anette had learned not to smile too much at him or laugh at his jokes or his stories. Mother Pedersen had a way of looking at her when she did that caused Anette to lose sleep at night, puzzling over it.

But Teacher had not learned these things. She was a schoolteacher; she carried all the knowledge of the world in her head. Yet she couldn't seem to understand the unspoken rules of Mother Pedersen's house. Anette longed to warn her. But Anette didn't have the words, even in her native tongue, to give voice to her concerns about what was happening in that two-story house. The air was so close, so stifling with things that she couldn't understand, but that still resonated in her heart, her head, her very bones. There was a vibration, all the time, a high, tense note, like a string on a violin being teased forever, and all you could hope for was that it would finally break. And yet, you also feared that day, had nightmares about it, entered that house with dread that today would be the day when that note was silenced forever.

Especially after last week, when there was no school and the air was so bitterly cold that Father Pedersen couldn't always escape to the barn where Teacher sometimes followed him, and they were all stuck together for long days and longer nights—Anette shuddered, thinking about it.

So it was such a relief, this morning, when the cold spell broke; everyone except Mother Pedersen had fled that house. Teacher had grabbed Anette's hand and run with her—neither wore their heavy coats, only thick shawls, and Anette had even dared to put on her regular petticoats, letting her flannel ones air out on the line where she'd hung the children's wash before breakfast. Teacher and Anette flew across the log bridge over the ravine at the back of the property, and their boots skimmed the packed, hard, snow-covered prairie, that little one-room school a beacon, drawing them away from the darkness of that house.

And now, at recess, Anette and Fredrik were running like they always did, like birds themselves, chasing and laughing, until Anette finally tagged him. When she did, she felt a stinging shock, heard a sizzle, and they both leapt apart, gasping.

Then they looked up at the sky. As Anette began to tremble, Fredrik ran to get Teacher.

CHAPTER 2

. . . . .

———

Come to Nebraska, the Garden of Eden! Acres for the taking, acres of a bountiful land that will surely yield a harvest fit for the gods. Have you ever seen the sun set behind rolling green hills, heard the prairie lark sing its glorious song, smelled the perfume of flowers so abundant, they make a veritable carpet of velvet petals? Have you longed for the magic of a prairie winter, gentle yet abundant snow to nourish the earth, neither too cold nor too warm, only perfection in every way? Have you longed to cultivate a land so yielding, the plow is scarcely needed to give up its rich earth? Then leave your Czars, your Kings, the shackles of the filthy city, and come to a land of fresh, healthy air, a land where every man can be his own king. Our agents of the Union Pacific Railroad will even meet you off the boat in New York Harbor and make arrangements for you to take the first train west to God's own country, Nebraska. The Homestead Act provides for any male or female head of a household one hundred and sixty of these heavenly acres for only a small filing

fee. In five years, those acres will be yours to pass on to
your children and their children's children.

Come to Nebraska, the Garden of Eden!

GAVIN WOODSON LEANED BACK IN HIS CHAIR, THE CIGAR
between his fingers forgotten so the ash now was about an
inch long. He had just pinned the *Come to Nebraska* newspaper clipping to the scarred wall to the left of his cluttered
desk. Blots of ink marred the other clippings he'd been pawing through, so that this was the only one he'd managed to
salvage. He didn't know why he'd pinned it. It was pabulum,
pure and simple. Maybe he'd decided to display it not as a
trophy but as a taunting reminder of how far he'd sunk, here
in Godforsaken Omaha.

He ought to be in New York right this minute, in the bustling offices of *The World*. Making plans for dinner at Del-
monico's, followed by drinks at the White Horse Tavern. Or
he might stroll along Fifth Avenue and gape at the mansions,
then watch a skating party in the park, maybe help a damsel
in distress on the ice and hope it would lead to a carriage
ride later. Or he could stay in his boardinghouse, a civilized
place with musicales in the parlor in the evenings, a gentleman's game of cards in the library, interesting and palatable
food produced by dimpling young Irish girls who let you put
an arm around them without automatically thinking you
were engaged.

Instead, after a falling-out with *The World*'s then-new
owner, Joseph Pulitzer, Gavin found himself in Godforsaken
Omaha. He couldn't say the name of the town any other way;

it was never merely "Omaha." It was godforsaken, pure and simple. As was this entire region, this desert, this prairie, these plains. And the poor sons of bitches he'd lured out here with his pen.

He glanced back up at the clipping and laughed. Jesus Christ, what a job he'd done! But that was actually his job writing for the state's boosters and railroad investors. Hammering out "news" articles that advertised this place as something it was not, pieces that got picked up by the wire services and placed in other newspapers or were used in pamphlets put out by the railroads. All with the same intent: To sell Nebraska. To sell all these acres, recently won from the Indians, to rubes and immigrants who didn't know any better. To settle this state, grow the population—because there weren't enough citizens in this country to fill up the ever-expanding territory, so they had to import bodies, pure and simple—and make the businessmen, the investors, and the railroads happy. And very rich. Because what good was a railroad snaking from coast to coast if there weren't towns along the way, grain and wheat and corn and livestock to transport, not to mention people? How else would you get enough bodies inside a territory to turn it into a state? So the railroads and the boosters employed washed-up reporters to lure those people across an ocean. Reporters like Gavin.

Gavin reached for his pen with a sigh. His desk here at the *Omaha Daily Bee* was the smallest, his cubbyhole the farthest away from the editor's desk. He wasn't technically employed by the *Bee,* but he was given a desk here, for appearance's sake. After all, to the public, he was a journalist.

But he wasn't, and he knew it. And while that had once outraged him, he was growing used to the insulating feeling—

like a ponderous buffalo coat keeping him warm while si-
multaneously weighing him down—of *acquiescence*. He even
felt, after a couple of whiskeys at the Gilded Lily down the
street, rather noble for admitting his failings. Wasn't it best
to acknowledge the limitations of a life and find a way to live
within them, rather than constantly trying to push up against
a fixed fate, like those ignorant sodbusters who'd believed
his seductive prose, trying and failing every year to make a
garden out of a desert?

It sure as hell was, Gavin had convinced himself. Most of
the time.

"Writing something up about that sleighing party?" Dan
Forsythe was standing next to him, in his usual sloppy
attire—frayed, black-stained cuffs (he refused to wear paper
cuffs to protect his shirts from the ink); heavy trousers, like
farmers wore; heavy boots, too, that Gavin could easily
imagine covered in muck and manure. Yet he was the star
reporter for the *Bee*, the publisher's pet.

"Yep."

"Hadn't you better go out there with them, then?"

Gavin had to laugh at this. "Why? That's not what I'm
paid to do and you know it. Nobody wants the truth from me.
I'll give 'em a pretty picture—*the gay party, accompanied by a
brass band, rode triumphantly east on Douglas Street toward the
river, the ladies' velvet outfits—one bright red, jaunty cap in particular stood out—providing splashes of color against the pure
white of the gently banked snow.*"

Forsythe laughed, and Gavin even enjoyed the admira-
tion in the man's eyes; he couldn't help it, he was proud of
his imaginative powers, even though they had no place in
real journalism.

"You've got it about right," Forsythe said, still chuckling.

"I saw them heading toward the river myself, right down to the jaunty red cap. And the brass band in the last sleigh. It's a helluva party—the whole town is having a holiday. Must have been a couple of hundred sleighs. The mayor's even out there."

"Well, it is big news, that bridge. It'll be good for everyone." Omaha was on the west bank of the Missouri River; Council Bluffs, Iowa, on the east. Originally, Council Bluffs was the bigger town; it was assumed that the new Union Pacific Railroad would build its terminus there. But Omaha won out, and there was a bitter rivalry between the two. Still, this new bridge could only help both towns. Previously, horses and wagons had to take a ferry across in summer, or trust the ice in winter; the only bridge had been the train bridge.

"Think I'll take a stroll," Forsythe said, scratching the back of his neck. Gavin knew what taking a stroll meant: heading down to one of the taverns, most likely the Lily. He decided to join Forsythe; he could write up that puff piece about the party in ten minutes and hand it over to be typeset. He'd have plenty of time after a snort or two.

The two men retrieved their coats and headed outdoors. The streets of Godforsaken Omaha were the usual mess of mud churned up and frozen into ruts covered with hard-packed snow that was brown with manure. In the business district near Douglas Street, there were wide planks for walking, although these, too, were treacherous no matter the season. The street here had tracks laid and a cable car, electrified by a wire dangling precariously above it, that chugged up and down, ringing its jolly bell at every stop; the city was inordinately proud of it, and it was crowded at all times. In the distance, the Paxton Hotel on Farnam rose a whopping five stories, and the new *Bee* building, almost complete next to the city hall, was going to top out at seven. There were restaurants and shops and busybody ladies' societies and churches and an opera house and schools and banks, as well as a decent red-light district for a man with money and particular preferences, but Omaha was still a cow town when you got right down to it. The stockyard stench marinated the town in summer and not even the most bracing winter winds could completely chase it away. Wild packs of dogs sometimes terrorized citizens; fistfights, canings, and the occasional gunfight were not unusual. And the only decent meal a fellow could have was steak. Steak for breakfast, steak for supper, steak for dinner.

Christ, what Gavin wouldn't give for a fresh oyster.

The two men stood for a moment outside; the sky was low but not threatening, a few soft snowflakes lazily drifted down, so sporadically that they barely registered. It was warm today, warmer than it had been, which was why the sleighing party had set out. It was only one o'clock, lunchtime, so he'd take advantage of the spread at the Lily, the usual boiled eggs and pickled beets and slices of tongue. His hunger roared to life and he patted his doughy stomach in embarrassment; he was going to seed here in Godforsaken Omaha, that was for damn sure. All he did was eat and drink and play cards and churn out ridiculous lies. The slim, taut young fellow he'd been in New York, vibrating with ambition and purpose, was only a memory now. A mocking memory.

Godforsaken Omaha—make that Godforsaken *Nebraska,* might as well throw in the entire state—had robbed him of his purpose. This damn West, with its damn stupid boosters and backroom deals and rubes falling for every scheme, every trick at the card table, every pamphlet filled with lies about the land and its opportunities—it had simply flattened him.

And still they came, those seekers and dreamers and swallowers of lies. Every day during the warm months, the train disgorged parties of them, families with grannies and babes in arms, wary bachelors. The depot was filled with the cacophony of other languages and the cries of hucksters trying to rob them of whatever meager savings they had brought with them—*Wagon for sale! Mules for transport! Claims filed here, no questions asked!*—and then they'd take the money and run. Or the wagon wouldn't have wheels. Or the mules would be tubercular.

But they all, eventually, left Omaha for points west, north, or south, sometimes on foot, sometimes on those sorry mules, sometimes in wagons that creaked and swayed and jolted. They left with paperwork in their hands, a promise that many would never fulfill.

And every day, the trains heading east filled up with those who had given up, had discovered the truth and been defeated by it: that this land of grasshoppers and fires and drought and monstrous blizzards would not be as easily tamed as Gavin and his fellow brothers-in-crime had promised.

Still, more came west than returned east. Land, no matter how hard and unyielding, was never short of those who wanted to own it. It was infantile, this belief, infantile and stupid, Gavin thought. Just like the rubes who believed it.

Just when had Gavin grown so cynical? Just when had he lost his love for his fellow man?

"I think I'll go for a stroll," Gavin said. Suddenly, he

couldn't bear being inside a stuffy bar full of cynics like himself. He stopped, turned around, and left Forsythe at the door of the Lily.

"What?" Forsythe looked puzzled, as well he might; Gavin was not one for taking exercise of any kind save for inside the bedroom of the closest bordello.

"It's nice, the weather." Gavin shrugged. "Warmer. I just want to walk around a bit, maybe go down to the river and walk across that new bridge myself, check in on the party."

"Suit yourself." Forsythe waved at someone at the bar and shut the door behind him.

Gavin turned, but he found himself tugged in the other direction, away from the river and toward the prairie. Something called to him—maybe it was the wind, gently stirring the few flat, lazy flakes; maybe it was the desire to get away from the stuffy indoors where he'd been cooped up the last week or so. Maybe it was the ghost of his conscience.

Whatever it was, he turned. And followed it.

CHAPTER 3

.....

ANETTE THOUGHT SHE WAS GOING TO CRY.

Only once had she done so. Only once in the time since her mother sent her away to the Pedersens'. Not when her hands blistered from the lye soap Mother Pedersen made her wash the floor with. Not even last week, when she saw and heard—

Not even last week.

But the moment that Tor Halvorsan slammed the door to the schoolhouse, she stuffed her fist into her mouth, stifling a sob; every nerve strained to erupt, the atmosphere was so suffocating, she was suddenly fretful, fearful. *This, she thought, is how it is when the world ends.*

The sun had vanished, swallowed by the cloud that wasn't a cloud, but a black wall of fury—sparks of lightning preceded it, bluish flashes of electricity tumbling over the snow like wagon wheels. She'd felt that shock, when she and Fredrik touched in the schoolyard; she swore she'd heard a hissing sound when she felt the jolt. They'd fled from it, leading the children back into the schoolhouse just in time.

And now, inside, the air was too close, squeezing her chest, and the howling sound wasn't just the fury of the

winds pounding the rickety building; it was also the strangled cries from the smaller students, tiny Sofia Nyquist sobbing uncontrollably, wrapping her arms around Teacher's
legs.

Teacher, too, looked shaken; she stared out the window,
at the blackness, the electric sparks—even the little stove in
the middle of the room was giving off eerie flares. What was
it that was so crushing, that made Anette want to clamp her
hands over her ears and fall to the floor? It was a blizzard,
for sure—but every one of them had seen prairie blizzards.
Every one of them had witnessed the furies of prairie
weather; the tornadoes in the spring, the fires, even grasshoppers forming living clouds and marching across the land
eating everything in their path. Floods when all the year's
rain fell at one time, and when all the snow melted.

But this was different and Anette couldn't begin to figure
out why; she only knew that the furious cloud that had now
completely blotted out the sun and was pummeling the
schoolhouse until the boards creaked and the windows rattled seemed to have overtaken her heart, too, and made her
want to howl with terror.

She was shivering, but it wasn't only from the fear; the
temperature had plummeted. Teacher shooed them all away
from the window toward the stove. But it didn't seem much
warmer there.

"Go put on your cloaks, children," Teacher said, her voice
unnaturally high and singsong.

They shuffled into the cloakroom—even colder there—
and hurriedly bundled themselves up before rushing back
to the stove. Anette looked around; hardly any of them had
worn their usual winter layers, heavy cloaks and coats and
wool stockings and petticoats, knit hats, mittens, scarves.

Only one or two children were adequately dressed; the rest of them, like Anette herself, had gleefully left most of the layers behind this morning. It was so warm—

It had been so warm.

"Good," Teacher said, but her pretty blue eyes betrayed some fear. Probably only Anette saw it, though; she'd seen it before, many times, back at the Pedersens'. "Now, Tor, can you fetch the rest of the wood?"

Tor went back to the cloakroom, where the sticks of wood were stored; he came back with one armful, dropped it, and when Teacher looked at him expectantly, he shook his head.

"It's all we have."

"Oh" was all that Teacher said. She went back to the window. Snow was swirling from all directions, violently enough that it pinged the thin glass. The heavy curtain of snow blocking the view only added to the stifling feeling pressing down on all of them inside.

"Well, let's sit down. It will probably blow over soon." She turned abruptly away from the window and went to the cloakroom, where she put on her own heavy shawl—all she'd worn this morning, Anette remembered. Teacher came back and opened the McGuffey Reader on her desk, but then she slammed it shut and went back to the window.

Anette wanted her to say something, anything. She looked around; all the students were gazing hopefully at Teacher, who must have felt it like a pressing weight on the back of her neck.

But Teacher was strangely silent.

RAINA WAS TRYING TO THINK, but the swirling snow and ice outside seemed to make the same swirling mess of her mind;

thoughts whirled about but she couldn't grab any one of them. *A blizzard. Fine. We've all seen blizzards before. But not at this time of day, during school. Wait it out. That's the thing. But the wood. The wood isn't enough. Burn the desks if we have to. But then what? No food. Little children crying—Enid, now little Sofia, weeping at their desks, weeping for their mothers. The boys. Send them out? Try to get help? They're big, especially Tor. He's bigger than I am. He's a good, sturdy boy and his farm is only, what—half a mile away? But people get lost in blizzards on the plains. Even patient, sturdy people.*

And above the chaos in her head, one thought, one sentence, one promise stood out.

I will take care of you.

It was the promise he made last week. After Anna Pedersen caught them—doing nothing but looking.

No, that wasn't true.

He had waited until Raina was in bed, trying to sleep but unable to, imagining his sure, strong hands touching her in places she herself hadn't ever been able to touch, for the shame of it. Anette was quiet, hopefully asleep, when he crept up the stairs and knelt beside Raina's bed, and he put his hand upon her shoulder—the only time he'd ever touched her—and he whispered, "I will take care of you, no matter what happens." And he leaned closer, his lips grazing her ear, she trembled, she quaked . . .

She believed him. Then she didn't. Then she did again—a chain between their hearts, that's what it felt like; it was so heavy, it tugged, then went slack, then tugged again. Yes, she believed him—his eyes were wet with emotion, his touch so gentle. Opportunity had presented itself before then and he'd never taken advantage of his desire to do more; at times, she'd ached for him to, and she'd been so angry when he hadn't, she'd wanted to slap him just to feel him beneath her hand.

But his honor invited her trust that night; it was like the fragile hope of peace that comes before a war. Peace destined to be shattered.

So surely, he would come for her now? Come for her and Anette—he loved Anette, he did, that was another sign of the goodness in him, he treated the little girl much more kindly than his wife did—he would come. To take them home, and then he could take the rest of the children, too. And although she cringed at the idea of bringing these innocents into that spider's web, right now she could think of no better alternative. They would freeze to death if they stayed here overnight. There was enough fuel to last a couple more hours, including the desks and books. But who knew how long this storm would last?

So. She had decided—just as she had decided upon him last week; she had decided.

He would come for them. For *her.*

"Children." She turned from the window. "It looks like we're going to stay in school late today, because of the storm. Let's pass the time by playing a game!" Maybe if they ran around, they'd stay warm. "Let's play tag—I haven't played it for so long! Tor, tag—you're it!" Tor, his eyebrows drawn together with worry, leapt in surprise when she tapped his shoulder. He looked startled, then shy; his face turned ruddy. She understood—she wasn't supposed to play games, she was *Miss Olsen*. They all looked embarrassed, but she nudged Tor and he obeyed, running slowly around in circles until the other children got into the spirit, began to giggle, began to run, too.

All except for Anette. Anette stood still, even when

Fredrik shouted at her to run. She chewed her lip and she shook her head. She would not move. Her wary pale blue eyes that saw everything that went on in the house with an intelligence that shocked Raina, yet always looked so confused and slow here in the schoolhouse, were turbulent. The little girl kept looking out the window, then over at the cloakroom, then back to the window, which continued to shake and rattle, as did the entire schoolhouse. At one point a gust hit it so assuredly that it seemed as if the two-by-fours—such a proud sight on the treeless prairie, signaling an investment by the homesteaders for they had to be brought in by train—might lift off the foundation.

Raina wished for a soddie all of a sudden, that symbol of poverty that yet was so much more sturdy, insulated, than these store-bought and tar-papered wooden planks. A soddie wouldn't blow over in a blizzard. A soddie, snug to the earth—made out of the earth itself, walls that were stacked mud and roofs that were strips of sod—was warmer.

But a soddie was a signal that a community was still transient, not permanent. And the homesteaders near Newman Grove were too proud for that. So this schoolhouse, while it looked fancier than the surrounding farmhouses, was not as warm nor as sturdy, because it was merely a place for children to spend whatever meager time they were not forced to spend working at home.

Raina clapped her hands, both to keep warm and to inspire the children to continue at their game, as they'd fallen silent once more, as if mesmerized by the howling wind. She consulted her watch, pinned neatly to the breast of her calico dress; it was one forty-five. Almost forty-five minutes since the blizzard had started. And still not a sign of rescue.

But he would come. She knew it.

"You are the most important thing to me in the world," he'd said last week, in those stolen moments they clung to whenever his wife—in all her golden-haired glory, so bright, so fierce, it was like looking at the sun itself, only no warmth emanated from her—had her back turned. Flying about the small two-story house like a fury, her hair in those elaborate coils, it must have taken her an extra hour each morning to arrange it so. Her vanity on display.

"You are the light, she is the dark," he'd whispered. He wrote it on a scrap of paper and handed it to Raina once. When they believed *she* wasn't looking.

He would rescue her.

But she needed an affirmation all the same. She whirled around and asked, "Anette . . ."

The girl was gone. She wasn't at the desk, nor was she running around with the others.

Then a blast of cold air froze everyone in their tracks; Raina dashed to the cloakroom. Anette's pail was gone, and there was fresh snow inside the door, which wasn't quite closed; the wind was too fierce.

"Anette!" Raina opened the door, gasped, shrank back from the howling wind, the snow as hard as pebbles against her bare skin and inadequate dress. She grit her teeth, tried to open her eyes, which had shut against the assaulting snow; she peered out, caught a glimpse of a red shawl, Anette's shawl, before it was swallowed up in the whirling, blinding void.

"Anette!"

What should she do? Run after the girl? But what about the others, standing still, no longer at play, confusion and fear on every face?

Oh, Gerda! Gerda would know. Gerda would do the right

thing, the smart thing. But Gerda wasn't here. Raina felt the weight of her responsibilities fall across her shoulders like an oxbow, and she stifled a cry. It wasn't fair, she was so small, she shouldn't have left home in the first place, she was too young—both for the dangerous games at the Pedersen home and for this. Children—some too young to do anything but cry for their mothers—in her care. When most of the time she felt unable to care for even the hardiest baby chick. It was only last year she was in braids! And now here she was, in a quaking, barely insulated schoolhouse with no fuel. And one of those children—the one most dear—running out into this storm that was unlike any other.

Gerda would know what to do, Raina was sure of it.

But Gerda was far, far away.

CHAPTER 4

· · · · ·

"LET'S GO!"

Gerda shouted at Tiny Svenson; she cupped her hands around her mouth so that her voice might carry through the howling wind. She giggled, grabbed both girls by the shoulders, and pulled them toward her, then settled down in the sleigh, ready for the journey.

Tiny waved a gloved hand at her—she could barely see it through the snow—and tightened the horse's bridle. His prize bay horse, the horse she teased that he loved even more than he loved her. Then he climbed back into the sleigh and wound the reins around his wrists; the wind was pummeling the sleigh so that it swayed back and forth like a small boat on a turbulent ocean. "Hang on," Tiny shouted at the three figures next to him, already shivering. The two little girls, Minna and Ingrid Nillssen, shuddered with cold; Gerda was vibrating with excitement.

She had planned it all this morning. The house where Gerda boarded as the district's schoolteacher would be blissfully free from the hovering presence of the Andersons. They were an elderly couple, one of the first homesteaders in this part of southeastern Dakota Territory not too far from Yankton, and they worried and fretted over Gerda more than her parents ever had. They did not like the fact that Tiny— not a thing like his name, a great, milk-fed oaf of a lad—had taken to courting the schoolmarm, despite the fact that both were of marriageable age. The Andersons had vowed to Gerda's parents that they would safeguard her virtue like two bulldogs, and they had succeeded, limiting Tiny's visits to a mere fifteen minutes after church, always supervised, Pa Anderson sitting in disapproval in the parlor or on the front porch, puffing on his pipe, short, throat-clearing puffs whenever he felt conversation was lagging or there were too many moony looks flying between the two young people.

But Pa and Ma Anderson were away today—the weather had been so nice and warm this morning, they declared that they would be in Yankton all day, laying in supplies. Ma Anderson even said she would look for a nice fabric, maybe lawn, so she could make Gerda a spring dress, something to look forward to during the endless prairie winter. And Gerda had turned her head to hide her joy at the opportunity before her. An opportunity that Gerda had revealed to Tiny when he arrived to take Gerda, along with the two little Nillssen girls who lived on the next farm, to school that morning. The Andersons allowed him this because of the presence of Gerda's pupils. And because their farm was the farthest away from the schoolhouse, about five miles, and Pa Anderson couldn't spare the time away from the farm. The Andersons had no son to help out; they had no children at all.

"I'll dismiss school early," Gerda whispered that morning into Tiny's red ear, so that the little girls wouldn't hear. "Pick me up at lunch; we'll have the rest of the afternoon to ourselves. We can play house!" For this was Gerda's latest weapon in the fight to keep Tiny from going west.

He wanted to be a cowboy, did Tiny; he devoured dime novels about them. Wild Bill Hickok was his favorite. Tiny despised homesteading, longing instead for an open range that didn't really exist any longer, except maybe farther west in Montana or Wyoming. He'd even trained the little bay to cut, like a cow pony; he had sent away last winter for an authentic cowboy hat from a mail order catalog. Gerda had to admit he looked quite dashing in it.

Tiny also harbored a desire to fight Indians, always moaning to her that he'd missed his only chance. Custer had been massacred years ago, when she and Tiny were just children. Tiny revered the man he looked at as a martyr to the point of trying to grow a long, droopy mustache like the one in the photographs. But at this, he could not succeed; Gerda had learned not to tease him about the patchy, fuzzy hair he insisted was soon to be a luxurious mustache.

Gerda tried to point out that most of the Indians had already been defeated, at least the ones in Dakota; Yankton was bordered to the west and north by the Great Sioux Reservation. She'd actually been asked to teach at a school for Indian children, like the one back in Genoa, Nebraska, not far from her family's homestead. Once, when she was younger, Papa had taken her and Raina to visit the new Indian school—it was about half a day's drive from their farm, and he thought it would be interesting to see. The Olsens had come to Nebraska from eastern Minnesota, where the family had first immigrated in 1876, the year of Custer's last stand. They hadn't had much dealing with Indians, beyond seeing them sometimes in town, peddling beautifully made baskets that could hold water—Mama marveled at the skill. And when Papa plowed, she and Raina often found finely carved arrowheads in the fields. But an entire school full of little Indian children in their clothes of buckskin and beads— Gerda remembered being so excited about it, she couldn't sleep the night before.

But it hadn't turned out the way she thought it would. The children weren't wearing their colorful beaded Indian costumes, after all. They were clad in somber uniforms, grey coat and pants for the boys, white homespun dresses for the girls. All the boys had their shining black hair cut short in a bowl shape; the girls wore their hair in severe braids devoid of pretty touches like feathers or beads. And none of them smiled at Gerda or Raina when the sisters stood at the back of the room with some other curious folks, watching the children seated at their desks, tonelessly chanting the alphabet. In fact, some of the littler ones were crying; one in particular, a tiny doll-like girl, looked so sad with her enormous brown eyes welling up with tears as she chewed the end of one of her braids, her birdlike shoulders heaving, that Gerda wanted to take her home with them.

But her father looked at her with such reproach when she asked him if she could keep the little girl, take her home and help her not feel so sad, that Gerda had felt sick with shame. He'd yanked her and Raina by the arms and dragged them out of the school; he pushed them away from the tall building, toward town, where he made them sit on the stoop of a dry goods store when he went to buy some thread for their mother. When he came out, he didn't have the usual sticks of hard candy; he curtly barked orders for them to get in the wagon so they could begin the journey home.

He sat silently, holding the reins, for the longest time while Gerda and Raina shared puzzled, worried looks. Normally Papa sang songs from the old country—*"Bonden og Kråka"* was a favorite—or talked through his hopes for the farm while he was driving, even though neither Gerda nor Raina was much help. But they didn't have to be; he simply liked to hear himself speak to someone other than the chickens—that's what he always said.

This day he was so quiet, for so long, that Gerda started to chew on her fingernails, and Raina couldn't hold back her tears, although she let them fall silently down her plump cheeks.

The wagon swayed on the rutty path; the sun was behind them now, so everything looked bathed in a warm, red glow— the tops of the grasses were already a russet hue, but they looked almost ruby in the fading sunlight. Only if you lived for a long time on the prairie did you know the landmarks; a newcomer's eye would only see mile after mile of barely undulating land, undisturbed by trees or buildings. But Gerda knew that particular clump of purple leadplant meant they only had an hour left to go if they didn't break a wheel or axle; she recognized the branch where another set of ruts went off to the north as the place where they would stop for the girls to use the bushes if they had to. She wondered if the prairie chickens scurrying across the trail in front of the wagon were the same that had scurried across it on the trip this morning.

Finally, Papa sighed so deeply his shoulders rose nearly to his ears. He pulled on the reins and the oxen ambled to a stop; he tugged on the hand brake and let the animals graze a bit. He peered down at Gerda for so long that she began to quake inside, wondering if she could hide in the tallgrass before he punished her.

"Those children back there," he finally said, removing his straw hat to wipe the perspiration along his forehead with his sleeve. "It's not right. I thought it was when I heard about it. A school where the wildness could be taught out of the child, where they would be taught English, taught to be part of a civilized society—that could only be a good thing. But I don't know now. It's hard, you know. Hard to be separated from your family."

Raina nodded eagerly, but Gerda knew she didn't understand. Papa was talking about himself, and how he'd left his mother in the old country, his brothers, too. He would never see them again. But he was a big, grown man and Gerda had never realized, until this moment, that a big, grown man could miss anything. Or anyone.

"And they are but little ones," her father continued, now staring ahead at the prairie, but Gerda knew he wasn't seeing it—he was seeing his village in Norway, tucked between steep mountains, the likes of which Gerda couldn't imagine, even though she'd been born there. But she had no memory of the old country other than vague snippets: a snug little bed in a whitewashed attic with a slanting roof; a Christmas dinner with a table full of uncles and aunts and older cousins who teased; her mother crying bitterly when they drove away in a wagon to the sea.

Now Papa was seeing his own mother, so far away—his father had died when he was younger—and the idea of that, of never seeing Papa and Mama again, squeezed her chest until it bruised her heart. "Little ones, taken from their families. Even if they be Indians, it's not right. And you, miss . . ." Papa turned to gaze again at Gerda, and she dropped her head, burning with shame, her eyes swimming with tears.

"Look at me, Gerda."

Slowly, she raised her face, only to weep even more because Papa was looking at her with the usual love light softening his blue eyes. She hiccupped as she sobbed, and he put his arm about her, pulling her close.

"People aren't to be treated like possessions. They shouldn't be bought and sold or contained or corralled. I thought you knew that, Gerda."

"Oh, Papa, I do! I just—she seemed so sad."

"Yes, and you wanted to make her feel better and that is a good notion to have. So maybe think about how you can accomplish that another way. Maybe not for this little girl, but others like her. Think about giving, not taking."

She'd nodded, and they continued the journey home, where Mama wanted to know all about the school. But none of them wanted to talk about it, and she stopped asking with one of her understanding looks.

Gerda had never forgotten what her father had said then, and when she heard of another Indian school, one to be built on a reservation so that the children would live with their parents, she'd applied.

But when she received an invitation to teach, she'd declined. She couldn't exactly say why—only that it seemed such an enormous leap from the world she knew into a world she didn't. A world she was more than a little afraid of. So she'd taken up this school, and boarded with the Andersons, and met Tiny—who wanted to go fight an enemy that was already defeated. All you had to do was see that school to know that.

But still she loved Tiny, maybe because he was so different from any other boy she'd known—placid cows, all of them, content to stay put and homestead. As if the imagination that had caused their parents to put an ocean between themselves and all that was familiar had skipped a generation. Tiny was the only boy she'd ever met who didn't want to stay exactly where he was. So she loved him for this—while trying to dissuade him from it, too. It wasn't as if she loved homesteading. But she knew there was no place for a woman on a cattle drive or riding with the cavalry.

Oh, Gerda didn't know exactly what she wanted, other than to do exactly as she pleased! And she wanted—she *needed*—to begin now, because the good Lord knew that life could be short and brutal—hadn't she stood graveside for a school chum who died from a bee sting, of all things? Hadn't her mother's best friend, Lydia Gunderson, died in childbed, delivering her sixth baby? Didn't children fall into wells, vanish forever in the tall prairie grass; didn't young men get kicked in the head by horses, people get bit by rattlers, or suffer unexpected bloody flux or step on rusty nails or fall into open fires? Didn't entire families get sucked up by tornadoes or perish in flash floods?

Life was hard, and short, and Gerda, at eighteen, lay awake at night sometimes, her mind too full of wanting to sleep. Mostly, she wanted Tiny. She wanted to cook for him, to shine his boots, to scold him for taking too much time with the animals, to make him trim his fingernails, to cut his hair for him, to read to him in front of the fire.

To sleep next to his sturdy body radiating warmth and strength in the depths of a feather bed covered with quilts, bridal quilts made just for her. To reach out to him in the night, bring him as close as it was possible between a husband and wife, only breaths and sighs and whispers apart.

Sometimes, Gerda moaned at night in her narrow bed next to Pa and Ma Anderson's room; she tossed and turned, burning with a fever, for her emotions, her desires, always had a way of stoking up the furnace of her strong heart, lungs, and blood. She was always ashamed at those moments, ashamed of her sinful desires. And she couldn't take comfort in the thought that soon they would be absolved through marriage. Because no matter how meaningfully he pressed her hand, Tiny kept talking about going west. Just last Sunday, he'd shown her an illustration of the rocky Colorado mountains that he'd cut out of a newspaper.

"That's a place where a man can breathe," he'd exulted. "Where a man can touch God!"

It was always "a man" who figured in Tiny's dreams and wants. Just one. Solo.

So Gerda had her plans for this unexpected gift of an afternoon. She would let Tiny kiss her today. And she would kiss him back.

She'd written Raina about Tiny, pouring out her frustrations. Raina's letters in reply, however, weren't at all like the sunny, understanding letters from Raina of old; they were full of dark thoughts and questions that Gerda could never begin to answer. Poor Raina! She was certainly having a tough time at her first school. Gerda, now in her third year as a teacher, wished she could give her some advice. But Gerda's teaching career had been uncomplicated, her previous boarding situations uneventful. And now, with the Andersons, she certainly couldn't complain about anything but their dogged protection; they treated her just like a daughter. Gerda had no advice at all to give to the little sister who had always looked up to her. To tell the truth, she'd tried to warn her parents that Raina might be a little young to board out, despite the fact that she was the same age as Gerda had been. But her parents couldn't see what Gerda saw, that Raina was too quick to feel—happiness, sadness, it didn't matter, emotions ran roughshod over her, leaving her gasping in their wake. Gerda's parents couldn't—or wouldn't— see that their younger girl with the dark blond hair was too trusting, that she never saw a reason to look beyond the surface of people's actions. A smile was enough to convince Raina that someone was kind; a funny story meant that the teller was the most humorous person she'd ever met. Raina's heart was simply too pliable, too eager to both receive and give.

Gerda had guarded her own heart fiercely from the country bumpkins she'd grown up with, the sons of the stoic Norwegians and Swedes of the community. Until she went to Dakota Territory—her father still didn't understand why she chose a school so far away from home, a long four-day journey—where she met Tiny.

This afternoon, Tiny had come jingling up to the schoolroom in the sleigh at exactly twelve o'clock, as she'd instructed him to; she was just bundling the children up to go home, having declared it a holiday due to the nice weather. It was easy work; they'd all come to school wearing light jackets or shawls, the heavy woolens airing out at home on the line. By this time of the year, wool was starting to smell briny after so many wearings, having gotten wet and then dried inside at close quarters, over and over again. Every homestead mother took the opportunity of a rare warm day to air winter clothing outdoors.

Gerda was just fastening the last button on little Minna's sweater when Tiny let out a whoop from the sleigh; he was standing, holding tight to the reins of the little bay as the cloud descended and curtained the sun. She gazed in a stupor as sparks sizzled from the runners of the sleigh and the children squealed at the sight—then she sprang into action.

"Children, make a run for it," she called out as she quickly doused the fire in the round-bellied stove with a pail of water. "You'd better hurry, it looks like a big one!"

It was the right thing to do, she decided; they were already bundled up and ready to go home, and she'd officially declared school out. There would be no teaching her disappointed pupils if she changed her mind and kept them inside.

And there would be no pretending with Tiny in the snug little farmhouse, cooking him the meal she'd planned—Ma Anderson had left a plucked and dressed chicken, saying they wouldn't be home until after dinner. There would be no snuggling together in the big rush rocker. No kisses designed to lasso her cowpoke.

"Go home," Gerda called gaily over the whine of the wind that was causing some of the students to halt in confusion. They looked at her, questions in their eyes. Homestead children understood weather. Shelter in place—wasn't that what they were taught to do in a blizzard?

But they were also taught to always obey Teacher.

It wasn't a blizzard yet, Gerda determined; it was only a startlingly dark cloud with no borders and a fierce wind whipping up the snow already on the ground; not much was falling from the sky. If everyone left now, they'd be home, snug and dry, in two shakes of a lamb's tail. "If you live too far away, stay with a friend who's nearer. But if you run now, you'll be fine!" She clapped her hands to make her point, hastily threw on her own shawl and the knitted blue hat with the jaunty pom-pom that Tiny loved, grabbed Minna and Ingrid by the hands, and ran out of the schoolhouse, the door shutting on its own as the wind kicked up something fierce.

Then she leapt into the sleigh with the two girls. Tiny jumped in beside her, and with a shout, he slapped the reins down on the haunches of the bay, and they took off, trying to outrace the storm.

There was a moment, when she turned around to look at the receding backs of her students only to find, to her astonishment, that the snow—suddenly tumbling down from the sky to mix with the snow kicked up from the ground—had already swallowed them up. She almost told Tiny to turn around; maybe she should run after them and bring them back to the schoolhouse, after all.

But then Tiny smiled down at her, and even though the temperature seemed to be plummeting by the heartbeat, and her eyelashes had little drops of ice on the ends weighing them down, she smiled back.

And she laughed as Tiny urged the bay to go faster.

CHAPTER 5

Don't ever lose that slate or that bucket! They cost a dime. A whole dime, do you understand? If you lose them, you can't go to school anymore. And come right home after. No dawdling.

The words were pounded into Anette's brain as thoroughly as if Mother Pedersen had taken a hammer to her skull. She never had lost the slate or bucket, and she never had dawdled, and she wouldn't begin now. She clutched the slate tightly to her chest, beneath her shawl, the bucket in her other hand, and bent into the wind. She couldn't open her eyes at all against the force of it, the hard pebbles of ice pounding her face. But her feet knew the way—hadn't she made this trip hundreds of times? All she had to worry about was the ravine at the edge of the farm. But that was a mile away. She just had to run, that was all—run faster than normal to chisel through the wall of wind blowing her backward with every other step.

But Teacher was yelling at her to come back inside—Teacher, who knew how Mother Pedersen was! Who knew that she meant what she said and that if you crossed her, even with a look, she would make your life miserable. Mother Pedersen would act on her threat, that was one thing Anette knew—she didn't like sending Anette to school at all. She only did it because it was the law or something—maybe because Teacher boarded with them, and so she couldn't very well keep Anette from attending. But Mother Pedersen never stopped talking about the expense of the slate and the pail and the clothes, and the work she had to do in Anette's absence.

Anette did wonder why Mother Pedersen was so unhappy. She had everything, to Anette's hungry eyes. A nice house, handsome children (although the oldest, a little girl very much like her mother, was already showing signs of coveting everything that didn't come to her). Mother Pedersen was so beautiful, sometimes it devastated Anette to look at her because she then had to go look at herself in the mirror and see her own pockmarked face, heavy eyebrows, square jaw. And Mother Pedersen had Father Pedersen, the nicest man Anette had ever known, so quick to help Anette lift a heavy pot or to open a door for her when she had her arms full of dirty laundry; so eager to make sure Teacher had enough light at night to mark the lessons, determined that she have a small vase of fresh flowers whenever they were blooming. His eyes—soft, brown—seemed to understand everything you could ever want to tell him, before you even opened your mouth. And he was just as sweet to Mother Pedersen, too—he always made sure she had pretty fabric to make clothes for herself. Why, once, he even rode all the way to Omaha to find fabric in the exact same shade of blue— almost as blue as a cornflower—of her eyes! If Anette ever had anyone like that all to her own—because she knew that Father Pedersen's kindness to her was only borrowed, as everything in her life was borrowed, her clothes, the roof over her head, any attention that was paid to her, good and bad— she would never be sad or angry.

But Mother Pedersen was both; she sometimes would stop what she was doing and sit down and cry, so fiercely it looked like her face might split in two while her narrow shoulders sliced through the air in sharp upward thrusts. And her anger! As much a part of her as her bright flaxen hair that she took such care of, her fury was like a harsh, metallic thread woven into her perfectly fitted dresses. You followed the glint of it throughout the house as she darted from bedroom to kitchen to parlor, only staying in one place when she concentrated on baking intricate, dainty pastries that were so light and airy they didn't seem to belong on the prairie. Their very beauty made Anette shy about eating them— not that she was often offered any. But when she did eat them, she was always disappointed; as sweet as they were, they never did fill her up.

Mother and Father Pedersen rarely visited the second floor. Mother Pedersen left clean linens at the bottom step of the crude stairs every week, but it was the job of Teacher and Anette to make the beds, empty the slop jugs, sweep and dust what little there was to dust. The rest of the house was nicely furnished, at least in Anette's opinion, since her old home— and funny how she now thought of it that way—had been sparse, with little furniture, no rugs, a dirt floor. But the upstairs, where the two boarders slept, was just the two bedsteads separated by a curtain. No pictures. The only decoration was the flowers that Father Pedersen brought Teacher.

But one night last week, Anette had awoken to sounds that were unfamiliar enough to pull her from her exhausted sleep; it had been laundry day but so cold that the water pump froze outside, so Anette had been forced to carry shovels full of snow inside instead, where they melted in a big tub by the stove. When she awoke, her arms and shoulders still ached so much that she couldn't move them right away, so she merely lay still, listening.

First she heard Teacher murmuring something—was she talking in her sleep? But then Anette heard more murmurs. Different murmurs. A voice that didn't belong—

It was Father Pedersen. Saying something so low, but so sweet that Anette felt her heart yearn for more. She could make out no words; she only knew that it was a song she would have loved to hear, if only she could.

Then Teacher said something that was interrupted by a creak of the stairs, and Father Pedersen was walking toward the top of the staircase—Anette by this time had pushed herself up on her elbow. She could only see his feet, in his sturdy boots that were dripping melting snow; he must have just come in from seeing to the horses. Although why he would have been doing that in the middle of the night, Anette had no idea. Then she saw Teacher's bare feet hit the floor, and she had been amazed at seeing the small, bony feet, the little pink toes; it was so cold, why didn't she sleep with her socks on as Anette did?

This fact—this odd, distracting thought—so puzzled Anette that she almost didn't hear Father Pedersen say, "Anna." Just the one word—Mother Pedersen's name—but the way he said it was terrible. Anette bolted upright, hugging the quilt to her chest for protection. His voice was vibrant with terror and supplication.

Teacher cried out.

There was another creak of the stairs, then something metallic clattered to the floor and Father Pedersen was rushing down, and Teacher must have flung herself back on her bed. She sobbed so piteously, Anette didn't know what to do. Should she go to her?

From downstairs she could hear the sound of voices being raised, and the littlest Pedersen wailing from his basket, and doors slamming, a sound like a scream cut off before it was uttered. So Anette remained in her own bed. It was as if a line had truly been drawn—a wall, bricked up—between the two beds. They seemed intended for different things, these two bedsteads. And Anette had never known that before, that beds might have purposes other than for sleeping.

The days after that strange night had made Anette want to scream; the house was too small for so many people with so many troubles. As the temperature remained well below zero, they were trapped, and everyone behaved so oddly. Father Pedersen wouldn't talk to Mother Pedersen, who wouldn't speak to Teacher, who acted terrified of both of them and suddenly both younger and older than she had been before, and no one thought of Anette at all. She felt like she was a ghost, almost; no one could see her, but she saw *everything*. More than she wanted to. But she wasn't invisible, at that; all the things she didn't want to see made her so confused that Mother Pedersen slapped her for allowing a pan of milk intended for the baby to scald.

Teacher, observing, rushed to Anette's side; she pulled her into her arms.

"You are a cruel, cruel person," she scolded Mother Pedersen. It was the first time Anette had ever heard her speak angrily to the older woman, and the pain of the slap was forgotten in her astonishment.

"You know nothing about me," Mother Pedersen responded coolly. "And despite your silly fantasies, you know nothing about *him.*"

Teacher had fled upstairs, sobbing. With a strangled cry, Mother Pedersen erupted in fury, becoming a demon before

Anette's very eyes—her face scarlet, the blue eyes blazing while the coils of her hair seemed to dance with electricity. Mother Pedersen snatched the scalded milk off the top of the cookstove and ran to the door to throw it out, only she closed the door on her hand and collapsed in a heap on the floor, pounding her chest with her fists and hissing, "This cursed place, this cursed land," over and over again. Teacher's sobs were audible and the baby started to cry and Liane, the oldest Pedersen child, hit Martin, the middle one, and the two started to scream and tear at each other's clothes. And Anette simply stood where she was, in the middle of hell.

There was no way out, nowhere for her to go; she couldn't even run away, because she would freeze. She could only shut her eyes and try to summon up something good, and she pictured herself running with Fredrik, the two of them skimming the prairie earth. Running was the most uncomplicated thing in the world; all you had to do was remember to breathe and cherish the ache in your chest that came from the freedom of your body carrying your mind and your thoughts somewhere else, your troubles, too—they were mobile, never burdensome, when you were running.

And Fredrik's happy face, the sandy hair tickling his arched eyebrows, the freckles on his face even more pronounced when he was running beside her, sometimes reaching out to grab her hand, as if the two of them together could run even faster than each alone—

"Anette! Anette!"

A tug on her sleeve, a hand in hers, and she stopped running, stopped remembering, and tried to breathe—but couldn't. She tried to inhale but only frigid air, grains of ice, invaded her lungs and she began to wheeze, her chest so tight, her throat stinging, her nostrils stuck together. Gasping for breath, Anette turned, tried to open her eyes wide but they were stuck together; she rubbed her eyes with her sleeve until some of the ice melted and she could see.

The world as she had known it was gone. Everywhere was now white, now grey, now white again. She was in the middle of that furious cloud and could not see anything that looked of this earth. She might have been sucked up in the storm, like a cyclone, were it not for the ground beneath her feet. Ground that was increasingly covered with snow.

"Anette!"

"Fredrik!" She could barely say his name, and the wind howled so that it was a miracle he heard it, but he held tight to her hand, leaned in close to her. His eyes were wide with recognition; recognition that this was not anything he had encountered before, this howling tunnel of wind almost knocking them off their feet, of no visibility, no markers at all. She wanted to scream at him—*How did you find me? Are you stupid? Go back!*

Please stay, stay with me, I don't know how to do this.

But she had to go home, she couldn't dawdle, it was the only consistent thought as her mind started to open up to the realization that it was foolish, what she had done, to try to outrace a blizzard. Only once did she think of going back, but as soon as she turned around to retrace her steps, she saw that they were already swallowed up by the drifting snow, and she couldn't see anything, anything at all, except for Fredrik's blue –frightened—eyes.

"We go," she managed to finally croak, then she shouted the words again, and Fredrik nodded.

We go. Forward, toward home.

We go, Anette said in her heart.

Together.

CHAPTER 6

· · · · ·

GAVIN HAD JUST TURNED THE CORNER OF FARNAM, ON his way back to the Gilded Lily, when the storm struck Omaha.

The force of it blew him off his feet and pushed him against a hitching post; he clung to it for a moment, stunned. Sure, the sky had grown dark in the northwest while he was out strolling, which was why he turned around in the first place. But weather, even in Godforsaken Nebraska, didn't move *that* fast, as fast as a steam engine on a flat track.

Grabbing on to the post until he could regain his balance, Gavin felt something like gravel hit the back of his neck. Turning around, ready to yell at some hooligan, he saw no one behind him at all, but when he reached up to touch his neck, he felt hard little pebbles of ice. He gaped in surprise as the buildings he'd just passed were swallowed up by a furious wall of snow, now mixed with the dirt of town so that it was streaked with brown and grey and black.

Gavin swore; he felt fear despite the fact that he was a mere few feet from shelter. And then, all he could think of was *her*. That young woman, the one he'd just tipped his hat to, what was it—God, only half an hour ago, it must have been. Dear God.

She'd be back out on the prairie now, she and her family; rubes they were, Swedes probably, maybe Germans; they all had that open, exposed expression of someone new to this land. Like baby chicks, needing to be taught everything. The family must have come into town for supplies; he'd spotted them out near the Catholic cemetery, at a little dry goods store that nobody who lived in town ever went to because the prices were too high. But the place did a splendid business jacking up the prices for homesteaders who were too overwhelmed to venture farther into town.

Hitched to a post in front of the store had been a wagon, the wheels replaced with crude sleigh runners; in the bed of the wagon were two small boys pummeling each other and jabbering in their native tongue. Next to them, sitting so that her back was against the driver seat of the wagon, was their older sister, Gavin supposed.

A young woman, maybe seventeen, who could tell? Gavin certainly couldn't. But she was wearing long skirts, her reddish blond hair braided into a crown atop her head. She was sitting so still, oblivious to the two hooligans fighting at her feet, her hands folded quietly in her lap, her face turned west, a longing kind of look in her eyes, a half smile playing at her lips. Her clothes were plain, homespun, her cloak a faded dark green. He couldn't see her feet, but he imagined she was wearing dirty men's boots, too big for her. Every material thing on her looked made for someone else.

It was her throat that made Gavin stop, look, *feel*. To his consternation and horror, tears sprang to his eyes. But her throat was so young, unlined, somehow tender and hopeful, if a throat could be that, but here it was, this womanly throat not yet weighed down by care and death and worry and fear. It held her delicate head aloft as she blinked her eyes dream ily, still looking out toward the prairie, like a stem holds a bud; it yearned.

Throats do not yearn, Gavin scolded himself. *You are giving emotions to things, and that is not what a journalist does. You are imbuing a rather ordinary part of the anatomy with poetry. This is ridiculous.*

Yet there it was. He couldn't take his eyes off her, she looked so detached from the plainness of her surroundings: the dirty snow, the weathered wagon. Her face belonged to another time and place. The girl must have sensed him staring, for she turned and met his gaze without fear or confusion or even wonder.

He tipped his hat to her, and she nodded regally. As if she had been expecting him.

Then the parents bustled up, handing packages to her, and suddenly she was just another young immigrant woman helping her mother and father, pulling apart her squabbling siblings. Gavin found himself, foolishly, hoping one of those brown paper–wrapped packages contained something sweet, something girlishly frivolous—a ribbon or a bottle of scent, a hair comb, a spool of pink thread, maybe. Something for her very own, to place under her pillow at night or maybe keep in a secret drawer.

But Gavin knew there was no such gift; he knew these people better than they knew themselves, he sometimes thought. There was no money set aside for an object designed to make a pretty girl feel even prettier—to make her aware of herself in a way that had nothing to do with hard labor, disappointment, suffering, sacrifice. And a future just like her mother's, who looked older, by twenty years, than she probably was.

Gavin turned and walked back toward town, brushing

away the ridiculous tears, laughing at himself. Godforsaken
Omaha was turning him into a fool. An old, sentimental goat
of a fool. It was long past time for a drink; he headed toward
the Lily.

But when the wind hit, all he could think of was the girl.
Out there. In this storm that had roared up so quickly. No
one today was dressed for it; she'd been wearing only a tattered cape, her brothers had only jackets patched at the elbows. Now they were out there in the midst of it, most likely
a long way from home.

He wished he'd asked her name.

Hugging the post, Gavin righted himself and threw himself up to the left, against the buildings, so that he could
make his way the three blocks to the Lily. Where the buildings ended, at the intersection of streets, was already haz-
ardous; when he stepped into the void, he could simply pray
no horse or wagon or trolley car was bearing down on him,
and it seemed only by the grace of somebody's god that he
regained the buildings on the other side of the street, continuing in this way—like a drunk sailor trying to navigate a
pitching, wave-washed deck—until he smelled the cigar
smoke and clove and beer aroma of the Lily. Pushing open
the door was easy as the wind was blowing against it, and he
tumbled into the blessedly warm room, slipped on a puddle
of melted snow, and fell flat on his ass.

A few fellows guffawed at him, but most were pressing
their dirty noses against the filthy windows, looking outside.

"Woodson, you all right?"

Dan Forsythe reached down to haul him up from the
floor. Gavin brushed off the ice and snow from his coat,
shaking his head.

"I am now. But God Almighty, that's a helluva storm out there."

"Blew up real quick, it did." Forsythe followed him to the bar, where Ol' Lieutenant, the Lily's owner, was already shoving a shot of whiskey at Gavin, who swallowed it greedily.

"It'll pass over just as quickly," someone staring out the window said. "Wasn't no cold wave issued for today, was there?"

Everyone then turned toward a man in a dark blue military uniform sitting at the end of the bar, nursing a beer. The man looked up, surprised. Just a touch guilty.

Corporal Findlay he was, one of the new "indicators" from the Army Signal Corps, whose job it was to take readings of the weather and send them to the new office in Saint Paul, Minnesota. Gavin had done a piece on them; how they had a division of these indicators, stationed all along the country at forts and railroad stations, who relayed wind direction and intensity, barometric pressure readings, temperature, sun or cloud coverage, via telegraph. These readings were collected in Saint Paul—previously, they had been gathered in Washington—and from these readings the officer in charge up there, a Lieutenant Woodruff, telegrammed his indication for the part of the country lying west of the Mississippi at various intervals throughout the day. The main prediction was the one transmitted just after midnight to the newspapers, post offices, and railroad stations.

It was a fairly new responsibility for the Army Signal Corps, and there were civilians—those claiming more scientific experience—who disagreed bitterly with the way the information was gathered and relayed. There was also some corruption—when wasn't there, when it came to the Grand Army of the Republic? Reports of soldiers who would fabri-

cate an entire week's worth of data in advance and pay someone to relay it for them while they went off to hunt or fish or
drink. The telegraph lines were often blown down by the
very weather they were supposed to try to indicate, delaying
readings until they were of no use.

But the railroads had demanded some kind of system to
at least try to keep the trains on schedule during these unpredictable, punishing prairie winters; and what the railroads demanded, the U.S. government was bound and
beholden to do. After all, the railroads had made this country, reshaped it along routes radiating north, west, and
south, like the rays of the sun. The railroads had given the
army something to do after it defeated the rebels; it had
given them a new, more exciting enemy in the Native. And
now that he was defeated, the army needed more to do. Like
trying to predict the weather.

In the winter, the worst indication was one for a "cold
wave," which meant that a front of plunging temperatures
following significant snow was to be expected. Today's indication had not called for a cold wave. No warning flags would
have been raised to warn anyone—but even if they had been,
Gavin knew, they were of little help except to those living
within sight of a train station. Or those who had access to
one of the major newspapers, like the *Bee.*

Homesteaders, naturally, did not.

"The readings last night and this morning didn't indicate
this, this—this disturbance from the west," Corporal Findlay
sputtered. "At least as far as I know. I'm not the one in charge,
that's Woodruff. Well, actually, Greely in Washington."

"Readings?" An old farmer—Sam Benson—guffawed.
"What the hell does that mean? I can predict the weather
just by looking at the sky."

"Did you predict this?" Findlay shot back.

Benson didn't say another word.

"Trust the red man when it comes to weather," Ol' Lieutenant chimed in as he pulled out a book—*Silas Marner*. The man was famous for reading whenever he wasn't pouring liquor; the book looked ridiculous in his giant hands the color of spring mud. He wore glasses, perched way down on the end of his nose; the glasses, with his tight, short coils of grey hair, gave him the look of a quiet schoolteacher. A look completely at odds with the rumors that he'd once shot ten Indians while out on patrol, even with his trigger hand bandaged after a horse bit him. Those Buffalo Soldiers sure were tough sons of bitches, Gavin knew. They had to be, back in the day. And now here was Ol' Lieutenant trying to better himself by reading books that men like Gavin had read long ago, in the quiet halls of eastern schools. You had to admire a man like that.

"Did you see any of them in town today?" Ol' Lieutenant asked, without glancing up from the page of his book.

There was silence as, one by one, men shook their heads.

"That means they knew."

"Well, how the hell am I supposed to plan my life around whether or not the Injuns come into town?" somebody asked, to the collected chuckles of men who normally spared no thoughts for the Natives now that they were all safely corralled on their reservations, only venturing out, with passes granted to them by their military guards, to sometimes sell their wares in town.

"It isn't letting up any," Forsythe said, pacing back and forth from the windows to the bar.

Findlay got up and started putting on his coat. "I need to get the latest readings in and telegraph them to Saint Paul."

He left without a word; the other men just shook their heads, still not willing to give this newfangled weather prediction any merit.

Of course, every man there recognized that it would be beneficial to know what the weather was going to be like from day to day. But out here on the plains, weather didn't cooperate like it did in the East, where you could look at the western sky, lick a finger and hold it up to the wind, sniff the air, and plan your day. Here, the weather might blow down straight from the Arctic Circle or roar up from the Gulf of Mexico or march in steadily from the Pacific, and some-times it did all three at once.

No civilized man could indicate it—not even an army man.

"I wonder if I should go to the schoolhouse," one shop-keeper mused, looking worried. "Davey can't walk home in this alone."

"They won't let school out in this kind of weather," some-one assured him.

"But maybe they will. That damn schoolteacher's from the East, he don't know our weather."

"I'm worried about my horse," Johnny Swanson fretted. "I don't like leaving her out there in this, if it ain't blowing over. I'm gone, gentlemen." And he threw on his hat and coat, opening the door and letting in a cold blast of air and snow that made more than a few swear. Others, thinking about their horses tied up to the hitching posts, too, fol-lowed him. So did Davey's father, the shopkeeper.

"That sleighing party, that's what's on my mind," For-sythe said quietly, as he drummed his fingers on the bar next to Gavin.

Gavin jerked his head up from his second shot of whis-key. "Damn. That's right. They're out there in this."

The two men exchanged looks. Then Gavin downed that shot, threw some money on the bar, and shrugged his arms back into his coat as Forsythe pulled his on.

"You two are going out in this? What are you, heroes?" Ol' Lieutenant snorted; the newspapermen were not exactly respected in a town like Omaha, where people were suspicious of those who made their living trading words, not goods. Gavin snorted. These rubes.

"Hardly." He could already imagine the headline—*Great Loss of Life! A Day of Pleasure Turns Deadly! Sleighing Party Becomes Funeral Party!*

And he didn't have to worry about Forsythe getting the headline alone this time; a storm like this was big enough for the two of them. Maybe this was it—maybe this was the event that would get Gavin back to New York, finally. A storm of epic, tragic proportions—the stories would write themselves! Pulitzer would have to bring him back to the fold; already he was thinking of how many ways he could describe what the wind was doing—*roaring, blowing, pummeling, assaulting, punching, whistling, screaming . . .*

The two prepared to head out into the storm that was not letting up, thank God; maybe this thing *was* going to turn out to be a tragedy, after all!

But as soon as he felt the first blast of ice slap his unprotected face, Gavin thought, once more, of that girl. How many ways could he come up with to describe what happened when young, hopeful—*yearning*—women were frozen to death out on the prairie?

Gavin looked up at the sky, hoping, to his own surprise, to see a break in the clouds, a glimpse of a fading sun.

But no such break occurred.

CHAPTER 7

. . . . .

OLLIE TENNANT WATCHED THE MEN FILE OUT OF HIS bar, successfully hiding his distaste. Not a one of them had mentioned the school where *his* children spent their days learning their lessons.

But Ollie was used to this; from the moment these idiots had mangled his name, assuming that he must be one of those Buffalo Soldiers whose legacies still loomed large in barely settled places like Omaha, he'd understood the way to deal with them. He'd understood that the only way to get a white man to respect you was to try to be as white as he was, at least in book learning. And you had to be braver, twenty times as brave as the average white gentleman, because the colored man was starting from a ways away from zero, in that category. At least in the white imagination.

So Ollie read his books, but he sometimes thought they were foolish—stories about the problems white people had, which couldn't hold a candle to the problems darker people had. He mostly read for the show of it, although now and then a book—like *The Adventures of Huckleberry Finn*— surprised him. But his reading soothed the customers somehow. It made them feel more inclined to spend.

And he'd smiled enigmatically when the stories sprang up about him—that he'd been a soldier, part of the famous 9th Cavalry that helped "tame" the Kiowa and Comanche down in Texas. All he'd done was buy a cavalry jacket off a drunk in Missouri, because the coat was warmer than the one he had on his back at the time. He'd never once said a word that wasn't true; all he had to do was smile or force a far-off look in his eye when white folk jumped to their own conclusions.

A colored man got a lot further in this world when he didn't open his mouth.

He wasn't no former slave, either; that was the other assumption folks in Omaha made about people with skin darker than an Indian or Mexican. Ollie had grown up in a tiny village in northern Indiana, a settlement of mostly coloreds who farmed small plots and kept to themselves. But just because his skin wasn't white didn't mean that he, too, didn't feel the tug of the West, like so many men. His first memories were of turning to face the setting sun, wanting to go with it, to see what it saw. He'd lit out as soon as he was able, wandering from outpost to outpost, finally ending up in Omaha, putting his money into this little bar that was fine for a while, sure, while the town was just itty-bitty, but now that it was booming, things were different.

First the railroad, then the stockyards; Omaha became a magnet for people who didn't want to farm but who would do—and do happily—the jobs that a lot of natural-born white Americans didn't want to do. The Irish, the Bohemians, the Poles, the Italians, the coloreds—they were willing to spend their days in a slaughterhouse or a canning facility, or bending over crooked rails and hammering them straight, or enduring the crippling fumes of a tanning house. Omaha had jobs like these in spades, and so they came, and the people who'd been here first, the white boomers and boosters, got rich off them, building rickety shacks for them to rent on the outskirts of town. There was Little Bohemia just south of here. Up north were the Hebrews, Italians, and people like Ollie himself; that was where the coloreds were starting to congregate.

Ollie had bought his little tavern right in the heart of the downtown area when there wasn't a downtown area. Back then, nobody seemed to care that they got their drinks from a colored man—one of the few in town at the time. But now, the city was *civilized. Tamed,* the newspapers trumpeted. Fine hotels and restaurants surrounded his little storefront. Just last week the *Bee* had run a story of a visiting colored man who tried to get a drink in a bar of one of those fine hotels, and—politely, the paper said—was asked to leave.

Ollie had been approached several times in recent months by groups of civic leaders pressuring him to sell. "Go north, Ollie. The land is cheap there; you could buy five lots for what we're able to pay you for the Lily."

Ollie was willing to admit he had a stubborn streak; he didn't like being told what to do. He'd once massacred a passel of fireflies, running after them, catching them in his big mitt of a hand, despite his mother warning him he would squeeze them to death. He'd clutched them even tighter in response, and when he finally released them into the glass jar she'd given him for just this purpose, he'd discovered she was right. They were lifeless, his hand faintly smeared with their yellow dust, still glowing in the dark. He'd squeezed the life out of them by wanting them too much.

He'd spent the rest of his life trying not to want too much. But he had a wife now, and two kids, and his wife hated living over the bar in this part of town where she wasn't wanted; she felt it much more keenly than Ollie. She kept pestering him to move to the North Side, where her friends were. (Ollie didn't have any friends and that was fine by him; he had no need for conversation. Nor did he have any love for some of the younger men coming to town, agitating for things like equal rights for the Negro. Ollie'd done just fine, hadn't he? Why upset the apple cart and make the whites nervous and angsty?) Still, he was considering the latest offer. Because he had a customer who had kindly told him that if he didn't, he could expect some kind of bill to pass in the town council that would annex his lot in the name of progress, and he wouldn't get even a single dime.

Besides, his kids went to school on the North Side, too. And it was a long walk back home. They weren't welcome on the new cable cars that ran up and down the main thorough-fares.

Ollie looked outside his now-empty bar. The storm wasn't getting any better; in fact, the wind seemed more in-tent on punishing everything standing upright. His win-dows creaked ominously, and despite the fact that the round-bellied stove was blazing away, full of coal, the air was getting colder by the minute. His kids couldn't come home in this. And Ollie didn't trust their teacher—a mania-cally cheerful white lady, daughter of an Episcopalian min-ister with a charitable bent—to keep them safe.

Ollie bundled up into his buffalo coat, pulled on some leather gloves, and prepared to go out in the storm to get his kids.

Because he couldn't trust the white men to spare a thought for them, that was for damn sure.

CHAPTER 8

"ANETTE! FREDRIK! ANETTE!" RAINA SCREAMED UNTIL her throat was raw; she stood on the doorstep to the school-house for as long as she could stand it, shouting after the two who had been sucked into the storm. All she could see was grey and white. The snow whipped up from the ground meeting the snow falling from the sky in a hellish, twisting dance. The wind kept pushing her off balance; she clung to the doorframe but finally had to shut the door. Her eyes watered and stung from the icy projectiles that assaulted them; she felt tears rushing down her cheeks.

"No—Tor! No!" She grabbed his arm and yanked him back from the door. Tor had buttoned up his jacket and was headed out to retrieve his brother.

"Let go of me," he yelled, fighting Raina. He was the larger, he could easily overpower her and leave. But desperation tightened her grip on his strong arm; she couldn't let him go, she couldn't do this alone.

"I say let go of me—Fredrik! Fredrik!" Tor wrested the door open again and shouted into the tempest, his voice ragged with tears that he tried to hide from Raina. Tor was fifteen, almost a man. No, a man already, by prairie standards; this was his last year in the schoolhouse. When he wasn't at school, Raina knew, a boy like Tor was laboring beside his father, sharing the hardest tasks. His body was already muscled and work-weathered, his hands callused, his nose sunburnt in the summer from spending days in the fields, his biceps like rocks. Only his mind still needed coaxing out of childhood.

Raina had noted in Tor a hunger, almost, but not quite, disguised by his manners, the same respect and obedience all the immigrant children had been brought up with. Tor was too polite to ask for more than his share in life, but Raina could tell by the way he gobbled up his assignments and spat them back out again that he had a desire to learn—and an ability for it—that she could never begin to satiate. In a different place, Tor would go to college. But not here, not in Nebraska. Not a poor farmer's oldest son. So she tried to slip him extra books when she could—her own books that she'd brought with her from home. *Ivanhoe, Oliver Twist.* Even *Jane Eyre* and *Vanity Fair,* which he seemed to enjoy despite that the fact that they were "girls' books."

But sometimes, Raina felt guilty about giving him more. What right did she have to enflame this boy's hunger when there was no way for him ever to satisfy it? He was born on a farm and he would die on a farm; he would stop reading words and searching for ideas and instead learn to read the weather in the sky, when a mare would foal by the way she walked, how often to switch crops from the color of the soil.

"Let go, I have to go after him! Mama and Papa—I have to, they'd never forgive me if I didn't; you don't understand, Fredrik's little, he's just a kid—"

"Tor." Raina's voice startled the boy, as it startled her; it came from a place she'd never had access to before. A deep well of authority and certainty. She started talking to him in Norwegian, forgetting the edict about English; it stopped Tor in his tracks to hear Miss Olsen speak his native language—she saw the confusion and curiosity in his eyes, giving Raina the advantage she needed. She quickly shut the door again. "Tor, you could get lost out there yourself. You might not be able to find them in all this—you know how fast those two are, they could be almost home by now, anyway—" She broke off, rubbing her stinging eyes; she didn't believe that, not with the fact of this monstrous wind rearranging the very landscape, and she knew Tor didn't believe it, either. But they both needed to pretend they did. "You have to stay here, do you understand?" Now her voice was urgent, conspiratorial. "The other children—I have to keep them safe now. We need to think of the greater good. We're going to run out of fuel soon, we'll have to think about what else we can use—break up the benches and tables, maybe. I can't do that without you. Do you understand?"

Tor's eyes, reddened from frustration and fear, looked anguished; Raina could see his thoughts fighting for prominence— the desire to protect his brother, the fear of disappointing his parents, the realization that what Raina was saying was true. All his responsibilities—and a homestead boy had so many, too many—claiming his heart, dividing it into little parcels. As she gazed into his face, about level with her own, she recognized how steady, how good a character he was. Clear blue eyes, unclouded by deception or prevarication. Strong eyebrows, darker than the reddish brown of his thick hair. No freckles, unlike his impish brother; Tor's skin was fair, yet his cheeks were ruddy and the peach fuzz on his upper lip starting to coarsen.

This was a boy, a man—a good man, he would be, just like

his father—who would never speak a seduction wrapped up in a compliment. Who would never say pretty things he shouldn't to a naïve young girl. Who would never dangle hope where none existed.

Nothing in his honest young face made her fearful. Or confused. She only knew an overwhelming sense of relief that he was here. Tor, she realized with an overdue slap of rational thinking, even at his young age, was everything that Gunner Pedersen was not. *Gunner*—suddenly she wanted to howl his name just as desperately as Tor had howled Fredrik's.

She and Tor were both missing people. People who had claim to their hearts. Despite what she thought about Gunner—his flaws as a husband, as a moral person—Raina still longed for him to come driving up with his fine horses and save her. Save them all.

She longed for him to act like the man she wanted him to be.

As she gently pulled Tor away from the door and back into the schoolroom toward the stove where the other children sat huddling, the youngest ones starting to sniff back tears, Raina still listened for the sound of horses whinnying, reins jingling, *his* teasing, musical voice calling out for her in that seductive way. Her heart actually seemed to reach toward the schoolyard, her hope, her need, was that strong. And she thought back to the other night—*that* night, when he did croon her name. "You're the most important thing to me in the world. Get dressed, my Raina," he'd whispered, pressing her hand when she sat up, wondering if she was dreaming, then hearing Anette turning over in her bed behind the curtain so that she knew she was not. "Get dressed, come to the barn. We're leaving this place, you and me. To-gether."

What gave him the right to say this? What had she ever done to indicate this was what she wanted? She'd tried so hard to be good, to be modest; she prayed every night to be released from this hell of temptation and despair. He gave her flowers, he manufactured ways for them to be alone, he stole her thoughts, her dreams, even her privacy, accompa-nying her whenever she tried to escape, whenever she found a dark corner to hide in. He did it all so smoothly, even deli-cately; no one would know there had been any words spoken between them that weren't harmless, any thoughts or hopes revealed that weren't innocent, what would normally occur between two chaste people living under the same roof.

No one but Anna, his wife. Anna saw and heard every-thing; she was a force of nature who never kept still, never hid herself away, seemed to be everywhere at once: now in the kitchen, dicing meat for stew; now in the little parlor, polishing the prize china lamps; now in the stable—his domain—rubbing the bits and bridles until they shone. Checking on the chickens, sending Anette through her paces, diapering the baby, braiding her daughter's hair so tight the girl cried, obsessively ironing her own pretty clothes, the only things she didn't make Anette launder. Sewing new aprons and bonnets for herself while Anette's clothes grew more and more threadbare, cooking dinner, each dish so pretty in a dainty bowl or platter, the table set like at a hotel, with many forks and spoons, even when the food was just plain farm food. She heard, she saw, she sus-pected, she scattered her withering words like hard, sharp pebbles throughout the house, you had to pick your way carefully through them, you never knew when you would face a new onslaught.

She never sat, never rested. Not even at night.

When Gunner crept back downstairs that awful night, Raina lay still for a long while. *I'll go back to sleep,* she told herself. *She may murder me in the night but I don't care anymore. I need to leave this house one way or another.*

She had never said a single word to Gunner that would indicate she was the type of woman who would run off with a married man. But words weren't the only way to communicate. And in her miserable heart she knew that had Anna not shown herself, she might have gone with him—after all, hadn't she already risen, her feet on the floor, ready to follow him, before Anna spoke?

A crash, a wail—Raina twitched as if she'd been poked with a barbed wire. She heard glass breaking, shattering her memories, and she looked about her. The largest schoolroom window had blown in with an explosion of glass; it was all over the floor. The greedy wind rushed through, howling now inside the schoolhouse as loudly as it did outside, and her hands flew to her ears to stifle it. She froze, trying to make sense of the scene: papers blowing all over the place and children screaming. Clara burned her hand on the stove as she ran to it for warmth. The snow piled in; the cold assaulted the room like an army of sharp knives. Tor rushed to gather the girl up as those icy knives slashed at Raina's shawl, her dress, her flesh, her bones. She was shivering now, her entire body shaking. Walter Blickenstaff ran to the window with his coat, trying to cover it up, but his coat was then sucked outside. Tor threw the last log into the stove, desperate, then turned to look at Raina for guidance while she still stood, freezing, shaking, children running to her, tugging on her skirt, crying, wailing, hysterical.

It hit her then. They couldn't remain here, after all. They would freeze to death. The time had come, and gone, when she could be rescued.

She was going to have to lead these ten children, not including Tor, outside. Into that storm.

Panicked, her gaze returned to Tor, who was comforting Clara. Raina knew that they would have to do it, the two of them. Together, these two children—yes, they were children, her heart cried out. How confusing that today she called herself a child while all those nights, in Gunner's eyes and her own desires, she had declared herself a woman. The irony did not escape her, but she only had a breath to realize it before returning to the desperate situation before her. Two young people, fifteen and sixteen, would have to get these even younger people somewhere safe.

Somewhere they wouldn't all freeze to death by morning.

CHAPTER 9

. . . . .

THE SLEIGH WAS NOT SKIMMING MERRILY OVER THE SNOW as it should have. The wind was too capricious, pummeling first this way, then the other, like a prizefighter taking out his revenge on an unworthy opponent. The little bay, Tiny's pride and joy, was frothing at the mouth, trying to keep up; his eyes kept getting crusted over with ice, causing him to stumble, so that every few yards, Tiny had to rein him in and climb down to cover the horse's eyes with his hands, thawing the ice.

"How close are we to home?" Gerda shouted over the wind as Tiny pulled on the reins, preparing to climb down and repeat this task. The little bay was whinnying piteously.

"A mile, maybe two," Tiny called back, and Gerda's heart sank. They must have been in the storm for nearly an hour. The two little girls sat on either side of her, their shawls—inadequate—pulled up over their heads. As Gerda gathered them closer to her, she could feel them shivering uncontrollably—or was that her own body trembling?

Then they were falling. Falling, the sleigh teetering on one runner, for a brief, hopeful moment balancing there while Gerda held her breath lest she blow the whole thing

over. But the sleigh tilted farther, heartlessly tossing its oc-
cupants out onto the prairie before it was yanked back upright by the horse. They hit the ground hard—the snow was
packed and icy—and the girls started to cry. Gerda pushed
herself up, stunned, and suddenly Tiny was leaping to his
feet and dashing after the little bay who was still trying to
outrun the storm; the horse and the sleigh disappeared into
a swirling mass of ice and snow.

"Tiny! Tiny!" Gerda didn't seem hurt from the fall, but
maybe she was too numb to feel pain? She wasn't too numb
to feel panic, however; panic rising up from her feet, rushing over her heart, squeezing her throat as Tiny disappeared
into the raging nightmare, shouting, "Poco! Poco!"

Poco. That horse of his, he'd named it after himself, saying that *poco* was the vaquero word for "small," and maybe it
was but it didn't matter now. What mattered was that Tiny
had vanished—she couldn't even hear him calling after the
horse—leaving her and the girls. Minna was crying while she
held on to Ingrid's hand, and the tears, Gerda saw to her
horror, froze on her cheeks. Gerda took her thumb, clad in
her wool gloves that were also frozen, and tried to rub the ice
away from the little girl's cheek.

She stopped, her stomach churning, when the flesh
peeled away, exposing a raw, red wound on Minna's face, although the girl didn't appear to feel anything; she kept sobbing, but it was from fear, not pain, as far as Gerda could tell.

"*Tiny!*" Gerda—holding tight to the girls, one in each
hand—took a few steps toward where Tiny had vanished, but
she wasn't sure of the direction. Maybe it was this way? She
turned, took more steps, stopped, dizzy; she didn't know
which way was north or south, east or west. Desperately she
looked at the ground, searching for tracks of the cutter

sleigh, of their footsteps in the blowing, drifting, oddly sand-like snow, but there were none. It was as if a giant broom had swept away any trace of their journey so far.

"Tiny!" Where was he? Why didn't he come back? He would, he must—they would wait for him. He'd be back in a moment, back with the horse and sleigh, of course he would. He wouldn't leave her, not Tiny—reliable, exasperating Tiny. Men like him didn't leave women and children to fend for themselves in a storm like this. He would be back. He had to come back.

Squatting down, she huddled with the two girls, drawing them close to her body; it was a little warmer this close to the ground, a little more visible as well, but still she couldn't see more than a couple of feet in any direction.

"Let's sing a song," she began, to keep the girls' minds off the deadening misery that must have grasped their very bones as it was now seizing hers. "Little drops of water, little grains of sand . . ." But she gave up; she couldn't keep shouting over the wailing squall. So they crouched as long as they could, Gerda's knees locking into place so thoroughly she wondered if she could ever stand straight again; finally, she collapsed onto the numbingly glacial earth, drawing the girls into her lap, the three of them one shuddering, miserable being, snow blowing so fiercely she worried they'd be covered completely, then she thought that might be preferable to being so exposed. . . .

She opened her eyes, her heart thumping but curiously weak; she must have drowsed off, and she knew that was deadly. She shook the girls, pinched them until they cried; little Minna's long eyelashes were frozen to her cheek and Gerda blew on them, rubbed them and more of the girl's tender flesh was exposed. Ingrid remained stoic, too stoic;

Gerda worried that the older girl might just topple over without giving her a chance to save her.

Because they were lost and alone. Tiny hadn't come back. She had no idea how long they'd been there on the ground but she had to dig them out of a small drift that came up to Minna's shoulders, in order for her to painfully rise and pull the girls to their feet.

Her entire body began to shudder, so that she could barely get the words out. "Girls, le-le-let's go," she forced herself to say. She couldn't wait for Tiny anymore. For one last moment she let him fill her thoughts—Tiny with shoulders so broad she teased that he could pull a plow himself; Tiny with a cocky smile at the ready, even in church; Tiny with strong hands that could span her waist; Tiny, his sparse mustache with a little white streak in it, like a bolt of lightning, that she imagined would tickle her lips when she allowed him to kiss her.

Tiny, out there shouting for his stupid horse, even though, rationally, Gerda understood that a horse was currency on the prairie. Tiny, alone in this, maybe as frightened as she was, although it was difficult for Gerda to imagine that.

Then she made her mind shut him out; she had to concentrate on the girls, on getting them to safety somehow. Although she couldn't shut her mind to a more ominous thought: What about the other children she'd urged—so gaily!—to run home in this fury of a blizzard?

But she couldn't think of them now. Gerda had to move, she had to get these two girls in her charge to some kind of shelter. No light penetrated the clouds, so she couldn't tell what time it was, and there was nothing to illuminate any familiar landmark. A creek bordered south of the line of homesteads that included the girls' farm and the Andersons', so if they'd been coming the usual way from the schoolhouse, that creek, and its little brace of elm trees that were just planted a couple of years ago so not very tall, should be on their right. If she could find that creek and walk along it, they would come to a house or a barn or even a stack of hay eventually.

But she felt like a mouse trapped in a bucket; no matter which way she turned, it all looked the same and there was no way out, no magic curtain of clouds parting, even for just a second, to show her the landscape beyond her own nose.

"Tiny," she called once more, but the words didn't carry, they were muffled, hollow; not even desperation could find a way out of this storm.

Minna was still crying, and now so was Ingrid, and they were both shivering violently. She tugged on them, taking a few steps forward, but Minna's feet were too small, they couldn't keep her upright in the force of the wind. So Gerda knelt down and told the child to climb up on her back. She staggered up with the additional weight, then stumbled, almost fell, but Ingrid grasped her hand, and she managed to stay upright.

"All right, all right," she repeated over and over. Ingrid didn't speak, neither did Minna, but at least Minna stopped crying as she buried her head in the back of Gerda's neck. Gerda was grateful for the child's warmth against her, shielding her a little from the wind.

"All right, all right," she kept chanting despite her teeth rattling so that she worried she would chip one of them. She had to walk with her head bowed, to try to keep the snow and ice from glazing over her eyes—she remembered the horse, Tiny getting out to melt the ice over his eyes, and panic, thoroughly part of her now, squeezed her heart. Where were they?

Where was she?

CHAPTER 10

. . . . . .

THE HOUSE WAS LOSING SOME OF ITS WARMTH, SO ANNA Pedersen went to the little lean-to off the kitchen to grab more wood. The lean-to was almost full; she thanked her foresight in having Gunner fill it up this morning, when it was warm, after those other two left for school.

She almost sang with joy when she saw them running away from the house this morning, the Schoolteacher—she refused to call her by her name—holding Anette by the hand as they flew away without a backward glance. If only they could truly flee and never come back! Even with the heavier workload, she would be glad to have both of these interlopers out of her house. She'd never asked for them to come here, had she? No. It was all *his* idea.

As it had been Gunner's brilliant plan to leave Minneapolis, which she had loved—it had reminded her a little bit of Kristiania, Norway's beautiful capital city, although it was not nearly so grand—to come here. To northeastern Nebraska, far from any city or town. A man who had never in his life tried to make a living from the earth, who had grown up in cities as had she, had gotten it into his idiotic head that owning acres of land was something he was owed now that he was an American. That living self-sufficiently, miles from any neighbor, was the true test of an American man. At least he hadn't tried to grow any crops; she could at least be thankful about that. No, Gunner, who had been in the horse guards in the army back in Norway—and hadn't she been smitten with him then, in his dashing uniform astride a sleek black horse?—had stuck with one thing he knew, anyway. And even Anna had to admit that breeding and selling horses was a reliable income in a land so newly settled, these Great Plains. People—poor farmers, too—had to have horses.

But he could have easily done this in Minneapolis. Oh, they had lived in a lovely neighborhood there, a little slice of home with bakeries and coffee shops and everyone speaking Norwegian. She was happy in Minneapolis; she had culture and streetcars and teas and parties. She'd had no desire to leave.

But he dragged her away from her family, her friends, to live like a peasant. To dirty her hands with daily labor, to have only him for companionship, to bear children alone with no help from her mother, her sisters. To nearly grow mad with the loneliness, the screeching of the wind driving her senseless; but the times when there were no sounds at all—not a wolf howling, a chicken scratching, a horse whinnying—were worse. Those times, with only her own heartbeat to remind her that she wasn't trapped in someone else's nightmare, that she was, in fact, alive and vulnerable, made her question her sanity. More than once, in such a state, she'd found a knife in her hand as she stood over her sleeping children's beds with no idea how—or why—it had gotten there.

She felt she was losing not only her sanity but herself. She kept looking in the mirror to reassure herself she was still Anna; Anna of the golden hair and the sparkling eyes and the brilliant laugh and the pretty ways who had been the envy of all her sisters, the belle of all the men. Anna who had chosen Gunner, not the other way around. She had many suitors, many chances, but she chose this man, and she must never let him forget that. He needed to know this every single day of this life out here in the middle of nowhere; he needed to be reminded that he was lucky to have her.

And he behaved like a lucky man, he truly did—at times. Yes, he brought her presents from town, planted a flower garden for her in the best soil around the house, relegating the vegetables to a more troublesome plot of land and doing the hard work of coaxing them to grow. He sang her songs in the evening and made his gratitude known to her in bed, when she permitted it.

But she could never forget the other times. The times when he put everything else on this dreadful scrap of land ahead of her. Like the time when she was giving birth to her youngest, the baby. Anna lay panting and grunting in the bed, the other two children standing in the doorway, dumb-struck, staring at her while she strained to bring forth this new life. And Gunner, where was he? In the barn, with his prize mare who was foaling at the same time. But the mare was having trouble, a breech birth, and her husband stuck his hands into the mare to pull out a foal, while she, Anna, lay alone. Split open with pain, clammy with terror, during childbirth. Alone, she gave birth to a son for him, she pulled the child out from between her legs with her own shaking hands, she held him there while she screamed. Their young-est son was born in a webbed, scarlet fury of blood and pain, and in that moment she couldn't help but feel this was his destiny.

That, she could not forget. Let alone forgive.

Then he brought *them,* those strangers, into her house. He presented each of them to her as he presented his pretty presents. With a flourish, a pleased flush on his handsome face. But with no real idea of how the practicalities of it all would work: who would feed them, clothe them, have to live with them day in and day out while he escaped to his ever-lasting stable.

"Anna, my love, you needed help, so I have arranged it," he told her the day that Anette's mother arrived with her in tow. "I heard of a woman who wanted to sell her girl—there's trouble at home, I gathered, and the mother thinks it's best to get rid of her. Someone in town told me, and I wrote to her, and she'll be here today. To help you, my love!" He must have seen the darkness overtake her face; that darkness she couldn't always control, even though she knew it distorted her pretty features, made her less than her usual self.

"A stranger? In *my* house?"

"You said you were lonely!"

"Lonely for my family, my sisters, my friends. Lonely for *you.* Not lonely for a girl her own mother doesn't even want! What do we know about the family? Is she slatternly, the mother? Is the girl a bastard child?"

"I don't know—I don't think—"

"You didn't even ask, did you?" Anna could have slapped his silly, stupid face right then; the man looked so surprised by her questions, so stunned at her refusal of his gift. Anna never refused gifts.

"It's too late, they'll be here today. I promised the mother. She was desperate—and so, my Anna, may I say, are you. You have too much to do with the children and this place, you know that's true."

"And why is that? Who dragged me out here to the ends of the earth?"

Gunner didn't respond, he never did when she reminded him of his folly. He only pressed his lips together, passed his hand over his eyes, so that when they were visible again a little light had gone out of them. They weren't such a polished, gleaming brown. Then he rose to go to the stable and tend to his horses, the only things he truly loved.

"Don't think that I will be good to this—creature," she called after him. "Don't think that I'll treat her as my own!"

And she hadn't; she never would. The girl was stupid, there was no other word for it; she had a habit of staring into space, her eyes dull. Her skin was pockmarked, her hair a mustardy brown and thin, stringy. Anna feared that her own children, a girl and two boys, would catch whatever had made Anette this way, but she had no choice but to rely on the girl for help. The child was a hard worker, there was no denying that, but she worked in as dull a way as she lived, her movements ploddingly methodical, her face expressionless. Anna would never be able to stop adding up the cost of an extra mouth to feed, an extra body to clothe, and then there was school to think of. But she had learned to live with the girl, absorb her status in the household—servant only. Not family.

But then, the Schoolteacher arrived. And that was Gunner's doing, too.

"Darling Anna, good news! I've been appointed to the school board—a sign of my importance in the community. Just you wait and see, I'll run for office one day, my dearest!" And he'd puffed his chest out, patted his mustache, and looked ridiculous. The vanity of man!

"And we've just decided on the new teacher for this term,"

he continued smugly. "This will be her first school, but her older sister has excellent references and she's from a good home. The Olsens over in the next county, they farm, immigrants, Norwegians like us. The father is a deacon in the church, an impeccable character. When we visited to tell the girl she was chosen, I was very impressed by the family."

"That's nice." She had been knitting a new muffler for him. Putting her pretty hands to labor for him. Completely unaware of the treachery he was about to deploy.

"And I volunteered our home, for her to board in. I felt it was the thing to do, being new to the school board. It's a good way to show my value to them. She'll start with the winter term, we can put her up in the attic with Anette. I thought I might insulate it, paint it up a bit—"

"You will not." Anna's voice was low and reasonable—but she felt the darkness blanket her face, the thick clouds impairing her vision. "You will not. How dare you, Gunner? How dare you do this without consulting me?" The man was too friendly, too stupid, too—everything. He wanted to make friends with these people, this community; he was putting down roots even when she was desperately trying to pull them up. She wanted to go *home.* She had not been reticent about telling him this, every single day. He knew her wishes, he knew he was lucky to have her—but he kept smiling and being neighborly and ingratiating himself with the community anyway. And now he wanted to introduce a young schoolteacher into this house? Because, of course, the schoolteacher would be pretty; she knew it. Not as pretty as herself. But still. Weren't schoolteachers in the stories she read always pretty?

And that turned out to be the case. Raina was petite, a doll-like young woman. Her hair had glints of red in it, and her nose was pert, charmingly turned up. Her prettiness was much quieter than Anna's; it wasn't flashy. Instead, it coaxed, it made you want to come closer to take another look, rather than blinding you at first glance.

From the very first moment she set eyes on the Schoolteacher—and saw her husband looking at the girl with something she hadn't seen in his eyes since they had courted back in Kristiania—Anna despised her. Despised *him*. She saw it all happen, right under her nose—the moony looks, the careful attention, the little presents, like flowers, fresh pencils. Gunner made a show every time he pulled the Schoolteacher's seat out for her at dinner. He insisted that she eat with them, too, and he even grew a bit of a spine and started insisting Anette do the same, even though, before, he didn't seem to care that Anette took her meals up in her attic. But once the Schoolteacher arrived, Gunner started to care about Anette, or at least to *pretend* to care about Anette. When before, he let Anna do as she liked regarding the girl.

At first, the Schoolteacher had been shy, and somewhat startled by the attention. But sure as the sun rises, the young woman began to blossom, color prettily, do her hair in elaborate twists instead of the simple braided coil she'd arrived with. She started to glare at Anna, defy her by speaking English to Anette, daring to help the girl with her lessons even after Anna told her not to. But she'd never spoken an impudent word to Anna, until last week.

And then came that dreadful night when she actually caught Gunner up in the attic in his coat and boots, kneeling beside her bed, preparing to take the Schoolteacher—where, exactly? He couldn't say.

He was a stupid, stupid man.

She'd stopped him, stopped them both that night—the

knife she'd started keeping beneath her mattress had done
the job, for the most part; she had only to show it. He coaxed
her down the stairs, wrested the knife out of her hand; it fell
with a clang. She slapped him and threatened to do the same
or worse to the Schoolteacher, but he said the right things:
He didn't know what had happened, he'd lost his head, it had
to be the cabin fever, being cooped up so long in the bitter
cold. He needed her, Anna; he needed his children, his family. His good name.

For a week he didn't say one word to the Schoolteacher.
But that didn't prevent Anna from taking out her fury on
them both—and Anette—at every chance.

Why didn't the strangers leave? When would the punishing temperatures rise so that they could leave her in peace
and give her a chance to breathe, to sit, to think—to plan?

Thank God the weather had cleared this morning, the
temperatures warming the little house so that the stove actually seemed to radiate heat. As the Schoolteacher and Anette fled the house, Gunner hadn't given either of them a
glance; he'd only sat at the breakfast table, talking earnestly
to Anna, something about the horses, she never truly listened to the words he said. She only needed to know that he
was paying attention to her, and her alone.

But now—

"I'm going to get them."

Gunner stood before her, wearing his heavy coat, carrying a buffalo robe, muffled up to his eyes, but still his words
destroyed her complacency, her growing contentment with
the storm raging outside while, inside, it was only her family
again. Blessedly. No interlopers. No vipers in the nest.

"No, you're not." She said it calmly; no blackness overcame her this time. She saw everything clearly, almost too

clearly; Gunner's eyes were too meltingly brown, the china too sparkling, the light from the kerosene lanterns too bright.

The gun in her hand too silver. Too cool, too heavy. She stared at it in surprise; she'd forgotten, until that moment, that she'd retrieved it earlier from the loose brick behind the stove. She'd forgotten that she'd been carrying it all morning as she stirred up the stove fire, set the table for the children, mixed the batter for the flapjacks. It had become part of her, soothing her. Keeping her intact, her mind rational. Her heart beating steadily.

She raised her arm, she aimed the gun right at him—right at his heart.

The heart that could only belong to her.

CHAPTER 11

"HOLY MOTHER OF GOD, THIS STORM." GAVIN PEERED
out the window, like everyone else was doing. As they'd been
doing for hours. Watching the weather. Waiting for some
kind of movement. Waiting for news to report. Waiting it
out, like sensible people.

There was no sign of the sleighing party; they must have
holed up over in Council Bluffs. The street was empty save
for flying pieces of trash, coming together in the air in a
crazy ballet.

"Why is everyone standing around like a damn herd of
cattle?" Suddenly Rosewater himself, Mr. Edward Rosewater, publisher and editor in chief of the *Omaha Daily Bee*,
was upon them. Immediately, everyone but Gavin and Dan
Forsythe scurried back to their desks, pretending to work.

Gavin wasn't technically employed by the man, but he respected him. Edward Rosewater was average in build, with
receding dark brown hair, the requisite luxuriant mustache,
and penetrating eyes that missed nothing. He'd built the *Bee*
from scratch, put his stamp on it and the town, was not
afraid to report on the most scandalous behavior of the town

fathers, and also not afraid to use his cane when the inevitable physical attacks came his way. He was a target of vitriol and not only because of his headlines; he was also a target because he was a Jew in a town that didn't have many of them and whose mostly Protestant citizens mistrusted those they knew.

But Rosewater didn't give a good goddamn about anyone but himself and his paper; despite his frequent altercations, gleefully reported by his competition, he strutted about town as though he owned it. He was currently building the tallest building, too, around the corner, to house the ever-expanding *Bee*.

"Forsythe," Rosewater bellowed, and Dan raised an eyebrow at him. As the ace reporter on staff, he could afford to pretend not to be afraid of his boss.

"Rosewater?"

Gavin grinned; nobody else got away without using the "Mr."

"Get your big ass outside and do what you're paid to do. Report. Go find that damn sleighing party—that's the story here. The town's finest, caught up in the biggest blizzard we've seen in ages—that's what will sell newspapers."

"What about those out on the prairie?" Gavin asked mildly.

Rosewater turned those penetrating eyes his way. "Good God, that won't sell papers, boy! So a few farmers lose their cattle or freeze to death in a haystack? So what? It's the peril of pretty ladies, damsels in distress in their finery, gentlemen with handlebar mustaches, dandies turned into heroes—that's what people want to read."

"I'm not sure I agree."

"I don't care if you do or don't. You don't work for me. It's a courtesy that you even have a desk here." And with that, Rosewater was done with him.

"Forsythe, are you gone yet?" Rosewater turned to Dan, who smiled, deliberately put on his coat, and saluted.

"At your service." And then he pushed his way out into the storm; Gavin glanced out the window and saw him disappear into the growing blackness.

"You!" Rosewater turned back to Gavin.

"Yes?"

"If you want to write something that the damn boosters will pay me for, write something funny. You know, something about how the outhouse will be mighty cold, or the ice supply will surely be guaranteed after this. Something cute. Although I hate cute. But people love that kind of thing, so do that. You're good at that, anyway."

Gavin winced as he watched Rosewater ascend the staircase, two steps at a time, to his office on the top floor. Yes, he was good at that. Anyway.

He went to his desk, put on his paper cuffs, pulled out a new bottle of ink from his bottom drawer. Bitterly, he uncorked it and unleashed a great blob of thick black India ink, splattering it all over his desk. He rubbed it into the wood, like a souvenir from a war.

Another piece of pabulum. That's what he was good at.

Overheard on the street after the massive storm . . . two fellows hitching up their horses stopped to observe that this year's supply of ice must be guaranteed after the events of yesterday . . .

Gavin dropped his pen, tore off his cuffs, crumpled up the paper, and gazed at it in his hand. He had the absurd notion that he should eat it, this feeble effort, this emblem of what he'd become. There were people out there dying. Losing their livelihood. Struggling to survive the night. And he was sitting in the overheated, stuffy offices of a newspaper writing *jokes*.

Because that's what these people had become to Rosewater, to the boosters who had counted them, head by head, when they got off the trains. No longer human beings, they were reduced first to numbers, and now to amusing anecdotes.

That's what they'd become to Gavin, too—until this afternoon.

That young woman. He couldn't get her out of his mind. Was it because she'd finally put a face, a real face, to the anonymous rubes and the jokes at their expense?

All he knew was that after seeing her, his previous empty promises filled him with shame. Because to this living, breathing yearning—young woman, and the others like her, this land that Gavin had falsely described was a land that stole not just their hearts but their very lives. It taunted and teased, sure, with its golden sunsets in the summer, the new wheat looking abundant, life-giving. Until the next day when either hail or grasshoppers or both tumbled from the sky, trampling that wheat to the earth, breaking the hearts of those who gazed at it, desperately, from the door of a miserable soddie.

Today, Gavin had finally seen their faces. The mother's face—a promise, or more precisely, a threat, of what the girl would look like in a few years: weathered lines, rough skin, a mouth turned down at the corners. Her shoulders stooped from carrying and fetching. And worrying. And they were out there on the prairie, still, in this storm.

Dropping back into his seat, Gavin rubbed his face with his hands, over and over—the actions of a man just one act shy of the asylum, he realized. Then he began to jiggle his left knee. He was ignited with the need to do something, anything—anything but write a joke. Or tell another lie. He needed to do something true, something heroic. Gavin rose, dropping his pen, scattering the blank pages; he hitched up his pants, filled with purpose.

But then he saw his reflection in the window—the soft jowls of his face, the expansive gut straining his suspenders to capacity. He plopped back down in his chair, stumped. What on earth could he do?

His only worth lay in his pen and his imagination. And for the life of him, he couldn't figure out how to use them for anything heroic, not while the storm was still raging.

Christ, he sure could use a snort. Maybe the Lily was still open, for what did a man like Ol' Lieutenant have to do but keep his doors open for poor sons of bitches with no real use in the world—

Like himself.

CHAPTER 12

OLLIE TENNANT, COATED IN SNOW, HIS LONG LASHES
beaded with ice, pushed the door open to the little storefront where his children attended school. He nearly fell inside, given a mighty shove by the bullying wind.

He had to take a few minutes to catch his breath, let his
lungs expand in the dry, marginally warmer air, blink his
glazed eyes until he could see again. The journey to the north
side of town from the Lily, even for a giant of a man like him,
had taken its toll. He'd never lost his way, but for damn sure,
the storm had played every trick it could on him, obscuring
street crossings, muffling the sound of horses and wagons,
tickling up the back of his coat with its icy fingers, kicking at
him from all sides so that he had to inch his way, holding on
to every available hitching post, streetlamp, street sign, and
doorway.

But he'd made it, and now he was aware that he was being
gaped at by a handful of children, including the two who resembled him and bore his last name. And by a young white
woman who was cowering in a far corner, away from the colored children; she seemed to press herself into the very

wall, her eyes wide with horror, as she registered his presence.

Finally his two children broke into a grin and shouted joyfully, "Papa!" as they ran to pull him farther into the room, closer to the small potbellied stove that radiated some heat.

"Papa! You've come!"

"Hasn't anybody else?" Ollie's coat and gloves began to thaw, dripping water on the floor; he went over to the row of empty pegs—the children all had on their coats and scarves or jackets and shawls—and hung up his ponderous coat. Returning to the stove, rubbing his hands together, he counted the children—there were six, including his own. Plus the teacher.

"Grayson's papa came and got him and his sister and then Jenny and Charles went home because they live down the street but the rest of us stayed put even though Teacher told us we could leave if we wanted to but we didn't and now you're here!" Little Francis, Ollie's boy of nine, finally paused to take a breath. Ollie rubbed his son's head and tugged gently on his ear, his sign to tell him to be quiet for now. Francis was well known for his ability to produce great quantities of speech on very little air.

"Teacher said that you could leave? In this weather?" Ollie looked at his daughter, Melissa, aged eleven. She nodded, her braids—curling up at the ends like little smiles—providing an emphasis.

"Miss?" Ollie, remembering his manners, took off his hat, shook out the melting snow. He took a step toward the schoolteacher—he had no idea what her name was, that was his wife's department—but stopped when she cowered farther into the corner of the room where she seemed to have set up camp.

She was a very young woman. A girl, barely more. Slight, no figure yet, but attired in women's clothing—a long green skirt, black belt, white shirtwaist with a cameo at the throat, and a big paisley shawl clutched tightly about her shoulders. Her eyes were wide with fear, and they only grew bigger with each step he took toward her. So Ollie—recognizing her behavior, for he encountered it too often, the behavior of a white woman terrified to be in such proximity to a colored man—instinctively gentled his voice and his movement. He must not give her any reason to fear him, because who knew what she would do or say? He had seen other men's lives ruined—or ended, swinging from a tree—because they had not read the signs, not until too late.

It was almost like dealing with a wounded animal, Ollie sometimes thought. You had to understand the mind of a creature, you had to anticipate its movements, and its fear. You had to know when to back off, when to duck your head, cross to the other side of the street, avert your eyes.

"Miss—" Ollie turned to his son and hissed, "What's her name?"

"Miss Carson!" Francis said too loudly, and Ollie winced.

"I'm sorry, Miss Carson, is it? I'm Mr. Tennant. Francis and Melissa's father. How are you all doing? Have the children eaten their lunch? Have you had anything to eat?"

"Stay away from me," Miss Carson said in a choked voice; she drew her knees up against her chest, pressing herself even farther against the wall, although Ollie hadn't thought that was possible. "I don't know—it's so awful outside—don't take one more step toward me, you—you—"

Ollie pressed his lips together, turned away so that he didn't have to see the terror in this young woman's eyes—and so that she wouldn't see the disgust in his. *This was who was*

teaching his kids? A girl who hated them, who was terrified
of them? Was she able to hide her disgust at the color of their
skin because they were small and couldn't hurt her? He tried
to remember what he knew about the school, newly open.
His children could legally go to the white schools but they
weren't welcome there, not as their numbers grew. Schools
were forming here on the North Side to accommodate the
growing population. He'd heard there was only one colored
teacher in all of Omaha, and she taught at a small high
school. So the younger children were being taught by white
teachers, mainly those who volunteered in, or were volunteered by, their churches. He'd never thought of it this way,
but it was true; teaching his children was considered an act
of charity. And Ollie knew people well enough to understand
that those performing a charitable act rarely had much love
or consideration for the recipients of it.

"I have to go home!" Miss Carson stood up abruptly; she
was trembling from head to toe. "I have to go home, they'll
be worried for me, I can't stay here, I don't care about—you
can take them home, get them out of here, get them away! All
of you, just go away!"

"Now, miss, listen to me." Ollie's voice could be as smooth
as honey when he wanted it to be, and right now he did. "It's
not possible, not with the way this storm is. Where do you
live, anyway?"

"Why do you want to know?" The girl's eyes narrowed,
her lips grew white.

"Just—is it on this side of town? Or somewhere else?"

"Near Fremont, the Episcopal Church—my papa is the
rector there. It was his idea that I teach here."

"Ah." Ollie nodded, unsurprised. "Well, miss, you won't

get there, is what I'm trying to tell you. The cable cars aren't running anymore, most of the streetlights are out, it's not fit for man or beast. You'd get lost, you might hurt yourself—you can't even see a horse coming around a corner. You need to stay here until it's over."

"Stay here—stay the night?" Her voice rose.

"At least until it's over."

"Will you take these—the children home?"

"No, miss, I won't. It's safest right where we are."

"Oh!" Miss Carson shut her eyes tight; she turned her head, hiding half her face against the wall.

Ollie took a few steps backward, allowing her time to absorb what he'd said. He turned toward the children, who were all holding hands near the stove, watching with big eyes. He joined them, holding his hands out toward the feeble fire, thinking.

The room was small. It had two rows of benches, no blackboard, no desks—not for the colored children, he thought grimly. Tell them they can learn but don't give them the tools they need. There were a few readers, and he deduced they had to share. His children had slates, but he knew—he'd overheard his wife—that some of the others didn't, and that she was thinking of taking up a collection for them. There were some pictures, childish drawings, pinned up on the whitewashed walls, but otherwise, it was a joyless place, dimly lit with a few dusty oil lamps.

He couldn't see any stacks of logs or buckets of coal for the stove.

"Where do you keep your fuel?" Ollie asked this casually, tossing it over his shoulder, still not turning toward the schoolteacher.

"We ran out about an hour ago. That's the last of it," she said, and he could hear her rapid breathing, like something caught in a trap, from across the increasingly cold room.

He rose—pretending to stretch, but really, he was searching for something to burn. There were the few books. He saw a stack of old newspapers in a far corner—probably intended for the outhouse behind the building. There was a massive desk—a heavy rolltop, like you'd find in a bank—for the teacher, and that counter along the back of the room. But that looked solid, not anything that would yield to his bare hands.

He turned his gaze to the two rows of benches. Putting his hands in his pockets, he casually strolled over to the first bench. He kicked at it, and it moved; it wasn't bolted to the floor. It wasn't solidly built, either, just planks nailed on either end to legs made of two-by-fours.

The six children shadowed him; he realized they'd been frightened by the teacher's behavior. Now that he was here, they weren't scared anymore—but they'd probably stick to him like glue until he could get them all home in the morning or whenever the storm stopped. When he stopped moving, they all did, too.

He turned, fixed them each with a kind gaze, then broke into a smile.

"Who wants to play a game?"

There were some grins, and then his son began to cheer as Ollie showed them how to break apart the benches, kicking at them, chopping them with their small hands. Sanctioned vandalism—every schoolchild's dream. Soon they were all laughing and shouting. It was good for them to run around, get their blood going, warm themselves up a little.

Ollie wasn't sure how long the fire would last, even with this new source of fuel.

"You can't—why, they can't do that! That's not right!" Miss Carson took a few steps out of her hiding place, outraged. "That's someone else's property—it belongs to the town!"

"I'll pay them back," Ollie said wryly. "Miss, we have to burn something, or freeze. Do you have any other ideas?"

"Yes—go home! All of you—go back to where you came from! I'm going home, I am!" With a wild cry she dashed across the room, headed for the door, and Ollie had a choice to make: Stop her, put his hands on a white woman and risk his very life—

Or let her go, this crazy person, to her doom.

"Miss! Miss Carson!" His voice could also fill a room—fill a church, his wife often hinted—if he wanted it to. It boomed, echoed in the nearly empty space, and he placed himself firmly between the wild-eyed young woman and the door.

She stopped a couple of feet in front of him, and so finally he was able to take a good look at her face. She was white—whiter than he'd ever seen a person—with terror, her lips pale, too. But her cheeks were still round with the last remnants of childhood; her pointed chin was trembling, like his own little girl's did when she was sad or afraid.

Children had come late in Ollie's life; he wasn't looking to have a family—he had few outright plans for living—but it had happened to him anyway, and he couldn't really remember having much choice in the matter. He'd met a girl: sweet, shrewd Alma, who didn't mind that he owned a bar and—most important—never went overboard in trying to get him to attend church. She only dropped a couple of subtle hints a month, which, given what Ollie knew about churchgoing women, made her a model of restraint. She tamed him in a different way by giving him two babies who turned his heart to mush the moment he held them as newborns; each one of them had pounded his chest with a tiny fist and made a conquest.

And ever since, Ollie had discovered he was putty in a child's hand; everything about children, their overabundance of emotion, their exhausting energy that would give way, without warning, to a sleep that could not be interrupted, delighted him. Especially their possibility. Who could tell what kind of a person a child will grow into? Some thought they could; Alma was particularly judgmental in this way: "That Francis, he will grow up to be a preacher, now mark my words, the way he can talk!" "You know little Peter, the Thompsons' boy? The way he looks at you—I can tell he's going to grow up to be no good!"

But Ollie held out hope for each and every one of them.

It was that quivering chin on this girl of no more than fifteen or sixteen—this girl, he had to acknowledge, who was most likely forced into this situation by her misguided parent who was trying to tick off an item on his own checklist to get into heaven—that did it. If she were an adult—for Ollie held out no such hope for change and goodness in adults—he would have let her go outside without a second thought. He wasn't there to save her. He was there to save the children.

He had not been prepared for the schoolteacher to be a child herself. But she was, and so he had to act.

"You can't go out there, miss." He softened his voice again. "You'll be going to your death. I don't want that to happen, these children don't want that to happen. Look at them."

Miss Carson, clutching her shawl so tightly her knuckles bulged, turned toward her pupils. None of them reacted in any way; they simply stared right back at her, faces neutral. There was no great love between teacher and pupils, that was evident. So Ollie made a gesture to Francis, who immediately understood and stepped forward, his hands clasped upon his chest like the actress who had played Little Eva in a production of *Uncle Tom's Cabin* that had passed through last summer, and Ollie had to stifle a grin. This boy of his! Maybe Alma was correct: Maybe a stage of some kind—in a church or in a theater—was part of his future.

But Ollie kept his face serious, for this wasn't make-believe; it was life and death.

"Please, Miss Carson, please don't go," Francis said, his voice full of pathos. "We want you to stay with us! If anything happened to you we would be so sad!"

Miss Carson, evidently no fool, cocked a skeptical eyebrow at him—but she also appeared to be considering the situation from another angle; she glanced out at the dark street. The glow of the oil lamps inside the building cast a weak light outside, so that the full fury of the storm wasn't visible. Fortunately the mercurial wind chose that moment to turn and pound on the huge glass storefront window; even Ollie let out a yelp of surprise. It seemed a miracle the window didn't break.

Miss Carson had jumped, too; she was crying again, twisting up the ends of her shawl in her small hands. "I don't know—I can't stay here—I want to go home! I miss my parents! Why don't they come for me?" She finally let her gaze meet Ollie's, tears streaming down her cheeks. "Why doesn't anyone come?"

"I did. I'm here. Let's all sit down by the fire—my, it's

cold, isn't it?" Ollie—he would not touch her, no sir—tried to lure her toward the stove with his voice, his movement. "I think I'll go put my coat on, yes, that's what I'm going to do." He gave her some room to get to the stove while he took his dripping coat off the wooden peg, shoving his arms into the sleeves. It really was cold.

She crept toward the stove, casting wary glances toward the children, who automatically stepped back to allow her the warmest spot. She huddled there, miserable, still sniffling, occasionally wiping her nose with her shawl.

Then his son took a step toward her, reaching out his hand. "Miss Carson, don't you worry. We'll be all right, now that my papa is here. This old storm will blow itself out sometime—it can't last forever!"

Miss Carson didn't take Francis's hand, but she did smile—a timid little smile; she kind of reminded Ollie of a rabbit, now that he thought about it, with her little red nose, quivering chin—and she nodded.

Ollie exhaled. He felt as if he'd been holding his breath the entire time, ever since he left the Lily, to tell the truth. First the physical exertion of tunneling his way through the storm, then the emotional tightrope he'd had to cross once he got here. But now he could breathe.

They'd be safe, they could survive the night. All of them, including that insensitive but frightened woman-child of Christian charity.

But for damn sure, he was going to have a talk with Alma tomorrow, when the storm cleared and they were all back safe and snug above the saloon. He wasn't going to allow his children to be taught out of pity. No, he wasn't. They deserved to be taught by someone who looked like them, thought like them. They deserved to be treated like people, not rungs on the ladder to heaven. There must be something the community could do—help more of their young women get teaching certificates or do a better job advertising for colored teachers. Something.

Maybe the storm had blown some good sense into him—he admitted that. No more could he hide behind his bar, stubbornly refusing to see that the landscape of polite society was being reconfigured as thoroughly as the wind was surely rearranging the physical landscape right now. Trees would be uprooted, fences blown down, roofs collapsed.

And cities like Omaha would continue to be divided up, like with like, languages not mixing. Certain streets not crossed by one kind or another.

Children learning different lessons, depending on the color of their skin.

CHAPTER 13

"ANETTE!"

Anette started, panicked. She'd almost fallen asleep, even as she was still walking, miraculously; still stumbling in a whirlwind of snow that stung her cheeks. Snow that wasn't snow, but pebbles. A wind that wasn't a wind, but a cyclone.

Fredrik held her hand—she saw it but couldn't feel it. In her other hand was the lunch pail, and she thought the slate was still snug against her chest—frozen to it, she imagined. Somehow, she was being tugged alongside him as he was crying, and calling her name, trying to wake her up out of her stupor.

She was shivering. But she was hot. She was falling. But she was on her feet. She had to go to the bathroom—urgently, she felt her bladder swell, knew it released, knew there must be warmth drizzling down her legs, soaking her underclothes, her petticoat, her stockings, dripping down into her shoes. She longed for that warmth, actually—but it never came, she didn't feel anything.

Fredrik was suddenly stopping, a strange look on his

face, embarrassment; he looked down at his pants. Anette looked, too, and there was a dark stain. The two gazed at each other for a moment; they shared the embarrassment—they'd never done this before, not in front of the other. And they were both crying now, but still bound together, hands entwined. And then they started moving again.

They had to be close to the Pedersen homestead. Didn't they? They'd been trudging through the snow for hours, it seemed to Anette. And it occurred to her she'd never spent this much time with Fredrik. Their time together, always, was so fleeting: a few minutes before school started, recess, their races home. They were always moving, never sitting still, even when talking—although it was Fredrik who mostly talked. Anette was simply content to listen to someone talking to her, not at her. Anyway, she didn't have much to share; she couldn't tell him how it was at the Pedersens'. She was ashamed to reveal that she was just a hired girl, really, but without pay. Unwanted.

Whereas Fredrik had a large, happy family he was always complaining about. Tor teased him mercilessly, put frogs in his boots, dropped snakes down his shirt. Fredrik, in turn, taunted his little brothers and sister, but Fredrik swore he got punished for it in a way Tor never did; his papa would look at him gravely and say he was disappointed in him before giving him a good whipping. And his mother would kiss away all his tears, but still she would deny him dessert that night.

"You have to be an example, Fredrik," she would say. But she never, ever punished Tor. Both his papa and his mama thought the sun rose and set on *him*. And what about the time Fredrik brought home the prize for spelling? Did his mama cry with pride over that, the way she did when Tor revealed that Miss Olsen said she couldn't teach him much more, that he learned too quickly?

No. Mama did make him his favorite dessert that night, Fredrik admitted—*stollen* with raisins—and excused him from bringing in the water for the dishes. But she didn't shed shining tears of joy.

Oh, the trials of poor Fredrik! Anette never betrayed to Fredrik how much she envied him, how silly, really, she thought his trials were. How, in sharing these stories, he was reminding Anette of all that was missing in her own life. A happy family, a mother and father who cared for you enough to punish you and then cry over it, a big brother who thought of you enough to play pranks on you. People who saw you as a *person,* not as a problem or an unasked-for solution, no better than a workhorse in a plow.

People who loved you.

If only Anette had an older sibling who teased her! A papa who punished her in order to make her a better person, because he loved her that much! But she would never, ever let it slip to Fredrik that she felt this way. Because Fredrik Halvorsan, freckled and naughty yet completely innocent of the bad things that could happen to people, had chosen Anette. He was the only person in the world who looked for her, and her alone, in a crowded room. The only person who fought to sit next to her, not to get away from her. The only person who considered her an ally, not an enemy or a stupid little donkey, plodding along doing all the work nobody else wanted to do.

The only person who said her name with happiness, not reluctance or anger.

"Anette!"

He tugged her arm painfully; she rubbed her eyes, which had crusted shut again, opening them with a thumb that didn't feel. She was shivering so thoroughly she couldn't remember what it was like not to; her inadequate shawl, her regular cotton petticoat, could not keep her warm. She could not imagine being warm again. But she still kept moving; those strong legs and heart that launched her toward school with joy kept her upright now. Linked with Fredrik, she proceeded, inch by inch. Head bent down, face stinging from the strange, gritty balls of snow. The two of them all alone in the echoing center of the storm, at once muffling all sound— she couldn't hear their footsteps, it was difficult to talk to each other—and assaulting her ears with the shrieking wind.

Anette took a deep breath, then shouted at Fredrik, "I think we're going the wrong way!"

She didn't know if that was true or not, but they'd been walking for hours without coming to anything that looked familiar.

"No, we're not," Fredrik shouted. He was so maddening sometimes, just because he was a boy and Anette was not. He wasn't shy about bossing her around, and most of the time Anette let him.

But now she found herself arguing back—she was not going to let this boy tell her what to do! "Yes, we are—it is my way home, I know it!"

"You stupid, we're lost right now!" Fredrik cried hoarsely.

And suddenly they were screaming at each other, tears freezing on their faces; she'd never known anyone more stupid than this boy! She was sick of people bullying her, bossing her around. Yes, she was terrified and the vicious winds were trying to pull her off her very feet, but this boy was not going to tell her how to get to her own home! For the moment she forgot that this was Fredrik, her only friend; he represented everyone who had told her what to do, how fast or how slow she should do it, where to live, how to think.

He was *everyone*. And before she knew what she was doing, she slapped him across the face.

"You stupid girl!" Fredrik clenched his fists but didn't strike her back. "You—you slavey! No better than a hired girl—worse than a hired girl! You know what everyone says about you at school—your own mother sold you for a pig. You're so ugly, that's all you were worth!"

"You take that back!" Anette was crying, but madder than she'd been since—since she could ever remember. She hadn't allowed herself to be angry at her mother, or at Mother Pedersen; all along, deep down, she'd agreed with Fredrik and all the others. She *was* stupid, she *was* ugly—but now, lost in a volcano of ash-like snow, stuck with this idiotic boy, she was also angrier than a hive of bees. She flew at him, shaking him by the shoulders, and he fought back, pushing her to the ground. She picked herself up and screamed at him.

"I am not—I wasn't sold! I wasn't, I wasn't, I wasn't!"

She flung her arm, the arm still grasping the pail, backward, prepared to strike. Fredrik saw, his eyes widened— then he turned around and ran off in the other direction, disappearing into the cloud of misery.

Leaving her alone once more.

She stood for a moment with her arm still in the air, poised to hit; she wanted something, *someone* to pummel. She screamed at the top of her lungs, one long, piercing cry that ended in hoarse whimpering. She panted, it was too hard to breathe in this whirlpool of ice and snow, yet she opened her mouth and let loose her fury again, a fury that rose up to meet the fury raining down, yet it hardly made a dent. She was too small, she was too insignificant. No one heard her.

No one cared.

Falling to her knees, she wept great heaving sobs. And she shivered, and she wept, and she burned with anger, and she froze with fear, and she knew she would die right there and no one would care. Would her mama ever know? Would she come claim her body and bury it near the dugout, a cave, really, carved into a riverbank? It must have been carved by the Indians, maybe it was a hiding place during the Indian wars, her stepfather said once. "Jesus, this place stinks of them, don't it?" And there were arrowheads everywhere, catching the glint of the sun in the summer so they were easy to find.

Even though she'd never known another dwelling until her mother gave her away, she'd understood how miserable the dugout was, and that most people didn't live that way, no better than gophers in holes. In the spring it flooded and in the summer snakes crawled through the dirt walls and in the autumn the wild pigs came and terrorized everyone and in the winter they all just sat and stared at one another; it was too cold to do anything else, and that was when her stepfather was the worst, in the winter. That was when he would alternate between making fun of Anette and coming too close. "To warm up," he would say with a sickening smile while her mother looked on with compressed lips and her little brothers laughed.

Her own family thought she wasn't good enough even for that hole in the ground, and they sent her away.

The Pedersens surely wouldn't care if she froze to death. They would find her lifeless, but with the slate and the lunch pail, the only two things Mother Pedersen cared about, and she would sigh with relief and let her husband deal with Anette's body; he'd probably bury it somewhere because he was decent. But then he would forget her as soon as the last spade full of earth covered her up, he wouldn't put up a marker or anything, and soon the grass would grow over her, and she would lie there in the cold earth alone for all eternity, forgotten.

Not even Fredrik would mourn her now—she'd made sure of that, she'd chased him away, she'd reminded him, the only person who hadn't yet discovered it on his own, that she wasn't worthy of love.

"Fredrik!" Seized by panic, she scrambled up, her anger forgotten, and she was herself again. No longer a fury raging at her fate, just a stupid girl unable to do anything on her own, lost. "Fredrik!"

She began to run in the direction she thought he'd gone, she kept screaming his name, and finally she heard something. She stopped, listened with all her might, and it was crying she heard, a boy crying, and her heart beat faster with hope, propelling her legs toward that sound.

"Fredrik!"

She found him seated in a little swallow of the earth, drifted over with snow—she didn't see him, she tripped over him. His legs were drawn up tightly against his chest and he was crying; he looked up at her—the snow had frosted over his eyebrows, was stuck on his eyelashes, his cheeks were unnaturally red from the biting cold, the burn of the snow. But he was Fredrik, all the same.

"I'm so-so-sorry," he wheezed, his voice quaking, but he got up and hugged her tightly, and the surprise of this made Anette gasp. He'd never hugged her. No one had—she was so shocked she forgot to hug him back, or maybe she didn't know how to. But either way, in a moment they were hand in hand again, and he meekly allowed her to pull him back in the direction that, a few moments ago, she had been so certain of that she'd nearly lost the only person in the world who would mourn her if she died.

But now, she wasn't so certain; in fact, she had no idea which way to go. But Fredrik didn't seem able to help; he was muttering something to himself and obediently held on to Anette's hand as she led him forward.

So she pretended that she knew the way home but the only thing she really knew was that they had to keep moving or else. So they continued to stumble on.

Together.

CHAPTER 14

"WE HAVE TO LEAVE."

Raina was surprised to hear her voice—a calm, rational voice—say the words out loud; she'd been sure she was only thinking them. But once she said them, they made sense; her mind, not her heart, was finally in control. Even as the snow kept blowing through the broken window, the temperature dropping with each heartbeat, she was sure of one thing. It was all up to her; no one would come to save her. Not her big sister, not her father. Not Gunner Pedersen.

"Children," Raina shouted over the wind and the sniffles and the wails—she did a quick headcount, just to make sure. Ten children, plus Tor. Sofia Nyquist was the youngest, only six, sobbing for her mother; her older sister, Enid, barely older, seven. Rosa and Eva Larsen, twins, eight years old; Albert Blickenstaff, nine; Clara Hagen and Tana Berg, ten; Albert's big brother, Walter, and his best friend, Daniel Hagen, eleven. Tall but painfully thin Arvid Dahl, thirteen; he was the biggest boy next to Tor but so frail from a lifetime of illnesses, and his asthma was already making his breathing squeak and rattle.

Surveying them, Raina found herself unaccountably

touched by small things: The crooked part in Daniel's hair—she imagined him refusing to let his mother part his hair anymore; that was for a baby and he was a big boy, he could do it himself. The way Clara and Tana held hands, as they always did, sitting side by side on the bench or out at recess skipping together. Enid's lopsided smile; one of her front teeth was missing, and she wasn't embarrassed about it at all, she smiled boldly, brilliantly, defying anyone to make fun of her. Walter's way of hitching up his suspenders, just like a man would, an unconscious yet proud little gesture, as if he was constantly surveying a field of bounty, mentally calculating the income from it. Yet he was a small child, finer boned than the other boys, better fitted for a general store than the farm that he'd been destined for since birth out here on the prairie.

Raina realized she'd not really taken the time to get to know her pupils; her mind had been so distracted, first by the excitement of leaving home, then by the oppressive atmosphere at the Pedersens', her fear of Anna, and then the cyclone of confusion, hope, desire, that Gunner stirred in her. Taunted her with, to be honest. Her pupils had been the least of everything; they had occupied the smallest space in her brain and heart, and she chided herself. Teaching was her *job,* and these children were her charges. It was only now that she was about to lead them out into the chaos of the storm that she fully realized it. Fully saw them as individuals.

"Miss Olsen, please, before we go—let me just run out for a minute to see if I can find Fredrik and Anette." Tor dared to take her hand—a big breach in manners, but he was so desperate. He clutched her hand until it hurt. "Please, Fredrik is so little, Mama and Papa have always told me I have to look out for him. Please!"

Raina longed to let him go, because she was thinking of Anette right then. Of all her pupils, Anette was the only one she really knew. Anette, unloved, misused; it was so rare to see any light behind her pale blue eyes, except when she was with Fredrik. Anette, terrified to displease Anna Pedersen; that's why she left, Raina knew that with certainty. How many times had that awful woman told the girl she couldn't linger after school, that she would be punished severely if she did? Anna was not the kind of person to threaten punishment if she didn't have one already in mind. Anette knew that better than anyone. No wonder she'd sprinted off for home.

"Tor, I can't stop you, you know that. I can only trust you to make the right decision." Raina had never spoken so honestly as she did in that moment—the moment that Tor Halvorsan shook off the last vestiges of childhood, squared his shoulders, met her gaze evenly, and promised to stay by her side.

Raina was moved to witness this transformation. She turned away, quickly, before he could see the tears in her eyes.

"Now," she said, going to the children, putting her arms, briefly, around each one, to give them some courage—she herself felt as if she had none, but she must pretend for their sakes. "Girls, untie your aprons, please."

Looking at her in surprise, they obeyed. Little Clara regarded her apron—a pretty, useless one, different from the other girls' in that it was of a dainty fabric, embroidered in colorful threads along the hem and the waistband—with a sigh. But she untied it.

"Good." Raina added her own apron to the bundle, then she told the children to stand in line, from tallest to smallest; Arvid to Sofia. They obeyed, shuddering, stamping their feet, the snow still blasting in from the huge open window and the temperature falling by the second. They were clad in the coats and shawls they'd come to school with, but none of them was adequately dressed; neither was Raina. She thought of her heavy woolen coat, which she'd carelessly left hanging outside to air. But at least she had a long skirt, and a petticoat; the little girls' skirts only hit their knees. Clara and Sofia had wool hats, and Tana had a scarf wound up to her eyes. So did Arvid. But only half the children wore mittens or gloves.

"Now, we're going to tie ourselves together, you see? Like a chain, a people chain." Without realizing it, Raina had started talking in Norwegian, and although Albert and Walter were German, they seemed to understand.

She handed the aprons out to most of the children, and they tied the strings first around their waists, then each new apron to the string of the one before it, so that when they were done, the children resembled one long—oddly gay, with Clara's festive apron right in the middle—insect with ten heads and twenty pairs of arms and legs. Albert started to giggle, and soon the others did, too, charmed with the novelty of it.

"Shhh!" Raina scolded them; they had to conserve their energy. She beckoned Tor over to where she was standing, shivering, searching outside; the landscape wasn't merely bleak, it was angry, a roiling, churning ocean. The flat Nebraska land that everyone joked about wasn't, really. There were still plenty of obstacles waiting to trip you up if you weren't careful; gopher holes and stubborn grass that didn't die off in the winter completely, little creeks, ravines, not to mention barbed-wire fencing. And there would be no way to see any of these, with the storm cloud touching the very ground, until you were upon them. Tangled up in them.

"Tor, your house is the nearest, I think?" She wasn't sure about this; she had been so caught up in her own drama that she'd never really gotten a good read on the land. Her father would be disappointed in her; he had always told her that you get the lay of the land first, then worry about the land-scape of emotions. The land was the most cruel, he'd always said.

But he was wrong, although Raina couldn't tell him just how.

"Yes, Miss Olsen. About half a mile southwest of here."

Southwest—that was good, they wouldn't be walking di-rectly into the teeth of the snarling demon outside. "So if we walk outside the door, we head at a diagonal, to our right?"

He nodded.

"Are there any landmarks—barns or fences or trees, maybe even a haystack, that might help us stay in the right direction?"

The boy pondered, his heavy eyebrows drawing together in a sharp "V" on his forehead. "There's a small creek right outside our barn, with some planks we use as a footbridge."

"But nothing before then?"

"No, I don't think so."

"All right."

The wind screamed louder, and the top piece of the stove blew off its mooring to the ceiling; the children cried, tried to run from it but got tangled up, each going in a different direction. Raina rushed to sort it out, and knew she couldn't put off their departure another minute. They would freeze to death here.

They would freeze to death outside, too, but please, God

in heaven, she would get them to the Halvorsans' before they did. They would have to move quickly; she shook her head at the little girls.

"Tor, you might have to carry Sofia. I'll take Enid up front with me." She untied Enid, smiled into her wide grey eyes, lips that trembled from cold, excitement, or fear, who could tell? She smoothed the little girl's copper braids. "Those are very pretty ribbons, Enid."

"Th-Thank you, Miss Olsen," she said, and braved a tiny smile, which pierced Raina's heart. The trust, the inno-cence, placed right into her very hands. The bravery of these sons and daughters of immigrants.

"All right, children! We're going now, but we're together. Nothing bad can happen to us if we're together. We're going to Tor's house, and when we get there I bet there will be some cookies and warm milk, and we'll play games until your parents come to get you. That will be fun, won't it?"

There were a few excited yelps but, for the most part, the children were silent. Trusting. Lifting Enid up, she nodded at Tor, who held on to Rosa Larsen, Sofia already on his back.

"Let's go," she cried, bending her head against the wind as she led them all through the doorway of the schoolhouse. She paused for a moment to get her bearing, then she faced the southwest, feeling the pull of the ten children and Tor behind her, all of them in her wake, but attached to her. The children were too stunned by the storm to do more than gasp.

Then she stepped into the howling void.

CHAPTER 15

. . . . . .

THE BIRDS AND BEASTS OF THE PRAIRIE TOOK SHELTER where they could.

They had sensed it first, long before the humans; they felt the change in the atmosphere, the wind moving like the hands of a clock from the south to the northwest. They smelled it, the subtle yet acrid whiff of electricity. Snow smelled different from rain; drier, less mossy. They felt the coming cold even before the temperature started to plummet.

The rattlesnakes and the toads and the salamanders didn't sense any of this; they were sleeping their winter sleep, burrowed deep beneath the ground, their hearts barely beating, only just enough to keep them alive until spring. They were unaware of the storm raging on top of them.

Prairie dogs, too, with their extra layer of winter fat, were lazing about in the subterranean burrows of their prairie towns; they may have noticed some changes in the air above them, but they didn't care. They would wait the storm out, families cuddling together in little nests made of grass. Once the storm was over, these curious critters would venture out to see what was what, but for now, dozing was the plan.

Even foxes, sporting an additional layer of fur for the winter, decided to cower in dens built against abandoned houses or in soddies, forgoing the delight of sleeping out on the plain at night under the stars. There was no hunting to be done in a storm like this; there was little enough hunting to be done in the winter anyway, which meant an extra reliance on the chicken eggs so prized by the homesteaders. But on a day like this, even a henhouse wasn't tempting; the mature foxes huddled with their young, for winter was high breeding time.

Coyotes also sought shelter in dens constructed in abandoned houses or in soddies or against what trees there were, or in ravines and creek banks. Hunting was difficult in the winter; the rodents buried deep in the ground, leaving only deer—skinny themselves now, months after the abundance of their autumn pillaging—to be brought down, divided up, consumed or hoarded.

It was the larger animals, the ones who couldn't hide in dens, that took the brunt of it. The deer and the elk and the pronghorn had to endure the worst of nature's fury, huddling together against what shelter they could find out on the pitiless prairie that left them so vulnerable with few trees, hills, or gullies for protection. The minute they smelled the change in the air, they clumped together in herds, snuggling low to the ground for warmth, heads down, eyes shut, the weakest and youngest in the middle for protection. Many wouldn't survive; neither would most of the rabbits trying to shelter together trapped far from their burrows.

The cows—what grazing cows there still were, that is,

since by this year of 1888, most bright-eyed ranchers, like an eager young New Yorker named Theodore Roosevelt, had learned the brutal lesson that cows were a losing investment on the merciless plains—had it the worst. The weather was too harsh; every year blizzards wiped out hundreds in one fell swoop. This blizzard was no exception, striking in its peculiarly heartless fashion. Some of the confused cows, not as adept at gathering together as deer and elk, found themselves encased in a hell of self-made ice, their blowing, moist breath freezing about them, suffocating them where they stood, then the elements finishing them off while they remained upright.

Most of the migratory birds from Canada—rough-legged hawks, a snowy owl or two—weathered the storm, somewhat stunned by its ferocity; they had their nests atop abandoned barns, the odd tree. They were used to the tundra, so they simply bent their heads against the elements and waited; once the weather cleared, the piercing blue sky against the dazzling white landscape would provide the perfect setting for hunting.

Horses caught outside, too, suffered in the storm, wandering farther from their barns in their confusion, some finally giving up and laying down to be covered by the snow, and, eventually, overcome by the plunging temperatures that would follow.

One horse in particular, dragging an empty cutter sleigh, had stopped trying to outrace the howling wall of fury nipping at his heels; it was now barely moving, swaying on its hooves, the weight of the sleigh terrible, so that every now and then the horse tried to buck it off. That took too much strength, though, and the horse became resigned to its burden, even as its heart slowed down, trying to conserve en-

ergy. Blind to his surroundings— eyes fully plastered shut by
ice—the horse kept moving by instinct, yet he was slowing
down with each step.

Slowing down enough so that someone could have caught
him. And the horse wondered why his owner had not; why
the exhausted cries of his name had stopped at some point,
so many painful steps back.

LIKE THE HORSE SHE CURSED, Gerda kept moving against
the force of the wind, just barely; staggering with each small
step, eyes tightly shut against the javelins of ice hurtling
down from the sky, tugging little Ingrid along, struggling to
keep the child upright. Minna had stopped crying, a silent
stone upon Gerda's back. Every now and then Gerda felt a
warm breath in her ear, so that she could tell Minna was still
alive, and she thanked God. Because now she knew, she fully
understood, that the three of them might not make it out of
this; she'd already given up on Tiny, or so she told herself.
She wasn't prone to foolish hope, no, not she. Not practical
Gerda—isn't that what Papa always called her? His little soldier, his rock. Papa had wanted a son so much, at least that's
what Mama said once, in a rare, disjointed act of desperation that Gerda still wondered about, years later.

One morning when Gerda was only about ten, Mama had
been airing out the bedstead that she and Papa slept on. But
all at once, Mama plopped down on it as if her legs had given
out on her, and suddenly a torrent of words—Norwegian
words—poured out of her. Mama was talking to *her*, Gerda,
who had been carefully washing the breakfast dishes in a
bucket of water, keeping an eye on Raina, who was outside,
singing a little song while she made her doll a blanket out of

tallgrass, weaving the long purplish stems in and out. It was a spring day, a soft one, as Mama sometimes called these rare, blessed days when everything—the sun, the breeze, the temperature—was moderate. Coaxing.

"Yes, I know, your papa, my Steffen, he wanted a son so badly to share the work, to keep his name alive, but he loves you girls, Gerda; he loves you with all his heart."

Gerda looked at her mother in confusion; she had never questioned her father's love, it was as constant as the rustling of the prairie grass. As perennial as the cry of a screech owl at night. As comforting as the patter of a gentle rain in spring.

"Oh, yes, he loves you," Mama repeated in a rush, mistaking Gerda's expression. "You especially, Gerda. He does look at you like his right arm sometimes, and I don't know that that is fair, but it is the way it is. Still you have the best papa around, but a son, a boy, it would have helped. He is a strong man but this place is too much even for him, he will work himself to death, that is the fate of a man here, but it is a fate your papa wanted, even so. At home, there wasn't enough for him, the farms were divided up among all the sons so that none of them had much. They weren't big farms like this, no, so your father had to up and leave, he took us away; my mother, my poor mother, I do miss her so. My sisters, my Breena and my Maja, the letters come too slowly, all the way across the ocean, they might be gone now, do you know? Gone—accidents happen, sickness, and Mama, she is old!" Gerda's mother looked stunned by this, she raised her hands up in a jerky movement and let them fall in her lap while her eyes were big and wondering, her mouth open in surprise. "Yes, they might be gone and, Gerda, I wouldn't know, would I? Maybe not for months."

"Mama!" Gerda dropped a tin cup in the dishwater and ran to her mother, putting an arm about her, but Mama didn't cry; she looked at Gerda, smiled, shook herself a little, and continued on with this strange conversation that seemed to spring from a hidden well, a conversation Gerda had never been part of before, the kind of talk you imagine goes on between a papa and a mama at night, after you're tucked into your bed with your sister and they're still up, sitting in front of the fire, their heads bent together, their voices low and murmuring and assuring you that someone is still awake and alert and will care for you even if there are wolves outside the door; you know you heard them, even though Papa scoffed and said it was a coyote. But as long as Papa and Mama were up and talking, you could go to sleep because you knew they wouldn't let a wolf inside.

But now, for the first time, Gerda suspected that perhaps those conversations weren't so comforting, after all; perhaps they were about urgent things, sad things. Heartbreaking things.

"But I have you and Raina, don't I? I have you and so I'm not as alone as Papa is; it's almost like my sisters but not quite. But Papa, he doesn't have men around him and that's a kind of loneliness, it is, Gerda, even though he loves us so. Do you think he is disappointed in me, because I didn't give him sons? Oh, there was one, yes, before you, but he died so little, so quickly, sometimes I almost forget. Of course, I won't ever forget but sometimes I get so busy and I have you two and so I do go a few hours without thinking of him; little Peter, we baptized him, or at least Papa did with our Bible, but he barely got it done before the baby died. He shuddered and whimpered and lay very still in my arms and then Papa took him from me. He wrapped him in something, and later we had a ceremony outside, but that was long ago, back home in Norway. I'll never see him again and I cried about that, yes I did, when we left; and perhaps I was even angry at your papa for taking us away from him, but of course I couldn't say that. And now we are here, so far away from him and Mama and my sisters, who might be dead, but that is the way of the Lord and all we can do is accept it."

Gerda was too stunned to say anything; she'd never heard of a brother. She'd never seen any sign of longing or sadness for him in either of her parents. She had no idea why her mother was so worried about the lack of him, or another son, all of a sudden. Did Mama have these thoughts all the time? And did she have to hide them, storing them up somewhere inside until they gushed out like now? Gerda understood that this was not part of the conversation that went on at night between her parents. Gerda knew that this was the kind of conversation that women had, and she remembered how sad Mama had been when her friend Lydia Gunderson, on the homestead next to theirs, had died giving birth. To a son, Gerda remembered. But both mother and child had died, and Mama, Gerda realized, must have been so lonely ever since. Even though they didn't see their neighbors all that often, especially during winter, still, Mama and Mrs. Gunderson must have been the kind of friends who talked about these things. And now, Mama only had her and Raina.

Mama suddenly rose and continued shaking out the mattress tick; she bent down and kissed Gerda on the head and gently told her to go back to the dishes, and the moment was over. Mama was Mama again, singing hymns as she went about her tasks, that odd, feverish gleam in her eyes gone. She welcomed Papa home from the fields that night as usual, with a table full of hearty food and a scolding for him to leave his work boots outside, as if he'd ever dared to wear them inside!

That night, as she and Raina lay next to each other, Raina already softly snoring, Gerda heard the familiar, low murmuring between her parents, felt the reflexive relaxing of her own limbs, her eyelids growing heavy. But for the first time, she understood that conversation didn't always bring about resolution. That people—all people—carried around inside them notions and thoughts and sadness that could not be alleviated simply by talking about them.

But that people—women, perhaps, especially—had to try. Or else . . . Gerda didn't really know. Maybe, when you carried those sad thoughts around forever, you could die from them?

Gerda's lips felt chapped and raw; she wanted to lick them but didn't dare for fear her tongue would freeze to them. She realized she'd been talking to herself. Just like Mama had on that strange day—and others like it. But as Raina got older it was upon her that Mama would shower these urgent, pent-up torrents of words, thoughts, feelings, memories. Gerda, by then, was spending too much time out in the fields or barn with Papa, doing her very best to keep up with him, although she couldn't. They both knew it, and in little glances and sighs from her father, Gerda did see what her mother meant; she did understand how much her father missed not having a son.

There she was again! Talking to herself, her thoughts strange and far away, while her body kept moving. Although she realized she was shuffling now, as was Ingrid, and she hadn't felt Minna stir at all for a while. Suddenly her heart seized, then it tried to race but it couldn't, her blood was too cold. But still panic flooded her, propelled her legs, her feet that could just as well have been cement blocks for all that Gerda could feel them, forward, forward. Now she was stumbling, shuffling instead of dragging. Her head still bent against the onslaught of this terrible, clogging snow; it filled her eyes, her nose, her mouth, her lungs, and she wondered if she could suffocate in it. She wondered if Minna already had.

"Come, come," she yelled, crazily, to poor Ingrid, who looked up at her once, and through the whirling snow Gerda saw horror—a face rubbed raw, eyes crusted over with ice. Ingrid's lips were blue and trembling. She emitted a faint, pitiful cry.

"Come!" Gerda had only one hand with which to drag the little girl, as her other arm was wrapped around one of Minna's limp legs. "Come, Ingrid, come!"

And with her head bent back down again, Gerda plunged forward into the nightmare. It was growing darker by the minute. It must be nearly dusk. They'd never see a light in a window, not shrouded in this curtain of misery.

She staggered on this way, one girl on her back, the other barely upright, crying constantly now, until suddenly Gerda smelled something. Something faintly sweet. She stopped, walked ahead, then turned blindly to her left; she dropped Ingrid's hand so that she could feel her way through the wind and snow, she inched ahead, arm outstretched, and it was a miracle that jolted through her body when she touched something—something hard, cold, little smooth ridges, an occasional sharp edge.

A haystack.

"Ingrid!" She whirled around, dropped Minna against the stack—the girl didn't move, she was as inert as a doll. Gerda ran back a few steps; she heard crying, grabbed something alive, and it was—another miracle!—Ingrid. Then she dragged the child back to the haystack, and with a fury—a hunger—Gerda began to paw at the hay. It was freezing, sharp, it bit at her hands, fighting back. But after how long, she did not know—she only knew that she was both drenched in perspiration and numb with cold—she had carved out an opening, a tiny cave barely large enough to shove Minna and Ingrid inside and maybe she could squeeze herself in there, too. It was something, anyway, and she crawled in after them as far as she could. She fell on her back, gazing up at darkness but it was quiet now, so quiet her ears popped; the wind was muffled, she heard her own breathing, and another ragged little breath beside her. But from the silent, frozen mound of clothes and flesh at her head, there came no sound.

"Minna," she croaked hoarsely, but a blanketing exhaustion overwhelmed her. She was sinking now, sinking in this tiny space, straw tickling her nose. It was still cold—colder down at her feet than at her head, although she could barely sense that, as she could not feel her feet—but they were out of the worst of it. They would stay here until it passed over. Minna was surely asleep, that was all; Ingrid had stopped crying, and must have fallen asleep, as well.

It was so quiet. She was only aware of her own breathing, shallow breaths coming further apart than she'd ever felt. It was like drowning, but she had never known anyone who had drowned, had only read about it in books. Her lungs filled up with something other than air, and she felt her eyes close, her body grow limp.

She tried to stay awake; she began to count backward from one hundred. Ninety-nine, ninety-eight, ninety-seven, ninety-six, ninety-five.

"Ingrid," she murmured, lips so numb she could barely move them. "Ingrid, now it's your turn, go on, keep counting. . . . Raina, why don't you ask her. . . ."

But Ingrid didn't answer; neither did Minna. And Raina was strangely silent, too.

Gerda didn't care any longer; she gave in, the waves crashed over her, pressing her down, down, down into the cold, hard earth.

. . . . . .

CHAPTER 16

SHE TIGHTENED THE SCARF ABOUT HER HEAD, TRIED to cover her ears, then quickly reached around to hold Enid firmly in place, even though the child's legs were wrapped around Raina's waist. Her other hand gripped Arvid's, whose wheezing was almost loud enough to compete with the roar of the wind.

Raina turned around, eyes shutting against the stinging wind and snow as hard as buckshot, but she forced her eyes open. She shouted, desperate to be heard, desperate to hear.

"Children! Roll call!"

Ears straining, she heard the tiny voices, weaker this time than the last. First Tor—reassuring, knowing he was there at the end of this bedraggled line—then Sofia, Rosa, Eva, Albert, Clara, Tana, Walter, Daniel, Arvid.

"Enid," the little girl whispered in her ear, and Raina closed her eyes, allowing herself to be thankful for this one moment, this moment when she knew they were all still alive, still together. Then she had to let go of that moment and forge ahead toward the next.

And it was in this way, inch by inch, stopping periodically for the children to claim their names, that Raina led her little band of schoolchildren toward what she desperately prayed was the Halvorsans' farm.

She couldn't rely on Tor for directions, although she trusted he would let her know if she was badly off. But he was there, was Tor; he was at her back, strong and steady and honest. Her guilt at not letting him run off after his brother was ever-present, whispering in her ear when Enid wasn't. She had let him down badly, and he would blame her for the rest of his days if something happened to Fredrik. But there were so many things to feel guilty for lately; one more seemed like nothing, just one more drop into an almost-full bucket.

Occasionally, as she kept struggling against the wind, the cold, the snow that was unlike any snow she'd ever known, these grainy pellets that clogged the eyes and nostrils and mouth, she thought of Anette and Fredrik, and worried about them. But then she forced herself to say, out loud, the names of each of the children soldiering on behind her, tied together with apron strings and pluck and luck. Her heart swelled with pride; none complained, not even the tiniest, as they trudged on, heads bent down like hers. They were one living, breathing unit. And she was the head. The heart.

Another step forward. Another. Another. Her thighs quivered, were on fire, but the rest of her legs and feet were senseless. The wind came at her from her left, now her right; punched her face with an icy blow, hit the back of her head. Her breathing was shallow, rapid; she didn't dare to breathe deeply, lest she inhale the sticky snow. Lest the frigid air burn her lungs from the inside.

Sometimes, she wondered about Gunner. Had he come for them, after all? Had he pulled up to the schoolhouse, seen the broken window, the chaos of scattered papers and books and lunch pails, and run to the closet, empty of clothes? What did he feel when he registered that she was gone, that they all were gone? Worry? Terror? Loss?

Or was he still at home, still warm and safe, sitting with Anna, laughing with his children? Had he ever, in all those feverish weeks, spared a thought for Raina once she left his house? Now she doubted that. Before, she would have passionately believed that his every waking moment was spent thinking only of her. But something had shifted in her today. Maybe it started that night, when he so quickly turned from her to Anna. Anna, her hair burning bright around her shoulders, her white nightgown, embroidered extravagantly with pale blue flowers. Anna, a butcher knife in her hand.

Gunner had not tried to overpower his wife; he'd quivered and crouched with fright, not stood tall with defiance. He'd knelt before Anna, coaxing her back down the stairs, until the knife fell to the floor with a clatter, and Gunner scooped Anna up in his arms, took her to their bedroom, and shut the door behind them. Leaving Raina alone in the attic, her mind still buzzing with all the unwanted thoughts and emotions he'd forced upon her. He'd invaded her bedroom, dared to kneel by her cot, rest his hands on her shoulders, whisper his plans in her ear. Tease her desires by telling her they were going to leave. Not asking her. Telling her.

Because to him, she was just a silly girl to whom he could do whatever he wanted. Because to him, she was a plaything. There was nothing noble in his devotion. It was vanity—she was a mirror, reassuring him that he was a man who could make a young girl lose her head. A reminder that as a man, he could take whatever he wanted.

The taste in her mouth was bitter, sour.

Suddenly she felt a tug; the apron string around her waist was taut. She stopped.

Tor was standing next to her, little Sofia in his arms, the other children, tied to them both, in a curved line between them. Only Sofia's eyes were visible; Tor had taken his own scarf and wrapped it about her head. Tor's face was red and raw, his ears a purplish hue. But his eyes were earnest and true. And worried.

"Miss Olsen, the little ones can't go much farther. Rosa and Eva and Albert are barely upright."

Raina glanced at Arvid, right behind her, manfully trying to conceal how wretched his breathing was, but his lips were nearly blue. She nodded.

"I know, we need to find shelter. How far do you think we are from your homestead?"

"If we can pick up the pace a little, I think we're not too far. We have to be careful of that creek, it's not deep but it wouldn't do to get wetter than we are. But I think we're only a few rods away."

"Right. Can you carry Rosa, too? Untie Eva and bring her up to me. I'll see if I can carry them both."

"Miss Olsen, I can walk," little Enid whispered, and Raina almost cried. She shook her head.

"No, dear, I don't think you can, but you're so brave, Enid! Such a brave girl!"

"Miss Olsen," Tor began, but Raina placed her hand on his arm.

"Raina," she said, looking into his eyes. He'd earned the right to call her by her name. Whatever happened after this, the two of them couldn't go back to being teacher and pupil. They were equal, now.

Tor might have blushed, had his face not already been

burned by the freezing wind and snow. He did look embarrassed.

"R-Raina. I don't know that you can carry them both."

"I can. So can you." And that was all there was to say; Tor
trudged back to the end of the line, untied Eva, and half carried, half dragged the child up to Raina. Raina smiled at her,
whispered into her ear, "We're almost there, we don't have
far to go." And then she—with Enid still on her back, the
girl's arms tightly around her neck—bent down and lifted
Eva up.

Raina snuggled the child in her arms. Then she shifted
her around until she could find the right balance, and started
moving again.

It was much harder to stay upright with both girls clinging to her, but there was the added benefit of their body heat,
such as it was; she wasn't as cold, at least her torso wasn't.
Her feet still felt like blocks of ice, and her fingers were losing feeling.

She walked and the children trudged behind her. One
more step. Another. Someone in the middle fell over, she
felt the tug at her waist, a jumble of cries, then whoever it
was scrambled back up, and the bunch of them inched forward, forward, forward.

How much longer? How long could they take it? Children
were crying behind her; she wanted to tell them not to, to
conserve their energy, their body fluids, but she couldn't
stop now. She didn't even dare pause to take the roll call; if
she stopped, she wouldn't be able to go on. Enid and Eva
were quiet, too quiet; they did occasionally stir, but she
could almost feel their heartbeats slowing, like clocks winding down. They were fragile, delicate. Bodies were sturdy
things—hadn't Papa always said that? But he was wrong.

Bodies were no match for this ferociousness, it wouldn't stop. There were no breaks at all in the snow dancing up from the ground to meet the snow plummeting from the sky. If only it would stop, just for a moment, so she could see something, anything. If only God would make it—

Stop.

For a miraculous moment, everything stilled; the winds paused, as if the heavens had taken a collective breath. It would be let out again in an instant, Raina knew, so she paused, and desperately looked about her; nothing was familiar. She didn't see anything of note, just the grey landscape, and she was about to burst into tears of frustration when she heard a shout behind her.

"There!" It was Tor; there was pure joy in his voice. "There—see, Miss Olsen! To the right! We're almost there!"

Squinting to her right, Raina looked and looked, and finally she saw it—a light. Faint, barely yellow, but a light, and then she could make out the greyish blob surrounding it, and she knew it was a house. Then she saw that there were more lights, lights in every window.

"That's our house! There! So close—we can make it now!"

She would have sworn it was miles away but then her eyes adjusted further, and she realized they were practically upon it. But they had been heading slightly to the left, south of it; if they'd continued on in that direction they would have missed it entirely. It was a miracle, pure and simple. A miracle that the clouds had parted to show them the way.

Raina had just enough time to see the footbridge over the little creek; she turned slightly, aimed right at it, and started forward just as the clouds descended once more, obscuring the house, the bridge; they were enshrouded again. But now she knew she was headed in the right direction, and all she

had to do was take about thirty steps and she'd be at the footbridge. She counted them, aloud—one, two, three.

She was at twenty-one when her foot hit the edge of the
rough wooden planks. She stopped, felt bodies running into
one another behind her, heard Arvid wheeze in surprise.
Turning, she shouted back at Tor, although she couldn't see
him; in the span of twenty-one steps the storm had de
scended with fury, more terrible than before.

"The bridge!" she shouted at the top of her lungs. "We're
at the bridge!"

Carefully, she knelt, settling Eva on the ground; the little
girl's eyelashes were glued together with sticky ice, so Raina
gently tried to melt the ice with her own frozen thumb until
she realized she was rubbing the child's cheeks raw. But Eva
was finally able to open her eyes; she looked dazed, stupid.
Raina tugged at Enid's arms, and the child slid down off of
her. "See the footbridge, Enid?"

Enid, her face pinched with fatigue, nodded.

"We have to cross it, and you get to be the first! I'll let you
children cross first in case it can't hold up for us all, and
then somehow I'll get over and we'll race to Tor's house,
where I bet there will be cookies and a hot fire! Don't you
want to be the first one there?"

Enid nodded, but looked terrified. With so much chaos
swirling about, this bridge—it barely deserved the name, for
in the summertime the children could leap over the creek,
skip across the planks, it would be a lark, a game. But now it
seemed a bridge to eternity itself; the far side was missing,
the destination appearing to vanish into the angry heavens.

"Go slowly, Enid. Just put one foot in front of the other."

Enid took a big breath, and she put one tiny foot on the
edge of the board; a gust of wind nearly pushed her over but

Raina grabbed her just in time, snatching the little girl back. These little ones couldn't do it, they wouldn't make it. She and Tor would have to carry each of them across.

Raina untied the apron string from her waist, shouted for the others to do the same. Tor came huffing up, Sofia clinging to his back, Rosa in his arms. He set the girls down.

"How far is it once we get over the bridge?" Raina asked, struggling for breath. All of a sudden, she felt as if she couldn't get enough oxygen inside her lungs; she was dizzy in an already-swirling landscape. She reached out for something to steady her, and Tor grabbed her arms so she didn't topple over.

They both stood that way, gasping for breath, linked together, for a moment that was both too brief and too long; there was not a second to be spared. The storm—the withering cold, the gravelly, icy snow, the exertion it had taken to get this far—was taking its toll on them all. Especially the children.

"It's about twenty yards," Tor said. "But we have to be careful; there's a gap between the barn and the house and if we miss either of them, we're back out on the prairie."

"I saw the lights in all the windows, back there. Hopefully we'll be able to see them again once we're closer. But we have to carry the little ones across the bridge, they're just too weak to do it on their own."

Tor nodded, picked up Sofia, who flung her arms about his neck and buried her face in his shoulder. "I'll go first."

He started across the bridge, one foot carefully feeling for the board. It was only about five feet across but once he got in the middle, an enormous gust pummeled him and he began to sway; Raina cried out.

But he bent his head down and remained upright; through the curtain of weather, Raina could just barely see that he scooted toward the end of the bridge and quickly set Sofia down on the other side, instructing her to remain where she was, not to move an inch. Then he was back across the bridge, reaching for Rosa, who shook her head and started to cry.

"No, no, no!" she screamed, and the poor thing was so tired, so disoriented, she tried to fight Tor off. But the young man patiently picked her up anyway and started back over the bridge on wobbly legs. Raina held her breath, but a taunting gust of wind blew up more snow that obscured him; she couldn't see if he made it, she could only wait. It seemed to her she didn't breathe at all until he was back. His eyes were tearing up and he had to keep rubbing them so they wouldn't freeze. His ears—uncovered since he'd given his scarf to Sofia—were dangerously purple, and Raina worried that there would be permanent damage. He was reaching out to get Enid when Raina stopped him; he had to rest.

"I'll take her," she said, and she picked up the child, who latched her arms about Raina's neck.

Suddenly Raina was aware of her skirts; heavy with snow and ice, they felt like an anchor about her legs. On the prairie, on solid ground, she'd rejoiced in their protection. But with one foot on the edge of a piece of wood ten inches wide, hovering above a pit of deadly snow and ice, even if it was only about three feet below, she panicked. She wanted to give the girl back to Tor but she had to do her part, she had to pull through with him; he couldn't do it all.

"Papa, Papa, I need you," she whispered. Because it was Papa who had always encouraged her to try harder, work harder, run faster, test her muscles to the limit; Mama might say he pushed her, pushed both girls, too hard, and maybe he had. But only out of necessity.

What she would do to have him here now, coaxing her, smiling down at her with his proud eyes, never for a moment entertaining the notion that she might not succeed. She could never let him down. Neither she nor Gerda could; it was a pact they'd made when they were smaller. They could never let their papa down.

So Raina took the first step onto the bridge; she tensed against the onslaught of the wind, the girl in her arms stirred enough to surprise her off her balance, and she tottered for a moment. Her skirts wrapped around her ankles in a sodden, frigid clump. But she fought them, took the next step, eyes open as far as they could be in the punishing wind, desperate to see something, anything, to help her stay balanced, stay on the right path.

Another step. Another. She heard sobbing right in front of her, and she knew the other girls were there, waiting miserably as Tor had told them; she was almost upon them. And then one more step, and she was bending down to deposit Enid when she heard a muffled cry, and a squishy thump, below.

In the creek. Someone had fallen in the creek.

"Enid? Sofia? Rosa?"

"It's Rosa," Sofia cried. "She fell down!"

"Tor! Tor?" Raina shouted, but she didn't know if he could hear her.

"Teacher, Teacher!" Rosa cried weakly, then she sobbed.

"Stay right there, Rosa! Don't move, I'm coming for you."

Raina pulled up her skirts, took a breath, and—praying she wouldn't fall on top of the girl—jumped into the creek.

. . . . . .

CHAPTER 17

Each step was a victory. Had she really run, free as she had ever been, across this endless prairie? It was impossible to remember now that each tiny step took all her concentration, seemed to deplete her heart and lungs so thoroughly she had to pause and rest before she could take the next step.

Fredrik, still clinging to her, had stopped crying; he could only keep saying, "I'm scared," but less and less often. Sometimes, he whimpered for his mother.

"I'm scared, too," Anette admitted, when her brain seemed to spark back up again, just for a quick second, before it was overcome by the cloud of confusion that was growing with each moment. Once she was able to pull her thoughts, which lay like fallen stalks of corn in her mind, together just enough to say, "We just have to find the ravine, the bridge, then we're home."

Fredrik, still crying, nodded.

Then they took another step.

At one point she became aware she was humming a song, something long forgotten—from the dugout, from her mama, from her babyhood. It had no words, it was just a simple tune, the notes rose and fell and rose and fell, and it wasn't pretty at all. It wasn't melodic. It was the sound a simple-minded person would make to comfort herself. And so maybe her stepfather had been right along: Maybe Anette was stupid. Sometimes she'd thought she wasn't, really—she was just constantly weary and lonely, trapped in a body so sturdy it fooled people. A girl built for work and nothing more, and her sadness made her not care what they thought, most of the time. It made her not care about much of anything.

Maybe she was leading Fredrik farther and farther away from home, maybe he was foolish to trust her, but he had given up. She could see that—feel it, as his hand was so limp in hers. He was only moving because he was linked to her. And she was too stupid to give up.

Maybe it was a good thing, then, that she was so dumb. She almost laughed.

But then she was falling, falling, Fredrik tumbling against her, knocking what little breath she still had out of her. They plunged through an ocean of snow, she was on her back looking up at churning clouds of snow that dumped their contents on top of her. Then they both stopped moving; they had reached the bottom.

Of the ravine, she realized, too stunned, too immobilized by panic to cry out. They'd found the ravine, after all. She had been right; she had been going in the right direction— but it was a hollow victory now.

Fredrik, next to her, began to moan as he pushed himself onto his elbow. He looked up—it was impossible to tell what was sky and what was earth, everything was one color, one substance—icy grey mixed with swirls of white. He pulled her into a sitting position, and they brushed the snow off their shoulders, their faces, their heads. Then he rose, looked around, tried to find a handhold to pull himself up the steep bank, but everything was coated in snow and ice. Not a blade of grass, not a stick, not a tree root showed itself. They couldn't be at the very bottom of the ravine, with its tiny, snake-sized rivulet of creek; it was filled with the snow of all the previous storms. But they still must be a long way down. Far enough that they would be hidden from the sight of anyone looking out a window or stumbling across the prairie.

Pushing herself up, she stood next to Fredrik. She tried to crawl back up the slope, but her hands were too numb, she had no strength; she slid backward, and still she tried. So did Fredrik; they were on their hands and knees together, two babies unable to balance on their feet, and they made it a few more inches before once again, they slid backward. There was no more strength in her, in him; she felt weak as a rag doll, and now she couldn't feel her feet anymore as she realized she was standing in a slushy pile of icy snow up to her thighs. The snow on the prairie had been hard-packed, and they hadn't stood still long enough to have it drift around them, but down here, protected from the wind and the stinging bullets of ice, the snowfall was more treacherous. Anette cried out, shouted for help, so did Fredrik, but their voices were hoarse and weak. The frustration that they might only be fifty yards from shelter, from the Pedersens' house or barn, almost flattened Anette; finally, wrung out, gasping for air but shivering too violently to get a good breath in, she fell backward into the snow. Her legs refused to propel her back up.

Fredrik fell down, too.

But he sidled next to her, and put his arm around her,

pulling her in close. And despite the cold, the dark—twilight seemed to have come in the middle of day, the clouds were so thick between earth and sun—Anette felt, in that moment, happy.

She wasn't alone anymore.

The storm raged above; she could hear the howling wind but it was muffled. Down here in this snow cave, the cold wasn't quite as shocking; it crept over her slowly, almost soothingly. Fredrik murmured something as his arm tightened around her. Anette couldn't muster the strength to ask him what he said, and then she didn't care. It didn't matter. The only thing that mattered was that he was there.

Anette sank a little into his embrace, closing her eyes. And then she slept.

CHAPTER 18

THE SHOCK OF THAT FRIGID MIX OF ICE AND SNOW reaching up to gobble her ankles and knees made Raina cry out loud and made her limbs shudder even more violently. But at least she hadn't landed on Rosa, who she could hear sobbing piteously, though each sob was fainter than the one before. Raina reached out, blindly pawing through the slush. It seemed to take an eternity, eating up her precious last reserves of sentient thoughts, a beating heart, and working lungs, but finally she felt the little girl's quivering shoulders. She sloshed over to her—down here the ice wasn't solid—and pulled the girl up; as she did, Rosa cried out weakly.

"My shoes! My shoes, Mama!"

"It doesn't matter," Raina said, as she desperately tried to cover the girl's wet stockings with her hands; her shoes were gone, and the water was already freezing into ice on her tiny, vulnerable feet. "We have to go."

But how? She shouted for Tor, for Arvid, for anybody. As she stood in about two feet of icy slush, there were no words to describe the shocking cold, there was no way to prevent it from racing up her legs, her torso, devouring her heart. She thought she might freeze where she stood, an icy statue with an equally frozen child in her arms, and no one would find them until spring.

"Hand her up to me!" It was Tor; somehow she could make out that he was on his stomach, leaning over the bank, his arms outstretched.

"I can't." Raina began to sob; she was reaching as high as she could, Rosa now ominously silent and limp in her arms, but she couldn't quite get the child to Tor. Her arms were like noodles, seemingly without bones to support them as they shook.

"Try, Raina, try!" And it was like Papa's voice in her ears, although she knew it was Tor's; even though she couldn't see him, she imagined Tor's encouraging eyes watching her, sure she wouldn't disappoint him. So she did try. With a strangled cry she heaved herself farther out of the slush, standing on her toes, straining every muscle in her torso and arms to raise up the deadweight of the child, and finally she felt Tor's arms mingled with hers as he reached down and, with a groan, hauled the girl up to the bank.

She was so relieved, so exhausted with emotion and exertion, that she was tempted to fall down where she was. Tor would get the others across, get them to the house. She knew this with the certainty that she knew the sun would rise in the morning. So Raina could simply sink into the bank of snow and ice, let the snow cover her up, and close her eyes and sleep. Every nerve, every muscle in her body cried out for this rest. Her eyelids began to flutter; she felt weak, limp—

Until an arm reached out and grabbed hers, and a fierce voice invaded her torpor.

"Raina, you have to keep going. I need you, Raina."

She shook her head, she tried to quiet the tremor that was rattling her entire body, but she couldn't. She reached up, and allowed Tor to help her up the bank, her feet stumbling, now feeling like entire blocks of ice, but somehow she made it.

She flopped like a fish beside an inert Rosa, and Enid and Sofia. She watched, numbly, as Tor made his way—even more unsteadily—across the bridge and returned with Clara in his arms.

Then she pushed herself up, and crossed the bridge again, too—she barely noticed her skirts this time, her entire lower body was so numb. She grabbed Eva, unceremoniously, into her arms and gingerly crossed the bridge, dropped the girl on the ground, and went back. Somehow. Her mind had stopped working—thank goodness, for that meant it stopped questioning, as well. She was operating on pure instinct now.

The older children were able to cross on their own, with Raina on one end of the bridge shouting encouragement, and Tor on the other doing the same. And finally, they were all across the creek.

Rosa wasn't moving at all, but the other little girls were able to stand; there wasn't time to tie them all together again. Tor picked Rosa up and he and Raina herded the children in the direction they thought led to the house. With every shuffle, every pitiful mewl, like a weak kitten, from an exhausted child who had come to school that morning happy and well and strong, Raina prayed that they were going in the right direction. But she simply couldn't tell.

Until she heard a ringing . . . faint, then getting stronger. A cowbell. Someone was desperately ringing a cowbell.

"That's Mama," Tor shouted, joyful. "That's Mama ringing the bell!"

Raina started to weep, although strangely there were no more tears in her, no more moisture inside; the vortex of ice and frigid air had sucked it all up, dried her out. She urged the children on. They all heard the bell ringing with a frenzy. They stumbled toward a faint light, now veiled, now clearly visible, now veiled again, until they were standing, dumbstruck, in front of a grey farmhouse with kerosene lamps burning in every window. A frantic woman in a big wool cap with earflaps on her head, shivering in a man's overcoat, was standing with the door open, ringing a cowbell with all her might. When she saw the bedraggled group materialize out of the storm like spirits, she gave a cry of joy, dropped the bell, and rushed out to grab Sofia, who was about to tumble over where she stood.

"Good God! Good God in heaven! You're here—Papa, they're here, they're here! Tor and Fredrik and all the children, they're here!"

Tor handed Rosa, who was deathly still, to his father who was towering and strong and so like her own papa, Raina wanted to weep again. After the others were all inside, Raina allowed Mrs. Halvorsan to grab her by the arms and pull her into the blessed protection of the house.

Raina stood, numb, while all around her was chaos. Mr. and Mrs. Halvorsan rushed about, crying out as they peeled icy layers off of their sons' schoolmates. Raina could only slump against a wall, steeling herself for what was about to come.

"But—Fredrik? Where is Fredrik?" Mrs. Halvorsan's voice rose higher and higher with panic.

"Tor, where is your brother?" Mr. Halvorsan's booming

voice almost shattered the windows. "Tell me, son, where is Fredrik?"

Raina shut her eyes as her body trembled even more than it had in the storm; she was still frozen. But not so frozen that her heart didn't thunder with guilt.

She opened her eyes and caught Tor's glance; he was looking at her accusingly. No longer were they the team that had brought these children to safety—she could only pray, because Rosa was barely breathing as Mrs. Halvorsan knelt before her, peeling off the icy stockings from her feet. Raina, once again, was the monster who had prevented Tor from following his little brother out into the storm.

"Fredrik went after Anette," Raina began to explain shakily; her voice was raspy and frail. "Anette Pedersen. She ran out into the storm for home. Fredrik followed her, and Tor was about to go after him, but I wouldn't let him. It's my fault. I needed Tor to get these children safely here. I couldn't have done this without him."

The Halvorsans exchanged stricken looks; Mrs. Halvorsan hid her face in her hands and began to sob. Mr. Halvorsan, without a word, went to a coatrack and began to pile clothing on—coat, scarf, gloves.

"Papa!" Tor stumbled toward him. "Let me go, it's my fault, let me—" But the boy was weak, too weak; Raina rushed after him, pulling him back. He turned on her, trying to push her away; he was fighting, still. But like a tired kitten fights, although his words contained venom.

"You!" He hit at Raina, his fist striking her shoulder, his eyes full of fury. "You stopped me! If something happened to him I'll never, ever forgive you! Papa—don't go out there! Don't—let me!"

He twisted out of Raina's grip, and flung himself at his

father, who picked the strapping lad up as if he were a baby. Tor writhed and struggled and finally began to cry, a jagged, hoarse cry, but his father placed him in a chair with finality—pausing to gently kiss his eldest son on the forehead.

"I hate you. I hate you." Tor threw the words at Raina, where they landed with surprising force, given his weakened state. "I'll never forgive you, never."

"I know," she whispered, unnoticed by anyone in the room but Tor. The children were crying and Mr. Halvorsan walked over to his wife, who was standing now, feverishly knotting her apron in her hands.

"I'm going after him," Mr. Halvorsan told his wife, who looked frantically out the window at the still raging storm and bit her lip. She couldn't tell her husband not to go—and she couldn't tell him he should, either.

But Raina could.

Weaker than ever, swaying on her own two feet, she stumbled after Fredrik's father as he went toward the door.

"It's madness. Look—it's night already. You'll never find him in the dark; they must be at the Pedersens' by now. It's suicide to go out there!"

"I have to find my son," Mr. Halvorsan told her. In his eyes, she saw Tor's determination and honor, and she knew she couldn't stop this giant of a man—a father; not as she had stopped Tor.

"Peter, I—" Mrs. Halvorsan began to sob as she tended to Tor, who was moaning feverishly in the chair, finally giving in to his exhaustion. "I don't know, I don't know. My God, we have the others to think of, if anything happens to— But Fredrik!"

"Don't go," Raina pleaded one last time. "And please, don't blame Tor—blame me!"

Peter Halvorsan paused as he was winding another scarf about his face, leaving room only for his eyes, which somehow looked down at her, kindly.

"I don't blame anything but this cursed land and my folly in coming here," he said. Then he was gone, the door slamming behind him.

Raina turned toward the nightmarish scene before her: children still shivering, some sobbing for their parents, as Mrs. Halvorsan was fetching a pan from a shelf near the stove; she dashed outside to fill the pan with snow, and she started bathing Rosa's feet in it. Arvid was hunched over by the fire, wheezing, his thin shoulders rising up to his ears. Rosa lay still, so still, and Raina glanced at the little girl's feet; they were purple. Purple as the sky must be outside, obscured by the still-raging storm that shook the little house and pounded the windows.

Tor was deeply asleep—he must have fainted. Raina crept over to him, picking her way among the children lying, like fallen soldiers, in the crowded room, too exhausted to take any of their frozen outer garments off. For a moment Raina allowed herself a morsel of satisfaction; she had gotten them all here anyway. Who knew what lay ahead—frostbite was a concern, of course, and she glanced again over to little Rosa with her tiny, blackening feet; she knew that once the feet thawed the girl would be in a torment of pain. But still, they were all here, and not lost on the prairie.

Except for Fredrik and Anette.

Raina knelt down next to Tor, and put her hand on his forehead, clammy with perspiration.

"I'm so sorry. But I couldn't have done it without you."

Then she felt light-headed, a fuzzy blackness clouding the outer corners of her vision. Sitting back on her heels, she took one last glimpse at his troubled young face. Her eyelids fluttered, and she felt herself falling, welcoming the exhaustion that overwhelmed her determination.

Finally, Raina slept.

CHAPTER 19

. . . . . .

THE BLIZZARD, CREATED WHEN AN ENORMOUS TROUGH of cold air rushing in from the Arctic had met up with an equally enormous influx of warm, wet air from the gulf, gobbled up everything in its path. The collision generated a force of energy no one could remember seeing in their lifetimes, but that all would talk about with wonder until the day they died. With so much energy, the storm kept on pulsating over the land, eventually reaching down all the way to Texas as it marched eastward.

And as it marched, something took its place: a high-pressure system of air so frigidly punishing, it froze exposed flesh within minutes.

AT SOME POINT, ANETTE SENSED something that brought her out of the deepest sleep she'd ever known. It wasn't a sound, but an absence of it—the wind had stopped howling. Her ears still rang from the memory of that noise but were trying, desperately, to understand the eerie silence that had replaced it.

She couldn't move, though, to see what had happened;

something heavy was pressing on her chest, keeping her pinned to the ground. Her entire torso was covered, save for her left hand, which she tried to move but couldn't; she couldn't feel for what was on top of her.

All she knew was that the storm was over, but it was still very dark. Nighttime.

And it was unbearably cold, but her eyes closed anyway; she was too exhausted, too thoroughly frigid, to register more. She gave up; she wanted to say Fredrik's name, but then she didn't care.

She fell back asleep.

GERDA, TOO, WAS DIMLY AWARE when the wind stopped roaring. She didn't wake up, but she'd been dreaming of Tiny riding his horse out on the prairie, the two of them racing a screaming locomotive. In her dream, the train abruptly stopped, as if it had run out of steam, and Tiny waved his cowboy hat in triumph, whooping and yelling; he pulled on the reins of little Poco, stood up in his saddle, and winked at Gerda. Then he dug his heels into the horse's sides and galloped away from her; she watched until he was a speck on the horizon.

She shivered in her sleep and thought that someone had left a door open somewhere because her feet were cold. She flung out an arm and it hit something, something covered in clothing, but the something didn't move or flinch, so she withdrew her arm, pulled it over her torso for warmth.

She murmured Tiny's name, although she didn't know it. She fell back asleep so she could resume her dream, so she could run after him, before he disappeared forever.

———

AT SOME POINT, RAINA opened her eyes; her clothes were thawing, damp now. The fireplace was roaring, and she turned her head. Mrs. Halvorsan was sitting on a chair next to it, watching the flames. The room was too cold to be cozy, but it was reassuring, with all the children sleeping soundly. But then Raina heard a tiny moaning—like a mouse crying— and she pushed herself up on her elbows.

Little Rosa was thrashing about, asleep but obviously in pain.

"How is she?" Raina asked, and Mrs. Halvorsan turned to her in surprise. She was a tall, lanky woman, with soft brown hair that, despite all her exertions, remained in a deter- mined bun at the nape of her neck. Her eyes were the same blue as Tor's, but they were anxious; even when she smiled at Raina, there was a worried "V" between them.

"The poor thing, she'll lose her feet. There's no saving them, and I've got nothing for her pain save for some whis- key we keep for medicine. I need to give her more."

"Is Mr. Halvorsan back?" Raina rose on shaking limbs; she was still shivering out all the cold. But it wasn't as vio- lent as before, so she could walk into the kitchen, over to the table where Mrs. Halvorsan was pouring the whiskey into a tin cup.

"No" was all Mrs. Halvorsan said. She was not inviting speculation.

"The storm stopped," Raina said with wonder, realizing, for the first time, that the house wasn't rattling with the wind.

"Yes, and the temperature has dropped. It must be twenty below."

The implication of this silenced Raina. Anyone caught out on the prairie—

No, she couldn't think of it. Besides Fredrik and Anette and now Mr. Halvorsan, she wondered, for the first time, about her family. Mama and Papa—had they had the good sense to stay inside? Or had they, too, been caught out, doing the usual chores—tending to the livestock, letting the horses have some time outside the barn, when the weather had seemed so innocent? Just this morning—no, yesterday. For it was three A.M. now, she saw from the mantel clock.

And Gerda, what had she done? She would have been with a schoolhouse full of students, too, up in Dakota Territory. There was a chance the storm had missed her, but Raina, having been out in the infinite wilderness of it, thought that chance was slim. Raina didn't know what kind of schoolhouse it was; Gerda had never said whether it was a soddie, or a small cabin, or a bigger house with wood but no insulation, like Raina's school. But Gerda was so sensible, so strong. Surely she had managed to stay out of the storm, keep her children safe, too. Unless, of course, something had happened beyond her control, like had happened to Raina.

She found herself yawning repeatedly and couldn't help herself; she knew she should stay up and keep Mrs. Halvorsan company until her husband came back. She should take her turn tending to Rosa. But she was still so exhausted, it was like she was walking through quicksand as she sheepishly crept back to the room full of children, and curled back up among them, next to Clara and Enid. She reached out a hand to pat both children, satisfied they were sleeping; alive.

The one person she didn't think about was Gunner Pedersen.

Then she fell back into a sleep with arms—arms that enfolded her, kept her still and warm, pinning her down against her will.

JANUARY 13, 1888, 12:15 A.M.

SIGNAL OFFICE
WAR DEPARTMENT
SAINT PAUL

———

Indications for 24 hours commencing at 7A.M. today.

FOR SAINT PAUL AND MINNEAPOLIS: snow, colder with a cold wave, fresh northerly winds.

FOR MINNESOTA: colder with a cold wave, snow followed in northern part by fair weather, fresh northerly winds.

FOR DAKOTA: local snows, colder with a cold wave, fresh northerly winds becoming variable.

CHAPTER 20

. . . . . .

THE SUN ROSE THAT MORNING AS EVER, PEEKING OVER the eastern horizon, taking its sweet time, painting the black sky purple, then pink, then with tendrils of faded blue that began to erase the night. It continued to rise, until a dome of the most brilliant blue encircled a prairie that was sparkling with new snow, the crystals catching and reflecting back up their blinding bursts of brilliance.

A hawk, one that had found shelter in a nest built in the top of a newly planted oak next to a little creek, emerged, shaking its wings lazily before taking to the sky, working to catch a current. The air was so still he had to climb higher than usual, but then he found it; he circled widely, flapping his wings slowly as he patrolled his patch of prairie, searching for something to eat.

As he soared high above, the blinding white of the landscape below seemed unbroken, a great undulating blanket of snow as far as the eye could see, except for a few far-flung houses and barns. Fences were completely obscured, so that it all seemed one parcel, one infinite landscape of shimmering diamonds.

But the hawk knew the landscape; there were vast areas

of it he avoided due to a scarcity of prey. Land that was overhunted—that land was the Great Sioux Reservation, bordered by the rugged Black Hills on the west, the Missouri River on the east. There, even scrawny squirrels and half-dead rabbits were precious. The smudges there were tepees, made out of fading buffalo hide, clustered together in groups, the groups too close to those from other tribes, but forced, due to the government, to live together. Misery hung over this landscape like a cloud, even on the sunniest day.

So he kept to the south, swooping closer to the ground, and finally the peaceful-seeming landscape gave up some secrets. A fence post here, a clump of bushes there, an upturned wagon, haystacks.

As his eyes adjusted, however, other secrets were discovered. What seemed like a line of small haystacks were, upon closer inspection as the hawk zeroed in, cows. Unmoving cows, statues; some on their sides, others standing, all frozen where they were.

The hawk turned, uninterested, to investigate more dark shapes emerging from the blinding white; horses, their legs collapsed under them, eyes closed forever.

Now the hawk swooped back up, circling ever wider, before zeroing in on the ground again, intent for food.

But nothing moved. Not a rabbit, not a gopher. Not a smaller bird, unaware.

A small smudge over there—the bird cruised down to see, hopeful, hungry. But he was disappointed; the smudge did not move. For it was an arm, sticking out of the snow, attached to a body buried beneath.

Another odd blot of lifelessness, another, another—the bird took it all in from his aerial vantage point. A yellow hat atop a grey head, eyes frozen shut. A hand, poking out of a drift; a child's hand, so small, so white, a deathly white, paler than the snow. A wagon wheel, a pale blue dress fluttering out of its spokes, and inside that dress, a lifeless female body.

Clothing fluttered, moving, tricking the hawk time and again into thinking it had found its breakfast. Clothing blown off bodies that were now naked to the elements, like the one over there, only a few heartbreaking steps away from a barn.

And more small hands, feet, faces upturned, eyes shut tight. That deathly pallor, blue grey against the dazzling white snow.

The hawk turned northward, hoping for better hunting grounds.

But he was doomed to be disappointed on this cold, sunny morning.

. . . . . .

CHAPTER 21

As the sun rose, its rays filled the Halvorsan house with cruel memories. A reminder of the previous morning, when everything seemed full of hope and promise. But despite the blinding rays, the house was no warmer than it had been the night before; there was ice inside the windowpanes because of the humidity from all the clothing that had thawed out during the night.

The children began to stir, sitting up, crying out their hunger, their longing for their parents. Raina rubbed the sleep from her eyes and looked down in surprise; her damp garments had been replaced by dry ones, a dress, one of Mrs. Halvorsan's own. Every muscle ached—pulsed with pain, actually; every joint protested movement, and she had a pounding headache. But she rose, and automatically went to the stove, where Mrs. Halvorsan stood before a pot of porridge, stirring it listlessly with one hand while with the other she clutched a dishtowel so tightly, her knuckles were white.

Tor wasn't among the children, and Raina could only assume that at some point he had gone to his own room, where his younger siblings slept.

"Has Mr.—"

"No," Mrs. Halvorsan said abruptly. "Peter has not returned. Tor is getting dressed to go out and look, now that the storm is gone."

"How is he? I was worried about his ears; did they get frostbit?"

"Only a little, he'll lose some skin but not the cartilage, so he'll be fine."

"Mrs. Halvorsan, I—I don't know what to say about Fredrik. He ran after Anette before I could even see that he was gone."

"Anette? That Pedersen girl, the one who's just a hired hand?" Mrs. Halvorsan put the spoon down, turning to Raina in surprise.

"Yes. They're very good friends, you know."

"I didn't know. Fredrik talks about her now and then, but I didn't know he was partial to her in any way."

"She doesn't have any friends, other than your son. The other children don't know how to treat her; they know she's—well, just a servant, really, at the Pedersens. It makes it awkward for them all."

"You board with them, don't you?" Mrs. Halvorsan's eyebrow arched, and Raina found herself blushing, as if the woman could know what had happened over the last few weeks.

"Yes, I do."

"I hear that woman—Anna Pedersen—is a handful. We tried to be neighborly when they first came, but she didn't want no part of us, or nobody else. Too good for us, she must think herself." Mrs. Halvorsan sniffed, then she turned back to the stove, picking up the spoon and attacking the porridge, the dishtowel now on the floor.

"It is—it is an unusual household. And Anette is not

treated well, but then her own mother was the one who gave her away."

"Sold her, I heard."

"I don't know about that. But she is unloved, that's true. Except by your Fredrik. So please, don't be angry with him for running after her. He has a kind heart."

"Yes." Mrs. Halvorsan's chin began to tremble, and she wiped her eyes with the back of her hand. "Yes, he has, that one."

"And Tor, he does, too. He so wanted to go after his brother, but I couldn't let him. It's my fault, not his." Raina desperately wanted Sara Halvorsan to tell her it was nobody's fault, but she didn't. She simply walked to the window and stared out at the pitiless prairie. The snow sparkled like fresh sugar, mounded up against the barn, the porch. Anyone out there—anyone who had been trapped overnight, lost in the storm—how could they survive the cold? Especially small, vulnerable bodies. Like Anette and Fredrik.

Tor lumbered down the crude stairs leading up to the attic; here in his own house, the biggest person there, he looked like a man. In a buffalo coat, a wool hat with earflaps, sturdy boots, leather gloves, a muffler he was in the process of winding about his neck and face, he appeared immense. Like a bear. Only his eyes, anxious, still sleepy, betrayed his youth.

His mother went to him, placed her hand on his arm.

"See if you can find Papa's tracks, but if not, head toward the Pedersen place. And try to find out where the doctor is. That little girl, Rosa—she's going to lose her foot, I think. I gave her some whiskey but I don't have any more."

"I will, Mama," Tor said, his voice muffled. "Don't worry, I'll find them."

"I know you'll do your best," she assured him, releasing him to his duty. Raina cleared her throat; she wanted to say something to Tor, too—if only "good luck"—but she knew he would never pay any mind to anything she said, ever again. They were no longer allies, and they couldn't go back to being teacher and pupil.

They were strangers, she guessed with a disappointment that surprised her. Or even worse, adversaries.

Tor did not look at her; he walked to the front door and left, and Raina watched him struggle through the drifted snow, in some places up to his waist; here, sheltered by buildings, the snow had things to pile against. But out on the prairie it would be different, somewhat easier; not as deep, as if a giant broom had swept the snow first one way, then another. She was about to turn away when she saw Tor suddenly stop; he put his hands to his mouth as if he was calling out to someone just out of view of the kitchen. Then he broke into an awkward run, falling once, before he staggered up and disappeared around the corner of the barn.

Ten seconds later, everyone in the house could hear his strangled cry, mixed with the startling sound of bells jingling, a horse neighing as, with a great fanfare, a sleigh roared up to the house; Raina ran outside, heedless of the cold, and locked eyes with the man holding the reins, bundled up in robes and skins. As she did, she felt the familiar flush of anger and confusion, desire and hate—

Just as Tor came running toward her, arms waving wildly in the air, shouting, "Papa! Papa!—Miss Olsen, Mama—come see, it's Papa!"

Before Raina could say a word to Gunner Pedersen, she was being pulled by Tor through the snow, the shock of plunging into the cold igniting memories of the night before. Mrs. Halvorsan was right behind her, calling her husband's name; Gunner had jumped out of the sleigh, shouting, "Raina? Raina—thank God!" But when they turned the corner of the barn, they all stopped, shocked into silence.

For there was the body of Peter Halvorsan, stuck in the snow like a frozen Norse god. He appeared to be seated, his great shoulders and head the only things visible. His skin was a sickly grey, his hair white with snow, and icicles beaded his shut eyes, his hair, his beard.

He was only ten feet from his own barn.

"Papa," Tor cried hoarsely as he tried, frantically, to dig his father out of his snowy grave. He ran to the barn for a shovel; he began to chip away at the snow, but he was sobbing too heavily. Gunner ran to the boy, gently pushed him away, knelt down and tried to shake Peter Halvorsan back into living. But it was too late.

"Peter!" Mrs. Halvorsan was on her knees, her hands patting her husband's still, icy face, trying to warm him up; desperate, she tried to pry his frozen lips open so she could blow breath into his body. But it was too late.

"Raina!" Gunner finally turned to her. "I thought—I didn't know . . . I worried myself sick when no one came home; you must come with me now. I'll take you back."

But it was too late.

Raina shook her head, backed away, her eyes glued to the tragic scene before her. "No," she whispered fiercely. "I won't go back to that house. I won't."

Gunner looked at her, puzzled, then turned around to help Tor pry his father's body off the ground—it was frozen into a sitting position, making it difficult to maneuver. The two of them stumbled, struggled to bear that icy giant into the house; Mrs. Halvorsan was still crying her husband's name, and Tor's tears froze on his cheeks. Somehow, they got Peter Halvorsan into the kitchen, and laid him on the floor next to the stove; the presence of this frozen form, lying on its side, knees drawn up, silenced the entire house of crying children.

"Peter," Mrs. Halvorsan whispered, kneeling next to him, gently covering him up with her own shawl. "My Peter, my boy—Fredrik, oh, where is he?"

Raina looked at Gunner; he shook his head, shrugged his shoulders. So Anette and Fredrik had not made it home, after all. She grabbed her coat, her gloves, and ran out the door, Gunner following her.

"We have to find them, Anette and Fredrik," she called over her shoulder as she climbed back into the sleigh, waving off his assist. "Oh, hurry up! Don't just stand there!"

Gunner was so shocked by her tone that any gallant speech froze on his tongue; he climbed in next to her but seemed incapable of action. She grabbed the reins herself and slapped them against the horse's back, jerking the sleigh into motion as she steered it out toward the prairie.

Praying it wasn't too late.

CHAPTER 22

. . . . . .

THE CHANGE IN ATMOSPHERE FINALLY ROUSED GERDA from her coma, although she couldn't open her eyes right away. They were frosted shut, as if she'd stitched her top and bottom eyelashes together. She was able to move her left arm, slowly, and she placed her hand—cold, a dead weight— on her eyes, and tried to pry her lids apart. Finally she was able to, although she knew she'd broken the skin some- where, as she felt a fresh sting of icy air around the corners of both eyes.

She remained on her back, and she waited for her eyes to adjust to the gloom, to tell her where she was. At first all she saw was darkness, but slowly she became aware of a glow of light at her feet, weak rays of sun snaking inside the shelter, which gradually showed her that the roof over her head was made of straw, and then she realized she was lying on straw, frozen and poking at her. Then she looked at her hands and saw that they were purplish red, and covered with pricks.

She couldn't feel her feet at all.

There was a deafening silence in her ears—there was no other way to describe it; her ears rang but there was no sound, and when she struggled to push herself upright on her elbows, both ears popped with a viciousness that made her cry out; she clamped her hands to her ears, then fearfully removed them, terrified she wouldn't be able to hear anything. And indeed, the terrible silence surrounding her made her heart seize up, and she was sure she was deaf. Until, from outside the haystack, she heard a hawk's cry.

She struggled up until she was sitting; her limbs felt frozen—her knees were locked, and painfully she maneuvered them, bending them. But her feet—she watched them with detachment, as if they no longer were part of her—were sticking out of the haystack. They were feet, they were clad in the boots she'd put on yesterday morning, but were they really hers? She painfully tried to pull them inside the stack, and she could, but there was no feeling at all below her knees, and she wondered how she would get Minna and Ingrid to safety, which couldn't be far away. After all, they were in a haystack, so they must be near a barn. And a house.

"Minna, Minna darling, Ingrid, wake up." Her voice was hoarse, a croak, and she was desperately thirsty; she couldn't remember when she last had a drink of water, or a morsel of food. But she must get help for the girls, who were still sleeping; she glanced at the two, merely lumps of clothing, curled up in slumber. She decided to let them remain asleep; it was better for them, given how weak and hungry they must be.

Now that the storm had stopped, she would be able to find her way back to them. So it was up to her, alone, to venture outside the shelter of the stack; it was up to her, alone, to find help.

Where was Tiny? Where had he spent the night? The thought blinded her, like a flash of lightning; she saw him, in the same flash, running away, shouting at that horse, chasing it into the vortex of snow and wind. He had left her, left the girls, to fend for themselves. He had abandoned her, as she knew, deep down, he always would. Whether for a horse or for an adventure, he would have left her eventually. The absence of him—for if he had survived, she would never be able to look at him in the same way again, so either way, he was lost to her for good—shocked her. He had been the stock of all her dreams these past few months; all her plans for the future included him. Now she must start over; she would have to find new castles to build.

And a strange foreboding also rattled her chest: What of the children she had so blithely sent home?

For a second her breath caught on the suggestion of loss beyond anything she could comprehend, her own actions the reason why. She shut her mind to it, lest it overwhelm her. She must think now only of Minna and Ingrid, so inert in their sleep. Their ordeal must have taken such a toll on them, no wonder they slept so soundly.

Turning about was painful—she cried out, but the girls didn't appear to hear—as sharp daggers slaughtered her knees. She was afraid she might break them, and she wondered about that—could a kneecap break? She'd never heard of such a thing, but every inch of her felt as brittle as thin glass. Still she had to get out of here, somehow.

Finally, she maneuvered herself until she was on her hands and knees, her lower legs dragging behind like sled runners as she crawled out of the haystack. The unfiltered air made her gasp, made her bronchial tubes seize up, her nostrils freeze; she had to pant to get any of that icy hot air inside her lungs. The blinding sun, the dazzling white snow—her eyes began to smart, to tear up, and she shut them, feeling tears roll and then freeze on her cheeks. Her ears began to burn, but she crawled away from the haystack with her eyes still squeezed shut; she crawled for a few more yards then dared to pry open her eyes once more, steeling herself for the shock of the sun—

And when she saw the house only twenty-five yards or so away, she shouted with all her might as she crawled, one painful movement at a time, toward it. It was the girls' house, for heaven's sake! All this time, shelter had been only one last march away, but they hadn't known. All this time, as the girls' parents must have been frantic with worry, their daughters were freezing in one of their own haystacks. There was no irony left in Gerda, for she couldn't bring herself to laugh about it. All she could do was inch forward like a wounded animal, her hands in the snow, no feeling left in them, her feet just dead things attached to her legs, shouting with all her might, knowing her voice wouldn't carry, not even in the frigid morning air that amplified everything else—that hawk circling above, still crying, the rustle of a frozen tumbleweed scooting over the snow, a faint, chirping sound, like a mouse that had found himself, unwillingly, forced out of his nest.

"Help, help," Gerda kept shouting, and finally a door opened. A worried man and woman peered out, horrified astonishment on their faces as they snatched at coats and rushed out of the house toward her. With her last ounce of strength she pointed toward the haystack and gasped, "Minna, Ingrid," and then she felt herself fading down into the snow until a strong arm hauled her out and she was being carried into the house and deposited in haste upon the floor nearest the kitchen stove, the faint warmth of the fire surprising her frozen skin into protesting with shocks of pure pain. The arms, attached to the body of Gustav Nillssen,

then left, and she heard him call for his girls, his cries min-
gling with his wife's.

Then they were silenced. No more calls; it was quiet.
Gerda imagined them lifting up their daughters and any
second they'd be back inside. But the seconds passed, the
silence continued.

Gerda's eyes fluttered, she fell back into what passed for
sleep when a body was so frozen and exhausted, her heart so
feeble she was aware of its every attempt to beat blood
through her body. . . . It was so tempting to just give in and
let her heart take a rest; she could sleep forever and ever. . . .

Then a cry startled her awake, shocking her heart into
beating more regularly, remembering its purpose.

The shrieking kept up, got louder, came closer. Then the
door burst open and two adults, their arms around two limp
bundles of clothing, were inside, kicking Gerda away from
the stove so they could kneel before it, frantically rubbing
the bundles, calling their names—Ingrid! Minna!

But the bundles didn't move, didn't stir.

Gerda pushed herself up on her elbows, confused; she,
too, called the girls' names. But no answer came, and she
caught a glimpse of Minna's deathly white face, blue lips,
doll-like blue hands. The stillness that Gerda had seen earlier but not been able to recognize in one so young, the stillness of a body ready for the grave.

Gerda fell back, shutting her eyes before she could see
the Nillssens' faces. She couldn't bear it, not now; not with
the still-fresh memory of Minna on her back as she took
each grueling step, thinking that as she did, she was one
step closer to getting her and Ingrid to shelter. Thinking
that Minna was still alive—and now she had to wonder. When

did the girl die? Was it before they even got in the haystack, that tunnel she'd dug with her own numb hands?

Had she been carrying a corpse on her back the entire time? The effigy of a child—of *all* the children—she'd been in charge of keeping safe?

Where were they? Where were all the others? Feverishly, she began to chant the names of all her pupils out loud, as she did every day when she took the roll: "Minna, Ingrid, Hardus, Johnny, Johannes, Karl, Walter, Sebastian, Lydia.

"Minna, Ingrid, Hardus, Johnny, Johannes, Karl, Walter, Sebastian, Lydia—"

"Shut up, shut up!" Someone was shaking her shoulders, forcing her to wake up, to see—

New grief, etching its way into weathered skin, in the faces of the girls' parents. Mrs. Nillssen would turn hard in her sorrow, Gerda thought, oddly, as she tried to make sense of the tragedy. Hard, silent, but she would endure. Mr. Nillssen would be plowed under it, just like the fields he worked every day. Maybe that was what truly did make this land yield up its meager harvest: the weight of unbearable sadness pressing down upon it.

Gerda shut her eyes, pushed Mrs. Nillssen away, desperate for sleep to overtake her. Instead, her feet began to awaken. First they throbbed, then they burned, then they itched, and finally it was as if angry ants were swarming over her flesh, tearing it away with their pincers; she gasped, she moaned, she sat up and screamed, tearing at her boots to get them off, begging for Mrs. Nillssen to cut off her boots because the laces had shrunk as they'd thawed out, anything to relieve the searing pain.

And when finally the boots were cut off—and some of her

flesh seemed to be sheared off with them—she saw skin that was purplish black, dying. Her very flesh was dying, and the metaphor seemed so apt she wanted to laugh.

But then the ants began their attack again, and all she could do was bite down on the towel Mrs. Nillssen shoved in her mouth to shut her up.

"*Shhh, shhh.* You mustn't disturb the girls," the woman whispered in Gerda's ear as she writhed in pain.

CHAPTER 23

......

THIS MORNING AT FIRST LIGHT, ANNA HAD WATCHED AS her husband harnessed the horse, strapped the blanket around its girth, then climbed up in the sleigh and rode off, fast as lightning, over the log bridge straddling the ravine, toward the tundra of the prairie. She couldn't watch him for long; the rising sun was already too fierce, little glints of ice reflecting it everywhere. Something blinding did catch her eye out by the ravine, but she had to cover her eyes with her hands, the glare actually hurt.

What a fool her husband was, going out there in this cold. But he thought himself a paragon of the community, so he had to ride to the rescue of the Schoolteacher, the girl, all the children who must have spent the night in the schoolhouse. The Great Gunner Pedersen, Hero of the Storm. Ha! What an idiot, a preening idiot, he was. At least now the storm was over; he wouldn't get lost, he wouldn't perish. Although she wished he would, at least five times a day, practicality had won out last night. She couldn't risk losing him in the middle of winter; she couldn't deal with the horses, the house, the children all by herself. In the spring, she could leave him—she knew that now. But until they were through the winter, she needed him.

So she'd held him at gunpoint all night. What a fantastic thing to recall! She'd pointed the gun, the one her sister had given her the night before they moved away from Minneapolis to this desolate wasteland—"To use if there is only one way out, my darling," Margit had whispered fiercely in Anna's ear—right at his heart. All night long, she held her husband hostage. She, Anna Pedersen, who used to weep whenever mice had to be killed, back when she was young and tender, untouched.

She blamed the prairie. She blamed her husband. She would not blame herself.

Let the man ride off now with his gallant steed; he wouldn't come to any harm. She was sure everyone was safe—maybe a little cold and hungry—at the schoolhouse. The Schoolteacher had sense; she wouldn't have risked the children's lives. What a simpleton Gunner was—he did not understand women at all. Only as figures of romance and fancy, to be saved, protected. Their strength downright terrified him, she had seen that herself too many times to count. So naturally, the moment a new woman came into his life, outwardly uncertain and shy, he had behaved like a romantic patsy. Oh, the poor, pretty young thing, this Raina Olsen, boarding out for the first time, so homesick! She needed his protection, his assurance—just as he'd thought Anna had, back when they were courting.

But Anna hadn't been deceived at all by the Schoolteacher. She could see the young woman was stronger than she appeared, even though her head had been decidedly turned by Gunner's ridiculous behavior. What Anna had feared was that the young woman would use that strength to persuade Gunner to run off, something that Gunner would never do on his own, despite his seductive words and actions.

Anna didn't fear that any longer. Something had happened during the long night while the wind broke against the windows and her husband sat like a hostage before the gun in her hand. She'd seen her husband for who he was. Six foot two, and terrified of a woman a full foot shorter. A boy who only pretended he was a man. She'd realized she could pull the trigger anytime, and she wouldn't feel remorse, only justification.

It was a powerful feeling. It gave her back control of her life.

Busy at the stove, baking a loaf of bread she'd set out to rise earlier, she bustled about the kitchen; anyone looking at her would see the Anna of old: the sweetheart, the dazzler, the icon of femininity. It was just her and the children. She was humming a contented little tune when she heard horses pull up outside. She looked out the window in surprise; Gunner couldn't be back so soon, could he?

The sleigh outside belonged to Doc Eriksen, the only physician around. He had practiced in the old country and was beyond the age when a man of medicine should be expected to retire peacefully. The prairie, of course, had forced him back into service; the ruthless prairie, with its endless dangers to people formerly used to living close together, relying upon one another. To have a doctor in a community out here was nothing less than a miracle, even if he was a doctor who looked as if he required medical care himself. He waved at Anna, shouted something; she glanced at the children—

they were sitting close to the stove, maybe too close, so she snapped at them to stay back—then she threw on a shawl and went outside.

The cold slapped her across the face, lifted her almost out of her shoes; she gasped, she wiped away tears. She didn't imagine how anyone could last out in it, and she thought of Gunner. And then—reluctantly—of the Schoolteacher. And finally, of Anette.

"Mrs. Pedersen, is your husband at home?" Doc Eriksen remained in his sleigh, even after she urged him to come inside and warm up. He was covered in robes, and only his eyes were visible; his brows were frosted over, his voice muffled.

"No, he went to the schoolhouse to get the children."

"Ah. I was just out at the Blickenstaffs'. Their children didn't come home. So I'm heading up to the schoolhouse, too. Are you all well here? Are you missing anyone?"

"No. Well . . ." She had to tell him, didn't she? "Except for the Schoolteacher. And Anette, of course. But certainly they're all together, with the others. Gunner and the children and I, we were inside all night."

"Good. I'm afraid there are many people who weren't inside last night. Well, I'm off." The doctor shook the reins, turned the horse around, and skimmed across the log bridge, heading out to where Gunner had gone earlier; the tracks were still visible in the snow, now that the wind had blown itself out.

Anna was turning to go inside—she could not remain in this cold one more minute—when that dancing light out on the other side of the ravine, about ten yards away from the bridge, caught her eye once more. Shading her eyes from the sun, she took several steps toward it, squinting, trying to make it out. She kept walking, the cold grabbing at her, snaking up her skirts, wrapping her limbs in its icy tendrils, but now she could make it out, that glint—it was something silver, maybe, or something steel. It was—

It couldn't be, surely? It couldn't be Anette's lunch pail?

Anna stopped, her hand on her heart; her breath came in short gasps. No, no, it wasn't that, it must be something else; she shook her head, blinked rapidly to clear her vision from that brilliant sun, then looked again. And she saw it, plain as day—the glistening lunch pail, sticking out of the snow.

"Anette? Anette!" Anna cupped her hands about her mouth, shouting with all her might. She listened; she concentrated on the air, she heard nothing but a gentle swoop of snow dancing across the landscape. She shouted once more.

Then she heard something—a faint cry. Like a kitten, or a newborn.

"Anette?"

The cry grew louder, and it seemed to be coming from beneath the earth—

It seemed to be coming from the ravine.

Anna's feet propelled her back to the house. She flew inside, and in no time she was in her coat, her scarf covered her face, her ears, and she had gloves on her hands. She shouted at the children to stay away from the stove, she grabbed every blanket she could find, and then she was racing out the door, plowing through the snow toward the ravine. She got to the edge, stopped herself just in time before tumbling over it; her chest was on fire from the exertion in this frigid air.

Dropping to her knees, she peered over the edge but at first couldn't make anything out; it was shadowy down there, and her eyes were blinded from the fierce whiteness of the snow, the sun. Snow blindness—that's what it was called, she thought crazily.

"Anette?" She called it softly, almost afraid to be heard.

"Ye-yes?"

It was her, she was down there! Anna leaned farther over the edge; it was only about five feet down, but with the snow, she knew that if she fell in, she might not get back out. She peered and peered into the gloom, and then she finally was able to make something out—a shape, two shapes, in the snow below.

"Anette, is that you?"

"Yes, ma'am," the voice called out, so tiny, so scared. Tinged with exhaustion, with tears. "I'm sorry, I tried—I left the others, so I could come home—I'm sorry."

"Don't—don't move, I'll be there in a moment." *Don't be sorry,* is what Anna nearly blurted out. *Don't apologize.*

For the lunch pail—she glanced over to the other lip of the ravine, to where it lay like an accusing stare—told her everything she didn't want to know. It was because of *her*—all the times she'd scolded Anette not to dawdle, nagged her about the cost of the pail, the slate—that Anette must have spent this past terrible night in the ravine. Alone.

No—Anna peered back down in the ravine, and now she could clearly see Anette, her head and hand the only things exposed, for she was buried in a pile of garments. Garments that were not all hers. There was an unfamiliar grey coat on top of her, boy's brown pants, a boy's crimson shirt.

And next to Anette, a nearly naked body. Grey, almost blue, against the snow.

Book Two

THE MAIDEN OF
THE PRAIRIE

. . . . . .

THE HORSE PLOWED ON, HEAD BOBBING WITH EACH steady step, sometimes nickering softly, his breath blowing puffs of air that turned into moist clouds that froze into tiny crystals that scattered like diamond dust in the air, and the effect was beautiful. If you overlooked the fact that it was horse snot. The hardware on his bridle jingled, the leather harness and reins creaked and moaned, and the runners on the sleigh swished through the snow like a constant admonition *shhh, shhh, shhh, shhh.*

The man plowed on, as well—a large man made larger by the massive buffalo robe that covered him from head to toe, a wild, mahogany-colored curly coat, surely having seen better days, since it was matted in patches, as if the beast had just rolled up from sleep. Perched atop a comically dainty sleigh being pulled by the horse—a sleigh more fitted for an elegant lady on her way to a tea party—the man loomed even more ponderously than usual. Faded, horsehair-covered blankets were piled up on his knees. He resembled nothing less than a humiliated bear in a circus, forced to wear human clothing and ride about in a pony-drawn kiddie sleigh.

He was alone. As far as the eye could see, there was this: an undulating carpet of various shades of white as pure as an angel's robes; a garish, vicious yellow-white sun that turned the snow into dangerous shards of brilliance, aiming right for the eye; telegraph poles; and the bear in the kiddie sleigh.

The runners swishing, the creaking, the jingling, his own occasional mutterings; those were the only sounds Gavin heard for a very long time as he kept his head bent against the cold. As he trusted to the horse and whatever God had time to spare for a miserable soul like himself, on a miserable mission for a miserable reason he couldn't begin to parse.

Gavin Woodson, tenderfoot extraordinaire, colossal joke of a man, was headed out onto the Great Plains by himself in a hired sleigh with a hired horse, a few feedbags of oats at his feet, a carpetbag full of paper and pens and ink and a change of woolen underwear by his side.

He, the horse, and the sleigh were the only creatures on this earth, or so he could easily believe; he saw no one else, heard not a sound save those mentioned.

He'd never felt so pathetic.

He was a city man who felt most at home in stifling, sweat-infused enclosures, on busy streets bordered with tall buildings that kept the horizon at bay. On the rare occasion that his lungs desired fresh air, he was content with a park or a street corner. But there was little fresh air in Omaha; the canning facilities, the stockyards filled the air with odors whose sources were best left unquestioned. That he'd been inspired, that morning of the blizzard, to walk away from the city and toward the prairie, had puzzled him. That he'd been so captivated by the sight of the girl had worried him.

That he could not shake her from his thoughts, no matter how much he tried through drink and poker and the machinations of the newspaper—well, that was the reason he was out here on the Godforsaken Prairie.

Heading out, to find her.

It was a fool's mission and he knew it. But Gavin Woodson was no stranger to fools' missions. It was the reason he'd been fired from *The World,* all over a bullish inability to back away from a story involving one of Pulitzer's college friends. "I know I'm a stubborn cuss, but . . ." he'd kept saying to anyone who would listen as he blundered on, but in the end, it didn't matter. It turned out that announcing your own stupidity was more than a little redundant.

In the first days after the blizzard, when reports started being telegraphed in from the north and west about casualties beyond imagination—entire schoolrooms of children frozen where they sat! trapped train passengers reduced to cannibalism!—Gavin became restless with an anxiety, a need. Of course, he scoffed at some of these reports as too ridiculous, but they gave him the chance he was looking for—the chance to head out and search for the girl, while also reporting, firsthand, on the aftermath. *Setting the record straight,* he assured Rosewater and his cronies, the men who paid his salary. *We don't want those eastern newspapers overreporting the damage, do we? They can only report on hearsay. We can do the responsible thing, be there on the ground, talk to the poor sons of bitches—the homesteaders—themselves. And mitigate the disaster before the eastern papers blow it out of proportion.*

They'd agreed, and he'd inwardly rejoiced although outwardly he remained his usual weary, jaded self. He was ashamed to share the real reason he wanted to go. For a man who had made a career of declaring his every intent and folly, he found himself surprisingly circumspect about his true mission.

Embarrassed, to be blunt.

Even when he had one last drink with Ol' Lieutenant and Dan Forsythe at the Lily before he headed out, he made sure to consume a smaller amount of whiskey than usual, lest the truth, prompted by his heart, push through his tight lips. It was only in the last few days that Gavin remembered he *had* a heart. He wasn't quite sure how to go about dealing with it, to be honest. Should he placate it? Make deals with it? For now, he thought it best to douse it in a moderate amount of alcohol and hope it might be pickled back into dormancy.

At the Lily, Forsythe, who had sheltered with the sleighing party in houses over in Council Bluffs—none of the party had perished in the blizzard—lamented the fact that it hadn't turned out to be much of a story.

"Rosewater has me in the doghouse about it. The man has ink for blood and a printing press for a heart. He expected nothing less sensational than cannibalism," Forsythe grumbled, shaking his head forlornly. "Like the Donner Party. Have you ever heard him envy the newspapers who got that story, back in the day? The amount of ink they sold over that?"

"He's a son of a bitch," Gavin agreed. "It's a fine line, though—he wants to keep the story alive, sell the papers— tragedy on the plains, all that. It's good for business—until it's not good for business, if you get my drift. The boosters are hovering, too, because none of them—the trains, the state, hell, even Rosewater—can afford to scare more of these poor sods off from coming out here. You can bet there's going to be an exodus of them come spring, all heading back

across the ocean. Land'll be even cheaper than it is now—
you might want to think about it." Gavin addressed this to
Ol' Lieutenant, who looked up from the book he was
reading—*Bleak House*—with an arched eyebrow. "And say,
why weren't you open the other day? I was in dire need of a
drink."

To Gavin's surprise, Ol' Lieutenant held his gaze for a
long moment, then deliberately closed the book and placed
it on the counter between Forsythe and Gavin.

The two men exchanged looks.

"I have kids like everybody else. I had to go get them.
And, boys, congratulate me. I'm selling the Lily but I'm not
going to homestead." Then Ol' Lieutenant did the unthink-
able: He poured himself a drink and leaned closer to the two
newspapermen. Gavin wasn't sure how to behave, sharing a
drink like this with a colored man; it was all well and good to
have him behind the counter, serving. But this was awkward; Forsythe leaned away from the bar a little. Gavin
smiled weakly but clinked his glass with Ol' Lieutenant's before taking a swig.

"No, after this storm, when I had to stay with the kids
over on the North Side at school—and it's a damn good thing
I did—leaving Alma . . ." Ol' Lieutenant looked up at the ceiling, toward the upper floor where evidently he lived, and
Gavin understood him to mean that Alma was his wife. He'd
never heard her name before. Or maybe he had, and he'd
never taken the time to note it?

"She was here alone in all that—I left her plenty of fuel
before I went out to find the kids, but nobody knew that, nobody checked in on her, even though there are plenty of
folks—white folks—livin' around here. So I'm moving to the
North Side. Isn't any place for someone like me here on this

side of town anymore. We have to stay with our own kind, take care of ourselves, our kids; this storm just kind of rein- forced that in my mind."

Forsythe looked annoyed by this speech, and took an- other drink.

"Was she all right? Your wife?" Gavin heard himself ask- ing, then blushing, afraid to say the woman's name for some reason. It seemed wrong—too familiar—when he'd only just learned it. When he'd only just acknowledged the fact that Ol' Lieutenant had a wife and she had a name and apparently they had children, too. Then he found himself wondering what Ol' Lieutenant's first name was, his real name—was it Marvin or Coleson or Harry or Sam?

Good God, this heart thing was going to be a real pain in the ass, wasn't it?

"Yeah, she's fine. Shaken up, worried about me and the kids all night, but fine. Still, she's the one been harping to move and now I see her point. These are the last drinks the Lily'll serve, gentlemen. Enjoy them." Then Ol' Lieutenant grinned, poured the men and himself another, and finally returned to his book, to Gavin and Forsythe's relief.

"Well, I wouldn't have expected a tenderfoot like you, Woodson, to head out there, not in winter. I don't care what Rosewater does to me, I'm staying in town."

"It was my idea," Gavin said mildly.

"You say," Forsythe replied with a smirk. "Well, I'll give you some advice—"

"Since you're such an adventurer yourself?" Gavin couldn't help himself.

"I'm no Greely, but I have ridden out on a cattle drive. Once. Partway. All right, it was just for a day, to get back- ground for a story. But still—stay close to the railroad tracks;

that way you won't get lost. You'll hear most of the news in the towns; they all know what's going on in their districts, even at the most remote homestead. I have no idea how but those Swedes and Norskis have their own telegraph system almost. Just don't head out away from the tracks without someone to guide you. You'll get lost and the wolves'll have a field day with your lard ass."

"Thanks." Gavin would have been irate at the insult, but the man had a point. He drained the last of his whiskey—probably the last he'd have for a while now because he couldn't imagine that the poor sons of bitches in soddies had the time or money for drink—and set the glass on the counter. He tipped his hat at Ol' Lieutenant.

"Bye—uh, sir," he said awkwardly; for some reason he couldn't bring himself to call the bartender by his usual handle, the moniker that Gavin and the others had given him without much thought. "Good luck on the North Side. I'll be sure to stop by once you open up your new place."

"Sure you will," Ol' Lieutenant said with unconcealed amusement, and Gavin was ashamed of the emptiness of the promise. "But do me a favor, will you, Mr. Woodson?"

"What?"

"While you're out there hunting for stories, make sure you tell about the colored folk, too. You know there's a settlement west of Yankton—in Sully County—that's mainly colored. Maybe you can get up that way? There are people here in town would like to hear about them, see if they made it through."

"I'll try," Gavin said. He had no idea there were Negro homesteaders, but the law didn't prevent it; the Homestead Act didn't specify race, except, of course, it excluded the Indians. So he'd lured them out here, too, had he? Jesus Christ.

He felt a strange twinge, and it occurred to him that it was his conscience—the annoying, hectoring better angel of his heart, he realized with a wince. He didn't know how far he'd have to go before he found what he was looking for—*who* he was looking for—so he offered no promise. But he thought that Ol' Lieutenant understood, by the way the man nodded.

Gavin impulsively reached across the counter to shake his hand, and he wasn't sure how to parse the gaze that Ol' Lieutenant bestowed upon him when he did. Then he shook hands with Forsythe, and headed out toward the livery stable, where his dainty sleigh and questionable horse awaited him.

And now here he was, as alone, as small, as he'd ever been despite the fact that he spilled over the seat of the sleigh. Experiencing, for the first time, the terrifying heartlessness of the Great Plains he'd sold thousands of suckers on.

Have you longed for the magic of a prairie winter, gentle yet abundant snow to nourish the earth, neither too cold nor too warm, only perfection in every way?

His stomach soured as he recalled his own words. He was all alone in a great dome of sky, trapped like an insect, unable to escape the evidence of the lie he'd perpetrated. No gentle snow was this; the train tracks to his right were completely obscured, only the adjacent telegraph poles sticking up, some at an angle, some broken completely, to keep him on the right path. He'd left the Union Pacific yard with the curses of railroad men in his ears; trains were stuck, they'd need to have work crews break up the snow to get those trains off the line before the great wedge plows, pushed by several locomotives, could come through and clear the tracks. Snow was the railroad's winter curse; the massive spring floods were nearly as much of a headache. Then the grasshoppers in the summer, drawn to the heat-retaining steel, their bodies clogging up the wheels. Really, sometimes Gavin wondered why in the hell these men had invested so much money and time in the endeavor.

But of course he knew why, and it was all around him— land. Too much land, it seemed to him, an astonishing amount; how could it ever be tamed and parceled, even by the hordes who had come here to do just that? He didn't dare gaze too much at it, for fear of becoming snow blind; he'd been instructed to keep his head down and trust his horse, outfitted with side blinkers to cut down the glare. But he did raise his head and let his eyes water in the cold and brilliance, now and then. Simply to gaze on a landscape he'd never fully understood—that he'd never tried to understand.

Everyone said the prairie was flat, but it wasn't. The snow-carpeted land swelled and dipped even though the horizon presented itself as one straight line. But the utter lack of natural landmarks, the unbrokenness of it all, made it seem so. And the air today, so still after the storm, also lent to the notion that he, the horse, and the sleigh were perched upon an infinite cloth-covered table, above the rest of the world. And yet, there would come a point where, if they weren't careful, they would fall off the edge and be lost forever.

Every once in a while, he did see tiny dark dots, far off, close to the edge of that table. Houses that, despite a thin trail of smoke from a chimney poking a tentative finger up in the sky, appeared utterly desolate, despairing. Those were homesteaders. Despite the temptation to veer off to talk to them, he stayed along the tracks as Forsythe had recommended.

And really, he asked himself—he was already aware that

he would be carrying on entire conversations with himself or the horse before this thing was over—what would he do if he did decide to turn the nag and take off over that landscape full of traps and obstacles buried by the snow? What would he say if he knocked on the door of one of those soddies or cabins?

Excuse me, I'm looking for a girl. Maybe you know her? Maybe she lives here? She's young and has reddish-blond hair, and her throat was yearning, and I don't know her name, and she doesn't know mine, either. But I need to find her, because—

Because why?

Well, that was it, wasn't it? Why on earth was he on such a fool's errand? Could it be that he was in love? With a girl at least half his age, whom he had seen for a couple of minutes?

No, he didn't think so, probing his feelings—a distasteful exercise he'd generally avoided until recently. He didn't long to enfold her in his arms or whisk her away to a homestead of his own. God, no.

Gavin had had romantic entanglements in the past, an almost-engagement back East, and a regular Sunday dinner invitation from the sister of one of the printers at the *Bee* that he had let peter out, sending his polite refusal one too many times. But he was no stranger to the softness of a woman's body—that softness he required, now and then, to reassure himself that he was still solid, a man of sinew and bone, despite all evidence to the contrary. Oh my, no, he was no stranger to the contours of a woman, pillows of flesh, excitable nipples, eager legs wrapping around him until he lost himself entirely, the moment always too brief, and then there was the brisk transaction of money, the quick ushering out the door and he was back in Godforsaken Omaha, his

disappointing self once more. And that transaction suf-
ficed—at least he'd thought so. Just the physical contact was
enough. Emotions, needs, yearnings, comfort, companionship, a sense of purpose, of being necessary to someone,
less alone in the swamp of his miserable thoughts and
actions—these he believed he'd outgrown. Or never needed
in the first place.

So no, he didn't want to *marry* the girl, it wasn't that. He
didn't want to marry at all. And to marry a Swedish or German homesteading daughter—he shuddered at the very notion of being entangled with a family still halfway stuck in
the Old World even while they battled, with spirit-breaking
results, the new. He tried to imagine himself living out here
on this callous flatland, trying to break it—he could feel its
unyielding surface beneath the runners of the sleigh—trying
to coax it into giving him something to live on, to keep going,
to do the same thing year after soul-sucking year. The
numbing repetitiveness of it, like Sisyphus, only instead of a
boulder, a plow. He tried to imagine living in one of those
squalid little soddies, surrounded by people needing something from you—your thoughts, your food, your sweat, your
dreams, your very breath; you'd never have your full share of
anything, ever again. And for what? One hundred and sixty
acres of land that was worth so little, the government was
practically giving it away.

God, no.

But the prairie—this desert masquerading as a grassland—
had its own beauty, he could admit. A cruel beauty, like that
of a breathtaking woman who will never remember your
name. The cloak of pure snow, like a cloud on the ground—no
footprints, not even a leaf print on it—made him feel as if he
were the first person to step onto an unexplored planet. A

horizon so far off it seemed like a mural. A sky so blue it seemed like a dream of blue; color shouldn't be this vivid in real life.

A cold so unnerving, he realized he was shivering and that he had been for longer than he had any idea of—damn, this place! What good was beauty when a man's balls were frozen? This godforsaken place!

The horse was slowing down, so Gavin tugged on the reins, pulled on the brake, and slid out, taking a feedbag with him; he unbridled the nag, strapped the bag over his big ugly face, but held on to the harness just in case the beast got a notion to run off toward one of those homesteads himself. Gavin needed to stay near the railroad, and he thought he was only about five miles to the next station. You'd think, though, that you'd be able to see five miles down the tracks in weather like this, but nothing was in sight, so maybe not.

The horse ate steadily, so Gavin dropped the harness to go off and answer the call of nature, but the thought of unbuttoning his pants to allow egress made him pause. Jesus Christ, in this ball-shriveling cold—should he just let loose and keep it inside? But no, he couldn't do that, it would freeze. So he tentatively poked himself out through the smallest opening he could allow, uttered epithets so vociferously the horse stopped eating and looked his way, then hastily buttoned himself back up again and raced back through snow above his knees to the sleigh. He slipped the bit back in the horse's mouth, dropped the half-empty feedbag onto the seat beside him, and slapped the reins, this time less tentatively.

And back to his contemplation of the girl. What was her allure? Not corporeal; he put that notion firmly to rest. She represented something ethereal. An idea. A notion. A prayer. A song. Something spiritual, something spectral. Something.

He simply had to find her, he supposed. To relieve his conscience, to absolve him of his sins. She was his church, this maiden of the prairie. And Gavin needed absolution. He hadn't known he'd needed it until he saw her the day of the blizzard.

He needed something good to come from this place, this place that, in his worst moments, he could almost believe he'd created all by himself—the Great God Gavin Woodson. Yes, that was it—maybe he'd started to feel that he'd populated these Great Plains all on his own, with no help from the government and the boosters and the railroads and the hustlers. Somehow he could make himself forget their part, especially after too much whiskey, too much sitting at an ink-stained desk with nothing to do but brood. He could convince himself that *he'd* done it, he'd created these home-steaders, they wouldn't exist without his pen.

Even God needed his Garden of Eden, his Adam, his Eve.

So Gavin Woodson needed his maiden, but unlike God, he had no wish to punish her. No—the realization became more potent with each step of the puffing nag—he needed to *save* her. Like a pudgy, dissolute Lochinvar, riding in on his noble steed to rescue her from the fate of the prairie.

And if not her, well, then someone else. Because some-thing good had to come out of the despair and tragedy in the wake of this blizzard that appeared to have struck with more ferocity, leaving more casualties, than any blizzard in the short history of these homesteaded plains. Not even the winter of 1880 to 1881, still talked about in hushed tones, surprised an entire region like this one had.

Now the old-timers had something new to talk about.

There would be a rush on wood for coffins as soon as the tracks cleared, he'd heard when he'd picked up the horse and sleigh. There just weren't enough trees for the poor souls to provide their own.

Frankly, Gavin wondered how they'd even go about digging graves in ground this solidly frozen. What would they do with the dead, then? Keep them in barns or lean-tos? The wolves would surely be after them.

This godforsaken place. It killed these poor bastards, then refused to receive their bodies with any kind of dignity.

The horse continued plodding. Gavin realized he'd been traveling north, so he'd picked the wrong goddamn train track to follow, since the girl and her family seemed to have gone due west; typical Gavin, he cursed himself. Finally, up ahead, he saw a cluster of buildings, spreading out on either side of the track for about a city block both ways.

There were people in those buildings. *His* people, he was starting to think of them.

Maybe they would know where she was.

. . . . . .

CHAPTER 25

RAINA WANTED TO RUN FROM THE STIFLING ROOM that smelled of fresh blood and decaying flesh; she tried not to look at the bucket where the tiny, blackened hand now lay. She pressed a handkerchief to her mouth and Doc Eriksen, busily sewing jagged flesh to flesh, gave her a look. In response, she stiffened her spine and transferred that handkerchief to Anette's clammy brow. The poor thing moaned, but didn't move or open her eyes.

Anna Pedersen was perspiring, too, but hadn't strayed from Doc's side as she handed him the instruments of torture he'd required—bone saw, clamps, needles. This was hell, Raina decided. To maim a young child in order to save her life—this was hell on earth.

How long had it been since the blizzard? Three or four days? An eternity ago. Yet there were still so many missing in the community—bodies hidden in snowdrifts, waiting silently for spring. It was actually a miracle they'd found Fredrik's father that morning—

That awful morning was the worst moment of Raina's life. She was ripped apart by it all—the grief; the desire to comfort Tor and his mother; the guilt she felt at being the cause of

everything; the relief, quickly doused by bitter disappointment, when she saw Gunner; the desperation when he didn't
know where Anette and Fredrik were. She grew up that
morning, Raina did. Grew up, grew out of childhood and un-
certainty and pretty notions and romantic foolishness. She
felt herself stand taller, her muscles harden, and a bitter
taste invade her mouth. It was life in all its terrible beauty
and terrible tragedy—that was what she tasted that morning.
She might know softness again, love, hope, happiness. But
she would also never know a world where Mama and Papa—
and especially Gerda—could make everything all right.

It was this grown-up Raina who had steered the sleigh
away from the Halvorsans', Gunner mute beside her, over
snow that looked so fetching now that it was the morning
after; she briefly noted the beauty, the sun dogs—one on either side of the sun—showing off in the sky, one lone hawk
swooping low over the ground.

She aimed the sleigh toward the Pedersen homestead,
skirting past the schoolhouse—it seemed only moments
away from the Halvorsans' and she closed her eyes, remembering the hours it had taken them to get there. If they'd had
a sleigh—if he'd come for them—

But he hadn't. She'd done her best. She'd tried.

Despite her earlier vow that she'd never go back to the
Pedersen house, it seemed the logical path to follow; Anette
had headed out that way in the storm. Raina held the horse
to a walk as they searched for signs of the two children's
progress; Gunner had most likely been in too much of a
hurry this morning to see anything and besides, he wouldn't
have known to look. Raina was relieved that it was too cold to
carry on a conversation; their mouths and noses were muf-

fled. Gunner seemed so strange to her now, shy, perhaps? There was something that made him not able to look her in the eye: an acknowledgment of failure, or of shame. Something had happened to him during that long, stormy night. She could only guess what, until she realized she didn't care at all, and the realization was both a thudding end of a dream and a soaring release. She didn't care anymore what happened to Gunner Pedersen.

The horse picked its way slowly across the prairie, struggling through drifts up to its knees, but sometimes finding its footing easier where the snow had been swept by wind. It plodded toward the homestead south of the school, the house growing bigger and bigger, but Raina was concentrating on the land they were gliding over, searching for anything—a mitten, a shawl, a slate. She didn't see any footprints in the snow, but that wasn't unusual, given the sweeping winds of the night before. But then, as they grew closer to the homestead, she did see something—she saw a pail, a lunch pail, sticking out of the snow, beckoning them.

"There!" She pointed at it, and Gunner grunted.

"Didn't see that this morning," he replied, as she drew the horse up beside it.

They were on the far side of the ravine; the log bridge, wide enough for a wagon or a sleigh, was just to the left; its surface had been tamped down a little by the runners of the sleigh when Gunner had left earlier. There was another set of hoofprints churning up the snow here, too. And boot prints. They both got out of the sleigh and approached the pail; the snow on the other side of the ravine, on the bank, was broken up; someone had been here, someone had scrambled down the steep incline.

Raina felt her feet taking her toward the edge, her heart seizing up with fear and hope, both, with every step. She forced herself to look down.

The small body, grey, almost blue, like his father. Curled up on his side with his eyes closed, like the child he was. His clothes in a pile next to him, he was only wearing his long johns, and they were ragged, as if he'd torn at them. She sank to her knees in the snow, and misery washed over her; the poor boy, funny little Fredrik—to have died like this, far from home.

But where was Anette? She'd expected to find them together. She started to scan the landscape, which was when she saw Anna Pedersen flying over the bridge, waving her arms wildly.

"I have her. I got her—Anette—I dragged her up, carried her inside, do you know where the doctor is? He was just here, Doc Eriksen, and I said we didn't need any help but that was before I found them!"

Anna's hair streamed down her back, her skirt was wet, her hands red and raw; her eyes were strange, frantic.

"It was my fault, do you see the pail? I told her to bring it home, she had the slate, too, but it broke and, oh! Oh, the boy! He covered her with his clothes, do you see? He took his own clothes off and covered Anette, that's how I found her, and she lives. For now—she isn't conscious, I don't know what to do with her hand, do you know?" Anna grabbed Raina by the shoulders, desperate. "Frostbite? Do you know what to do?"

Raina nodded. Gunner stood staring down at poor Fredrik as Anna grabbed Raina by the hand and dragged her across the bridge. Raina glanced back.

"Bring him in, for pity's sake!" she cried, because Gun-

ner looked as if he'd forgotten how to move his own arms
and legs; he just stood there, dumbstruck.

Finally he raised his head, nodded, and slid down into
the ravine as Anna and Raina reached the house. Anette
lived! She was alive! Raina felt something loosen inside her;
she was close to weeping, but she couldn't let herself. She
had to concentrate on Anette now.

And strangely, she knew that she had an ally in the woman
whose presence had been such torture. For Anna Pedersen
was behaving in a manner Raina had never before seen;
she was clucking about, dashing in her usual way, but this
time it was in service to another. To poor Anette, the burden, the unwanted, overworked, unloved little girl.

Anna had wrapped her up in blankets as close to the stove
as she could get her without lighting her on fire; Anette's
face was the only thing visible, poking out of a quilt of stars.
She had a blackish spot on her nose, and another on one
cheek—frostbite, of course.

"It's her hand," Anna whispered as if she was afraid to
awaken Anette, even as Raina wondered if they should.

"Has she been sleeping all this time?" Raina asked, and
Anna nodded.

"Mostly. She was crying when I found her, but she was
half asleep, and she moaned when I carried her out—she
weighs nothing!" Anna's eyes were wide with astonishment,
as if she was finally understanding that her beast of burden
was just a little girl, after all. "But she's been asleep since,
although she is in pain, she cries some."

"All right," Raina said, running out to get a pail of snow.
Gingerly, she and Anna unwrapped Anette; when Raina saw
the purple hand, she gasped, but packed it in snow.

They got Anette undressed and into one of Anna's nightgowns; Anna insisted she lie in her bed, in the downstairs bedroom. At some point Raina registered that her entire body was shivering, her coat and gloves thawing out, soaking her skin, but there was no chance to take them off.

Because now she had to take Fredrik home.

Tenderly, she wrapped blankets around his tiny frame, with the sharp, birdlike shoulder blades of childhood, the still-round cheek, the skinny legs limp. He was so small. So still—Fredrik Halvorsan, still! He'd always been a whir of activity, even seated: kicking his feet and tapping his fingers against the desk, fidgeting, twisting, looking around. Running on the playground with Anette, the two of them caught up in a perpetual game of tag that had ended in this cruel fashion—Raina had to shut her eyes to his lifeless body. What would she say to his mother—and to Tor?

Gunner shuffled his feet, cleared his throat. "Raina," he said in that silky, mesmerizing way, and her eyes flew open, her heart jolted with a warning. "My dear, you are exhausted. I'll take him home, you stay here. Let me take care of you—"

"Enough of that!" Raina cried out, wanting to pummel this man who lived while those like Peter and Fredrik Halvorsan did not. "I waited for you to save me in the schoolroom when the blizzard struck. What a fool I was, what a fool I've been, to think you would actually come!"

"I—Anna—it was her. Let me explain." Gunner dropped his voice to a whisper, looking furtive all of a sudden. "Anna—she convinced me—I could not leave her alone with my children. I had to think of my family—"

"Oh, don't blame your wife! You're a man, you could have come. But she was right, you should have thought of your family in the first place. I should have, too. I won't be so silly—so selfish—again. I don't need you to rescue me anymore, Gunner, and I don't think I ever really did. I'm taking Fredrik home myself. He was my responsibility."

"But dearest Raina, you're—"

"Listen to the girl, you imbecile." Anna appeared, carrying a slop bucket from Anette's sickroom. "Why either of us ever thought we needed you is a mystery. At least one of us has come to her senses. Go!" She shooed Raina toward her mission. "I'll deal with him. But come back soon—and try to bring the doctor!" There was desperation in Anna's eyes as she looked to where Anette lay, moaning and shivering.

"I will. And—I'm sorry, Anna, for things I may have done—"

Anna cut her off. "I have much to be sorry for myself." They looked at each other; it was wariness between them, but respect now, too. Raina had no idea how long it would last.

Then she left with Fredrik's body in the sleigh. Every moment since the blizzard first struck, it seemed she'd had to do the hardest thing she'd ever done, each task escalating, dragging her further out of childhood. But this, taking Fredrik home to his mother and Tor this was the most wrenching by far. Her hands shook as they held the reins, her throat was dry, she wondered if she would collapse beneath the weight of the misery she was bringing with her. But she managed to steer the horse on the right path, focusing on his broad flanks, the flecks of ice in his mane. He must be exhausted, too.

As she approached the farmhouse she'd left only hours before, Tor and Sara Halvorsan came rushing to the door, desperate hope on their faces.

"We have found them," Raina said, climbing out of the sleigh, but holding on to the reins to steady herself before delivering the blow. "Fredrik is dead, but Anette is saved. Because of him, because of your son. He saved her life."

Tor buried his face in his hands, and she couldn't look at him; instead, she watched Sara Halvorsan intently, ready to catch her if she fell. But Sara did not. She had aged overnight; deep grooves surrounded her mouth, her eyes permanently bracketed with grief. She gasped but did not falter.

And it was anger that swept her past Raina and the sleigh, to the edge of the prairie, just past the barn—just past where her husband had fallen. She raised one hand, fisted in rage, at the sky. She screamed—one raging curse at the land.

Slowly, she walked back toward the sleigh, and waited patiently as Tor picked up his little brother—stiffly frozen like his father had been, but so much smaller—and, with a sudden tender look on his face, gave him up to their mother. She took her younger son into her arms and carried him—as gently as she must have when he was first born—into the house.

Tor finally looked at Raina; she steeled herself as he raised his head, but did not turn away. Whatever he would say, however he looked at her—she would take it, she would give him that relief.

He had no tears in his eyes; he was sad—oh, so sad! Grief held him in its grip, but not so tightly that he didn't look like himself, like who he was. No longer a schoolboy; a man forever now, just as Raina was a woman. A man who had lost too much. He stared at her with such heartbreaking sadness, sharing it with her as if it were the bread of life. And she took it as solemnly as she'd taken her first communion.

Then the sadness was replaced with disgust, followed by the flickering flame of hatred; he looked away from her, dismissing her.

"Please, Tor, I'm so sorry—"

"Go, now. Leave us alone," he said in a choked voice, his arm thrust toward her, warding her off as if she were a witch.

She nodded, unable to think of a single thing to say that could help this broken family. So she turned to go, to find the doctor, because there was still Anette—the only person left that she could help.

She knew that she'd never see Tor in her schoolroom again.

NOW IN THE MAKESHIFT operating room, Doc was bandaging Anette's stitched-up stump, warning the women of the days to come.

"She'll feel as if she still has her hand, at first. It's a phantom pain. It will itch and burn. She may get a fever; these things can't be predicted. She might yet die, of course, if the infection's too far gone. We can't tell if it is or isn't, there's nothing more I can do for her. Watch her. If she seems to do better quickly, that's often a sign that, in fact, it's worse than we thought, and there will be a relapse. That's the danger time."

"How will she—how will she get about, without the hand?" Anna asked in a choked whisper.

"She'll learn. People do. She's younger than most who go through this—although I've never had to amputate so many children's limbs as I have these last couple of days." The poor man, for a moment, let his mask of professionalism drop, and his face was scored with defeat and grief. "But children learn new things rapidly. They have wooden hands now, too; and maybe someday, she can afford one. But they're just for show, not functional."

"But to get a man—not whole like this—I don't see how?" Anna shook her head. "Who would want a woman not whole?"

"You'd be surprised," Doc said matter-of-factly, packing up his instruments of torture and placing them inside his worn leather satchel. "We're not in a big city, she's a child of this place, and there are more incomplete people on the prairie than anywhere I've ever seen. This place, it devours people, spits them out missing things like hands and feet. There'll be a lot like her from now on, I'm afraid. This storm—" But he shook his head and chose not to finish his thought.

"Rosa—what happened with her?" Raina asked as she walked him out of the stifling bedroom. Doc Eriksen looked too exhausted to stand; she offered him some coffee but he declined.

"I think she'll recover all right—she won't lose her feet, just some toes. She's one of the lucky ones."

"That's a blessing, anyway."

"Like I said, this land chews people up and spits them out in pieces. Even children."

"Why—why did you come here, then?" Raina asked the question she'd never dared ask her own parents but had always longed to. Why leave what you knew, a land that was familiar, your family, your friends, problems you could predict because you'd encountered them before? Why start over in a barren desert of cruelty? And subject your children to it, or bring new children into its prickly bosom?

Why did men believe that land was worth the human toll it extracted?

"You were born here?" Doc asked as he wound a muffler about his neck, groaning and flexing his stiff hands.

"No, but I was so little, I don't remember the old country."

"Then you don't know what it was like. It wasn't bad, don't get me wrong. But there wasn't much opportunity for a man to change the path he was set on from birth. Here, there is. And for many men, that's enough."

"What about you? You were a doctor there, you're a doctor here."

"And a homesteader. A piss-poor one—I'm sorry, excuse me, Raina. But I own land, and I never would have in Norway. It's not good land, though. That's the fact of it. I think of those articles that started showing up in the papers back home, promising us the moon and the stars. None of them were the truth, but why were we so eager to believe them? We have to answer for that ourselves. But we're here now. Some will go back, after this. Every year, many go back, I think. But the ones that stick it out—stubborn old fools like me—"

"Like Papa," Raina broke in, frowning.

"I've never met your papa but I imagine he is stubborn, because his daughter seems to have a streak of it." Doc Eriksen laughed, but his rueful amusement only highlighted how weary he was, how old; his teeth were yellow, his cheeks hollow, the bags under his eyes as droopy as a hound's. "Us stubborn men, if we stick it out, if somehow we make this earth do what it *should,* and not what it *wants* . . . Think of the reward. Not in riches, but in satisfaction, in dying knowing you have tamed nature itself. Of knowing your children"— and here Doc Eriksen lay a gnarled but kind hand on Raina's shoulder—"will have more than you ever dreamed of, because of you."

Raina smiled and lay her cheek on the old man's hand,

before seeing him to the door. But she didn't agree with what he said, because she couldn't imagine having more than her parents did back in Norway—how many stories had she heard about the fun they'd had there surrounded by family, for all the farms were close together in the old country, not separated by one hundred and sixty acres like they were here? Back there, they never wanted for food or clothing; there was always someone to borrow from, hand-me-downs passed from one cousin to another. They were not rich, no— not in the things men value. Still, she knew her mother had been happier there, richer in the things that women know as worthy—sympathy, conversation, community. But a married woman had no choices of her own. A married woman's future was her husband's, no matter where she lived.

What was Raina's future now?

Mama's dream of sending her girls to a teaching college so they could at least find a position somewhere other than a country schoolhouse full of poor children who would need nothing more than a cursory education—

Well, that dream was vanishing just as the sun was vanishing outside. After this winter, there would be the usual floods that would mean the usual delay in planting, the rush to harvest before the next winter arrived. How could they save enough? There'd never be enough money for college now, especially since Gerda . . .

Oh, what was she doing, thinking of college in the face of such loss? But as Raina patted the letter in her apron, the letter that had brought the unfathomable news about her sister, she still couldn't bring herself to believe it. She had initially longed to rush home to her parents, to comfort them and be comforted. But now, she was afraid.

Afraid that her parents would see into her heart and

know she was not the same person she'd been when she left home. Afraid to add to their grief in this way. Afraid to be thrust into the reality that her family was not the same, either—and would never be again.

Raina couldn't bear it, she couldn't hold off her grief any longer; she fell onto a sofa and wept for her sister—and also for herself. Why couldn't her parents have settled in a city like Omaha or Saint Paul? In a city, she and Gerda could have worked together in a little store, or taken a secretarial course, or taught in a school where the children didn't fall asleep from exhaustion.

Or where the wrong decision didn't lead to unimaginable tragedy.

Suddenly she could hear her sister's voice in her ears, scoffing. *Poor Raina,* the voice said—but there was warmth in it, love. *Such a baby, such a princess.* And Raina stopped crying, and she laughed instead as she blew her nose and dried her eyes.

No matter what, Gerda would always be with her; the bond of sisters was eternal. This letter was simply paper and ink, nothing more; her heart knew the real truth of her sister. These words could not change that.

From the bedroom, Anna was calling her name; Raina rose with a sigh, reaching into her pocket. She took the letter—neatly folded, no need to read it again—and went to the kitchen. Opening the door of the woodstove, she threw the letter inside. She did not remain to watch the flames consume it.

Instead, she resolutely went back inside the sickroom to care for Anette.

CHAPTER 26

ANETTE WAS DREAMING NOW, AGAIN, ALWAYS. FOR A GIRL who had not been given to dreaming before—how could anyone sleep so lightly as to dream, when she was so exhausted every night her sleep was as heavy as a ton of bricks, blotting out any fancies?—she was currently entangled in so many she couldn't make sense of them.

There was the dream of being yanked out of an ice house and into someone's arms, a woman's arms, not Mama's, but someone else's. And when she opened her eyes, just once, she saw that she was in Mother Pedersen's arms, but that couldn't be possible, because, well—that just couldn't be possible. And then Mother Pedersen was crying and saying she was sorry, but that, too, could not be. Then the nightmare of fire licking at her hands, devouring them in its fierce, gaping mouth, and she cried and screamed, and maybe someone held her down because she wanted to get up and stab that flaming monster in the eyes, but she couldn't because she couldn't move her arms.

Another bout of dreams and fantasies—past, present, future, she had no idea: Fredrik taunting her, telling her to get up, she was a baby, just a girl, a stupid girl, why didn't she get up and go with him? A recurring sensation of falling from a ledge up in the sky into the very earth itself, the soil rising up to catch her was soft as a feather bed. She fell deep into it, afraid that it would hurt when she finally landed, but she never did, she just kept tumbling down in its pillowy embrace. Teacher calling her name over and over, sternly, like Anette had done something bad. And her slate! Her pail! Where were they? She patted her chest, felt for the slate—hadn't she wrapped her shawl over it?

Mrs. Halvorsan, Tor Halvorsan, they knocked at the door of her turbulent mind, they cried Fredrik's name, they gazed at her and put something in her arms, they cried again, they left, they came back. They were only notions, not real people, of course. Real people did not come to see her, did not treat her kindly. Except for Fredrik, who kept running in and out of her dreams like he did when they played tag together; he'd dart around the corner of the schoolhouse, then reappear behind her like a demon. She'd laugh and dash away from his outstretched hand, and he'd call her name. He called her name now. His was the voice she heard the most, rising above all the others she might have recognized and might not have, but it seemed there was a babbling stew of praying, crying, talking all around her, never letting her sleep as she longed to.

Then they stopped. The dreams. The voices were silenced, too, and that's when she knew that the voices hadn't really been in her dreams, they had been real people, talking. But it was quiet now. And she thought that she had died. For wasn't that what death was, the silencing of all things?

"I don't know how we'll tell her," a voice said. So she wasn't dead, after all. She tried to open one eye, to see who was talking, but it took too much effort, so she lay quietly, her old trick of not being noticeable so she couldn't offend.

"Maybe she knows already, somehow," another voice whispered, and Anette couldn't help it, her eyes wrenched open—painfully—because the voices belonged to Mother Pedersen and Teacher, and they sounded like they were . . . well, not exactly friends, but united in something.

The light—feeble as it was in whatever unfamiliar room she was in—stung her eyes. Then she realized she was lying in a brass bed and so, astonishingly, must be in the Pedersens' bedroom. Her lashes felt heavy, then instant tears obscured her vision. She wondered how long she'd been lying in the Pedersens' bed, and what had happened to her own. Shouldn't she be upstairs? She started to shiver, her teeth rattled and she moaned, and that silenced the voices.

"She's awake!" Mother Pedersen looked at Teacher with what might have been joy, except that Anette had never before seen joy in Mother Pedersen's eyes. Blinking, trying to clear her vision, she struggled to recall the last thing she had seen before falling asleep.

Fredrik! Where was he? Where—they'd been outside, in the storm, the storm—oh, the storm! The howling and the swirling, gritty ice-snow, the cold—she was shivering more violently, again as if she was outside and not inside. They'd fallen, she remembered that—they'd fallen into the ravine.

But that was all she remembered.

Anette pressed her hands against the mattress to raise herself up to a sitting position, but there was a bolt of pain in her left hand when she did and she fell over on her left side as if her hand had simply given out; she couldn't get the leverage she needed. So she rolled over on her back, blinked some more, and stared at the ceiling.

"Don't move, Anette, you're not strong enough. Stay quiet, *kjaereste*," Teacher whispered, and Anette's head spun again.

No one had ever called her that before. She realized she was being talked to in her native tongue, and she relaxed a little.

"But Fredrik . . ." Anette mumbled. She turned her head to gaze at Teacher, who was right next to the bed. Mother Pedersen was hovering over Teacher, clasping and unclasping her hands. Both of them looked tired—even Mother Pedersen's lively hair looked limp. Teacher was thinner than before, and paler, and the tip of her nose was blistered, like she'd had a sunburn.

At the mention of Fredrik, both of them looked away.

"I don't think . . ." Teacher whispered to Mother Pedersen. But Mother Pedersen shook her head.

"We have to tell the truth, she deserves that." Then Mother Pedersen came to the other side of the bed, and she knelt down; she took Anette's right hand in hers, and Anette marveled at how callused Mother Pedersen's hands were, just like Mama's hands had been. But Mother Pedersen's nails were so pretty and pink and buffed; Anette had never suspected the palms were rough from work.

"Where is Fredrik?" Anette whispered; her throat was parched, she longed for water.

"Fredrik died, Anette," Mother Pedersen said, her voice matter-of-fact but not cruel. "He died, in the storm. I found you both, together, the morning after—over a week ago, now. You were in the ravine. He had—" Mother Pedersen had to look away for a moment, and Anette—despite the deepening misery reaching out to draw her back into the nightmare she'd only just left—was astonished to see that she had tears running down her cheeks.

Mother Pedersen took a breath and forced herself to look at Anette. "He had taken his clothes off, Anette. He covered you with them. He saved your life."

And Anette, in that moment before she lost consciousness again, was filled with bitter anger; she wanted to slap
Fredrik in the face and call him a stupid, careless boy.

Because didn't he know that hers wasn't a life worth saving?

THE NEXT TIME ANETTE opened her eyes, the light was different; it was late afternoon, and there were so many oil
lamps lit all around her that she wondered if someone had
died, then she remembered someone had, and it was
Fredrik, and she turned her face to muffle a moan as the
grief hit her anew. Her anger at his self-sacrifice had vanished, replaced by loss. Loss more pure and uncomplicated
than any she'd known before. Her loss of her real family, her
former life—that had been too diluted, murky as it was with
questions that seemingly had no answers, stunned surprise
at the rapid change in her environment, the immediate, exhausting work that Mother Pedersen shoveled her way. Her
mama was still alive in the world—that, too, made the loss
difficult to process. Losing Fredrik was different; she would
never see his freckled face again, never make fun of his
donkey ears sticking out from his head, never see his eyes
light up with happiness.

She'd never have another friend, she thought miserably.
From now on, she would truly be alone in the world.

There were hot tears streaming down her face and into
her ears and so she raised her left hand to wipe them away—
but the tears still remained, nothing touched her cheek at
all. It was almost as if she'd missed her own face! Puzzled,
she tried again, and again she missed. Then she looked at
her hand—

It wasn't there. Her arm, mostly covered by an unfamiliar nightgown that was soft and scented, ended in a bandaged stump where her hand should have been.

She struggled up, leveraging herself with her right hand, which was also bandaged but still attached, and she held out her left arm, moving it left, then right, up, then down, wriggling her fingers—she felt them! They did wriggle! She felt pain, too, when she moved her wrist.

But there was no hand, there were no fingers.

Where was it? Had someone taken it without her permission—was *nothing* her very own, not even her flesh? She was jabbering in Norwegian, enraged by everything that had happened, Fredrik gone and now her hand, and this was too much to take. All the months of being treated like an unwanted old dog at best, but overworked and despised at worst—she had had enough. What a stupid turn of events! She must leave this place, go somewhere, to Fredrik's house; but no, he wasn't there—her heart seized up in an odd way and then it fluttered. She placed her left hand on her chest. Then she looked down and saw it again—that queer, bandaged end of her arm, as if—as if—someone had sawed off her hand?

She was falling, falling, and with a thud, she hit the floor, heard excited voices, arms lifting her up, cool hands on her hot forehead, and then she was back in the cushioned earth again, dreaming her dreams.

WHEN ANETTE PEDERSEN WOKE a third time, it was morning, and the oil lamps were extinguished. The usual voices were in the kitchen. They weren't bothering to whisper. This was a conversation that had been going on a long time, she could tell by the weariness in the voices, the circling back to topics.

There was a grunt at the foot of the bed, and Anette tried to lift her head, then she pushed herself up on her right hand, and she saw once more the absence of her left.

She also saw a man. Seated on a chair that was much too small for him. He was a large person, with a soft, doughy shape she'd never seen before in a man. All the men she knew—and there weren't that many—were solidly muscular. But this one looked as if he had never handled a shovel or a hoe in his life. He was grunting again, and his breath was labored, as if he'd tired himself out just by sitting.

But he wasn't only sitting. He was writing something, furiously scribbling with a pencil across a sheet of paper.

Finally, he raised his head and saw her watching him.

He grinned—it was a funny grin, and it tickled something inside Anette, something she had only ever felt with Fredrik. She found herself grinning back. Then he said something in English, and to her astonishment, she understood it.

"Well, here she is, finally, wide awake! The plucky little girl herself!"

And the voices stopped in the kitchen. Anette heard a general stampede of feet, and she was suddenly surrounded— Mother and Father Pedersen, Teacher, Doc Eriksen. They all gaped at her like she was the answer to a question. She blushed at all those eyes, and she turned again to the man. Who beamed at her like she was a prize, someone worth knowing.

Who looked at her the same way Fredrik did, with pure happiness.

CHAPTER 27

THE FIRST COUPLE OF DAYS THAT GAVIN WOODSON SPENT on the Godforsaken Prairie had yielded nothing but unbroken horror.

Every small settlement—you couldn't call them towns, since they were only a handful of buildings, sometimes only repurposed abandoned train cars—gave up, all too readily, its tragedies to his pencil and notepad. It was as if he'd given these people permission to drop that fabled stoicism and pour forth so much pent-up grief and trouble, his pencil could barely keep up. After a while, the stories all began to blur but still he wrote them down. He had to. He had to bear witness.

The men lost, out tending livestock. The livestock gone, too; another disastrous year for cattle and who in his right mind would continue to pursue that folly?

There were people who miraculously survived the night in a cold that froze the cattle where they stood, only to drop dead in the morning when they rose to find their way home— something about the change in pressure on the heart; he'd have to look it up or ask a doctor when he got back to Omaha. It was a mystery to Gavin and it seemed improbable, but too many people had witnessed it, had looked out their windows to see someone rise from the snow like a wraith, take a step or two, then drop deader than a stone.

Men who survived, who got home—only to find their wives and children frozen beside a cold and empty stove, maybe the windows had blown out, maybe not; the cold was so relentless it had no fear of windows and walls. Or men who found their wives steps from the house, almost covered entirely by the snow. They'd become disoriented, lost their way between house and barn if they hadn't thought to tie up a line between the two, and many hadn't because the storm had come upon them so abruptly.

Entire families were caught out on the plains, driving home from getting supplies on that deceptively warm morning. Like the family of his maiden; he could imagine it only too well.

But it was the children that everyone talked about.

The storm hit at precisely the wrong time here in northeastern Nebraska, southeastern Dakota. Earlier, and there would have been no question of sheltering in place. But it hit right when most schools were about to disgorge their pupils for the day, or just had.

Gavin scurried from town to town, house to house, following breadcrumbs like in the old children's fairy tale. But this time, the breadcrumbs were the children themselves: their lost bodies, frozen. He'd pull up in one settlement, hear the tales of woe, then someone would say something along the lines of "But I heard that the schoolteacher there up in Holt County let them all go home, alone," and he'd be back in his ridiculous sleigh—it had definitely elicited a few snorts of amusement—trying to figure out how the hell to get up to Holt County. Most of the time, someone took pity on him—they had relatives up that way, anyway, and wanted to check in on them—and would ride alongside him. These men—so lean they looked starved, and indeed some did have the telltale signs of malnutrition: the distended stomach, the sunken cheeks and haunted eyes—wouldn't say a word, they'd just ride. Ploddingly, horses breaking through the snow, they'd point off in one direction and then peel away in another, and Gavin would have no choice but to aim his nag and trudge off, steeling himself for the inevitable.

A stranger knocking on a dugout door elicited less astonishment than he would have thought. Perhaps it was the grief, permeating every frigid dugout, every poorly insulated cabin or shed that opened its door to Gavin and his pad of paper, that dulled any other senses. Grief so palpable it soured the air. The adult homesteaders rarely spoke English but there was usually a child or two who did, who translated.

"I'm sorry, I'm here because I heard . . ." Gavin only had to begin, and then the child—who had, by some grace of some god, stayed home from school that fateful day or had made it home safely—would immediately start jabbering in both English and Norwegian. And then the stories would be shared—the boy sent out to bring the horse in from pasture. The father who had gone out to the barn at the height of the storm to make sure there was hay, to break the ice in the troughs. The mother who just had to check on the chickens—they were so fragile, she wondered if she should bring them in.

And there were many still missing. Many families resigned to not knowing the truth until the spring thaw.

Several times, he found himself knocking on a door just in time to witness the simplicity of a Norwegian funeral. A pine box, at best; often just a body wrapped in a blanket. A few hymns sung in a language he didn't understand, a prayer, then the body removed, taken to a plot of land next to the barn, usually; a place that already had crude gravestones dotting it. This was never the first death a family had experienced. The ground, despite the cold, could usually be coerced into giving up enough topsoil to lower the box or body deep enough to keep predators out.

So many of the boxes were small. Three feet, four.

In every house, Gavin hoped, right before he knocked on the door, to see the face he sought. There were glimpses of it, stray pieces of an incomplete puzzle—pretty blue eyes in a young woman's face, a thick blond braid the right shade, even throats that yearned, dammit. But never the complete picture.

Gavin would write it all down, and then move on to the nearest train station where he could telegraph the more sensational stories to the *Bee*—the ones that Rosewater was now, in opposition to his earlier stance, clamoring for, because the public's hunger for these tragedies was proving to be voracious. He slept many a night on the floor of one of those stations. There were few hotels or boardinghouses in these strange, bleak settlements.

But God Almighty, what he'd give for a good snort back at the Lily; hot shots of whiskey burning his throat, blotting his senses, making him forget everything he was forced to record. Because the tragedies started to blur together into one infinite shroud of misery that he wondered if he could ever shrug off. Oh, there were stories with happy endings— the dog who spent the night out with his young master, whose barking led searchers to the unconscious boy, saving his life. Those who had miraculously survived that frigid night with nothing more than some numb fingers or a slightly frostbit nose. These survivors would keep the blizzard alive in memory, passed from one generation to the next.

The other stories haunted his dreams, made him question the folly of man; not just himself, but man in general. This great age in which he lived—the age of *Go West, Young Man*, the age of industry with enormous factories bellowing up volcanos of black smoke and creating rivers of sludge, of railroads trampling the landscape; new inventions like telegraphs and telephones and typewriters and electric light and steam engines—it had brainwashed them all into thinking there was nothing that man couldn't conquer or bend to his will.

Even the weather itself.

Death toll not exaggerated, he telegraphed to Rosewater. *Hard to get exact number. Many still missing.*

Good work so far, Rosewater telegraphed in reply. Then one day, this: *Great interest from all but stories starting to blur. Need new angle.*

Gavin's desire to bear witness did not abate; he still sought the tragedies, he wrote them all down: *Olaf Gustoffsen, aged ten, ran back to the schoolhouse after his teacher dismissed school to retrieve a book; found frozen to death the next morning. Maria Jorgensen, aged thirteen, and her sister Helga, expired on the prairie, huddled together, big sister with her arm wrapped about her younger sibling.* But he was a newspaperman to his very bones, and he understood Rosewater's request. There was no way to spin "cute" out of this tragedy, but he did need to find some new angle to keep the story alive—and the papers selling.

So it was providential when he ran into a man called Doc Eriksen in a settlement a couple of counties south of the Dakota border in northeastern Nebraska. The man was old, bent, exhausted; Gavin met him in the farmhouse of a family that had lost a son and a father. The son had died saving his friend, a little girl. He'd covered her up with his own clothing during the night.

Eriksen was tending to the mother, who had collapsed with grief after the twin funeral. A polite, tall young man with floppy sandy hair, maybe fifteen, was tending to two younger brothers and a sister until his mother got up again.

"Will she?" Gavin asked, because grief of that sort might be too heavy ever to stand up under.

"Oh, yes, she will," Eriksen replied. "You don't know these homesteaders the way I do. She has a family to care for, a farm to run—she won't stay down for long. She just needed some laudanum so she could rest, because she wasn't sleeping."

The young man studied Gavin warily, even though his manners remained excruciatingly proper; he'd obviously been loath to let Gavin in, but the presence of the doctor seemed to assure him that this stranger wasn't going to steal anything other than his family's grief. Gavin, pulling out his notebook, turned to him.

"So I heard your brother, he was a hero? He saved his friend?"

The boy, named Tor, nodded. "Fredrik, that is—was—his name. They ran out in the storm, Miss Olsen couldn't stop them. I should have—I should have—" But he turned abruptly to give his little sister, just a toddler, a wooden spoon to play with.

"Between you and me," Doc said, in a precise English that was surprising for an immigrant his age, "I don't know about these stories. Like this boy. He was indeed found with most of his clothes off, piled on top of his friend. But I've seen this in others who froze to death out there alone—and their clothes were torn off, too. I don't think it was animals that did it, either, but I can't quite understand it. It's as if, in the moments before they lost consciousness, they were burning with fever instead of freezing to death. Maybe cold that severe does something to the mind. I don't know, I just think—"

"Fredrik was a hero," Tor said, his eyes flashing dangerously. "He saved Anette."

"Well, let's hope so, son—that little girl might not make it. I'm on my way there now. Care to come with me, Mr. Woodson?"

"Yes, if you don't mind," Gavin replied gratefully; he was beginning to feel claustrophobic in the stifling kitchen; the stove was too hot, there were stacks of dirty dishes on the table. The boy was obviously trying his best but was outnumbered by his needy siblings. Gavin looked around the small farmhouse—just two rooms downstairs, a kitchen and a small bedroom; upstairs, there must be another room. The funeral had come and gone and now all that was left to do was to continue living, he supposed. The mother was apparently strong, despite the laudanum; the boy was almost a man in body, although his flash of emotion betrayed that he was yet a boy in spirit. This was a family devastated by grief, but it looked to be a family that would find some way to go on. And that was what Gavin was discovering about these "rubes" he'd so dismissed; they had the strength to go on. Despite the cruelty of the land and weather, the best of them would find a way to keep at it instead of going back to the softer lands from where they'd come. The unyielding soil had seeped into their skins, their backbones.

"I'll tell the story of your brother, don't worry," he assured the boy, and there was a flush in the lad's cheeks, sudden, embarrassing tears in his eyes as he nodded. Then Tor held out his hand.

"Thank you," he said, shaking Gavin's paw firmly. *"Tusen takk."*

Then the boy turned to the stove, throwing in some wood; he grabbed a pan of potatoes and began to peel them.

"Come, let's go, I need to check on this girl. You might find something there of interest," the doctor mused, "for that paper of yours."

"I'm not sure I can keep filling columns with these stories of loss," Gavin said, rubbing his eyes because they were suddenly misty. It must have been the heat from the stove.

"Then you definitely need to come with me to the Pedersens'," Doc Eriksen said as he and Gavin threw on their layers—the wet wool, the perpetually musky buffalo coat, everything was beginning to smell, as was he. He should find a place to bathe soon. Then they ventured out to the tundra, as he had begun to call this battered, frozen land.

CHAPTER 28

. . . . . .

Wʜᴇɴ ᴛʜᴇ ʏᴏᴜɴɢ ᴡᴏᴍᴀɴ ᴏᴘᴇɴᴇᴅ ᴛʜᴇ ᴅᴏᴏʀ, ɢᴀᴠɪɴ's heart leapt. It was impossible, but—could it really be her? His maiden in the flesh?

She had the same dark blond hair that would surely have streaks of gold and russet in it in summer. She was slight but not delicate, and there was an air of patience about her. She had a pretty face—not flashily pretty, not like the woman he glimpsed behind her, a woman whose beauty seemed out of place in this setting—but a restful pretty. He could, he realized, spend a lifetime gazing at that face.

But then she wrinkled her nose, crossed her arms, and planted her feet widely, not at all inclined to let a strange man into the home. No, she wasn't his maiden, after all; this competent young woman needed no saving.

"Miss Olsen, Mrs. Pedersen," Doc Eriksen introduced the two women, "this is Mr. Woodson. He's a newspaperman, come all the way from Omaha to report on the storm."

The girl raised an eyebrow, looked him up and down skeptically.

"Miss Olsen is the schoolteacher hereabouts," Doc Eriksen explained, gesturing to the younger woman.

Gavin was startled; this was a schoolteacher? He'd taken her to be a pupil, she was so young. She couldn't be much older than the Halvorsan boy he'd just seen.

"Miss," Gavin said, removing his hat, and for some reason this struck the young woman as funny; she smiled, relaxed, and let him in.

"How is the little girl today?" Doc asked anxiously as he removed his coat and scarf and gloves with lightning speed, not pausing to hear the answer as he rushed toward a back bedroom on the other side of the house.

Miss Olsen's face darkened; worry creased her smooth forehead. "The same."

Mrs. Pedersen took Gavin's coat and woolens, sniffed them without embarrassment, then shook her head. She turned and darted away with them in her arms, putting them in a little closet of a room outside the kitchen. Then she came back with a proper smile and welcome.

"Welcome to my home. My husband is out with the horses. Please come in, won't you? I'm afraid I don't have anything proper to offer you but if you don't mind plain coffee cake, I can give you that." She said it so precisely and prettily, Gavin was startled. Her English was halting but understandable. This was a city girl, and Gavin knew city girls. This was a woman used to entertaining in her own parlor, holding musicales or teas. A woman accustomed to the company of females, because a speech like this was the kind of thing a woman said to impress other women, not men.

Gavin nodded, and she dashed off to slice him a piece of the cake; he sat down with it at the kitchen table—he glimpsed a tiny parlor of sorts, but it seemed to be occupied by three small children all staring at him as if he had descended from the heavens on a ladder made of candy—then Mrs. Pedersen started chattering in Norwegian, a rush of words that Miss Olsen patiently translated.

"I'm sorry, you'll excuse me. Everything is a mess but it doesn't matter because of Anette. I need to go to her now, Raina will keep you company. My husband is perfectly useless except with horses." Mrs. Pedersen said these last words with such forthrightness, and Miss Olsen translated them with equal directness, that Gavin almost swallowed a bite of cake whole. While his sample size was small, he had yet to hear a Norwegian speak this way about a spouse.

Raina, too, seemed suddenly uncomfortable by the statement she'd just translated; she sat with downcast eyes while Gavin pulled out his pencil and paper. Then she looked at him with interest. "You're from Omaha? Oh, such a big city! And you write for the paper? You get to see your words in print?"

"Yes, I do," he answered, amused. Women weren't generally impressed by what he did for a living, especially not the women of Omaha.

"It must be such an honor, to do that job. You must be a very respected man."

Gavin stifled a sudden cough.

"Well, yes, perhaps—so tell me, Miss Olsen, you are a schoolteacher? How old are you, if you don't mind? You look so young. And what did you do during the blizzard, then? When it struck? Tell me everything."

"I'm sixteen," Raina said, blushing again. "I just did my job."

"That's not true. She's a heroine," another voice interrupted, and Gavin looked up. A tall man, handsome, not as weathered and bent as the other Norskis he'd encountered, was standing in the doorway to the kitchen. He had a bridle in his hand. So this must be the useless husband.

Raina stared at her hands folded in her lap; she did not look pleased or flattered. The man continued, in a truly awkward fashion; even Gavin sensed that he was putting his foot in it somehow, but neither Raina nor the wife—who kept darting in and out of the kitchen fetching things for Doc Eriksen—appeared to afford him any stature.

"This pretty young woman here, she got her pupils to safety. She tied them all together with their aprons, can you imagine? And she got them all to the Halvorsans' in the storm."

"Not all," Raina said softly. "And Tor helped."

"*Ja, ja,* the boy helped. And poor Anette"—Mr. Pedersen nodded toward the bedroom—"she and Fredrik ran off toward home instead."

"I couldn't stop them," Raina said, bitterness creeping into her voice. "I tried. I couldn't stop them. Anette felt—"

"Anette came home because of me," Mrs. Pedersen, her arms full of linen, chimed in. "She knew I would be angry if she didn't come home to do her chores. It is my fault that she is maimed for life."

"Anette is your child?" Gavin was puzzled; none of these people really seemed related to one another. He couldn't explain it other than they seemed to treat each other warily, as if they were all on edge. None of the loving affection or long-suffering hatred that springs up between people who share a name or blood.

"No, no, she's just a girl, you know—" Mrs. Pedersen replied, but was evidently frustrated by her lack of English.

"Her mother abandoned her," Gunner said.

"She lives here, as do I," Raina patiently explained to the bewildered Gavin. "We board. I'm the teacher, so I have to board out. I don't live in this district. Anette was—is—somewhat of a hired girl."

"I go to her," Mrs. Pedersen said abruptly, and left the room. Raina, watching her, shook her head; her expression was bemused.

"She is trying," Raina murmured, and Gavin didn't know what or who she meant.

"I don't quite—I would like to write about this, with your permission. You see"—and an idea took shape in his mind. That word that Mr. Pedersen had used—*heroine*—struck him as useful. Extremely useful—*of course*! There had to be heroes and heroines among all the tragedy; stories of triumph, stories to keep readers interested instead of tuning out the endless misery. Stories to sell papers. Gavin knew the public; while they liked to read about heroes, the appeal of a heroine—a young, pretty woman like Raina who had, against all odds, saved the lives of her pupils—was far greater. And then there was the child fighting for her life—that was a story people could get behind, too. A story of hope; someone they would invest in and keep buying papers to read about. It really was astonishing, this girl's story—a child who had been abandoned by her own mother only to be saved by the selfless act of her only friend in the world, a young, innocent boy—

It wasn't a story, it was a goddamn gold mine. Pulitzer would surely take notice of this back East.

"Are all schoolteachers out here like you?" he asked Raina.

"Like me? We all have to have a certificate, yes, after an examination."

"No, no." Gavin was too excited now to remember to be a

gentleman and that he was a guest in this house. He heaved himself out of the small wooden chair he was in—it creaked dangerously—and began to pace the room. "I mean, are they all girls like you? Pretty? I always thought teachers were men, for some reason. That's how it was back East."

"We can't convince many eastern teachers to come out here, you know," Gunner explained. "We take care of our own, we school our own."

"But you're so young!" He couldn't help himself, even though the girl looked very uncomfortable. "Barely a child yourself and look at you, you saved—how many?—other children!"

"Ten. Eleven, if you count Tor but he helped me, you see—"

Gavin didn't care about Tor.

"Ten children! Ten saved! This is wonderful! I want to know everything. The boss'll eat it up!" Gavin couldn't believe he hadn't thought of this before. "There must be others like you—do you know any other teachers?"

Raina rose, trembling; her face was scarlet, her eyes downcast and ashamed. Then she sank back down to the chair and hid her face in her hands.

"Yes," she said, raising her head, and worry lines crisscrossed her forehead. "Yes, I know another schoolteacher."

But that's all she would say about it; he couldn't get the story out of her. It didn't matter, there would surely be others and he would find them. Meanwhile, there was the little girl in the room, suffering from something, no one had told him what.

"Can I see her?" He pointed toward the bedroom. Raina nodded wearily, then she led him to the threshold. She acted reluctant to cross it.

The room was too crowded with a suite of fancy furniture—
brass bedstead, carved mahogany dresser, horsehair-
covered chair. Furniture like this was completely out of
place on the plains; it belonged in a city. On either side of
the bed were the doctor and Mrs. Pedersen. The room was
hot, it smelled of sickness—vomit, excrement, the sour
smell of fever. In the middle of the bed lay a tiny form, covered by blankets. She was propped up on two pillows, both
arms over the coverlet. Her left arm ended in a stump that
looked freshly rendered; the bandage had brownish stains
on it.

The tiny form was moaning, and Gavin didn't dare go too
close; he feared catching whatever fever gripped her in its
vise. Doc saw his fear and shook his head.

"No, it's the infection, from the amputation. It's not
catching."

"This is the little girl? The one who was covered by the
boy's clothes?"

Doc nodded.

Gavin crept closer.

The little face was red, although the lips were white.
Sweat glistened on her brow, her eyes were shut but swollen.
Her cheeks were pockmarked, her jaw was heavy, her eyebrows thick. Beneath the sheen of sweat, he perceived that
her hair was a mousy brown color.

But Gavin knew, the moment he saw her, that here she
was. In the midst of misery, in a tiny house full of wary people, he had found her; the girl he would save—and who would
save him, too, from his previous self.

Gavin Woodson had found his maiden of the prairie.

CHAPTER 29

HOW DO YOU GROW OLD ON THE PRAIRIE?

You become bent with work, you watch your crops fail and succeed and fail again. You marry, you have children, they have children. There are celebrations—marriages, births, good crops, new roofs. There is grief. Death, always that shadow stalking the celebrations, making them even more necessary, more desperately gay—the music louder, the dancing faster, the laughter brighter, anything to ignore its presence. You learn to parcel out your heart, cautiously, because of the certainty that one day, a part of it will be wrenched from you forever. You grow older, quieter, and stern because of this caution. But you still survive, you do the work, you see your children go off on their own to repeat the cycle, but maybe this time, the results will be different— abundant years, better crops, maybe one of their children finds a way to own an even bigger piece of land, maybe buy a new threshing machine. Maybe build a house with five rooms, not three. Fulfill the promise that lured you here in the first place.

Eventually, your incomplete heart—because of those fragments that have been torn off like the last leaves of autumn through the years—weakens. The work is too much for frail bones and papery skin. All you can do is live quietly with your memories in the back room of one of your children's houses, and you help while you can, doing things like cooking and mending, until eventually those tasks are taken from you. You sit in a chair by the fire and doze, remembering it all over and over again, if you're lucky. Or forgetting everything—and maybe that is the luckier thing, after all— puzzled by the strangers hovering over you, spooning broth into your mouth, bathing you once a week. But you are not alone. Even if you no longer recognize the people you had birthed, the husband who still grips your hand at night, tenderly, you are not alone.

That was how you grew old on the prairie, if you were a woman.

The one spinster Gerda had known, the spinster homesteader she had boarded with a year ago, had never envisioned staying out here on the land. She was going to prove up her place, and hire hands to do all the work, then sell it for a good profit and return to Chicago, where she was from. She never spoke of marrying, but maybe in Chicago she had had a beau, or at least family to go back to. Her plans certainly were not to grow old out here alone.

Gerda hadn't planned to do that, either. Even if Tiny had gone west without her, there would have been others. Less appealing, but she would never have reached the age of twenty-one still unattached. The math didn't add up. There were too many men who needed wives.

But who would have her now?

In the shock of all the news that fell on her head like hammers raining from the sky, forcing its way through the agonizing pain she suffered physically from her foot being severed from her leg; throughout the torment of guilt and woe, the averted gazes, the tightly pressed lips of those who were forced only through Christian charity to tend to her—this was the one taunting, destroying thought that stood out from all the others.

Who would have her now?

It wasn't her lost foot that had branded her undesirable. A one-legged wife was still useful to someone; a one-legged wife could still cook and clean and bear children, tend to chickens, garden.

Gerda had never known a criminal. Had there ever even been one in her district? She couldn't remember anything close to it, no chicken or horse thieves. One far neighbor had shot another neighbor's dog, causing some hard feelings, but the dog was known for eating eggs, and so most had thought it was a justifiable act.

Tiny's books had been full of tales of daring bandits like Jesse James and Belle Starr, but they had been depicted in such a thrilling, one-sided way that you had no choice but to sympathize with the bandit. The stories were outlandish, fictional, even if they were based on real people. But they were too far removed from the prairie—these stories happened in other places like Texas or Arizona Territory, in fantastic landscapes featuring canyons and arroyos and sagebrush and cacti, places so unimaginable to Gerda it was as if they existed on other planets. None of it—the bandits or the landscape—was real.

But now, intimately, Gerda knew a criminal. A *murderess*. She knew herself.

The first day after she'd crawled up to the house, she was still the schoolteacher, a victim of the storm like so many.

Yes, Minna and Ingrid had died in her care, but she had carried the girls on her very back, she had carved out a shelter in a haystack, nearly destroying her hands in the process. She had *tried*. She was valiant. The storm was too big; no one could have done more, or better. She was too gripped by the fiery pain of a dying foot to know anything but that; the pain was all-encompassing, it drove every other sensation away— she didn't even know how to breathe, how to keep her eyes open, roasting in the flames of it. She succumbed to it, almost gratefully.

When she opened her eyes, finally freed from its torment, she was no longer in the Nillssens' kitchen. She was back at the Andersons', in her own bed. And Mama and Papa were with her, Mama seated next to her, clutching her hand, humming a hymn: "How Blest Are They Who Hear God's Word."

Papa was standing at the foot of the bed, but strangely he wouldn't look at her directly, not even when she croaked his name—the first word out of her mouth, it must have been for days, because her lips were dry, her voice a rasp.

"Papa?"

He turned toward her, she saw a flicker of relief on his face, but then he quickly turned away.

"Mama?"

"Shhh, we're here, we're here," Mama responded—but she, too, looked troubled. Gerda's left foot began to itch, to burn, but when she struggled to touch it with her other foot, there was nothing there; she looked at her mother in bewilderment.

"They had to amputate it, my dear heart. I'm so sorry, Gerda—my child, my poor child!" Mama stifled a sob, gently smoothed Gerda's damp hair. Gerda could see that only one foot, her right, stuck up through the covers; there was nothing where her other foot should be.

"That night," she murmured, trying to process the information—would she be able to walk? To teach again? "I remember . . . it was so cold . . ."

"Yes, darling, yes. Don't talk now." Mama gave her a glass of water, which Gerda gulped gratefully, then she felt as if it might come right back up; she turned on her side, leaned over the bed, but managed to keep it down. She rolled over again.

"Papa, Papa—" She reached her hand out toward her father, who walked away and stared out a window. Sharply did her mother speak to him in Norwegian. "Stop behaving like this, she is still our daughter."

"What, Mama?" Gerda struggled to sit up, her foot—the foot that was no longer part of her—still throbbing, but how could that be?

Mama must have read her thoughts, for, as she helped her up into a seated position, shoving a pillow behind her back, she explained. "You will still feel the foot, the doctor says. It's normal, but eventually it will go away, that feeling."

"Oh."

Gerda shut her eyes, too exhausted to ask more. Her mind was turning over this information like a child turns over a handful of pebbles, searching for the one that feels best in her hand; the smoothest, coolest one. She couldn't find anything that felt right, however. She was maimed for life. Never before had she imagined this for herself—she'd imagined pretty dresses, bright hair ribbons, a house of her own, with Tiny—

"Tiny!" Her eyes flew open and for now, her foot was forgotten. "Where is he? Tiny—did he—was he—?"

"They found his body a couple of days ago," Papa said
coldly, still gazing out the window, his big, work-scarred
hands grasped behind his back.

"No, no!" Gerda felt the impact of his words in her solar
plexus, knocking the breath out of her—not Tiny! Yes, she'd
told herself he was probably lost when he didn't come back
for her and the girls, but that was then, during the pinnacle
of the storm when her resolve was focused only on survival. Now she could feel the pain exquisitely, viscerally—she
struggled to control herself because she didn't want to share
her grief with her parents. It was *hers,* hers alone, they would
never understand it. They would never understand *them,*
Gerda and Tiny, because Mama and Papa had never been
young and in love, had never had hopes and dreams—

But these were *her* hopes and dreams, not Tiny's. If only
they'd been able to have that one day together, the day she'd
planned; the two of them playing house so she could show
him what he would miss if he ran away, she could convince
him with her domesticity—with her lips, if necessary—what
a wife could give him that a life of adventure couldn't . . . if
only . . .

Her face was wet with hot tears, her head pounded, and
her foot was beginning to tingle again; her stomach was so
empty she felt faint but also sick, but she swallowed the bile,
the grief. There was something else, some other worry buzzing about her aching head, and then she remembered, and
she looked at Papa. She began to shake with dread—she understood why he was acting so strangely toward her. But she
had to ask, she had to know.

"The other children?" she whispered pleadingly. "The others—what about them?"

"Finally you ask what you should have asked the moment you awoke?" Papa's voice bounced off the glass window-panes and thundered about the room, tormenting her ears, her heart. "Finally you want to know about your students and not your beau?"

She nodded.

"They are gone, Gerda. All of them, lost in the storm. Three boys found together frozen, their arms about each other—the Gerber boys. A brother and sister—the Borstads—found only a few feet from the schoolhouse. And two little boys, Hardus Hummel and Johnny Rolstad, found together, too, not far from the Rolstad farm."

The names were too much; she felt herself receding from the room, from her father's accusing voice, and she began to chant as she had during the storm—"Minna, Ingrid, Hardus, Johnny, Johannes, Karl, Walter, Sebastian, Lydia . . . Minna, Ingrid, Hardus, Johnny, Johannes, Karl, Walter, Sebastian, Lydia."

"Stop it!" Papa was beside her in one great inhuman stride; as she continued to mumble the names, their little faces spinning through her mind, she was trapped on a carousel of the dead—

A sting, a gasp. Papa had slapped her across the face.

"Steffen!" Mama rose, her voice terrible; she pushed her husband away from her daughter. Gerda was stunned, although she didn't feel pain from the slap itself; her torture was that, for the first time in her life, her father had struck her.

And she deserved it, more than he would ever know—more than he ever *could* know.

"Why, Gerda—why?" Papa's voice was hoarse; he sank down into a chair and let his shoulders slump so that he seemed like an old man, but he raised his head and finally looked her in the eye. "What were you thinking when you let them all go, when you left with Tiny and the two little girls?"

Now she couldn't meet *his* gaze. She also couldn't answer his question—never could he know what she was thinking that day. So she only shook her head.

"We must get you back to our farm soon," Papa said, rising once more, roaming the little room—where were the Andersons? She didn't even hear Ma Anderson bustling about in the kitchen. "You're not safe here."

"What do you mean?" Gerda's head ached as if someone had put it in a vise; she rubbed her temples but brushed her mother's hands away when that good woman tried to do it for her. She didn't deserve to be touched or soothed—not by decent people, people like her parents. People who would die from grief and disappointment if they could see inside her blackened, sinful heart.

"They want to kill you," Papa muttered. "I can't blame them."

Once more Mama's great and terrible voice boomed out her father's name. "Steffen!"

"It's true, she ought to know. The father of the three boys came here, wild with grief. He had a shotgun. He would have killed you if I hadn't been here."

"You exaggerate—Papa exaggerates," Mama clucked in her gentle way. "The man came here, yes, but he would not have shot you! To think of that, to shoot a schoolteacher because of—because of this storm. Everyone with any sense knows it wasn't your fault, that the storm was worse than anyone could predict. Do not think of it."

But Gerda was irritated by her mother's love and protection and she continued to swat at her ministering hands as if they were flies. She preferred the way Papa was speaking to her, not bothering to conceal his disgust. He spoke to her as if she were a criminal. And she knew that she was, forevermore.

"You will have to come home with us soon, and you will never teach again. Not near here, at any rate. I don't know what we'll do with you. Or how we'll show our faces again to anyone."

Once again his anger drained from him and his shoulders sagged, his head bent, and Gerda's misery was complete. She had done this to him. She had tarnished his name in the community, forever.

"A man has only his name, Gerda," Papa'd once told her when they were in the barn, mucking out the ox stalls. He'd smiled proudly at her when she staggered beneath a shovel full of manure without flinching; that smile she'd learned to hoard, smug that it was hers alone and not Raina's; that smile that told her, *I know you're not a son, but you are as fine a daughter as a man could have.*

"A man has only his name, that's why he wants sons. But if he can't have sons, he still has his name until he dies and so he must make sure he does nothing to ruin it—he must make sure those in his care behave in a certain way. You understand, don't you, daughter?"

She must have been nearing thirteen or fourteen when this conversation occurred, she realized. Nearing womanhood, and all the delicate navigation that entailed, and she'd blushed, understanding what he couldn't bring himself to say. But she'd also nodded—of course she understood! It was so easy, she'd thought then. She was unable to imagine a scenario when she wouldn't behave in a way to bring him honor. The world was simple then—right and wrong. You don't steal, you don't lie, you don't hurt anyone, you do your chores, you don't talk back to your parents. You don't covet your sister's fancy handkerchief that an aunt back home sent for Christmas; you don't feel like your lot in life is worse than anyone else's. You don't want more than your fair share—

Ah. But that was what tripped her up in the end. Wasn't it? She'd wanted *more.* Asked for *more.* More time with Tiny. More of him than he wanted to give. That wanting had led her to making the worst possible decision; it had led her to put herself first, her students last.

It had led her to murder.

Would she actually face trial for the deaths of her students? Her heart began to palpitate, her throat constrict. She asked her mother for another glass of water but she couldn't begin to ask her that question. Papa would know—

But Papa wouldn't look at her.

She would have to wait to know the full impact of her actions, then—but she couldn't imagine that anything could be worse than this guilt she would have to bear in secret. Papa and Mama could never know how thoroughly bad she was. It was hard enough on them as it was. She would have to carry the boulder of her evil—for that's what it was, selfishness that had led to unimaginable ruin, the deaths of innocents, of innocence itself—on her back, alone, for the rest of her life. No one would see it but her, she would never be able to let someone else hold it, not even for the briefest of moments.

As she lay for three more long days in the darkened room—the curtains drawn tight against anguished eyes—

tended by her mother while her father prowled the Andersons' house like a caged tiger, she tried to sleep, to rest her body, but she couldn't. In the middle of the night she would sit bolt upright, prodded with electric shocks of fear and guilt, imagining herself in a jail cell, the gallows awaiting her the next morning. She couldn't stop this nightmare, this torment.

She began to hate her mother for loving her, for staying by her side even through the nightmares. This good woman— she had lost a son in the old country. And now, she had lost a daughter. A woman, a mother—she looks forward to the day a daughter marries. Hadn't Mama been stockpiling a hope chest for years, for both Gerda and Raina? Whenever she had a spare second, she had knitted shawls and blankets, pressed flowers and put them under glass, made sachets of dried prairie grass, saved precious ribbons from stray packages or gifts. All for her daughters, to set them up in their own homes when their time came. And then, of course, there would come the longed-for grandchildren, the next generation, the hope for the future.

But Gerda had deprived her of this. At least there still was Raina.

Finally, the Andersons asked Mama and Papa to take Gerda home. She overheard them one evening, as the four of them miserably shared a meal. "We can't keep her here any longer, we have our own place in the community to think of," Pa Anderson said, not bothering to lower his voice. "She was a good girl, though, at least what we saw. But after this . . ."

So the next day, despite the fact that Gerda was still weak with fever from the surgery, still unable to eat more than broth, she was packed up—unceremoniously, like the rest of her clothing and things that were hastily thrown in a carpetbag—and bundled into blankets. It was so strange, she could feel the weight of the blankets on her missing foot, she was certain of it. But she was just as certain that she had only buttoned one shoe, not two. The four-day-long journey back to their homestead was so torturous to her weak, mutilated body she almost bit through her lower lip to hide her screams, tasting blood along with the tears the entire journey. That was when she began to hate Papa, too. For he seemed to go out of the way to hit the bumpiest parts of the trail.

But she never hated anyone more than she despised herself.

Over and over, she forced herself to remember her students' joy when she released them early. Johannes Gerber had thrown his cap in the air with a shout, and actually picked his little brother up in his arms and swung him around until Gerda had to tell him, laughingly, to stop. The way Minna and Ingrid had smiled their secret smile, because they alone would be riding with Teacher and her beau, and Gerda had long known how much that honor meant to them, how they whispered about it in the middle of a circle of gaping admirers at almost every recess.

And then she would force herself to imagine how lost they must have felt, alone, forsaken by the person in charge of them when they were not at home. Forsaken by Teacher, who was too absorbed in her own plans to understand the growing, growling threat of the storm as it swirled about them all. She had only that last glimpse of them all being swallowed by the greedy cloud. After that, she could only speculate—had they cried? Argued, the three brothers who almost always argued? Had the big children put their arms about the small ones? Had they all called out for their mothers and fathers?

Had they called out for her? *Miss Olsen, what do we do? Where are you? Why did you send us away?*

Finally she was home, back in her own room, still recuperating—it would be a long while, the home doctor told her with a shake of his head. But she would recover, she was strong, she would learn to get by with the crutch or the wooden boot.

Back home, and from her small room that would only grow more constrictive with each passing year, she heard her parents going about the business of farming in the winter. There were more storms—and the first time she heard the howling wind outside her walls, she sat up and began to shiver, her body automatically reacting just to the thought of being out there again, in that pummeling, knifelike wind. Despite the pile of quilts on top of her, she wondered if she would ever feel warm again.

The livestock was always a worry in the winter—would the hay last until they could graze again? Mama had to bring new chicks into the kitchen, to keep them warm close to the stove. Food would run low—extra low this winter, because she was no longer able to help out with her teacher's salary, and she was an unexpected mouth to feed. But she had little appetite, anyway.

No longer did Papa sing his booming songs while he worked. Now, when she heard her parents huddled together by the hearth at night when they thought she was asleep, Gerda knew that they were talking about her. There were sounds of muffled sobs. Of broken prayers. Of wondering, "Why did she do it? What will become of her now?"

How do you grow old on the prairie?

Watching your parents fall apart a little every day, and then witnessing them valiantly try to mend themselves again on the morrow, each time losing a stitch or two until they didn't resemble people so much as rag dolls, the stuffing falling out. Hiding alone in your room with the curtains drawn, ashamed to show your face to the sun. Terrified to behold another human being, unable to bear the look in their eyes— *This is her, she's the one I was telling you about. Remember her? Gerda Olsen? She used to be so proud, that one. And we were proud of her, too, I'll admit. A shining example, a good teacher.*

Did you hear that she murdered nine children?

Then one day, the papers from Omaha began to arrive. And just when Gerda thought she could suffer no more—

She had to read about her sister.

CHAPTER 30

The Heroine of
the Prairie

In the midst of such unspeakable horror when words have sometimes failed us, one shining example of Glorious Womanhood has come to light to this reporter. Raina Olsen, a young schoolteacher only sixteen years of age, was one of those quick-thinking pioneer women we herald in song and poem. Unable to keep her pupils safe when the Savage Storm gnashed its teeth and blew in the window of her one-room schoolhouse, she was tasked with getting them all to safety in the middle of the Most Ferocious Blizzard ever recorded in Nebraska. This courageous young woman tied her pupils together using all the little girls' apron strings and led them to the safety of a nearby farmhouse. The way was full of danger, and all nearly perished while crossing a treacherous bridge over a raging river. But this brave daughter of pioneers managed to get her flock to safety.

The courage and wisdom displayed by this pretty young woman has touched the hearts of all involved, and she has been the recipient of much gratitude in the tiny community of Newman Grove, where she saved so many young lives.

Her ambition, she states modestly, is to return to the schoolhouse as soon as it is repaired. A chance to study further, perhaps even at the university in Lincoln, would not be dismissed outright. When asked about plans to marry, the modest young lady blushes and demurs, although there is many a young man in the area who has lost his heart to this Heroine of the Prairie.

"EXCELLENT WORK, WOODSON," ROSEWATER SAID WITH undisguised surprise that rankled. He peered at Gavin over the top of the latest edition. Gavin was seated in the great man's office, while Forsythe cooled his heels outside. "We were desperate for something like this. We need to keep circulation up, but God Almighty it was getting dreary, day after day some new tragedy. Christ, they all begin to blur together don't they? Amputations, frozen babies, trains stuck for days with no food, dead farmers, all those children, on and on and on. People get tired of constant bad news, they shut it out after a while, become immune to it. It takes something new to excite them and get them buying papers again. And, by God, man, you've done it! This is wonderful. We need to find some other young women—the prettier the better—like this Olsen girl."

"We also need to find a way to spin this whole disaster so as not to scare people out of the state." Jonas Munchin, one of the town's boosters and thus Gavin's actual boss, spoke gravely. "The eastern papers are still reporting high casualties—one of them said nearly a thousand have perished. We can't have that kind of thing reported. There've been some angry citizens out here who keep writing to those papers back East with figures that won't help us at all. Some quack in Dakota said about a hundred died in the southern part of that territory alone. Now, how he can know that, I can't comprehend—did he go out and count them all himself? Maybe he included some of the Natives on the reservation, but really, who cares about them? Still, the papers are running with those figures. We have to counterattack."

"We can do some opinion pieces," Rosewater mused, drumming his ink-stained fingers on his desk. "To contradict those kinds of figures, talk about the benefits of the storm—you know, how snow is welcome; it means we're assured a good crop this summer, all that water. Something like that. Something about the freshness of the air after a blizzard, compared to the smoke-filled cities back East— keep that kind of thing up. You know what to do, Woodson— that's what you're paid for. Forget the facts of the matter, concentrate on the distracting stuff that people want to believe in, like the heroines. I think there's something in it for you if you do, don't you, Munchin?"

"Of course." Munchin threw his arms open expansively, as if the state's coffers were his very own to do whatever he wanted with, and that was probably the simple truth, Gavin thought wryly. "All that tragedy was good for a while, but we have to be careful. Whatever the actual death toll is, report only about a third of it, if you even have to do that. Maybe forget the facts entirely and just do those puff opinion pieces—people think those are the news, anyway, espe-

cially if they're printed in a newspaper. And soon enough
the eastern newspapers will move on to something else.
They sit in judgment back there, they criticize us in the West
at every turn, they make fun of us, but what do they really
know? They only send someone out here when he's in dis-
grace." And the man looked pointedly at Gavin. "We're the
end of the road, the flophouse, for those eastern elites. They
don't care about us unless something like this happens, then
they have a field day at our expense."

Gavin actually agreed with Munchin's point; he just dis-
liked the man himself, and the not-so-subtle disparagement
of his own character, which he had to admit was accurate. Or
least it had been, until *her.* His maiden.

Gavin rose, shook hands, and left the stale office with its
cigar smoke, and its smugness that stank just as much. He
ignored Forsythe's questioning glance and stepped outside,
inhaling fresh air—although the air in Omaha was not fresh,
not like it was out there on the prairie, where it was so pure
it stung the nostrils and ignited every sense. Here, even in
winter, there was still the stench of the stockyards and the
human and animal waste that came when men and horses
and pigs and dogs all lived together in one contained area,
no matter how large, how growing. How thriving.

Gavin took another walk, but this time it was to the train
depot; the trains were back to running, between storms. He
and that nag had had their last communion; he wasn't going
to rent a sleigh again. There were people on the prairie who
would take him where he needed to be.

People, not numbers. Some of them more special to him
than others.

ANOTHER HEROINE
DISCOVERED

Young Minnie Freeman is another of these intrepid maids who managed to save her students against all odds in the Worst Nature Can Imagine. When the soddie that served as a schoolhouse had its roof blown off by the Fury of the Storm, Miss Freeman acted with courage and re-solve. Faced with certain Death by Freezing, she—like her fellow Heroine Raina Olsen—tied her pupils to-gether with a length of rope found in the schoolhouse. Then she bravely led her pupils through the storm to safety.

We at the *Bee* feel strongly that Raina Olsen and Min-nie Freeman should each get a medal, at the least, for their heroism. If not for their acts of bravery, more would have perished. But because of them, the list of casualties is far smaller than is being reported by some newspapers back East. We should honor these young ladies and en-sure their future. Donations can be sent c/o the *Omaha Daily Bee*.

(Letters to the *Omaha Daily Bee*)

Dear Sir,
I wish to donate to Miss Olsen the sum of three dollars so she can realize her goal of attaining an education. Her story has touched my heart. We need more women like her.

Dear Sir,
Please accept one cow, to be given to Miss Raina Olsen for
her bravery. She can do what she pleases with the cow,
which is a good milk cow.

Dear Sir,
I would like to donate two dollars each to Minnie Free-
man and Raina Olsen in gratitude for their bravery.

THE HEROINE FUND

We at the *Bee* have been inundated with letters concerning the heroines Minnie Freeman and Raina
Olsen. There have been poems and songs written for
them. There have been many generous gifts of goods
and money, as well, and we continue to urge those who
can to contribute to their futures. We have been sent so
many gifts in care of these two brave lasses that we have
taken the liberty of setting up a fund for them, and we
will duly note, in each issue of the *Bee*, the donor and
the amount in a column titled "The Heroine Fund." You
may send all donations c/o the *Omaha Daily Bee*.

"More good work, Woodson," Rosewater said ten days
later, with a genuine smile. "The Heroine Fund—brilliant! I
think we need one or two more young ladies, though, to truly
capture the imagination and keep this thing going. We're
falling off a little, although not too much. People keep do
nating because they want to see their names in print—that
was a hell of an idea, you son of a bitch! One more big story,

don't you think? A tale of woe, someone people can rally around—that's the very thing we need."

Gavin nodded. It was precisely what he'd been waiting to hear; now it was time.

AN INCREDIBLE STORY OF A
LITTLE GIRL'S SUFFERING

It has come to our attention of the Great Suffering of another victim of the storm, a young girl named Anette Pedersen. This poor unfortunate girl had her life saved due to the bravery of her closest friend, a boy named Fredrik Halvorsan. Young Halvorsan tragically died a hero's death protecting his little companion. In the worst of the storm, he gallantly covered his young friend with his own coat and other clothing, ensuring her survival by his sacrifice. Anette Pedersen is a girl of just eleven who has been in a household that was forced to take her in after she was abandoned by her own mother. She has suffered an Amputation of the Hand due to frostbite and continues to suffer greatly, although it is now hoped that she will live. We will provide updates of her condition as warranted.

Dear Sir,
I would be happy to take in the little girl I read about in your paper, Anette Pedersen. I will give her a good home and all the care she needs. I am a widow with a tender heart and good fortune enough to share, and a nice snug home in Lincoln where she wouldn't have to do a lick of work, the poor child.

Dear Sir,
I am sending a dollar to Anette Pedersen, the little child
who has lost a hand. Please make sure it gets to her.

To the General Public:
We have added Anette Pedersen to the roll of the Heroine
Fund. All donations earmarked for her will go directly
to her and she will share, along with the others, any
donations that are given without any recipient desig-
nated.

THE HEROINE FUND

We are pleased to announce that the following Good and
Generous citizens have made contributions to the Heroine Fund, originally started here at the *Bee:*

Mrs. Charles Wentworth donated $5 to Raina Olsen
Mr. Reed Garner donated $7 to Minnie Freeman
Mr. and Mrs. James Farmer donated $2 to Raina
    Olsen
The Bastable Boarding School in Lincoln has offered
    free tuition, room, and board to Anette Pedersen
Mr. Jacob Pendergrast donated $2 each to Raina
    Olsen and Minnie Freeman, and sets aside $5 for
    the education of Anette Pedersen
The Presbyterian Congregation of Grunby, Ne-
    braska, took up a collection, the sum of which ($10)
    is to be divided equally between the three heroines
A former medical officer in the Grand Army of the
    Republic, who wishes to remain anonymous, do-

nates a custom-made wooden hand to Anette Pedersen once she is recovered

The Heroine Fund
Update

As of this date, it totals nearly $15,000, spread nearly
evenly among the three heroines.

Raina Olsen and
Her Pupils

Today, February 5, Raina Olsen reopened her schoolroom, the scene of much horror and drama during the
Great Blizzard. The *Bee* sent a photographer out to capture the moment. Pictured is Miss Olsen with most of
her students. Since the creation of the Heroine Fund,
Miss Olsen has been inundated with many proposals of
marriage, although the innocent maid protests, stating
that she is too focused on her pupils right now to think of
anything else.

The exploits of the heroines were picked up by the wire
services and ran everywhere, east and west, although it was
the *Bee* that saw the greatest increase in readership because
Nebraskans thought of them as their own. Everyone was
touched by the girls' plight; everyone on the prairie was
proud of the schoolteachers. The updates on Anette's health,
which continued to improve, were followed as anxiously as
the travails of a maiden in a dime novel.

One woman, in particular, followed those updates, although how she first became aware of them, no one, later, would be able to say. The woman could not read English and wouldn't have been able to afford to buy a newspaper anyway. Or have access to one. Perhaps a neighbor had braved the weather to alert her to the news of this child. Perhaps someone recognized her name, now forgotten by most—if, indeed, they even knew she had a name—until the girl became famous overnight.

But this woman got on a mule one day, according to her husband. She told him and her sons that she would be back in a week, perhaps—she was hazy on that, that was what the husband remembered, later. In fact, she'd done some things to make him wonder if she planned on coming back at all—she took her meager wardrobe with her, her one comb that still had a few teeth in it, a tarnished silver spoon she'd brought from the old country. She told him to try and remember to feed the boys, for heaven's sake. And then she was gone.

What no one knew but her was that she had seen something bright, something possibly beautiful, glistening on the horizon. She'd never had anything bright or beautiful in her life—except for that spoon, which, in truth, she'd stolen. She'd only known misery, poverty, hunger. She couldn't remember why she came to America in the first place. Poverty was poverty wherever you lived. Maybe she'd just been swept up in the tide of others coming. She wasn't the type of person to display initiative on her own. Life was short and cruel; it had its own plans and it was only fools who tried to outsmart it.

But this was different. This was providence. And she'd be a fool *not* to take advantage of it.

The woman aimed her mule in the direction she had traveled only a year and a half before. Did she have any shame when she remembered that previous journey? Any remorse, when she recalled her daughter's questions, her bewildered eyes—her pathetic tears?

There was no remorse, no shame; she'd done what she had to do, what would make her life easier.

She snorted, thinking that her journey this time was so similar. She had troubles—that hadn't changed much in the ensuing months, not even with one less mouth to feed—and a solution had presented itself yet again. All she had to do was go to the same house she'd gone to before. Tying her nag of a mule up outside the prosperous two-story home, she realized that if all went according to plan, she had left her husband and sons without any means of transportation. Oh, well. Maybe, if she was feeling particularly generous, she would drag the beast home behind a new carriage, a farewell present before she turned her back on that damned miserable cave and rode off to live in a grand house with servants, a house full of gleaming furniture and plush carpets and china plates, a house that didn't smell of shit and sweat and boiled potatoes. That didn't smell of *him* and the brats, still unable to make it outside—they didn't have an outhouse, only holes in the ground—before they pissed themselves.

But probably she wouldn't do that, after all. Her husband was a lot like her; it wouldn't be smart to let him know she was suddenly rolling in money.

If all went according to plan.

She walked to the front door and knocked. And when the door was answered by the woman she remembered—that beautiful woman who had looked at her with such distaste the other time, too—she calmly stated her business.

"I am Anette's mother. I heard about her from the papers. And I am here to take her home."

. . . . . .

CHAPTER 31

ANETTE HAD GROWN USED TO THE FUNNY MAN WHO kept coming to sit by her bedside. He read her many letters from strange people who were worried about her and prayed for her and sent her presents of dolls and books. She was getting better with her English, thanks to Mother Pedersen letting Teacher give her lessons. The funny man—Mr. Woodson—didn't know any Norwegian.

But Mr. Woodson liked her; Anette could tell. The pain of losing Fredrik never left her; she too easily could conjure up his laughing face, his flashing feet, the way he had of pushing his hair up from his forehead until it stood straight on end. Tor and his mother came to visit once—they had come before, she was told, when she was sick—and they reminded her so much of him that it had hurt her inside, like bees stinging her heart. Tor looked so like his little brother, except he had a calm, soothing presence, unlike the whirligig Fredrik had been. Fredrik's mother had been so sad, and had taken Anette's hand in hers and asked, urgently, "But he saved you, didn't he, my Fredrik? He saved your life, my boy did."

Anette nodded, and this made Mrs. Halvorsan smile, finally, and she spent the afternoon telling story after story of Fredrik—the time when he was three, when they thought they'd lost him in the tallgrass, but he was asleep in the barn and never heard them calling for him; the time he almost tumbled down the well but got his foot tangled up in the bucket rope, which saved him; the time he found a toad and put it in his mother's drawer where she kept the good linen, because he thought it was the nicest place in the world for a toad to live. Anette loved the stories and could have listened to them forever, although Tor didn't seem to enjoy them. He watched his mother anxiously, and Anette didn't know what he was afraid of, only that he relaxed when his mother stopped telling the stories and decided it was time to go back home to get supper. That was when his mother was brisk and more like, well—a mother, and Tor looked almost like his old self.

Anette had never really paid much attention to Tor at school, other than to take Fredrik's side against him whenever the two brothers bickered. Tor was just one of the big boys, outside of her thoughts. He was friendly, he was helpful to Teacher, but he was older and smarter and almost gone from the schoolhouse anyway.

But now it was different; they shared something, it seemed to Anette. Even though he didn't say much to her—really, he didn't seem all that interested in her, his attention was all on his mother during the visit. Still, when he gruffly said goodbye, Anette knew she didn't imagine some connection between them, some different way he looked at her—as if seeing inside her, straight to her grief. And there was something to that look that made her miss Fredrik less, that night.

But she wouldn't see Tor again, not for a very long time.

She wouldn't be going back to school for a while, not with her wound that, while getting better, still was a long way off from allowing her out of doors. By the time she got back to school, Tor would be gone, working in the fields. Taking the place of his father.

Anette began to get restless, stuck in the bed. Now that she was awake and aware, she was very uncomfortable with Mother Pedersen's nursing. To have this woman, who had never before uttered a kind word to her, bathe her was embarrassing to the extreme. Anette wished she could bathe herself but she couldn't yet manage it with one hand, although Doc Eriksen assured her that in time, she would be able to do almost everything she'd been able to do with two hands. For now, she had to squeeze her eyes shut so she didn't see Mother Pedersen's face when she removed her nightshirt and helped her into the tub, and rubbed at her, gently, with a big sponge and soft soap that smelled like lavender. Anette did like the soap; she'd never known anything like it, a soap that did not hurt her skin, something so fragrant it made her smell nice for days after. Sometimes Mother Pedersen dabbed at Anette's neck and wrists with cologne, and Anette giggled and felt very grown up. But still so strange! This new way of being treated lovingly, like a special guest, startled her almost more than it soothed her.

But then it began to worry her, no matter what Mr. Woodson said, with his letters promising all sorts of things she'd never imagined—money, schooling (which frankly terrified her). If Anette wasn't of use to anyone, if she couldn't work, who would want her? All those people writing—surely they would demand something back in return, cooking and scrubbing and cleaning and sewing, and how could she do that with only one hand? The last two years had taught her some things, mostly things she hadn't wanted to learn. But primarily it had taught her that, with the exception of Fredrik, the only thing people liked about her was her ability to work hard without complaint. It was her only value. And even that wasn't enough, because look at her own mother. Anette had always worked hard back in the dugout, but that hadn't been enough for her mother to keep her. And Mother Pedersen, before—before—

Anette understood that something had happened to her surrogate mother during the blizzard. Just as if Mother Pedersen, too, had been lost in it, turned around like she and Fredrik had been so that she had no idea what was earth and what was sky. Something had happened to change her, too. It was what made her prone to weeping when she caught sight of Anette's still-raw stump, the stitches still black against her skin. It was what caused her, one night when she must have thought Anette was sleeping, to creep in and kneel by the bed and lay an anguished head on the mattress and whisper, "I'm so sorry, you poor creature. Can you ever forgive me? I will never forgive myself." And then she'd sobbed noisily, as if there was an untapped well of bitter tears she'd just discovered within.

Anette didn't know what she should forgive, although she did feel pity for her, in a way. But she couldn't forget the harsh words and backbreaking work, either. The strange, stifling atmosphere in that house was gone, but it was, in Anette's mind, only banished temporarily, lurking outside like another inevitable storm. Maybe Mother Pedersen could change overnight, but Anette doubted it; it was more like one obsession had been replaced by another. Just as she'd once been violently angry, now she was sorry. And violently caring; her focus on Anette was almost suffocating.

Yet everyone treated Anette as if *she* were the one who
had changed. Teacher, too, was the recipient of this attention; people came from miles around to bring the two of
them presents, to shake Teacher's hand, to gaze in at Anette
as she lay there like a prize pig. Anette simply didn't under
stand it, even though Mr. Woodson tried to explain it to
her—the people had read about them in his newspaper. Mr.
Woodson had shared their stories, because he liked them
both very much and thought they deserved something special for what they'd gone through. He even showed her one
of his newspapers and she saw her own name in the tiny
black print. But still, she couldn't quite understand it all.

He was so nice to her, Mr. Woodson was! Nicer than anyone had ever been. He never failed to break into an enormous grin when he saw her. He was always glad to see
Teacher, polite enough to the Pedersens, but only when he
held Anette's hand did he laugh as if she brought him—joy,
was it?

He visited a lot, traveling back and forth from the big city
of Omaha, which he sometimes tried to describe to Anette,
but she couldn't grasp it. Tall buildings! Something called a
cable car that carried people about! Stores of untold riches
and goods—one entire store just for shoes! Another just for
hats! Many churches of many different kinds, people called
Jews, Bohemians, Italians, all with different customs and
languages and foods and ways of living, yet they were all still
part of one city! And when he began to tell her about a place
called New York that was about one hundred times the size of
Omaha, with even more cable cars and a place called Wall
Street where all the money in the United States was made—
she guessed he meant that was where all the dollars were
printed up and the coins produced by some kind of magic—

well! It all overwhelmed her imagination and she pleaded
with him to stop because her brain was too small to keep it
all in, which made him laugh heartily, although she didn't
know why.

Every time he visited he brought satchels of letters, baskets of fruit. The first time in her life that Anette saw a pine-
apple, she laughed so hard tears came to her eyes. Who could
eat such a prickly fruit, like a porcupine? But then Mr.
Woodson showed Mother Pedersen how to chop the top off,
slice away the prickly skin, and remove the core of sweet,
juicy fruit; and when they all tasted it, Anette thought she'd
never eaten anything so heavenly in her life. It tasted like all
the dreams she'd never had.

But sometimes, when he thought she wasn't watching,
Mr. Woodson would study her with a troubled frown. He
would look at her, then at Mother Pedersen, and shake his
head. As if he didn't quite trust the situation in front of his
own eyes. As if he somehow could see into the past, see how
it was before the blizzard. Then he would grow silent, and
thoughtful.

There came a day when Anette was allowed to sit in a
chair for an entire afternoon, with real clothes on, not a
nightgown. She'd expected to put on her old clothes, but instead there was a bright blue gingham dress with rows of
buttons up the back that Mother Pedersen fastened for her.
She had new underthings, too—pretty, snow-white underthings with little frills. And new black slippers with red ribbons across the instep—Anette could not stop looking at
them; she sat in the chair and extended her legs, pointing
her feet, admiring them. Her hair had been washed and
brushed. It was like a holiday, if she'd ever known what a
holiday was before, which she didn't. But that was how Mr.

Woodson described it, the day she got out of bed for the first time.

She heard Mother Pedersen flying about the house in her usual way, and once it was time to start dinner Anette came out of the bedroom on unsteady legs, gingerly crossing the floor in her pretty new shoes; she held her one hand against the wall for balance. She had no idea how long she'd been in bed; she'd never thought to ask, but her legs felt like jelly that hadn't jelled. Still, now that she was dressed and up, she knew she ought to be helping get dinner.

"Anette! What are you doing?" Mother Pedersen asked, aghast, as Anette tried to grasp a pail; she could at least bring in some snow to melt on the stove.

"Helping."

"You sit right down! You're too weak. Let me." And Mother Pedersen snatched the pail from her hand with something like her old anger, and marched outside to get the snow, bringing it inside to melt by the stove.

"I—I don't know. . . ." Anette had no idea what to say, how to ask the question she was desperate to ask: Would she be able to stay here, now that she couldn't work so much? If not, where would she go—who would take her in? She just wished someone would explain it to her. Mr. Woodson might be able to tell her, but he wasn't here today, and Teacher wasn't yet back from school.

"You don't know what?" Mother Pedersen—obviously harried and tired—snapped. But then she caught herself, brought the back of her hand up to her red face as if to cool it, and presented a forced, but not malicious, smile to Anette. It struck her that Mother Pedersen, too, was uncertain about how to proceed with this new—softness?—between them.

"I don't know—"

But then there was a knock at the door. Mother Pedersen frowned, put down the skillet of cornbread she was about to slide into the hot oven, and dashed to answer it, muttering, "Now what?" All the visitors were beginning to wear on her, Anette could tell.

Anette heard a commotion at the door, then a voice, a voice from her memory, or a dream, perhaps. Then into the kitchen rushed someone radiating emotion and exuding a familiar smell—a combination of potatoes and horse and sweat. Before she knew what was happening, Anette felt arms around her neck and for a moment, the world turned black as she was enfolded into those arms that might have once rocked her, but probably not. Still, the sensation she felt with them around her reached back to before she'd been born. It was both familiar and startlingly strange.

But her heart knew; her heart forced the cry of "Mama!" out of her throat before her mind could put everything together. Anette was astonished to feel a rush of tears flood down her cheeks; longing—pent up this last year and a half, longing for something she'd never truly known—nearly burst her chest wide open. She sobbed with pure relief, a feeling as basic as breathing, as natural as seeing, to be in her mother's arms.

Other emotions—anger, hurt—beckoned at her across this great gulf of belonging, but for now she shut her eyes to them. Wasn't this what she'd wanted? Wasn't this what she'd forbidden herself to cry for, because she knew it would never happen? And yet here she was!

"Mama!"

"My Anette! My poor girl! Oh, to have you in my arms again, my poor thing! What have they done to you?"

At this, Mother Pedersen began to sputter angrily. But before she could say anything, Anette's mama was pulling her down on her lap and rocking her, none too gently—Anette winced as her mother touched her stump too roughly—and Anette laid her head against her mother's shoulder and allowed herself to feel like someone's daughter again. Or maybe for the first time?

Because even as she fell into this womb-like embrace, she couldn't help but think that never, not once that she could remember, had she been cuddled and exclaimed over. Loved.

So why was her mother being so nice to her now?

CHAPTER 32

WHEN GAVIN WOODSON MADE THE NOW-FAMILIAR journey from the Newman Grove train station to the Pedersen homestead on a borrowed horse, lugging all the letters and gifts that were small enough to carry (Christ, this good deed of his, while it may have given him a conscience, a soul, and a heart, was about to break his back), the last thing he expected to find was Anette's mother sitting on a chair in the kitchen like a queen on a throne—and Anette cuddled on her lap.

Good Lord, the woman was ugly—that was his first, uncharitable thought. He actively flinched from her. His Anette—yes, that was how he thought of her now, with no embarrassment—was not a pretty creature, not at all. But she was not ugly, he would never hear her called that. She was as yet unformed; she still had time to grow into a beauty—he knew he had an idiot's touching faith in the transformative power of a few years. But when Gavin beheld Anette's mother, for the first time he doubted whether that would happen.

The woman hadn't seen a bath in weeks; her hair was greasy and scraped into a bun, and she had a round, porous nose, few teeth, heavy eyebrows. She obviously had not put on her good clothes for the occasion—then it struck him with horror that maybe she *had*. Misery and poverty clung to her like the ragged shawl she was wearing, the dirty apron, the soiled dress. She was the most pathetic creature he'd ever laid eyes on.

But there was a gleam in her eyes, which were small and shrewd. She smelled opportunity, that was immediately obvious even to someone who played poker as badly as Gavin did. Opportunity in the being of the daughter she had sold to the Pedersens a year and a half ago.

"Sold her for two chickens and a pig," Gunner confirmed when he came in from the barn a few minutes later. The two men were in the parlor, while Anette's mother fawned over the girl in the kitchen. "The woman sold me her child for livestock. I heard of the situation through a neighbor, that there was this family that lived about a day's ride away in a hovel. The mother was eager to get Anette out of the house— she didn't seem able to stand the sight of her; she didn't shed a tear when she left the girl here. We've not heard a peep from her since."

"Why did you do it? Why were you a party to this—" Gavin couldn't even find the right word, he was so disgusted by the entire transaction.

Gunner's face reddened; he turned away to pour himself some coffee. "For my wife—Anna—it's not quite so simple. You're from the city. You don't know how it is out here."

"No, I don't suppose I do." And Gavin didn't hide his sneer. He also didn't reveal that Raina had told him some of the story already, how Anette had been overworked by the Pedersens to the point of abuse.

And now this—what to do with this woman who obviously

thought to get her hands on the money being deposited in her daughter's name in a bank account in Omaha? Or maybe even wanted to take her back to the terrible place from where she'd come, and there was no way that Gavin Woodson was going to let that happen.

Over his dead body would anything bad happen to Anette.

Anette, who kept him coming back to the Pedersens time and time again. Anette who, in his mind, had assumed the characteristics of an orphan in a Dickens story. This little girl, so dear and amusing—she did not realize she had a sense of humor, which was one of her most endearing qualities. But she said the funniest things, like when he had given her a single glove, right hand, of course; the left glove thoughtfully missing. Anette mused that perhaps there was someone out there with two left hands who needed an extra glove. Or when he told her that someone had wanted to give her a piano, and she laughed and said she'd never been able to play before and she certainly couldn't now, could she?

The funny little waif had stolen his curmudgeonly old heart. His maiden of the prairie—the original one—was only a distant memory. But the idea she had inspired was still with him and was now embodied in this little girl who had suffered mightily, and not only in the blizzard. When Gavin was back in Omaha writing these stories, the stories that were driving subscriptions through the roof, the stories that might, if he were lucky, get him back in the good graces of Pulitzer back East, he fretted about Anette. He wondered if she was going to bed early enough. He worried if she was eating healthy, hearty food—the Pedersens didn't seem pinched for money, but, still, he could never know for certain. Anna Pedersen acted like a woman who had repented for a great sin—almost too eager to please, to nurture, to nurse. She seemed genuinely sorrowful, desperate to atone for her past behavior toward the little girl, but a woman like that, well—Gavin knew women like that, or so he believed he did. Women who had relied on their looks for so long that they'd gotten spoiled and selfish. And then, too, she was obviously a hothouse flower plunked down in the middle of the cold, withering prairie soil. What resentment she might have about that he couldn't begin to know—but he could guess.

But as long as Raina remained there to watch over her, he was reasonably assured of Anette's well-being. However, Raina couldn't stay forever. School would be out in the early spring, in time for planting, and Raina now had options before her: proposals and money and an education, the world was truly hers for the taking. She would leave the Pedersens. And where would that leave Anette?

That Gavin could take her in, make her his ward—again, something out of Dickens—did cross his mind. But his situation in Omaha—a stifling room in a boardinghouse—didn't seem proper for a little girl. What he wanted for her was a life she'd never known nor could ever have expected before the storm and its aftermath—a life of ease, of love, of stability. Gavin couldn't provide that. He was a man without close relations. He had no idea how to do family things like carving a turkey at Christmas or saying prayers at night or making sure children bathed often enough—Christ, he could barely remember to do that himself.

But who *could* be Anette's family? It couldn't be the Pedersens, no matter how penitent Mrs. Pedersen acted; not people who had bought this child for labor.

Spying Gavin, Anette beckoned for him to come into the kitchen, where she introduced him to her mother in her funny way. "The Newspaper Man," she declared, as if he were the only one in the world, the original. Suddenly the mother was gazing at him as if he was about to give her not just a chicken and a hog but an entire barnyard full of animals, and he recoiled. He didn't care how happy Anette was to see her, he was not going to let this woman get her hands on Anette or her money.

But how could he prevent it?

"I am Mrs. Thorkelsen," the mother said with ridiculous dignity. Then she dabbed at her eyes with a grubby handkerchief. "Ah, so good, this man!" Raina, who was home from school by now, translated. "You see my poor, poor child, my daughter? What she has been through? The loss of her hand? And she almost died? These people!" Mrs. Thorkelsen gestured angrily at the Pedersens. "I gave Anette to them thinking they would give her a better life than I could—see my sacrifice? How I suffered, the mama? But not as much as my poor daughter."

"You—you—" Anna Pedersen could barely contain her fury; her hands were fisted, her face nearly purple. She kept glancing at the stove in the kitchen for some reason. But she managed to swallow her angry words, because of Anette.

"And now, thanks to you and all those kind people from the newspaper," Mrs. Thorkelsen continued smugly, "we won't have to suffer again, will we, *min datter*?"

Gavin took a step backward; his nostrils flared as she smiled a mostly toothless, cunning smile. "We? What do you mean, *we*?"

Anette's mother stopped smiling. She pushed her child off her lap so she could stand up, her hands on her hips—

And Gavin shuddered at the undistilled hatred in her small, shrewd eyes.

CHAPTER 33

. . . . . .

Anna's nerves were strung so tightly, she thought she might fly apart if anyone brushed against her. Her household had been disrupted enough by the events of the past weeks, what with Anette taking over the bedroom— she didn't begrudge her that, no, it was the least she could do for the child she had maimed. But there was also the fact that she and Gunner had to sleep somewhere, and she'd banished him to the parlor while she slept with her children; Raina was still upstairs in the attic. And then the Newspaper Man, always underfoot now, bringing more and more *things* into the house, things that needed to be stored somewhere the letters and toys and clothes and odd trinkets like the beads the Catholics used for prayer, someone's mother's old Bible, framed needlework samplers spouting prayers. Even a milk cow—well, that was actually useful, and the cow was a welcome addition to the barn. But the house simply couldn't hold any more of these things, yet they still came, along with *him*.

The Newspaper Man. He had turned their lives upside down more thoroughly than the blizzard. What would happen to Anette—to them all—after the blizzard, Anna hadn't had time to imagine, not in all the turbulence of the sick-room. But even if she had, she'd never have been able to imagine this—the sudden, unwanted glare of notoriety.

People—strangers as well as neighbors—came knocking on her very door asking to see Raina or Anette, "the hero-ines"! As if they could just stare at the two, like animals in the zoo back in Kristiania. As if she, Anna Pedersen, would be happy to let them trample all kinds of slush and snow into her house, would be thrilled to be ignored, treated as a hired girl, in order to satisfy the incomprehensible hunger to be-hold two ordinary humans who had survived an extraordi-nary situation.

Yet even as her skin pricked with resentment—no one ever asked about Anna, no one ever complimented *her* or praised her devotion—she was also consumed by guilt. Every time she remembered the sight of that pail, gleaming in the snow, she had to sit down, press her handkerchief into her mouth to stifle her cry. She had banished the pail to the barn, where Gunner could use it for slop. She would buy An-ette a new one—a shinier, bigger one—when she went back to school. And a new slate, too, and new dresses, hair rib-bons, stockings—anything, to atone for her sins.

But it wouldn't suffice; she would still have this gaping, pulsating hole within, a hole where her goodness, her Chris-tian charity—her untouched soul—used to reside. She could never make it up to Anette. She was going to hell, and Anna did believe in hell, the old-fashioned kind she was taught in the Lutheran church. Demons and flames and eternal suf-fering.

Unless . . .

She could have another chance.

She'd not told anyone—least of all her husband—but she

was determined that Anette remain with them despite the opportunities the Newspaper Man brought with every visit: offers from well-off people to adopt Anette, give her an education, not to mention all the money being set aside for her future. It wasn't the money that Anna desired, it was the chance for redemption. Fierce was that determination—it propelled her about the sickroom just as her fury at Gunner and the Schoolteacher used to fuel her housekeeping before—to give Anette a good life, the best life possible. She would do what she could to try to make up for the loss of the limb; she would help her with her lessons, provide her with the best food, pretty clothes; she would curl the girl's hair, massage creams into her rough skin, turn her into a living doll, anything to make up for the fact that she was forever less than whole.

Because what good was a woman if she wasn't complete? What man would have her? Anna had been brought up to believe that a woman was only as prized as the man who made her his wife. Of course, that belief made her tie herself to a man who was enviable on the surface, but underneath, weak as pudding. Still, she couldn't shake her upbringing.

In maiming Anette, she had spoiled any chance the girl might have for a good marriage. So it was up to Anna to fix her as best she could—to save her. And in doing so, she would save herself.

The moment she opened the door and beheld Anette's mother—that horrifying hag, that heartless shrew—Anna's mind started whirling, trying to stay one step ahead of her. This was danger. This was evil; evil as black as Anna's own.

Maybe that's why she recognized it instantly.

"You see my poor, poor child, my daughter? What she has been through?" Mrs. Thorkelsen was saying now as she cuddled Anette—actually putting the girl in a kind of stranglehold. The Newspaper Man looked at her skeptically. "And now, thanks to you and all those kind people, we won't have to suffer again, will we, *min datter*?"

"What do you mean, *we*?" the Newspaper Man replied.

Anna watched as the hag shoved Anette off her lap and rose to glare at the Newspaper Man, who took a step back, unprepared for the look of repulsion in the woman's eyes.

Fool, Anna thought. What a fool that man was. He was not a worthy opponent for this woman, despite his big city airs and his words in the newspapers that had lured her here in the first place—couldn't he see how he himself was to blame? No, of course he couldn't; he was just a man. It would take a woman to save Anette.

"I assume you're after the money?" Anna asked the woman, ignoring the sputtering Newspaper Man. Raina and Gunner were also in the kitchen now but silent. Witnessing.

"I am only concerned about *min datter,* who has suffered so in your care, losing her hand! Almost dying! I will take her with me and give her all that she desires, thanks to the kind people. The things only a mama can provide."

"Oh, Mama!" Anette's little face radiated joy—Anna had never seen her look this way. The girl had never smiled, she had never laughed before the blizzard. But first the Newspaper Man, and now the arrival of her mother, had done this. Transformed a sullen—no, desperately unhappy—creature into a real child. One who could laugh and smile.

One who knew that she belonged to someone—Anna's heart pinched with guilt again, remembering how she'd treated the girl from the start.

"You really have come for me then, Mama? You really do want me? And we can go back home?"

"Yes, or maybe even—how would you like to go some-where else, just you and me? Maybe not back to the old place, not back to that bast—your stepfather? Maybe we start over somewhere nice, just the two of us?"

Anette nodded and buried her face in her mother's bosom. She began to cry, softly, but they were tears of hap-piness. Anna couldn't bear it, she couldn't look at this heart-rending tableau—the mother was now patting Anette on the back, murmuring *"Min datter, min datter,"* over and over; she even managed to produce touching tears. Crocodile tears, more like it.

Oh, Anna knew this woman. And she could imagine, too well, what would happen if she took Anette away. She'd burn through all the money, she'd drag the girl from flophouse to flophouse, she'd never see that Anette got an education. She would most likely sell her again, but by that time, Anette would be a young woman. And the kind of selling that en tailed made Anna shake with fury. It took all her self-control not to tear that hag's eyes out right now.

Anna glanced at the others—Raina, Gunner, the Newspa-per Man. Their faces, too, revealed their fear—but also their helplessness.

"She is her mother." Raina was the first to break the spell; she spoke in English, so Mrs. Thorkelsen couldn't under stand. But the woman was so busy clucking over her daugh-ter, she didn't take notice—she was putting on a show, staking her claim—and Anette was loving it, believing every false declaration of endearment and devotion. *Ach,* that poor child! Another thing she must do—teach Anette not to be so gullible.

"A mother can take her own child," Raina continued. "What can we do?"

"We signed no papers," Gunner admitted. "Legally, Anette is not ours. I doubt there are any birth certificates or marriage certificates in that woman's possession—papers don't seem to mean much out here, other than land claims—but if this went to any kind of court, no judge would deny that it's the mother's right to take Anette back."

"I'll be damned if she takes her," grumbled the Newspaper Man. "She sold her own daughter. She'll take the money and the girl and run, and we'll never find Anette again. That is not going to happen, I promise. I can . . . I can write something up about her in the newspaper, expose her for who she is." But he, too, looked helpless in spite of his anger, and Anna snorted. A pen, mighty as his appeared to be, was nothing on the prairie. It was no weapon against the basest elements of humankind, and those were what the prairie brought out in people. There was no refinement here. Only the elemental instincts and emotions: greed, evil, might, right. A pen was no weapon against a determined woman.

Pffft!

Anna had no time for these blathering idiots who couldn't see the danger in front of them, who held on to useless niceties and legalities and idealistic notions of mother love. Turning her back on them—her gaze lingering, just for a moment, on the stove in the kitchen—Anna sighed. She really had enough to do with all these people in the house—cook, clean, sew, nurse—and now this cunning wench disguised as a pitiful mother. Anna thought that Raina, at least, would have had more sense. But no, it would be up to her alone.

"It is time for dinner," she announced, putting an end to all the babbling. It hurt her ears, it made her skin itch, all these stupid people in her house. "Anette needs to eat so she can go to bed and get her rest." Anna shooed them all out of her kitchen, grabbed the skillet of cornbread and shoved it into the oven.

The sooner these idiots were fed, the sooner they would go to sleep.

And then she could do what must be done.

CHAPTER 34

. . . . . .

PEOPLE DISAPPEAR IN THE PRAIRIE. THAT IS ONE THING everyone understands from the moment they get off the train. Just one look at the endless, unmarked land stretching out on either side of the tracks—no buildings in sight, no fences, just space—and a person can't help but think that it is a good place to vanish, willingly or unwillingly.

Indeed, it was not unusual to hear of people who had walked away from home, never to be seen again. Every community had its tale—the man near Gibbon who had been surveying his withering crops, last spotted with a scythe in his hand walking through the rows of dust-choked stalks. Never to be seen again, despite notices put up by his frantic family. The mother up around Beatrice who put her baby down for a nap, went out the door with a bucket for water, and never returned. The baby was found by its father, red in the face from crying all day but otherwise unharmed.

Bodies, frozen to death in a blizzard, swallowed up by it— some would be found come spring. But others wouldn't; those who had been caught in remote areas, trapped in gullies or ravines or ground caves where the snow took longer to thaw, where people wouldn't necessarily be searching. Perhaps bones would be found, a year or so later, stripped of identifying flesh, clothing long torn away, only a few remnants of fabric left and that weathered beyond recognition. There were wolves, of course. Cougars.

The Great Plains were immense enough to inspire the grandest, most foolish of dreams—but they were also vast enough that no one could ever explore every corner. Some people disappeared because they wanted to, because they recognized an opportunity to start over somewhere else with no risk of being traced. Some vanished because they simply gave up.

And some people disappeared because someone else wanted them to.

Anna Pedersen had one chance for redemption, that night. One chance to make up for everything she'd ever done to Anette. One chance to ensure the girl the future she deserved because no one else seemed able to.

By acting, she wouldn't redeem her own soul—she would further destroy it. But she was already damned for eternity. What was one more sin upon her shoulders, to bear for the rest of her life here in this cursed place?

She was strong enough.

It was easy to get the mother outside—simply whisper that she was going to be given a gift of a horse, one of Gunner's prize mares; it was only the beginning of the bounties awaiting her. That beast she'd ridden, it should be shot. But she should come with Anna now, since Gunner had already bedded down the horses for the night. Raina was upstairs, the Newspaper Man gone back to town. It was a secret gift, between two women! Anna would make sure she got to pick the best horse; if she waited for Gunner to do it, he would try to talk her into an inferior nag, not worthy of her.

Anna glanced at Anette, who was sleeping peacefully as her mother sat on the side of the bed, gazing about the room, most likely wondering what she could fit into that ragged carpetbag of hers.

Mrs. Thorkelsen—she never gave her first name and Anna was glad for that—nodded eagerly and obediently followed her outside. She gabbled on about the money, how good life would be from now on—occasionally she caught herself and thought to mention how good life would be for *Anette* from now on. But mostly she talked of clothing for herself, a house, a carriage, more food than she had ever eaten before, cakes and cookies and enormous joints of beef. A life of ease and luxury, that's what she would have! And no more men—she laughed about that and Anna begrudgingly chuckled, as well, woman to woman. No more men! She wouldn't need a husband now!

After they were inside the barn, the door latched behind them, Mrs. Thorkelsen scurried up and down the stalls, perusing the horses as if she were the judge at a livestock show. Anna watched her, let her take the time to choose—that one, the little black mare with the white diamond on her face. She would do just fine—what an elegant horse!

Anna nodded. As she walked over to where the woman was standing and smiling at her prize, Anna reached into her apron pocket. The cool metal of the gun soothed her once more—mesmerized her, as it had when she'd trained it on Gunner that night of the blizzard. The blizzard that was, she realized, not merely a storm but also the physical manifestation of the torment of her own soul, the turbulent struggle for it bursting out and over the prairie. She, Anna, had stirred up the very gods, dooming her to hell while they had destroyed children like Fredrik and taken Anette's hand.

She knew her fate, and she knew Mrs. Thorkelsen's.

The woman never grasped it, though—she had no time to see the flash of steel, Anna's finger curling around the trigger. She must have felt the muzzle against the back of her cloak, for Anna knew she had to muffle the sound as best she could. But Anna pulled the trigger quickly, and the woman fell without a sound, although the horses did react and so Anna had to run from stall to stall, soothing them, praying Gunner wouldn't hear and come out—how stupid, she hadn't thought of the horses!

But he didn't come out, and soon she had them quiet again, and all Anna had to do was haul the woman's body over the swaying back of her pathetic mule that had been stabled. She was heavier in death. Anna struggled, her muscles quivered, but she managed it—and then, bundling up in Gunner's coat and hat and gloves and boots, which she'd stashed away out here after dinner, she led the beast out of the barn.

Turning her head against the slight wind—it wasn't so bitterly cold, it was simply a February night in Nebraska—Anna led the unsteady mule with its silenced burden out on the prairie. Anna's feet swam in her husband's boots, making the journey more difficult. She glanced up, grateful for the full moon illuminating her path. She led the mule out for what seemed like miles, before she reached a small ravine, far from any homestead in the area. After studying it for a long moment, she began to dig out the snow, two or three feet of it—it took longer than she thought it would. Her hands, even in Gunner's rawhide work gloves, grew numb with cold, and her arms ached.

Finally, she had carved out a well large enough for the body of a small, hateful woman. She dumped Mrs. Thorkelsen into the snowy grave, and suddenly Anna felt nauseated. She saw once more the small, almost blue body of Fredrik Halvorsan lying in a similar grave, next to Anette. But then she closed her eyes for a moment, and when she opened them she found she could get on with her work. She pushed and kicked the snow over the body until it was completely covered.

She was hot now, perspiring beneath the heavy coat. But she would cool off on the walk back home—she slapped the mule, sending it stumbling farther out on the prairie. It wouldn't last more than a day or two and then it, too, would be a pile of bones come spring. There was no saddle on it; she'd remembered to unbridle it, so that there was nothing identifiable, just in case.

And it would snow again, soon; she sniffed the air. It had that heavy, moist scent. Oh yes, it would snow again soon, and cover every track.

Satisfied now—content that she had saved Anette once and for all—Anna was resigned to her own fate. But she wasn't in any hurry to meet it, so she kept the pistol in her pocket as she started the long walk back to her house. She would get there before dawn, the household still asleep. She would clean herself up, take the woman's carpetbag and hide it somewhere until she could burn it. Then she would sneak into the makeshift cot next to her children where she'd been sleeping for weeks now. Gunner would never notice she hadn't spent the night inside.

There would be questions in the morning—but not too many. No one would be sorry that the mother was gone; Anna could easily make up a story about giving her some money and sending her back, everyone would believe her. The mule, of course, would be gone, too. Anette might be sad, but not for long. After all, she'd been abandoned before.

Soon everyone would be gone from the house: the Newspaper Man, the Schoolteacher, Anette. She had to give the girl up; she'd saved her life twice now. That was enough. Someone else—someone without a mortal sin on her soul— would have to see the girl through to adulthood. So it would be just her family again, no interlopers, no strangers coming to gawk. Anna felt a soaring within, anticipating the house back to normal, everything polished and shiny, everything—and *everyone*—in its place. Including the pistol, tucked back in the loose brick behind the stove, where it would remain until the next time she needed it. Now she understood why her sister had given it to her before she left Minneapolis. In the city she would have had no use for it. But out here, well—

Out here, a woman needed an ally that would ask no questions. And tell no tales.

Anna stopped for a moment, halfway home; she stood, breathing heavily, and she looked up at the sky. The moon was so bright that she could see her shadow, but even so the stars were visible, and so numerous she gasped. How had she never looked up at them before? The prairie sky was a dazzling display of flickering ice, leaving scarcely any room between the stars. She felt that if she was up there among them she wouldn't be able to take a step without touching one—she raised her hand, pointed a finger, imagining how cold they must be, icy to the touch, so far away from the sun.

There was a low hooting sound, an owl, off somewhere. Dropping her gaze from the illuminated sky, Anna searched for it but saw nothing but the tundra encircling her. She was the very middle, the eye. The frigid, frosty land stretched in all directions, and it was beautiful—graceful, even. Fingers of dried tallgrass broke through the snow and waved gently; there were little dips and swales, like on a cake gaily frosted. The excited whisper of loose snow dancing in the distance. The feeling of being the only person in the world—Anna loved that feeling, and she wondered why she'd never thought of looking for it out here.

My God, but the prairie is beautiful, she thought. *One day I, too, might disappear in it.*

Placing her man-sized boots into the tracks she'd made on the way out, she continued to walk toward home.

CHAPTER 35

Bᴙ ᴛʜᴇ ᴛɪᴍᴇ sᴘʀɪɴɢ ᴀʀʀɪᴠᴇᴅ ᴏɴ ᴛʜᴇ ᴘʀᴀɪʀɪᴇ, ᴡɪᴛʜ the Chinook winds sweeping over snow-smothered plains, snaking along the frozen creeks and up the sandhills, rattling houses anew, it was the melting that people worried about. And indeed, that year there was massive flooding, entire towns afloat, creeks rushing over their banks and turning soddies into muddy memories. But that was part of a prairie spring, everyone was prepared for it. After the snow came the floods, then the jolting dry, the spring fires, the summer and the grasshoppers and then the fall fires . . . it went on and on. It was simply what happened.

By the end of spring, life had, for the most part, returned to normal. The dead were buried. There were always dead after a prairie winter; babies who couldn't survive, the elderly. The weak were ripe for the picking in the depths of the prairie winter.

This year, there were just more healthy people lost. And too many children.

More empty places at tables, fewer hands to try to work the fields after the floods finally abated. Schools emptied out anyway in the spring, so the surviving children could help with the planting. By then, they'd all gotten used to the empty desks.

To be sure, when the snows melted, bodies were found, and there was a fresh round of grief, but it was muted. These bodies had already been mourned by the practical souls of the plains. No one still held out hope that a lost loved one was simply waiting for a bout of good weather to return home after sheltering in some stranger's house. So more funerals, more burnt cork to blacken the coffin, but at least now the ground was softer, the digging easier, everything sped up so they could get back to what was important, what was *life*—the spring planting.

At the few celebrations that spring—a wedding here, a christening there, church when people could be spared from the fields—it was noted, ruefully, how many incomplete people were there. Friends and relations missing ears, wearing hats pulled down low to cover up the raw wound. Grotesque holes where once there was a nose. Missing digits abounded; it was almost, but not quite, rare to see someone with ten fingers or ten toes, they joked. They grew used to wooden hands, like the one Anette Pedersen sported proudly.

To wooden boots, like the one that Gerda Olsen stomped about on, miserably.

But those who experienced the storm would never forget it; they would pass the stories down from one generation to the next, and they wouldn't embellish them because they didn't need to. And embellishing was not their way regard-less.

Life must go on.

But many lives had irrevocably changed. Some for the better.

Most not.

THE HALVORSAN FARM CONTINUED to eke out an existence. Tor did not go back to school, although he was missed. Raina went out to the house one day before the spring term was over. She needed to talk to him, to see for herself how the family was doing—she couldn't quite explain why. It was part of her general leavetaking, she supposed; she felt a compulsion to wrap things up before journeying back to her family and all that awaited her there—most important, Gerda.

But she wanted to see Tor and Mrs. Halvorsan, she wanted one last chance to say how sorry she was for their losses. She no longer felt responsible for Fredrik's fate, but she did feel, keenly, the family's grief because she had been witness to its inception, the first oozing cut of it.

When she walked to their house one warm spring day, after letting the children out—and smiling to see little Rosa being fought over as to which big boy would carry her home because she was still using a crutch—once again Raina marveled at how short a distance their house was from the schoolhouse. You could make out the buildings, the well, even the clothesline from the steps of the schoolhouse. It was a walk of about fifteen minutes.

Yet it had been a lifetime that day in January.

Mrs. Halvorsan was out hanging clothes when she saw Raina coming; the good lady immediately ran into the house but Raina smiled; she knew women, she knew there would be a plate of cookies or a slice of coffee cake, warmed up, waiting for her, with a cup of tea. It was inconceivable to allow a visitor inside your house without food to welcome her.

By the time Raina knocked on the door, carefully scraping the spring mud from her boots, Mrs. Halvorsan had smoothed her hair and put on a clean apron. She let Raina inside with a shy smile—that shy smile most prairie women had upon greeting guests, especially after a long winter, because they were so unused to company. By the end of summer, people would be freer with their smiles, their laughter. But the isolating, demoralizing winter was still too recent.

"Good, good, Miss Olsen, it is good of you to come! You have been on our minds!"

"I have?" Raina laughed, shook off her cloak, took the proffered seat at the kitchen table, sipped some tea. Two little Halvorsans—one looking so like Fredrik that her heart seized, just for a moment—were chasing each other about the kitchen but all it took was for Mrs. Halvorsan to glance at them once and say, "It is the *Teacher*!" and they quieted down.

"They will be at school next term," Mrs. Halvorsan said proudly. "So you can teach them!"

"That was one reason I wanted to visit," Raina said, shifting uncomfortably in the narrow ladder-backed chair. "I won't be back next term. I've given my notice."

"Oh, heavens." Mrs. Halvorsan appeared truly distressed; she twisted the apron in her lap and there was a flash of tears in her eyes that she turned away to hide, but not quickly enough. Then she tried to laugh at herself. "I cry so easily these days."

"That's understandable—so do I," Raina admitted, reaching over to clasp the woman's hand. It was a hand that was red from scrubbing, the fingers long and sinewy, very little fat in the pads. There were shiny spots where burns—from cooking—had healed. The nails were short, but not dirty. There was strength in this hand.

"I am sorry you won't be back. But you have so many nice things ahead of you, I don't blame you." The woman turned to face Raina, the tears wiped away. "Get away from here while you can. Once you break the ground with a hoe, you will never be able to leave." And she looked out the window, to where Tor was in the fields, slapping the reins against an ox pulling a plow.

"I love the prairie," Raina said, and it was true. She loved the beauty of it, the wide openness, the songbirds and flowers, the waving, russet grasses in the fall. The shadows falling across the land, like patchwork, as the clouds danced beneath the sun. The people. But she still felt trapped like an insect beneath a glass jar whenever she truly took in the scope of it. Despite its optimistic vastness, there was little to do with it but stay and plow and hope for the best.

"I love it, but I am excited to go to college. I'm going to Lincoln on a scholarship to the Latin School there, to prepare for the university in two years. I'll be able to save the sum I was given, by all the kind people. And that's what I wanted to see you about—I don't think I deserved all that. Tor was just as responsible for getting the children here safely. Mrs. Halvorsan, please, won't you let me give Tor some of the funds so he can go to college, too?"

"Tor? College?" Mrs. Halvorsan was so startled, she had to clutch the table for support. She rose and rushed to the window to watch her oldest son in the fields. She stayed there for a very long time, and when she finally turned around, her eyes were shining, proud. "You think he could get in? The entrance exams—like to this Latin school?"

"He could if I helped him study, and I would be privileged to."

"My Tor! In college—imagine!" Again that shining light in her tired but resolute eyes. She shook her head and repeated herself. "I wonder what he could be? Maybe a doctor, you think?"

"Maybe." Raina smiled.

Then Mrs. Halvorsan's smile faded; she looked around the small house until her gaze fell on the kitchen table where Raina still sat. Once, there had been a father at the head of that table. Now the chair was empty. Once, there had been another boy—still needing to grow into his strength, but he would—to help out.

Now there was only Tor. For several years, it would be only him; the other children were too young.

Raina understood the struggle evident on the older woman's face—the pride, the unexpected gift of opportunity. The reality of the money and time already sunk into the homestead, which was theirs now, outright; they had proved it up, it was a working farm now. Could she afford to hire hands to do the work when Tor was gone? Raina didn't know but suspected not.

"I would never stand in the way of any of my children," Mrs. Halvorsan was saying, as if to herself. "That would make me a bad mother. But now . . ." And she didn't have to say more.

"I can't presume to know how it is here, now that Mr. Halvorsan and Fredrik are gone. I know that they are missed, for so many reasons. All I can do is offer this to Tor."

"I will let Tor decide," Mrs. Halvorsan said reluctantly.

Raina didn't know if she was fearful that Tor would take the offer or that he wouldn't, and maybe Mrs. Halvorsan didn't know this herself. The thing was, as she herself had learned ever since Gavin Woodson showed up at the Pedersens' door, choice and opportunity were not the uncomplicated gifts most people thought they were.

They were burdens, different but no less heavy than the burden of getting a good crop in, of fighting off a prairie fire, of worrying how to make it through a long winter with little fuel or food. The weight of making the right choice wore heavily on someone with a conscience.

"How is Anette?" Mrs. Halvorsan asked.

"Anette is doing well. Her hand looks very natural, especially when she wears long sleeves and gloves. She's learned to button herself up in the back with a special button hook that also helps with her shoes." Raina shook her head, remembering how quickly Anette had adapted to her loss, coming up with little tricks and cunning shortcuts—like jamming a knitting needle cast with yarn into a jar filled with dried corn to keep it upright, while she maneuvered the other needle with her one hand. This way, she could knit simple patterns, pot holders, and scarves. "Anette is just—stronger, somehow. I used to think that Fredrik was the one who gave her courage. She didn't seem to possess any on her own. But now I see that Fredrik just gave her the key to unlock it herself."

"And her mother?" Mrs. Halvorsan's brows drew together in disapproval. Raina had no idea how the neighborhood had heard about Mrs. Thorkelsen's visit, but somehow they had.

Raina still didn't quite understand what happened to Anette's mother; she simply didn't believe she could have been paid off, as Anna Pedersen insisted, by all the pin money she'd been saving up. And that she disappeared in the middle of the night, depriving herself of a touching scene of farewell for all to witness—that, too, made little sense.

"We've not heard anything more from her," Raina finally said. And that was the truth. "And Anette will be leaving the Pedersens soon. She's going to have a holiday in Omaha with Mr. Woodson! Then she'll go to boarding school in Lincoln, but I'll be nearby, so she won't feel so out of place. Mr. Woodson has found someone he knows in Omaha to be her legal guardian, to see to the trust that they put the money in, and protect it until she is finished with her schooling—I hope she will go to college, too, when the time comes. But she will be free to make her own choices—imagine all that! For Anette—it's simply wonderful."

"That is good." Mrs. Halvorsan nodded, clearly pleased. "That something like this happened because of my Fredrik— that is good." And she looked as proud as if it had been Fredrik himself offered a scholarship.

"Yes, it is. Now, I would like to discuss this with Tor, if that's all right with you?"

"Yes, do." Still Mrs. Halvorsan struggled, obviously, over the dilemma before her. This woman! To have lost so much in such a short time, to have gone through her own dark night of the soul, to emerge from it because of her oldest son who wouldn't let her succumb—and now to have to contemplate him leaving, as well. Even though it was for his own good. It could not be easy.

Nothing about this place was easy, even when good fortune fell from the sky, no less disorienting than a blizzard.

Raina bundled up in her shawl—it was spring, the sun shining, but still the winds carried the memory of winter.

She went out to find Tor, who, when he saw her coming, yelled at the ox to stop. He remained in the field, however, patiently holding the reins, so Raina had to pick her way through the mud, careful not to destroy any of the neat furrows he had already produced, ready for planting.

The earth smelled of manure and promise. The same promise it held every spring. Raina automatically said the farmer's prayer for a good crop this year. She would always be a farmer's daughter, she understood. No matter what fate awaited her in Lincoln.

As she approached, suddenly Raina felt shy; she and Tor hadn't spoken since his father died, when Tor had been so angry at her.

"Hello, Tor."

"Hello, Miss Olsen." Tor nodded respectfully.

"You look well—are you?" Anxiously, Raina studied him; he was taller, thinner than he was the last time she'd seen him. But his neck looked thicker, more like a man's; his jaw, too, had a set to it that hadn't been there before.

His eyes—

They shone softly with forgiveness, his gaze once again frank and blameless, and Raina had to look away, she was afraid to show him how joyful she was to see it.

There was a long pause, while Tor—like the man he suddenly was—looked at his boots, patiently waiting for Raina—like the woman she had become—to gather herself, blink away her tears. Then she turned to him and they smiled at each other, and Raina felt some missing piece of her heart settle back into place; it was a small piece, but surprisingly important.

"Tor, I've been talking with your mother. She seems so much better!"

"She does?" Tor looked so relieved, and Raina under-stood how much he had suffered this winter, not just with the loss of his brother and father, but with worry for his mother.

"Yes, she does! Almost like her old self!"

"I hoped—I thought so, too. But it is good to hear that from someone else."

"We've missed you in the schoolroom these past weeks."

Tor hung his head, gestured about him at the field. "Yes, but—you see how it is. I am the man here now."

"I know. It's not fair, but I know."

"I do miss school, though. I have some of your books, that you lent me—I've read them many times this winter, but I guess you want them back now?" He couldn't keep the hungry question out of his voice, and Raina smiled, pleased.

"No, you may keep them. They're not enough, though—it's not enough to reread something over and over again. Not for someone like you."

"Like me?" Tor looked up, astonished. Raina knew that he had never considered himself different from any farm boy. *Different, special, deserving*—these were not words that homesteaders, particularly Norwegians, approved of when discussing themselves or others. In fact, they rarely dis-cussed themselves at all; introspection was not an asset here.

"Yes, someone who likes to learn. I know you do, Tor. I saw it in the schoolroom, even though I only taught you for such a short time. And that's why I'm here. You see, I have—these funds. From those silly things in the newspapers." And now it was Raina's turn to blush.

"Yes, yes, I know. Did you really get a proposal from a rajah?" Tor grinned.

"Oh, goodness. Yes, and so many others! What fools they are. What kind of person do they think I am?" Raina's skin felt hot with anger. So much of the Heroine Fund had been ridiculous; the milk cow and the gold medals and the stories which were pure fabrication that others wrote about her. Mr. Woodson hadn't written anything false, but he had set the whole thing in motion, and the very worst part of it had been the ridiculous proposals of marriage. They made her feel too much on display; she found herself looking in the mirror too often, trying different ways of doing her hair, of curling the ribbons that she tied about her throat, which was also a new habit. They made her feel too special—and she was very much on guard against that feeling.

It was what had brought her so much trouble, earlier, with Gunner Pedersen.

"I am not going to marry anyone," Raina retorted, concentrating on the worms crawling out of the freshly turned earth, nudging a particularly fat one along with the toe of her boot. "In fact, I'm going to college. And that's what I wanted to talk to you about. I was hoping you would go to college, too. The money that is mine should be half yours. That is fair to me, and I asked those in charge if I could help with your education, and they said yes. I think you could get a scholarship, and the money could go to your room and board and maybe you could even send some back home."

"I—a—scholarship? College?" He looked so bewildered, so overwhelmed, Raina realized this was an idea he'd never even formed before; he'd never dreamed this. No boy his age, in his situation, in this place, dreamed such a thing. Tor dropped the reins of the ox, but the animal didn't move; Tor did, however. He began to walk up and down the furrows, making a mess of them, rubbing his forehead, and Raina wanted to tell him to stop, he was ruining his work. But she kept silent, allowing him to work out this monumental puzzle she'd just placed before him.

As she watched, she thought again how different the fate was of a boy versus a girl, a man versus a woman. There was a time—fleeting, like the flutter of a butterfly's wings—when women did have a choice, she realized. She'd never thought that before, but now she knew, there was that one moment, after school was over. The choice then—to become a teacher for a couple of years before marrying, or to stay at home—wasn't much of one, at that. But it was still a choice, a chance—a young woman could travel beyond her own farm, boarding out, meeting new people.

But on the prairie, most young men—these sons of immigrants—didn't have even that meager opportunity. The land waited, it was always waiting, for the next pair of strong hands, unbent back, sturdy legs and heart. It was only the odd ones—what little Gerda had said of her beau, Tiny, those like him—who got away from it at all. The land made boys become men too soon, turned young men old before their time, so it always needed more men.

Maybe it was different in the city—after all, she knew someone now from Omaha, and he wasn't a farmer; the notion of Gavin Woodson plowing a furrow made her want to double up with laughter. But while the geographic distance between city and homestead wasn't all that great, the landscape of possibility was impossible to breach.

"I don't know—college?" Tor stopped before her, scratching his head, his face red with excitement. "What did Mama say about it?"

"She said it was your decision."

"I don't know if it is. I'm not the only one that would be

affected. There's been too much—Papa, Fredrik—and there are the little ones. I can't think—what would happen to them if I wasn't here?"

"I can't answer that, Tor, and I can't tell you not to think of them, that wouldn't be right. But I also can't tell you not to think of yourself."

Raina allowed his big hands, not yet as rough as they would be in even a few months of this work, to grasp hers tightly; then he released them and sat down on the plow. He watched the ox standing so complacently. He looked up at the sky, squinting; he reached down and picked up the muddy earth he'd plowed. Then he looked back at his house, and Raina followed his gaze. Mrs. Halvorsan was standing in the kitchen window, gazing out at the two of them, but the glare on the window obscured whatever expression was on her face.

There was no sound other than the rustle of the wind, the constant music of the prairie, kicking up dust and rustling grass and causing clothes to flap on the line. But Raina could have sworn she heard gears turning in Tor's head. New, stiff gears, creaking in protest.

Finally Tor rose; he wiped his hands on his dungarees, and stood halfway between the plow and Raina. He looked back at the farmhouse.

"I can't," he said, shaking his head. "I know it's ungrateful of me, but I can't. I can't leave them, I can't leave the farm now that it's proved up, actually making a yield. It's still such a thin line, between good and bad here—success and failure, I mean. If there was more of a cushion, if Mama had the means to hire some hands, maybe. But even then, I think I would be torn, all the time—my head in school but my heart here. If I stay home, I'll be here, my whole self. I won't be missing anything. Do you see?" He looked so desperate for her understanding, maybe her absolution, that Raina could not let him know how disappointed she was. Unsurprised, but disappointed nonetheless. She wanted her time in the schoolhouse to have meant something to someone—like one of those preachy stories of how a teacher inspired a student to go on to greatness. But Tor's decision shouldn't be about her in any way, and she had to give him the gift of not letting him see her disappointment.

"Of course I understand, Tor. But I couldn't have lived with myself if I didn't give you the chance."

"Then it is good, between us?" Once more he reached for her hands.

"Yes, Tor, it is good between us." She smiled up at him and felt her heart twist a little. She would go off, come back sometimes to her own home to visit. But she couldn't see herself coming back here to this community—the Pedersens, the Halvorsans, the schoolhouse. And that was a shame, because here was a decent person whom she would always miss, even when she filled her life with other things, other people. Other goodness.

"You will write to me?"

He nodded eagerly. "I would like a postcard from Lincoln," he asked shyly. "If you can? I've never had a postcard before."

"Of course I will! As many as you want, for as long as you want. I wish . . . goodbye, Tor."

"Goodbye, Miss—Raina." He lifted his hand in farewell, as she picked up her skirts to trudge back across the land, still soft with melted snow, that softness that was so fleeting, for soon it would be as hard as pavement, baked dry. She headed toward the Pedersens', where her trunk was already packed, and in the morning Papa would come for her. Waving at Tor, she watched as he went inside the house to tell his mother his decision. And she moved over the prairie, feeling strange as she did so—almost as if she were a ghost, revisiting a lost life. Even though she stopped to pick flowers, sticking them in her hair like she was a little girl again; even though she paused now and then to inspect a gopher hole; even though she waded into a patch of prairie grass, not yet waist high, but still she felt the grasses tickling her knees, embraced that feeling, from her childhood, that if she just kept walking, she would be swallowed up, which might not be a bad thing.

And when she got to the ravine behind the Pedersens', she stopped to peer into it one last time, seeing once again the body of Fredrik Halvorsan. Then she shut her eyes resolutely to memory, marched across the log bridge—

And looked forward to tomorrow.

"RAINA IS HOME! RAINA IS HOME!" THE WORDS RANG
out like bells clanging as Mama ran outside to welcome her
daughter. Soon the little house would be filled with neighbors to welcome home the prodigal schoolteacher, and
Gerda was already planning her escape. She would take her
crutch and stomp around to the barn and hide out there until
the party was over.

She wasn't angry; she didn't begrudge her sister or her
parents their celebration. Mama and Papa deserved, finally,
to bask in the glow of a daughter who had done them proud.
Gerda no more had it in her to feel jealous of their happiness
than she had it in her to feel jealous of her sister. Her
emotions—dulled these last few months of confinement, of
banishment—never reached out to embrace or hurt anyone
else but herself. Her mind was a constant waterwheel, ever
churning up the same pattern of guilt, recrimination, the
desire to go back in time and change that fateful decision,
and fear for her future. It went round and round, churning
up the waters of her soul.

As soon as Mama flew out of the house to greet Raina,
Gerda took her crutch and a basket of knitting and slipped—

well, stomped—out the back door. The crutch still hurt beneath her armpit; it had rubbed her skin almost raw, despite all the various materials—calico, sheepskin—that Mama had tied on it, hoping to find the perfect one that wouldn't cause her daughter any extra pain. But nothing would help, except time, she supposed. In the same way that now the phantom pains of her missing foot had dulled to an ache, not electric jolts, the pain beneath her arm would dim, as well.

Gerda actually wished that it wouldn't.

She heard Raina's happy cry at seeing Mama, and then the voices dropped and she knew they were talking about *her*. Gerda could not bear it one more second, this constant discussion of what was to become of her, a conversation that never included her at all, for she was assumed, apparently, to be unable to make decisions anymore, since she'd made such a tragic one. She thumped hastily through the yard to escape it, scattering the chicks and chickens in her wake. Her movements were uneven as her new boot, strapped to the stump just above where her ankle had been, made such a heavy track in the dirt while her other foot left only the ball of it as an imprint. The heavy fake boot wasn't quite tall enough to match the length of her other leg so she was always slightly tilted, swaying as she walked.

The crutch wasn't necessary inside the house; there, she could hobble about enough so that she had two good arms to use to work, to help, to seek atonement through extra sewing, feverish sweeping, scrubbing the clothes on the washboard so intently, Mama teased her that she might scrub them into rags. Anything that she could do with her arms and one good leg, she would do, and do it better than anyone else, and maybe then Papa would look at her again with that pride in his eyes. So far, he had not.

He still couldn't meet her gaze; it made mealtimes especially awkward. He could talk to her, say her name, but he always looked down at his plate or the bread in his hands or his cup of coffee or at Mama. But not at Gerda.

She was almost to the barn now; there was a special little corner she had fashioned into a hiding place. It was silly, really, as if she were still a little girl, playing house with Raina. The two of them were always making a little playhouse out of corners and shadows, fixing it up with twig furniture and cups made of grass; they got so good at weaving these tiny fairy cups that they actually did hold water. What was it about children and hiding places? But here she was, eighteen, nineteen in a month, and she was still hiding away. During the winter, there had been no visitors, naturally. But once the thaws and the floods were through, some of the neighbors did come around, ostensibly to see how everyone had gotten through the winter, to ask if Mama's preserves had lasted, if they had any laying hens to trade for some seed—and to ask about Raina. But also, to gape at Gerda. She imagined they were hoping to find she'd grown a horn, or warts, or some outward symbol of evil. But she looked the same. The few that caught a glimpse of her always seemed disappointed by that. She didn't let many catch her, though.

Now she heard her name being called by Raina—"Gerda! Gerda?"—so she hobbled even faster to her corner, where there was a milk stool, a lantern, a blanket, some of her schoolteacher books. She reread them—she'd memorized them. Anything to try to take her mind off . . . things.

Or course, she couldn't teach again, not anywhere around here in northeastern Nebraska or Dakota. But she also couldn't imagine remaining in her parents' house much

longer. She couldn't forever blot out the sun that still shone
on her parents and her sister. She had received several letters that Mama and Papa would not allow her to read, they'd
burned them up without a word after they had read them
first, but she knew what was in them. *How could you? My son
is gone forever, my daughter. How could you do that to them?
How could you let them go to their deaths?*

Tiny's parents never wrote, however. Her parents never
spoke his name. She couldn't allow herself to, either, for
fear she would let slip the damning truth behind her actions
that day and kill her parents on the spot.

Sometimes she let her imagination loose, picturing herself older, odder every year that she remained here. Children would make up songs about her, cruel songs. They
would sneak around at night to see if they could catch a
glimpse of her—afraid but excited, too, to see her face. They
would shriek and run off in the night when she came to the
window to see who was throwing pebbles at it. In their telling, she would grow uglier and crazier each year, until she
was a witch, an ogress.

But also in her imagination, she sometimes saw herself
curled up on her bed, shrinking with the passing seasons.
Doing her best to take up less air, less space. Withering away
until she was like one of those creepy apple-head dolls that
Mrs. Kristiansen made, dolls with wizened, wrinkled faces
as if all substance had been sucked from them.

"Gerda!" Raina had crept into the barn while she'd been
arranging herself—not an easy thing to do—on the low milk
stool, preparing to wait out the party. "Gerda, you are trying
my patience—oh, there you are!"

There was scolding in Raina's voice. And other things—
adult things, maturity and weariness and resoluteness, too.

No nonsense. This was not the slightly singsong voice of the little sister she'd last seen months ago. Gerda steeled herself to look up into her sister's face.

There was no accusation in it. No hate. A steeliness—new—in her eyes, but it didn't obscure the love she'd always seen there. Her sister would never look up to her again, but she would still love her. And Gerda assumed that burden, too—just when had her family's love and care started feeling like the worst punishment she could imagine?

"Gerda, why are you hiding away? And oh—how thin you are!" Raina clucked like a mother hen; she shook her head. She was dusty from the trip, her braided bun slightly un-done, she hadn't even paused to splash water on her face. But she looked well; she looked pretty—prettier than she had when she left, her cheeks less full, her cheekbones more pronounced. She looked somewhat guarded, too; it was evi-dent that she had not come through these months unscathed emotionally. Gerda remembered her odd letters when she first left home, and she wondered.

Raina looked tested, that was it—and she'd obviously passed that test, spectacularly. The two of them had never been equals; Gerda had always been the leader, Raina the docile follower. But now their positions were reversed, their relationship redefined, and Gerda frankly didn't think she had the strength to adjust to its new parameters.

"I'm not hiding, I'm—" But then Gerda sighed. "Yes, I'm hiding."

"Not from me, I hope?"

"No, but from the others. You know Mama invited some neighbors to welcome you home."

"To show me off, you mean."

Gerda had to laugh. "Yes, that's what I mean."

"*Ach,* I thought I was through with all that, once I came home." And Raina slid down next to her sister, not caring that she was sitting in murky straw. She even took a piece of straw and began to suck on it, just like she used to when she was small. "I am tired of it, these people looking at me like I'm some saint. When all I did was what anyone would have done—" Then she stopped, and looked away.

"Why did you send them home, Gerda?" Raina finally asked the question that no one else had dared. In all this time, all the accusation and anger, no one had asked her *why* she'd let the children out early; they all just assumed she'd gotten confused in the storm and made the wrong decision, and that was bad enough.

But Gerda had been carrying the answer around in her stomach like a heavy stone; it weighed her down, it filled her up so that she couldn't eat, couldn't do anything but be aware of it, always. Here was a chance to give it to someone else, at least for a brief moment—and she took it, almost crying with the relief of unburdening herself.

"Oh, Raina—it was because of Tiny! I wanted to be alone with him, and I knew that the Andersons were going to be gone for the day, it was so nice, so much warmer than it had been—remember?" And Gerda shut her eyes and felt, again, the surprising gift of the soft air that morning, bearing with it promises. Promises of the future. "I told Tiny, that morning, that I was going to let school out early and he should come for me and the girls, and then the storm came. So suddenly! But the children were already wearing their cloaks and had all their slates and pails—I'd already rung the bell. I told them to run. As if they could have, those little things. Then I jumped in the sleigh with Minna and Ingrid and Tiny and we went off. Laughing—laughing, Raina! It seemed exciting, in that moment, to outrun the storm. But I did turn back, once. And I saw that the children had already disappeared in the snow and wind, and I worried, then. I wondered if I should make Tiny turn around so we could call them back. But I didn't. I told Tiny to keep going, I didn't want to spoil my plans. And that is why I am a criminal. A murderess."

"Oh, Gerda." Raina looked as shocked as a person could, and Gerda was glad. She'd longed to tell someone, but the only people around were Papa and Mama, and she just couldn't hurt them any more. But now that she had told Raina, she was strangely relieved and free.

"So you see, Raina, I am not like you, I'm not like anyone. I am evil. I am lost. I haven't told Papa and Mama this—about Tiny. I haven't told anyone. Just you. You're the only one who knows the truth about me." Gerda shifted on her stool; her lower leg ached in this position, but she welcomed the pain.

"It's good that you told me, you needed to tell someone. You're not bad, Gerda, you just let—you just let a boy turn your head for a minute." Raina seemed thoughtful; she tucked her legs up and hugged them against her chest. "That could happen to anyone."

"Not you. You wouldn't have endangered those children for a man."

Raina took a very long time to answer this. She opened her mouth to speak, shut it, then finally lay her head in her hands before looking at her again. "No, you are not evil. I—I almost ran off with a man. The husband of the family I boarded with. I tell you, Gerda, it was awful in that house, he paid me too much attention and I was a fool, I let him. The first man to give me flowers, I put all my heart in his hands. And one night, right before the storm—when it had been so cold, remember? And we couldn't leave the house for days, I thought I might go mad. He came to me and he told me we would leave, just the two of us. And even though he was a man who would leave his wife and family alone on the prairie—God help me, Gerda, I would have gone with him. I might have, I think. All that time in that house—those terrible weeks—I always asked myself, 'What would Gerda do?' Because you were the strong one, you always told me what to do, my sister." Raina reached for Gerda's hand.

"Why—what stopped you?"

"His wife. She came at him with a knife."

"Good Lord! I had no idea—your letters were odd, but I had no idea you landed in such an evil place." The two Olsen girls sat hand in hand for a long while. Gerda remembered their uncomplicated childhood, being loved, being wanted. How had these two, raised in such a manner, ended up here—both of them wracked with guilt over a man?

But just like a fairy tale, one sister remained good, while the other was branded forever.

"You didn't go," Gerda reminded her sister.

"I might have."

"You didn't. For whatever reason, you didn't."

"And then when the storm hit, I thought he would come for me and the children at the schoolhouse. I waited, hoping he would. But of course, he didn't." Raina raised her head and stared at the barn wall, tracking the movement of a small brown mouse that had poked its head out from a hollow in one of the slats. "Only when the wind blew the window out did I finally act on my own. I might have waited there all night, letting the children freeze to death."

"You didn't. You did the right thing in the end. Don't forget that, Raina. Don't ever forget that. I did not." Gerda embraced her guilt once more, returned to its rightful place in the pit of her stomach. Raina would walk around with little bits of it—the jagged, painful edges of knowledge—but this stone was hers alone.

"What do you plan to do now?" Raina asked after a long moment. "Teach again?"

"Not here, no. I can't. No one would hire me."

"You could—I could help you—let me help you!" Raina looked up, her eyes sparkling. "I could take you to Lincoln with me, help with your education. You could go to college, too!"

"No!" Gerda didn't mean to shout, but she couldn't bear this—her little sister so eager to help, to give her absolution. "No, Raina, no—you don't understand. I cannot stay in Nebraska."

"What do you mean?"

"I am outside now—an outcast. This community, they will not have me, nor should they. There's a pact out here, I've come to believe. Unwritten, but still. You don't think of yourself first. And you don't *want* too much. The people here—good people, don't get me wrong—they abide by these rules, they never ask for more than what Providence has given them. Other than sailing across an ocean to take a piece of the earth as their own, they have never asked for more. They have never thought of themselves first. But I did, you see. I broke the pact. I can't stay here."

"So where will you go, Gerda? Not too far away?"

"I have a plan, I think. I've written to the Bureau of Indian Affairs. Do you remember that school we visited long ago, where the little Indian children were? With Papa?"

"Yes, and Papa got so angry?"

"There are other schools like it. Out west—I mean to go

west. Tiny always wanted to—" Gerda felt tears threaten. It did not help that Raina immediately scooted over and put her arms around her; Gerda stiffened, tried to push her sister away, but Raina refused to let go and finally, Gerda dissolved into tears for her beau, missing him so much, more than she had thought she would. She missed the children, of course, but Tiny—the thought of him dying out there alone; they'd found his body up against a fence post, far from his pony's, he'd never even gotten close—caused her to muffle a scream of agony, feeling everything he must have felt. Terror, confusion, pain. Love and worry for her, too. She hoped.

The two sisters sat in this embrace for a long while, and finally, Gerda felt the last tears drain from her. She was cleansed, although this feeling wouldn't last. She would fill up again with the guilt and the grief and the shame, always the shame. As long as she had to look at her mama and especially her papa. So she had to leave. And live—alone.

How do you grow old on the prairie?

She wouldn't stay around long enough to find out.

"Raina? Raina!" Their mother was calling. Both sisters registered that she was only calling one of their names; Gerda smiled ruefully, already used to being forgotten. "Come, people are arriving!"

"Oh, I don't want to go!" Raina let go of her sister, and Gerda was amused to see her face in a familiar, childish pout.

"You have to," she admonished, for the last time the big sister scolding the little one; she wiped Raina's dusty face with her apron, tried to corral the loose locks about her face, tucking them into the braided knot at her neck. "Now stand up, wipe your eyes, put on a smile. Mama and Papa are waiting for you. You have to do this for them. For me."

"All right," Raina said reluctantly, scrambling up. "I must look a fright."

"You do, but such a pretty fright! And no one will care. They'll see what they want to see—the heroine of the prairie."

"Still, I need to wash up. You'll come in, too?"

Gerda shook her head firmly; she picked up a book and held it up. "They don't want me. They want you. I'm fine out here, believe me—content, even. In my own way."

"Well . . ." Raina looked doubtful.

"Raina!" It was Papa's booming voice now, and there was something in it that Gerda hadn't heard since she'd been home—pride.

"Go—go!" Gerda shooed her little sister away like she was a mouse. "You'll see me at supper."

Raina nodded, brushed the dust and hay off her dress, looked at her dirty hands with a shudder, and ran off to be welcomed back home—to be admired and petted. To be the joy of Mama and Papa.

Gerda returned to her book, settling down in her little corner.

Outside.

CHAPTER 37

A NETTE HAD NEVER BEEN SO OVERWHELMED IN HER
life. Not even when Mama took her to the Pedersens' and left
her there had she been so bewildered.

But this was different; this was a treat, she'd been told. A
holiday! Anette had no idea what a holiday was, but evidently
it was this—taking a train for the first time and oh, how terrifying it was! That great engine snorting and hissing and
belching black steam into the air. Told to step up and into
that live, sputtering monster, she hung back, frightened,
but Mr. Woodson took her hand and helped her in. They
picked a seat and he told her she could sit by the window as
if this was a prize, although she didn't really want to. But she
did, to please him.

The train started up with a shudder and more hissing,
more steam, and it took off, the wheels clacking, jolting her
in her seat as the car swayed from side to side. So fast! Too
fast! The landscape out the window started to rush by in a
dizzy, colorful blur. She didn't know which direction they
were going, forward or backward, and she squeezed her eyes
shut. Then she opened them, and the land rushed by her

again, greedily, but this time she kept her eyes open. Those tall poles—the telegraph, Mr. Woodson told her—seemed so close to the train, she was afraid they would hit them. There were times when the train slowed, then stopped, then other people got off or on before it sped up again, too soon. It kept going for a long time in this way—starting and stopping, starting and stopping, until they got to a great place with many tracks going in different directions, and other trains at rest but still steaming, and this was Omaha, Mr. Woodson said.

He got their bags—Anette only had one, because he said there would be things waiting for her at the house where she was going to stay until school started—and he helped her climb down the big steps. It felt strange to walk on ground that didn't move beneath her feet and for a few minutes she felt a little off-kilter. They walked toward a big house—it was the depot, he said—full of people. So many people! Anette had never seen so many people in her life.

Once, Mr. Woodson stopped and pointed to a cluster of families, all looking weary and defeated, waiting to get on one of the trains. "Homesteaders," he said, almost sadly. "Giving up, going back East or across the sea. A lot of them go back, you know."

Anette didn't know. She'd never been told how her mother had come to this new land, and she herself had been born here. That you could leave it had never seemed possible to her, until now.

When they exited through the doors of the crowded depot—people bumped into her, stepped on her feet, jostled her wooden hand, so she kept it close by her side—they got on what Mr. Woodson called a horsecar. It was a big train car only with wagon wheels, pulled by a horse, and it made many stops. It was full of people, too, mostly speaking English but so quickly and loudly that Anette couldn't quite keep up with it. There were other languages, though, mixed in; she did recognize a few snatches of Norwegian but then there were different words, with harsher accents, that she didn't recognize at all. And the people were all pressed together so tightly! She smelled their odors, some with food smells clinging to them that were unfamiliar to her—very pungent, sharp, some exotically sweet.

Then Mr. Woodson took her hand again, and they stepped down out of the horsecar and got on another, but this one was attached to some wires running overhead, and it went so fast! Not as fast as the train, but almost, and he said this was a cable car; it was new, Omaha was very proud of it, but back where he came from—New York City—they had many of these, he said so casually. As if it were not the most miraculous, terrifying thing he had ever seen! But by now, her senses were so overwhelmed all she could do was nod dumbly and hope that soon everything would stop and she could go somewhere quiet and sleep.

And that's what happened; they got off the cable car and walked a little way to a neighborhood with houses so close together, Anette marveled, and it made her uncomfortable. Was she supposed to live in a place like this, so close to other houses that you could see inside them? See how happy they were, all these fancy people?

These houses were so enormous, many families must live in them together—they had one, two, three stories! They even had large outdoor rooms stuck on them that Mr. Woodson, noticing how she stared at them, called verandas.

"Verandas," she repeated; it was such a pretty word, and she wondered if even Teacher knew it.

They went up the steps to one of these homes with a *veranda* that stretched around the corner of the house, maybe clear all the way around, she couldn't tell. They were welcomed inside by a man and a woman and the woman knelt beside Anette very tenderly, but she didn't put her arms around her, which Anette appreciated. Because she just didn't think she could stand one more unfamiliar sensation right then.

These people, the Johnsons, were what Mr. Woodson called her guardians, and when he said it, Anette caught a sadness in his voice. He had explained it to her when she'd asked why she couldn't live with him if she had to go to the city.

"Oh, you wouldn't want to live with an old bachelor, a working stiff like me," he'd sputtered, but he also looked pleased that she'd asked. "I have no business taking care of a little girl!" But he promised he would remain in Omaha for a while and show her all the sights before he went back to New York, so she would still see him. For a few weeks.

Anette didn't want to think about him leaving, not yet—so much had happened in such a short time! She was too tired to think—Mrs. Johnson saw that immediately while the two men stood chatting, and she rose with a cluck of her tongue.

"Oh, you two! Can't you see the little girl is asleep on her feet? I'm taking her up to her room now so she can take a nap."

As the nice lady led her up the stairs, suddenly Anette was seized with panic—who was this lady, really? Where was she taking her—to lock her up somewhere? She stopped and turned to Mr. Woodson and began to talk in Norwegian, forgetting he didn't speak it.

"You will come, too? Don't let me be alone—I'm afraid!"

But he seemed to understand her anyway, because he went up the steps to her and knelt down.

"I'll be back for dinner. It's a celebration, Anette—for you! A party! Don't be afraid of the Johnsons, they are very kind people and Mrs. Johnson only wants you to rest for a while. But I'll be back, I promise."

Anette nodded; her heart stopped squeezing with fear, and she continued up the stairs to be shown a room that was so splendid, once more all she could do was gape. There was so much furniture! She'd never seen so much furniture in her life, many chairs and bureaus and what Mrs. Johnson called a dressing table, and also what she called a wardrobe, and then a bed so huge, Anette was afraid of it. She might be swallowed up in the middle of this ocean of a bed!

She held herself perfectly still, afraid to move, her eyes taking in everything, but she still didn't quite comprehend, even when Mrs. Johnson repeated it, that this was *her* room. She was still trying to make sense of it as the kind woman helped her change out of her traveling clothes. That's what Mrs. Johnson called them, although to Anette they were simply clothes, but evidently rich people had clothes for different occasions. Then she was shown a wardrobe full of new dresses to choose from, and bureaus full of nightgowns, so she put one of those over her head and climbed into the bed for a nap.

Oh, how nice it was! It was softer and smelled better than anything she'd ever known in her life—it smelled like flowers and rainwater. She arranged herself on her pillow and shut her eyes, so Mrs. Johnson could get the hint and leave her alone. But sleep didn't come immediately.

How was it that just this morning she had said goodbye to the Pedersens? Mother Pedersen had actually wept and held her close, which Anette had not liked at all. Father Pedersen had given her a little present of flowers to take on the train, which she lost somewhere along the way. Then she had been driven away from that house that she'd been told, once, to call home.

And she would never see the other place—that dirty soddie that had once been home—ever again, either. Nor, probably, her mama. Who had left in the middle of the night as mysteriously as she had arrived.

But Anette had not been surprised.

Nothing really surprised her anymore. Too much was strange. Too much had happened to her. She ached with a longing for something, but she wasn't sure what. This place, this grand palace, was to be her home now, and then the school in the fall would be another home of sorts—but she couldn't bring herself to think of that. Although Teacher would be nearby then, in Lincoln, at something called a college, and she promised she would visit Anette often.

But she felt lonely anyway, mostly, despite the fact that she had been surrounded by people ever since the blizzard. Missing something. Missing someone. Not her mama, not anymore—oh, yes, she'd been so happy to see her that day! But almost immediately, she'd waited for the bad thing to happen, because it always did. And when she was told that her mother had left in the middle of the night without a goodbye—just like the other time—it didn't hurt as much. The wound this time was already inside her, it wasn't being carved into her with a dull knife like it had been the first time.

She would never see her mother again, but the difference was—she didn't want to see her mother again.

So it must be Fredrik she missed, then; Fredrik she thought of when she thought of "home." But she could bring his memories with her wherever she went, that's what Teacher had said to her once. So "home" would be that—anywhere she could think of Fredrik. But already his image was fading at an alarming rate; sometimes all she could remember of him were those dreadful moments when they were both crying, mad at each other, in the middle of the blizzard.

Or sometimes, all she could remember was his body, sleeping so still beside her when she opened her eyes the next morning in the ravine, and she was so cold, she was beyond feeling.

AS THE DAYS PASSED, Anette saw so many new things, experienced so many wondrous moments, she wondered if she would ever be able to remember them. She wished she was clever enough to write them down—in a diary, that's what it was called. Mrs. Johnson had given her one the first night she was in Omaha, but she didn't have the right words to explain all the images parading through her mind. She could see them clearly, but she couldn't pin them down upon the page. Everything happened so quickly, one after another, an assault. But people meant well, they liked her, they were kind, Mr. Woodson kept reminding her whenever he saw her grow still, her eyes dull, retreating into herself.

Take that dinner in her honor, when she had been the only child present. There were so many things to eat and it was evident she was supposed to try them all and make happy noises, but all she'd felt was sick by the time it was all over. And all those shining, grown-up faces turned her way! She'd squirmed, she'd wriggled, she'd wanted nothing as much as she wanted to run away right then, just sprint out of the house and keep running. But Omaha, she soon found out, was not a place for that; there were too many people and wagons and things called carriages and drays and cable cars, all going their own ways, taking turns crisscrossing the street, and Anette couldn't figure out the pattern, so she couldn't just run. She'd be hit by something, that was clear as day.

They took many outings, she and Mr. Woodson, and he did try, very patiently, to explain what he called traffic to her. There were corners where everything had to stop, where some people and carriages were allowed to proceed while others waited, but she just couldn't get the hang of it; she always wanted to cross when it wasn't her turn.

There were parties for her, where other children were all dressed up in party clothes, as was she; Mrs. Johnson had helped her understand, or at least try to, which clothes were supposed to be worn when. And every piece of clothing was only worn once at the Johnsons' before it was whisked away to be laundered! By someone else, not Anette! Mrs. Johnson did sit her down and explain that the boarding school wouldn't quite be the same; she would have a uniform and would wear it for a week before it was laundered, but again she wouldn't have to do it herself, which seemed fantastic.

At those parties, Anette was simply too shy to play any of the games the other children knew, games they seemed to have been born knowing how to play. What she'd heard someone call "playtime" was not anything she had been acquainted with, except for recess at school. While she wasn't ashamed of how hard she'd once worked—one of the most amazing things was that her body no longer got stiff and achy when she sat too long, her back no longer throbbed, she didn't get headaches anymore—she was sometimes filled with a sadness that she had missed out on what seemed an important part of childhood. At least childhood for girls and boys who had grown up in Omaha.

The other children's screaming—city children were definitely more excitable than prairie children—did make her ears ache, though; she hadn't been prepared for how *loud* the city was compared to the prairie. All the voices in the streets and the wheels of the carriages and wagons and cable cars, outdoor clocks with bells that chimed, and not all at the same time, harnesses on storefront doors that jingled when the doors opened and closed, jangly music coming out of buildings Mr. Woodson wouldn't take her to, people shouting, selling things on every corner—

Even Mother Pedersen at her most furious couldn't have made her voice heard over all that noise.

One day they went to what Mr. Woodson called a circus—P. T. Barnum's circus, he said proudly, he'd seen it back in New York at something called the Hippodrome. It was all under a big tent, and there was a parade full of the oddest people she'd ever seen—giants and tiny people and what Mr. Woodson pointed out as clowns, people with funny faces who piled out of carriages and jumped around and hit one another with pig bladders and sacks of flour. And then there were the fantastic animals; he pointed them out to her, too. Elephants and tigers and lions, the most beautiful horses she'd ever seen ridden bareback by elegant ladies on their tiptoes. Anette couldn't take her eyes off those graceful figures, she thought she might cry, she'd never seen such prettiness in her life. She was given peanuts and popcorn and something called spun sugar, and she ate it all and then got sick later, but Mr. Woodson didn't mind. "That's how you see your first circus," he said, tickled. "I got sick the first time I went to one, too."

He took her to where he worked, once. An enormous building surrounded by even taller ones. It had a big sign at the entrance that read *Home of the Omaha Daily Bee.* He was very proud when he took her inside and introduced her to so many men and ladies; one man in particular Mr. Woodson called "the boss," and he was very happy to meet her and shook her hand solemnly and said, "Thank you, little lady, for all the subscription renewals."

She had no idea what that meant.

Her favorite part was when Mr. Woodson showed her the printing press, a monster of a machine, taller than any man—well, maybe not as tall as the giant she'd seen in the circus—with a huge roll of paper that continuously flowed over the gears and what Mr. Woodson called "the slug," which seemed to be made of raised metal letters. The paper never stopped rolling over it, and then it was folded and cut into pages and it just kept going and going and going. The sound of it was like what she imagined a dragon sounded like. But she wasn't afraid of it; she could have looked at that never-ending roll of paper being stamped and folded and cut, over and over, forever. When Mr. Woodson saw how much she liked it, he chortled. "Another Nellie Bly, by God!"

She didn't know who Nellie Bly was, of course, and he explained that she was a woman who did what he did, and that made her stand very still. The other women she'd met at the office had done things like fetching coffee and hanging up hats and coats and writing down things for the men. That a woman could go out in the world like Mr. Woodson did, all by herself, and write her own words that so many people would read—she couldn't believe such a thing!

Mr. Woodson also took her to another part of town to meet one of his friends. This part of the city was different; the buildings looked newer, they were closer together and not as grand as where the Johnsons lived. And the people who lived there had skin that was dark, brown and caramel and every shade in between. At first she was a little afraid of them, they looked so different even from the Natives she'd seen, these dusky people in regular clothes, and so she cringed walking among them. But Mr. Woodson tightened his grip on her hand and told her, in a half whisper, to behave herself. He didn't seem afraid, but he did look a little nervous.

They walked into a saloon—"If the Johnsons found out they'd have my head so mum's the word!"—and Mr. Woodson picked her up and sat her on a stool in front of a long bar. Behind the bar was another dark man, and Mr. Woodson introduced him as "Mr. Ollie Tennant."

"Pleased to meet you, young lady," Mr. Tennant said solemnly, holding out his hand.

Anette looked at Mr. Woodson, who nodded. She held out her own hand, and Mr. Tennant shook it politely. Then she relaxed, because Mr. Tennant smiled kindly at her and gave her a glass of something called sarsaparilla, which was bitter at first, then surprised her with a smooth sweetness as it went down her throat. She liked it.

"I have a little girl about the same age as you," Mr. Tennant said proudly. "Melissa. She's out playing with her friends, though."

"That's nice," Anette said. "Does she look like you?"

Mr. Tennant seemed perplexed by this question, but then he smiled—he had a nice smile, it went all the way up to his eyes—and he nodded.

"Dark as midnight," he replied. "You might say it runs in the family."

Mr. Woodson chuckled at this, and then the two of them chatted a little—Mr. Woodson asked Mr. Tennant how business was on this side of town, and Mr. Tennant said it was good, better than it had been at the Lily, and that his wife was happier here. So was he.

"We look after one another," he said with satisfaction. "And we have some Negro schoolteachers here now, we're building a fine new high school. You were always good to me, Woodson. You're the only one of my old customers to stop by and say hello. I really appreciate that."

"I hear there's going to be a newspaper for the colored population. You should try your hand at writing for it, Ollie. I mean that. You're a well-read cuss, that's for sure. And people on the other side of town know you, they might actually read it if you're part of it."

"Maybe." Mr. Tennant nodded thoughtfully, and Anette thought she saw a little gleam in his soft brown eyes that was still there when she and Mr. Woodson said goodbye.

AS THE WEEKS RACED by in this way, she discovered some surprising things. First of all, how dirty the city was! There was soot and grime everywhere, and animal waste in the streets. The prairie was dirty, of course—goodness, it was all dirt! Even the walls where she'd once lived were composed entirely of dirt. But that kind of dirt came up from the earth, which she could never think of as anything other than good.

The dirt in the city came from the sky and from people. City dirt was dirtier than country dirt, it just was.

She also learned that you could get tired from good things almost as much as you can get tired from bad things. While her body felt stronger, more rested, than she could ever remember it feeling, the truth was that sometimes she grew weary just the same. She could get exhausted just from too much laughing, she found out. Too many outings, too many new experiences. Too many emotions—they could wear a person out. She thought she'd never be tired again, once it had been explained to her that she wouldn't have to work like she used to. She had been wrong about that.

Eventually, she got used to the Johnsons, as she'd gotten used to the Pedersens, and while there was a world of difference between them, the one constant was that she still felt as if she didn't belong. And now that she was growing up—she was twelve, they'd had a birthday party for her with presents and ice cream and an organ grinder with a monkey—she was starting to realize that she might never feel as if she belonged anywhere. That maybe she had never had the chance to, or that she didn't have it in her, and she was destined always to be a stranger in someone else's house. And this realization troubled her.

Especially when she had to say goodbye to Mr. Woodson, who was going back to New York City. He seemed excited about it, although sad, too.

The day before he was to get on one of those terrifying trains and head east, he took her for a walk. It was a long walk, the longest she'd had since coming to Omaha, but she liked that; her legs stretched out, they ached in a good way, and when she asked, as they came to the outskirts of town, whether she could run, he laughed and said, "Go ahead!"

And she did! She stretched out her legs and ran, her wooden hand didn't impede her at all, she ran and imagined that Fredrik was chasing her, and for a moment, she could feel him on her heels, ready to overtake her. And in the next moment, he had; he'd run on ahead of her, and once he turned back to wave at her, then he rounded a corner and disappeared. She stopped, then; tears filled her eyes as her heart followed him for a moment. Then her heart let him go. He was really gone now, gone forever—she wiped her tears, wrenched by his loss again, and the impending loss of Mr. Woodson, who'd been so kind, who made her laugh, who— maybe even loved her.

She hugged herself as she cried. Because no one was left to do so.

Mr. Woodson was beside her in a jiffy, though. He didn't hug her—he never had; he seemed awkward around her in that way. But he did pat her shoulder and she heard him sniff, too, as he managed to say, thickly, "There, there."

Then he took her hand, and they stood for a long moment together, as if waiting for someone. But finally, the two of them started walking again.

After a few minutes Mr. Woodson stopped, and he pointed at a little store.

"That's where I first saw her," he told Anette, staring at the shabby little store with a couple of weathered wagons and sturdy farm horses hitched in front of it. "That young girl. My maiden of the prairie. I thought I was an old fool, to be so taken with her. But she opened my eyes and led me out there. She led me to you." He squeezed her hand but kept on staring, still looking for someone who was not there. Anette understood, so she squeezed his hand back. He had a ghost, just like she did.

"At least I got to save you," he continued thoughtfully. "At least I got to do some good, after all." He sighed. It was a deep sigh, the kind of sigh that settled something.

Then they turned around and, hand in hand, walked back to town.

CHAPTER 38

. . . . . .

RAINA DECIDED TO TAKE ANETTE SHOPPING TODAY, THIS sunny Saturday in early August; they could both use some new things for fall, hats and scarves, perhaps some new shirtwaists. Anette had taken the short train ride from Omaha to Lincoln to spend the day with her as she did most every summer Saturday. University—Raina was in her final year, studying English—would start up again soon, so this was a good time. And a good time to sit Anette down and have a talk about her future.

Anette had graduated from the high school this past spring; it hadn't been easy, for even though her circumstances had improved so vastly, she had remained somewhat of a slow learner. Raina had helped her along as much as she could, and so had Anette's classmates, who all acted protective of the country girl with the wooden hand. Anette had passed her final examinations, but barely. She simply wasn't a scholar. She'd been given such an opportunity, but sometimes Raina felt it had been wasted on her, that there were so many homestead children who could have benefited more from the windfall, the education, the Heroine Fund. Anette had been the chosen one—as she herself had been—but in Anette's case, Raina feared she had been sent down a path that she shouldn't have been.

What to do, now that the journey was over?

There was no possibility that Anette would go to college, that was the one thing for sure. But what else could she do? Raina didn't want this responsibility, but there was no one else Anette could turn to.

Anette had kept in touch with Mr. Woodson over the years, and the Johnsons, of course, still welcomed Anette in their home during school holidays. They had Anette's welfare in mind, but they didn't know her as Raina did—they had never met the Anette from before. Raina was the only one who understood how ill at ease Anette was in the city, how withdrawn she sometimes was. How, when she entered a room, she always seemed to be holding her breath, looking for something. Or someone.

The only time Raina saw Anette truly happy was when she brought her out to the farm to visit Mama and Papa. There on the prairie, her hair streaming down her back, the shy, awkward city mouse became a country hawk, flying over the earth, miraculously never breaking an ankle in gopher holes or stepping in cow patties. Raina, as much as she would always feel at home on the farm, found herself, with each passing year, less at ease in the country, less used to the different rhythms, the obstacles—like those cursed cow patties!—she'd never known as obstacles when she was a child. She could navigate her way easily across a crowded city street, deftly stepping over manure left by horse-drawn carriages. But on the farm, visiting, she'd once stepped into a pail of milk, which made Papa laugh until tears streamed down his face.

City girl, he'd called her with affection—and regret.

The homestead was looking good; they'd added another barn, there were more milk cows, more chickens, an entire coop of them, neat little rows of laying hens. With the money from the Heroine Fund, she had been able to hire two hands to help with the work, now that Papa was starting to show his age. No longer could he tie a fence without suffering from it the next day, barely able to flex his fingers in his arthritic hands. He had a difficult time ceding work to anyone, but Mama, with her gentler, coaxing ways, was able to get him to once in a while.

Mama, too, was showing stiffness in her hands and snow in her hair. Sadness in her eyes, when she didn't think Raina was looking. Sadness over the empty chair, empty room. Sadness over Gerda.

Raina shook her head and concentrated on the problem at hand, on how she was going to broach the subject with Anette about her future. She supposed the girl could stay in Omaha with the Johnsons; that seemed a possibility. With a high school education she could surely work in a post office or maybe even answer telephones for a company. Maybe she could even work in a store like this one, a neat, bright little dry goods store that catered to women, particularly to university students with limited funds but unlimited appetite for fashion. It was a cheerful, pretty store with enormous feathered hats in the window, dresses on dummies, rolls and rolls of satin and silk and cotton and braided ribbons, so pretty and gay in all the colors of the rainbow. Raina glanced over at Anette, who was looking at some ribbons, and tried to picture her working in a dainty place like this.

Anette had grown tall, she had matured with a full bosom—fuller than Raina's own—and wide hips. Despite her

sophisticated dress, her fashionable bonnet and gloves—
covering up the wooden hand—she looked out of place here.
She was no beauty, but she had grown out of much of her ug-
liness. The pockmarks had faded and were less pronounced;
her eyebrows weren't so heavy, her hair had darkened to a
honey brown. She had full lips and high cheekbones that
enhanced her clear blue eyes. But it would have been a
stretch to call her pretty according to the current fashion of
delicate bones and tiny waists and pale faces. Anette's
cheeks were always stubbornly ruddy, even though it had
been years since she'd worked outdoors with any regularity.

Raina stopped by the fabric counter and fingered a very
pretty tartan plaid; it would do for a good winter dress. She
was searching for a pattern when she heard her name spoken by a hesitant, masculine, voice.

"Miss Olsen? Raina?"

"Yes?" She turned, expecting it to be a former or current
pupil of hers, for she took tutoring jobs fairly often. Despite
the money still available to her from the Heroine Fund, she
could not stop herself from squirreling away more for the
future. It was in her thrifty blood.

And it was a former pupil of hers who had called her
name, but not one that she expected. To her astonishment,
she found herself staring up into the face of Tor Halvorsan.

"Tor!" she cried out, very undignified, before she could
stop herself. She resisted an urge to throw her arms around
him.

Then she felt herself unaccountably shy, for here was a
man. Of course—he was only a year younger than she was, so
that made him, what—twenty? He was handsome with the
Halvorsan looks—jutting chin, glossy eyebrows, thick hair,
honest eyes. He was wearing city clothes that looked bor-

rowed, the jacket slightly snug across his broad shoulders, his collared shirt gaping a little across his chest. The pants, however, were too big and were hitched up with suspenders. And he was wearing his dusty farmer's boots.

He looked as out of place here as Anette did, Raina mused, gazing at him a bit too long as he began to color; and for a moment, he resembled that earnest young man he had been the last time she'd seen him. The good boy, who had given up an education to remain with his mother and siblings.

"What brings you all this way? And in a shop like this— the last place on earth I'd expect to find you!"

"Just a trip to look at some new plows. There are some newfangled ones that run on steam now, you don't even need horses or oxen. Imagine!" And the way his eyes sparkled at this, Raina knew that he was a farmer now, through and through. Only a farmer could get moony over a new plow.

"How is your mother? Your brothers and sister?" It had been a long time since Raina had heard news of the family, for she and Tor had never really written to each other. She sent him a postcard when she first got to Lincoln, but he hadn't replied. After a couple more postcards, she'd given up, knowing that he was probably too busy to correspond. And too shy.

"Fine, fine. We are good. I haven't been to town in a while, so I wanted to bring something back for Mama. I saw this store across from the hotel where I'm staying, so I thought I'd buy something here. I thought she might like a hat. Do you think? Although there are so many!" He pointed to the hat section, such a glazed, helpless expression in his eyes, Raina had to laugh.

"I think she would love a hat, and I'll help you pick one out." They walked over to the hat display, looking at all the

concoctions that sang out to Raina, but that would be ridiculous for a farm woman. Still, she handed him a pretty blue
silk bonnet with only a few ruffles on it. "This might do.
Now tell me, how are you?" She held him in her gaze; she
would not let him off with a Norski's stoic "Fine." And as she
dared him to tell her the truth, she felt something in her
heart begin to unfurl.

She didn't like to dwell on it, but the truth was, Raina was
lonely. Despite the camaraderie of the university, the tight-
knit group of female students, outnumbered by the males to
a pathetic degree—she was lonely. Although she was the
same age as her friends, she felt far older. She'd arrived in
Lincoln full of hope and optimism, yet still holding some
piece of her heart back. She'd had beaus but had never been
serious about any of them. Sometimes she wondered if it
was because of that early foolishness with Gunner Pedersen.
The first time a man had paid her any attention she had gotten swept up into a nightmare. A twisted, gothic ordeal that
only a devastating storm could put an end to.

Gunner Pedersen. Where was he now? Last she'd heard,
he'd disappeared left his wife and children, no one knew
where he'd gone. She never thought he'd have the strength to
actually leave. She'd assumed Anna would be the one to finally have enough and return to Minneapolis. But apparently it was Gunner who had vanished in the middle of the
night. Where to? She honestly didn't care. The truth was,
she hadn't thought of him in years.

Still, perhaps it was that experience that caused her to
ration herself—not that she felt that she herself was tainted,
no. She had enough sense and self-worth not to think that!
Foolish, yes, and she'd guarded against that folly in herself
ever since—perhaps too much, some of her friends might

scold. But she could admit she'd constructed a little cage around her heart, to keep it from leaping too quickly again.

Maybe, too, she kept that cage locked in the hope that someone was waiting for her—or that she was waiting for him. Someone she had already dreamed of or imagined. Or perhaps known? As she watched Tor so intently, she found herself wondering, for the first time—was it him? They'd gone through the very trials of hell together. Had she been waiting for him, all this time, to catch up with her so they could be equals, not pupil and teacher?

"I am well. Still on the farm, still helping Mother," he said with modest pride, and she had to smile at the way he called his mama "Mother"—like an adult would. A man who was respectful of, yet responsible for, her.

"Are you—have you—married?"

"No, not me. I don't know, Mother teases me that I'll turn into one of those bachelor farmers, the ones that nobody knows what to do with at Christmas or Thanksgiving. Maybe she's right." He grinned, but blushed, and Raina found that she was blushing, too. She wondered how long he was to be in Lincoln. She didn't have classes for another week; she had time to get to know him again.

Oh, she *knew* him, knew him like the weather—the constancy of him, his bravery, his goodness. But she had no idea what made him laugh, what his favorite food was, if he still read books, if he liked girls with brown hair or blond, if he dreamed of someone to sit by the fire with him. And she had no idea if she was capable of sitting by the fire, out on the prairie, with him. Still, for the first time since she left home, she was picturing herself with a man beyond just a nice meal at a restaurant or a walk in the park or a picnic. For the first time, she allowed herself to wonder what it would feel like to be two instead of one.

For the first time—

"Tor?"

Anette had joined them, a spool of pink and white checked ribbon in her hand. Raina had forgotten all about her.

"Oh, look, Anette—isn't it good to see him?"

Anette didn't speak; it appeared that she couldn't. Raina was used to that, of course; Anette was still shy about calling attention to herself, still prone to silent watching instead of participating. What Raina wasn't familiar with was the way the girl's breast was heaving, the way her eyes were shining, the way she looked at Tor as if, as if—

As if she were home.

Anette gazed at Tor with wonder, and maybe she was seeing Fredrik—Raina well remembered how strong the resemblance was. But then she kept gazing at him, and a sweet blush crept into those dusky cheeks, and the girl actually leaned toward him, yearning—wanting.

And Tor was looking at her in the same way. As if he'd found something lost so long ago, he'd given up hope. Until now, when the hope fairly vibrated in him—he grinned at Anette unreservedly, no timidity there. He openly admired the woman she'd become—his eyes widened as he took her in. He shook his head. Raina thought he was about to whistle, but then caught himself just in time.

"Anette! I never would have recognized you!"

And then Anette did the most surprising thing she could have done—

Anette Pedersen *twirled*. Daintily, girlishly, she picked

up her skirts and twirled. And Raina had to brush away a few surprising tears. All these years, she had never seen Anette be coquettish, be girlish—be joyful or light. But now a beatific glow radiated from her face. She stopped, letting her skirts swish about her flirtatiously, and she laughed at herself, then Tor laughed, too, and the two of them, together—

They looked perfect. Together.

Quietly did Raina lock that cage again, feel her heart settle down to its usual waiting perch. She allowed herself a moment of sadness.

She also allowed herself to imagine the future for them—Tor would take Anette back to the prairie, where she had always belonged. These two had shared so much loss, but loss binds people together just as tightly as happiness does. And the happiness would come. Anette would be a dutiful daughter to Mrs. Halvorsan and her very presence would be a welcome reminder that her son did not die in vain. There would be contented evenings sitting on the porch, watching the sun in its fiery glory descending behind fields rustling with hope, a songbird singing softly. There would be storms and floods, yes, of course. But there would also be love.

What would happen to Raina?

Papa and Mama would sell the farm eventually; they would have enough to move to Newman Grove, they already talked of that. Without a son to keep the farm in the family, they couldn't remain on the land they'd labored so painfully to own. The circular nature of their lives—moving back to a settled community like the one they'd left behind in Norway—maybe it was like life itself.

Raina thought sometimes of going to a bigger city like Chicago after she had her degree. Mr. Woodson, although he hadn't written to her in a while, still influenced her—she thought maybe she would write for a newspaper, too. Sometimes she wished to disappear, like her sister had, and maybe by going to a big city, she could accomplish that more easily.

But no, she didn't wish to disappear quite as thoroughly as had Gerda. Unlike her sister, Raina knew she would always be welcomed wherever she wished to go. And she would be there for her parents in their old age. Maybe in the city Raina would finally meet someone who would unlock her heart and throw away the key for good.

Maybe she wouldn't. Maybe she would live for her work or go back to teaching so she could live through her pupils, become one of those respected spinsters who was awarded a nice brooch upon her retirement, during a ceremony where her former pupils sang songs in her honor. After all, she was a heroine. Once.

Quietly, Raina picked up her shopping basket and tiptoed over to the cash register as Tor and Anette continued to chat happily, freely—these two silent children of the prairie, together chirping like lovebirds. Raina smiled, despite the aching loneliness she knew awaited her the moment she stepped out of the store. Anette and Tor—it was right. It was fitting.

They would name their first son Fredrik.

CHAPTER 39

· · · · · ·

Dear Raina,
I know it has been a long time since you've heard from
me. How are Mama and Papa? Are they angry with me
for leaving? I never wanted to hurt them but since I
already had, it seemed to me that it was best that the
break be swift and permanent. I could never again be the
daughter they had known. Every time they looked at me,
they would feel pain. And I've caused enough people
pain.

Let me tell you a little of what I've been doing, dearest
sister. First of all, I went to Colorado. Tiny showed me a
picture of the Rocky Mountains once—he said a fellow
could touch God there. So I thought I would go for him. I
thought maybe I could touch him somehow.

The mountains, Raina! Oh, the mountains! You've
never seen anything like them! They are so vast, so mag-
nificent, that at first you cannot breathe. They appear
like a smudge on the horizon—the train chugs west
through Nebraska, then goes a little south, and the land
is flat, like we know. But all along you have been climb-

ing, and that smudge becomes an unbroken, jagged line,
like a pencil drawing, and then you are suddenly up in
some foothills with these majestic mountains in front of
you, a long line north to south, repeating itself, endlessly,
to the west. I got off the train in Colorado Springs and
took a cog train—it's like a locomotive but it runs differ-
ently, it's smaller, so it can wind its way up through the
mountains. The air here smells of pine and cold—it's
hard to describe. It's not cold like the winter cold we're
used to, more like peppermint, I suppose, like the candy
we sometimes got in our stockings at Christmas—it's just
so pure! I went up all the way to the top of Pike's Peak,
one of the tallest mountains in Colorado, and the air is
thin that high up—above the tree line! Too high for anything to grow, the mountains are bare there, with patches
of snow and alpine flowers, but no trees. But when the
moon rises, it seems like you can walk right into it, it's so
close.

I didn't really touch God here, though. I thought, for a
minute, that I could. But I did feel close to Tiny then. I
said goodbye to him at the top of that mountain.

Then I went to Montana, to the Indian school that
had hired me.

This is when I learned that I am not the worst person
in the world. There is such evil there, Raina. The school is
mismanaged, the funds are misused. The children
mistreated—they are spanked regularly by the principal
and there is nothing I can do about it. I know that some
of the girls have been assaulted and ruined forever by
some of the male teachers and administrators—it's as if
that's one of the reasons they are there. Not only to be

schooled, but to be used, ruined, by some of these men who know they don't have to answer to anyone but other men just like them. I'm supposed to look away, like the other female teachers. They don't bother us—why should they, when they have helpless young girls who are too terrified to fight back?

Sometimes, when I see these men, I am filled with such rage, I want to do something to them—but I'm just the strange teacher with the wooden foot who couldn't get hired anywhere else. They laugh at me, call me names behind my back. I thought the children would do this, but it turns out that it's the adults who are the cruel ones.

The food is not parceled out equally and some children do not get enough to eat. I try to help, to sneak them some, to soothe, but even if they don't mock me, they do recoil from my touch—they recoil from all of us who truly want to help them. But maybe they can't tell the difference between us and the evil ones; maybe we look the same to them. I try to teach these children, I even try to make them smile with songs and games, but they are sullen and sad. Rows and rows of brown eyes in brown faces, eyes that are dull, that are lost, that are missing their families, their homes, their culture. They look out of place in our clothes. They look as out of place here as I feel, myself.

I do think we share this, this feeling of being outside what is called "civilized" society, but that society isn't so civilized, after all. I have seen that firsthand, now. Still, I have what they call a "pale face," and blond hair, so they distrust me, and rightly so given how other pale faces have treated them. My wooden boot is a source of curios-

*ity, but if I thought it would bind me to these miserable
children, make me one of their tribe, I was mistaken. As
much as I have suffered, those eyes tell me I haven't suffered like them. I still think that teaching them how to
live in society is a noble idea; what future will they have
if they revert back to their old tribal ways? The country
isn't wild any longer. But this is not the way to do it, I
know that now. And I can't save them, nor can they
save me.*

    *I think I will leave this place soon. For where, I do not
yet know.*

    *I hope this letter finds you well, Raina. I know that
whatever you do, you will succeed.*

    *I can only trust that this is the correct address for you
now, in Lincoln. And if it isn't, someone will forward it to
you.*

Your loving sister,
Gerda

Dear Raina,
*So you are in Chicago now! The big city! You are so much
braver than I am. Is it everything you hoped it would be? I
trust that by now—it has been so many years, what is it,
seven, since we parted?—you have a good husband, children, a loving home. You did not mention these things,
but I know you, dear sister. You might be trying to spare
my feelings by not revealing your own contentment.
Please don't do that! Your happiness will be my own.*

    *But why do I hope that you are married with a fam-
ily? It's not the only happiness for a woman, but it is the*

*one we are taught to believe in, the ending of the fairy
tale. It's what Mama and Papa would want for you, I
know that.*

*I wonder what they want for me? I wonder if they
think of me every day? I'm sure Mama does. I don't know
about Papa, I disappointed him so.*

*I am still in Montana; your letter was forwarded to
me from the Indian school. Montana is such a vast place,
there is room to wander and wander. You would be surprised to know how I live now, Raina. I live in a tent. By a
river, near a mining camp. I take in washing for the men,
and I teach those who want to learn, too. You should see
my classes—such a mixture of misfits from many different places, all come to Montana to make their fortune in
silver. But most of the mining is now being done by large
corporations, so there aren't many mining camps left for
the men who use a pickax. Still, there are enough for me
to make my living. I don't require much, after all.*

*During the winter months, which are hard here, I go
into the town of Butte, where I board. That is where your
letter was forwarded to me, so it took a long while to find
me out here in the camps. I don't have many friends, just
one or two other souls who are adrift, as I am. I don't ask
them why, and they don't ask me, and that's why we are
companionable.*

*Sometimes I think of going to live with the Indians on
a reservation. Why, I don't know—is it to teach them?
Even after my experience at that school? I still think an
education is a worthwhile thing and will only help them,
but they need to be with their families. They need to be
taught the things their ancestors knew, as well as the*

things that will help them in the future. But I don't know if they would let me in. After all, I look like the enemy to them, like the people who took their land and killed their ancestors. What they don't understand is that I am just as sorrowful as they are. But perhaps it's not up to them to understand me. Or help me.

I wonder if there is any place where I will feel as if I belong.

Do you ever think of the storm now, Raina? Or are you too far removed from it, snug in a city surrounded by tall buildings that block out the weather?

I do. I sometimes stay in my tent too long into the snow season, just so I will never forget how it was that awful night. Just so I can shiver and shake with cold once more, and remember every step I took with Minna on my back, Ingrid clutching my hand. I remember how the storm made me forget everything else, except for taking just one more step. Just one more. Then the one after that. And that was all that mattered. To take one more step.

At night, in my tent that quivers in the wind, I bundle up in blankets and robes. I have a pistol by my side. A woman can't be in the camps without one. I haven't had to use it but I can go to sleep knowing it's there. But before I go to sleep, I make myself say their names: Minna, Ingrid, Hardus, Johnny, Johannes, Karl, Walter, Sebastian, Lydia.

Do you think I will go to hell, Raina? Do you even believe in hell anymore? We did as children, didn't we? Papa would read from the Bible when we couldn't make it to church on Sunday, and I believed in hell then, oh, I did! I believed in heaven and hell, that they were two

separate places, one above and one below, and that I
would either be eternally lost or eternally saved in the
end.

But hell is this life we lead now, not later. So I suppose
that means there really is no heaven either, is there?
There never was, we were told a lie.

But maybe you are living your heaven now. I hope you
are.

Your loving sister,
Gerda

Dear Raina,

I suppose you are surprised to hear from me after so many
years! I don't know if you are still in Chicago. I can't
imagine that you are not, because where does a person go
after Chicago? It is beyond my imagination. I can't pic-
ture you going home to Nebraska, that is for certain. If
home is still there, even.

I don't know, but I feel it in my bones—which are so
sharp now, I don't seem to need as much food as I used
to—that Mama and Papa are gone by now. It seems likely.
I hope they were at peace, and happy, in the twilight of
their lives. I know they were together, and that is a bless-
ing. I can't imagine the two of them ever parting. I know
Mama wasn't always happy, I know she didn't want to
leave Norway. Have you ever thought about that—how it
was always the men who left, taking the women with
them? I never once heard of a woman leaving the old
country on her own accord. It was the men who had to
have more. I saw that in Montana, when I was there. No
woman wanted to mine for silver. There were smart

women who took advantage of the men who did, how-
ever. Many were wanton women, but I did not see them
that way (although there were many temperance groups
and society women who did, mercy!). I saw them as
women smarter than anyone else, who knew what men
wanted and found a way to make a living providing it. I
have shocked you, haven't I, dearest baby sister! Do not
worry, I myself am not a wanton woman.

Sometimes I wonder if I am a woman at all. Some-
times I think I am just a wraith. Roaming this earth until
one day, I will stop.

Minna, Ingrid, Hardus, Johnny, Johannes, Karl, Wal-
ter, Sebastian, Lydia. I haven't forgotten them, I still say
their names every night before I lay down wherever I hap-
pen to be.

I left Montana. For no real reason other than I felt like
wandering again. I knew too many people in Montana
and it has started to trouble me, to be in the company of
others. So I am starting over again, in Idaho. They have
mountains in Idaho, too. I don't think I shall ever come
down from the mountains.

Do you ever think how odd it is that we both left
home? Just when I said it's what men do, it struck me
that we did, too. Two women, two sisters. Because when I
think about us, and the others our age, born homestead-
ers, born of parents who chose to leave somewhere, I think
that most of us really didn't have a choice. That by leav-
ing all they'd known on their own accord, our parents
ended up enslaving their children to the land, just so they
could have a piece of paper saying that they possessed it.
Most of our generation are still there, I am certain. I used
to think of the boys we knew, how they had no imagina-

tion, they were too content to stay. But now I think it was so unfair to them. They had no choice; their parents lived and died to prove the land, and they left it to their children to continue the cycle. What could those boys do, other than stay there and try?

But you and I got out. It still mystifies me. It was the storm, of course—it blew us out of there, in a way. You because you did the right thing; me, because I didn't.

I don't know what you are doing now, Raina. I move around too much to ever get a letter back, and I have little hope that my previous letter got to you. I have even less hope that this one will. I suppose I wanted to say goodbye to you finally. Oh, don't worry, I am not dying!

I just feel less and less of this world somehow.

Maybe we will meet again, dear sister. But I don't think we will. You wouldn't recognize me anyway. You would pass me on the street. No, you would look at me and ask yourself, "Who is that poor excuse of a woman? That ghost in tattered clothing, stringy grey hair, a pain in her heart that makes her press her hand to her chest now and then to ease it?"

Up here in the mountains, higher and higher—maybe I will touch God one of these days, after all!—nobody cares. There are so few people, anyway. And they all have their own versions of hell to contend with.

I do hope you are happy, Raina. You deserve it.

> *Goodbye from your*
> *loving sister,*
> *Gerda*

Occasionally, in the years to come, Raina would receive odd gifts in the mail. A packet of eagle's feathers. A few stones of turquoise. A cowboy hat with silver disks stitched along its brim. Pebbles washed smooth by spring water.

A yellowed news clipping about a madwoman in the mountains whom no one has ever seen, but who sends presents to the schoolchildren in the nearest town.

The last thing she ever received, no return address like the others, was just a list, scrawled in a weak hand on brown paper, in pencil: *Minna, Ingrid, Hardus, Johnny, Johannes, Karl, Walter, Sebastian, Lydia.*

To that list, Raina added in her own precise, schoolteacher's hand:

Gerda.

THE CHILDREN'S BLIZZARD OF 1888—SOMETIMES KNOWN as the Schoolchildren's Blizzard or the Schoolhouse Blizzard—has long been known to me by its name, although I didn't truly grasp its scope and terror. But when my editor at the time and I were looking for a new idea for a novel, and she mused that it might be interesting to write about children, I replied, "The Children's Blizzard!" And when she asked what that was, I admitted I didn't exactly know.

I set off to do the research, and almost immediately, I started to construct a story around it.

For the first time in my career as a historical novelist, I wanted to write about an actual historical event, but invent the people caught up in it. My other books have all been created around real people—Anne Morrow Lindbergh, the real Alice in Wonderland, Truman Capote, Mary Pickford, etc. I was looking for a new challenge as a writer, and this subject, so vast with possibility, ignited my imagination. So I stuck to the actual timeline of the blizzard but invented most of the characters, basing many of them on the oral histories of those who remembered the storm and the newspaper articles about it.

The facts: In 1888, there was no National Weather Service. Meteorology didn't quite exist as a science. But the Army Signal Corps did have a branch of weather "indicators," career soldiers who had been selected to train, as much as the science of the time allowed, to try to indicate the weather. (They did not use words like *predict* or *forecast* then.) The Signal Corps was, at the time of the blizzard, under the command of Brigadier General Adolphus Greely, who had famously commanded a tragic expedition to the Arctic; most of his men perished, but he and a handful survived. The expedition was known as the Lady Franklin Bay Expedition. Despite controversy, he returned home a hero, and President Grover Cleveland appointed him chief signal officer of the army.

At the time, weather indicating consisted of an array of stations, many at army forts and railroad depots, each manned by a member of the Signal Corps whose job it was to take weather readings—barometric pressure, wind direction and speed, temperature—and telegraph the readings, at various intervals during the day, to Washington, D.C. There, soldiers would map out all the readings and indicate the weather for the next few hours. The time it took to gather the readings, form an indication, then telegraph it back out to various stations and newspapers, meant that the indications rarely got to where they should be in a timely manner. Too, there was much corruption in the Signal Corps: false readings, mismanagement, unmanned stations. In 1887, Greely felt pressure by the railroads to open up a western branch, to better serve the railway west of the Mississippi and, to a far lesser extent, the homesteaders there. He opened an office in Saint Paul, Minnesota, under the command of Lieutenant Thomas Woodruff.

The Homestead Act of 1862, signed into law by President Lincoln, encouraged the settlement of what was then known as the West—primarily Nebraska, Minnesota, Dakota Territory, then later Montana and Wyoming and Colorado. Anyone who could afford a small filing fee was given the opportunity to own one hundred and sixty acres of land. All that was required was to live on the land continuously for five years and prove it up—build a livable structure on it—and then the land was theirs. Of course, this land came at the expense of the Native Americans who had roamed it freely for thousands of years; this, and the discovery of pockets of gold and silver, ignited the post–Civil War Indian Wars, the genocide at the hands of the U.S. Army that resulted in relocating Native Americans to reservations.

The railroads were the great investment and marvel of the age, and they, along with the territories and states in this area, needed people—white people—to settle there. Territories wanted to become states; railroads needed people and goods to move up and down their lines. So a great propaganda—"fake news," if you will—campaign was waged to get people to homestead. Many of those targeted were northern Europeans eager to leave their homeland and go to this allegedly bountiful new land of milk and honey. They were sold a false bill of goods to get them there—the character of Gavin Woodson is not based on anyone in particular, but he represents those who engaged in this fake news and propaganda. But conditions in the countries of Germany and Norway and Sweden, or in the slums of New York, too—many homesteaders were from the crowded cities of the East—were difficult. Farms in Europe were generally divided up among all the children of a family so that in each succeeding generation, there was precious little land left to farm. And there was forced conscription in the army, as well. Thus, at the time, immigrants were welcomed to this country; the country needed them, their bodies were needed to grow the population, prove up the land, and make the railroads a profit.

During the 1880s, the weather in the Great Plains was especially daunting; this was what was known as the Little Ice Age. The weather there was both severe and wildly unpredictable. And it had hardly turned out to be the land of milk and honey that was promised; it was actually—it still is actually—a desert. The land could not be tamed by the methods the immigrants brought with them from their homelands. The crops they were used to planting simply wouldn't grow. There were prairie fires, grasshoppers that rained down, floods in the spring, tornados in the summer. And terrifying blizzards in the winter. Eventually, the homesteaders who persisted adapted their methods and crops; the introduction of dryland farming, and then the discovery of the Ogallala Aquifer, eventually turned this region into the breadbasket of America.

Many immigrants didn't stay for these advances; in the 1880s and 1890s, over sixty percent of homesteaders abandoned their property.

That left forty percent who did stay.

English was not the native tongue for most of the homesteaders who staked their claim. But their children were forced to speak the language in school—school so often taught by children themselves. One of the things that most intrigued me about this tragedy is that life-and-death decisions were made by young women, for the most part, barely out of school; teachers only sixteen, seventeen, eighteen years of age.

When the blizzard struck on January 12, 1888, no one had any advance notice. The weather indication for that day did not call for any unusual warnings, and of course, even if it had, most homesteaders lived far from the stations that would hoist these weather flags. And most did not get the city newspapers like the *Omaha Daily Bee,* which ran the indications. Even if they had received the papers, they wouldn't have been able to read them.

Blizzards were not unusual on the prairie, of course, especially not during the Little Ice Age. What made this one different was the fact that the morning of the twelfth was unusually balmy after an extended period of below-zero cold. Homesteaders were able to leave their homes for the first time in weeks, and they did. Farmers took their livestock out for exercise, people went to town to get supplies. Children went to school for the first time in days.

And most of them left home wearing only the minimal clothing for a prairie winter; shawls instead of coats, light scarves instead of wool mufflers.

When the blizzard struck central and eastern Nebraska and southeastern Dakota—the places that had the most casualties—it struck at a particularly devastating time: the hour when school was about to let out, or just had. This led to an unusually high proportion of casualties being children— thus the name, the Children's Blizzard.

Many details in my book are recorded history: the facts of the blizzard itself, the timeline, the details about the Army Signal Corps. Edward Rosewater and the *Omaha Daily Bee* really did exist and play a big part in the aftermath of the storm. There really was a Heroine Fund established by the *Bee.* The character of Raina Olsen in my novel is loosely based on the real-life heroine Minnie Freeman, who is also mentioned. The character of Anette Pedersen is based on another survivor, Lena Woebbecke.

The death toll is another story. Officially, the deaths are listed at 235, with most sources saying, vaguely, "and many or most of them were children." But there were worries among the newspapers and boosters that the actual toll, thought by most to be much higher, would scare off new immigrants. Too, it was difficult to take an official count. Many people didn't report deaths, or bodies weren't discovered until the spring. Many died after lingering illnesses brought on by the storm, as well, and weren't officially counted. And it appears no one really took count of those who perished on Indian reservations like the Great Sioux Reservation in what is now South Dakota.

My primary sources for research were the excellent nonfiction book by David Laskin called *The Children's Blizzard*, published in 2004, and the collection of memories of those who survived and witnessed the storm, titled *In All Its Fury: A History of the Blizzard of January 12th, 1888*, published in 1947. Archives of the *Omaha Daily Bee* were helpful as well.

Considering the era in which we live, I was intrigued and moved by this tragedy involving immigrants, who were welcomed to this country, without whom America would not be what it is today—and who were lured here, in many cases, by outright falsehoods masquerading as news and fact. I was also fascinated by the touching stories of these young women—girls, really—teachers who were faced with impossible decisions. Some made the correct ones—and others did not.

It is a fact that the Ogallala Aquifer is drying up, due to overfarming, faster than it is being replenished, and that someday soon, the Great Plains will be even more of an inland desert than it was when the first homesteaders arrived. And as we are faced with challenges of a climate and planet that are continuing to change due to human carelessness, we must take action now, before more lives are lost.

ACKNOWLEDGMENTS

My FAVORITE PART OF WRITING ANY BOOK IS THANKing all those who helped make it possible:

My deepest gratitude goes to Susanna Porter, who guided me along this thrilling journey. And as always, I wouldn't even have a career if it wasn't for Laura Langlie, my literary agent.

I am so lucky to have the best team in the world at Penguin Random House: Kara Welsh, Kim Hovey, Gina Wachtel, Sharon Propson, Jennifer Garza, Susan Corcoran, Quinne Rogers, Leigh Marchant, Allyson Pearl, Robbin Schiff, Benjamin Dreyer, Loren Noveck, Allison Schuster, Emily Hartley, and Gina Centrello.

Thank you to Kate Miciak, who coaxed this idea out of me.

Much gratitude to the team at Authors Unbound, and to the wonderful sales reps at Penguin Random House.

I couldn't do this without my family, particularly Dennis Hauser, who is the best author whisperer in the world. He is assisted by Alec Hauser, Ben Hauser, Emily Curtis, and Norman Miller.

And as always, thank you to the booksellers and readers who make it possible for me to do what I love.

ABOUT THE AUTHOR

MELANIE BENJAMIN has written the *New York Times* bestselling historical novels *The Aviator's Wife* and *The Swans of Fifth Avenue,* the nationally bestselling *Alice I Have Been,* and *Mistress of the Ritz, The Girls in the Picture,* and *The Autobiography of Mrs. Tom Thumb.* She lives in Chicago with her husband. When she isn't writing, she's reading.

Melaniebenjamin.com

Twitter: @MelanieBen

Look for Melanie Benjamin on Facebook

ABOUT THE TYPE

The text of this book was set in Filosofia, a typeface designed in 1996 by Zuzana Licko, who created it for digital typesetting as an interpretation of the eighteenth-century typeface Bodoni, designed by Giambattista Bodoni (1740–1813). Filosofia, an example of Licko's unusual font designs, has classical proportions with a strong vertical feeling, softened by rounded droplike serifs. She has designed many typefaces and is the cofounder of *Emigre* magazine, where many of them first appeared. Born in Bratislava, Czechoslovakia, in 1961, Licko came to the United States in 1968. She studied graphic communications at the University of California, Berkeley, graduating in 1984.

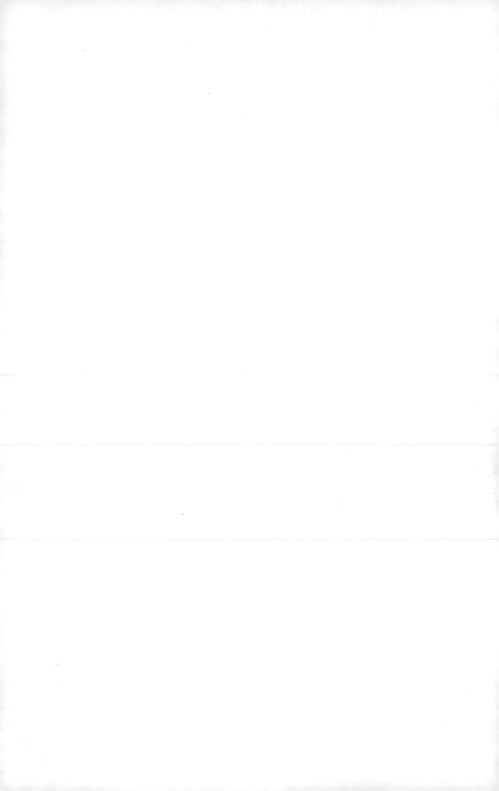